GALILEE RISING

BOOK TWO OF
THE GALILEE FALLS TRILOGY

CHRONICLED BY JENNIFER HARLOW

DEVIL ON THE LEFT BOOKS

COPYRIGHT

To all who championed this series,
You're My Heroes

ALSO BY JENNIFER HARLOW

THE GALILEE FALLS TRILOGY

In The Beginning...A Galilee Falls Short
Justice
Galilee Rising

THE F.R.E.A.K.S. SQUAD SERIES

Mind Over Monsters
To Catch a Vampire
Death Takes A Holiday

THE MIDNIGHT MAGIC MYSTERY SERIES

What's A Witch To Do?
Werewolf Sings The Blues (Out 3/14)

"The evil that men do lives after them; the good is oft interred with their bones."

-*Julius Caesar* by William Shakespeare

God, how I love this city. And how I am going to miss her.

I stand at the edge of the rooftop where I've spent many a night gazing down at her lifeblood, her citizens going about their lives as I watch over them. The group of women giggling as they step into the bar, searching for companionship. The man in the business suit screaming into his mobile phone, trying his hardest to hold onto his share of the proverbial pie. The musician carrying his guitar case, off to pursue his dream of immortality. The lone woman plowing through them all without a glimpse, head up and scowl affixed as if showing vulnerability even amongst these strangers would result in catastrophe. She knows it can, no doubt discovering this years ago the hard way. I can always spot my own kind.

"Lord Nightingale."

"White Night." *I spin around.* "You're late."

Independence's newest hero waits by the open door, his black and white clad figure filling its frame. I envy him that. Him simply standing is intimidating, whereas I had to build that reputation through years of painful, grueling work. Though he's only three inches taller than my six feet, I feel like a stringy pygmy around him. Less than. Always have. "I'm sorry. I was on surveillance, lost track of time. Tentacle and some goons."

"Watch out for that fourth arm. He rarely uses it, so it's difficult to remember it's there."

"Thank you," *he says with a reverent nod as he strides over to me.* "So, last night in town. Having any second thoughts about leaving?"

"On occasion. There are moments, but I know it's for the best. We're needed. It's our duty to answer that call."

"I'd go," *he says apologetically, showing momentary weakness that doesn't become him,* "I want to go, but I just can't. It's—"

"I know," *I say.* "We're proud to do it. That you trust us enough to."

He studies what is visible of my face for subterfuge. His shoulders relax when he finds none. "If you need anything, please call me."

"You're given us a detailed rundown on the players and layout. You know better than I do that the location may change, but the game remains the same. We'll be fine."

"I don't doubt it." He holds out his gloved hand, and I shake it. "Take care of her for me." His Caribbean blue eyes meet mine, as serious as a nuclear bomb as he squeezes my hand hard enough tendons crack. "Both of them."

Her image flashes into my mind, as always making me uncomfortable among other emotions I don't care to dwell upon. "I will guard them with my life," I say, meaning every word.

His vice-like grip eases before pulling away. "Thank you. From the bottom of my heart, thank you."

And he super-speeds away, off to be my city's new champion. This should make me resentful or bitter like Tesla must have felt when Edison came onto the scene but doesn't. Odd. Instead, I'm...excited. Dare I say it? Hopeful. I'd forgotten how lovely that feeling can be.

I turn around, taking one last look at my city. "Good-bye, Independence." I take off like a rocket into the sky, circling around the presidential monument's arches once before zooming away into the night.

Galilee Falls, here I come.

CHAPTER ONE

THE HEIRESS

Jesus Christ, just what we need. More fucking supers.

I kick off my heels and toss my jacket on the huge four-poster bed, but don't take my eyes off the news footage they must have been recycling since it happened. The players may change, but the game remains the same. "Our top story tonight," Anchorman Murray Marshall says. "Has Galilee Falls hero population increased by three? Earlier this afternoon, the super-criminal Gigantor and his gang of Giants, in a reported attempt to show their civic pride, donned Galilee Angels jerseys and attacked the Jericho Warriors bus as it pulled into Pendergast Stadium. Sports reporter Frank Casabian was on the scene and recorded the attack. Parental guidance is suggested."

On the screen, the nine-foot, thousand pound behemoth tips over the bus with little effort as the frightened cameraman and Frank Casabian shriek bleeped obscenities. Gigantor and his crew don't care about them, they're too busy demolishing the bus with barbwire clubs, attempting to reach the players inside. As glass smashes and a dozen frightened men holler and cry, two security guards come racing up, guns raised but shaking. Gigantor barrels at them like a bull on steroids taking a few hits to his costume but it must be bullet resistant as he doesn't slow a whit. He reaches the now petrified guards, swatting them like flies into the wall. They're knocked out, or that's what I choose to believe. I've seen enough death for a lifetime. The trembling camera stays trained on the mêlée as the man holding it prays.

Thirty seconds in, all windows are nothing but shards and henchmen leap into the bus as Gigantor struts back. "Bring me Tobias!" he bellows. A few seconds later, a bleeding and shaken man is pushed out of the broken bus window, collapsing to the ground in a small heap. Gary Tobias, National MVP two years running, cowers on the pavement amid shards of glass, slicing his ten million dollar a year hands. Gigantor laughs at the sight. Yeah, Tobias won't be playing tonight.

"Please don't kill me," he cries, no longer the cocky jerk his interviews make him out to be.

"I won't kill all of you," Gigantor says as he reaches the man. Looming over the sobbing football player, he slowly presses his foot down on the quarterback's kneecap as Tobias howls in pain. That howl socks me right in the gut. I know it too well.

"What the hell is that?" one of the henchmen shouts. The camera swings to where he's pointing. Here comes the money shot.

In perfect formation, the Royal Triumvirate swoop down from the heavens, capes flapping in the breeze to kick ass. Their leader, King Tempest, in his navy blue and white costume jets into Gigantor, knocking him off his feet. The ground quakes when they land. The cameraman doesn't know where to shoot. He pans from King Tempest pounding the hell out of the dazed giant to Lord Nightingale and Lady Liberty dispatching henchmen with punches and elegant roundhouse kicks. A few of the braver Jericho Warriors join in, grabbing discarded clubs to bludgeon their attackers. Good for them.

The carnage ends less than a minute later. The bad guys lie bleeding on the ground, Gigantor included. Tempest hog-ties the unconscious giant as sirens and flashing lights pull up. I count fifteen squad cars, a SWAT van, and two ambulances. It wouldn't be enough.

A young patrolman is the first to approach King Tempest, who smiles at the boy. "I gave him an extremely powerful sedative," the hero says. He removes three vials from his belt. "One every five hours." He pats the officer's shoulder. "Guess the game's cancelled tonight, huh? Too bad. I was really looking forward to it. It was going to be a hell of a battle." The awed officer nods. "Well then," Tempest says as he turns around, "team?"

The other two heroes nod, and all at once, the three take off into the air without another word. The footage ends there. Anchorman Murray Marshall once again sits behind his anchor desk, staring at the camera. "Sources report that Bridger Davis, A.K.A. Gigantor was transported to Xavier Maximum Security Prison shortly after for holding and has not yet regained consciousness. The other men involved in the attack have also been arrested and several players of the Jericho Warriors, including quarterback Gary Tobias, were taken to Our Lady of Perpetual Sorrow Hospital with minor injuries. Tonight's game has been cancelled and all tickets will be refunded. Commissioner—"

I shut off the television. Great. Those Tokyo businessmen we gave box seats to are going to be pissed. I'll bet Lane is shitting himself. I'm shocked I haven't received a frantic phone call. As if I would have a clue what to do if he did. From my perspective we don't need to purchase another telecommunications company. We have three. Or maybe it's four. Even after almost a year I don't know all of Pendergast Industries holdings. We're always in flux. Yesterday I was worth one billion, today they tell me it's three. And that's just my personal holdings. The company's worth four times that. It all gives me a headache. If Justin wasn't dead I'd kill him for doing this to me.

I mean, what the hell was he smoking when he wrote his will, leaving me controlling interest in Pendergast? I could barely balance my checkbook. He'd try to talk business, and my eyes would glaze over. He should have left it to one of those horrible cousins instead of willing them a hundred million each. At least then I wouldn't have three assholes contesting the will. Only people who have had money all their lives would be pissed they only got a hundred million bucks. Should have just given in, but I was just numb. One minute I had three grand to my name, and the next I was a billionaire with ten houses around the world, twelve cars, a jet, three boats, a baseball team, and was the figurehead of an international company employing twenty thousand people. At least I haven't fucked it up. Yet.

But no more work tonight. I've been in and out of meetings since six this morning. Lane, the CFO since Justin's dad, insists I don't need to be there at all. I told him to stuff it. If the business generations of Pendergasts poured their blood, sweat, and tears into it fails on my watch, I'll never forgive myself. The staff does the brunt of the work, so I just step in on the big deals or when a charity needs press coverage. The infamous Joanna Fallon is quite the draw. The upper crust and reporters from all divisions will pay good money and newsbytes to rub shoulders with the disgraced cop turned billionaire. If I'm feeling particularly nice, I'll even wear a sleeveless gown so they can all check out the burn scar on my upper arm from when a psychopath shot acid at me. At least the men look at my arm and not my boobs for once.

Off comes my Prada suit and on slip my old sweats from the Academy. I pull my long, curly black hair into a ponytail, wash off a hundred dollars worth of make-up, and stroll out of my bedroom the size of my old apartment into the equally gigantic, dark hallway with oil paintings and ancient tapestries hanging between the six doors. Unlike the rest, the master bedroom is modern and light with white walls, comfortable furniture, and electronic gadgets galore. Justin didn't see the point of messing with the rest of the hundred-year-old mansion when he inherited it, and I didn't either. Everything is exactly how he left it. My cousin Veronica says it's unhealthy. The few times she's come over, she comments it's like walking into a mausoleum with shrines to my dead friend in every room. She actually gave me the name of a therapist when she found out I refused to throw out his clothes and I was sleeping in his old bed. I changed the sheets!

As I descend the grand marble staircase, my butler Dobbs strolls out from the kitchen carrying a tray of food. I inherited him as well. Justin left him seven million dollars and the Rolls Royce, but he insisted on sticking around to serve the house's owner as he had for over forty years. His wife died before I met him twenty years ago, and like me the Pendergasts were all he really had. I thank God everyday he decided to stay. He's family. "Miss Joanna, cook made you chicken breast, steamed cauliflower, and an apple for desert. I hope this is satisfactory."

I grimace. "I hate diets."

"If I may be so forward, I will say it appears to be working."

I take the tray. "Thanks. I still have fifteen pounds to go." I gained twenty-five this year and have been in a dozen gossip rags, none flattering. My favorite was that I was pregnant with Justin's love child. He would have gotten a kick out of that. "I'll eat this then go for a run. Have you had dinner?"

"I was about to," Dobbs says.

"Then you can keep me company. Let's eat outside. Take advantage of the weather."

"Yes, miss," he says before disappearing back into the kitchen. I really don't feel like having dinner with anyone but the few nights I'm home at a reasonable time I try to dine with him. He's stuck in this monstrosity all day with no one but the servants under him to talk to, who he just orders around. The man's probably lonelier than even I. If that's possible.

I turn on the TV in the living room and up the volume before opening the sliding glass door and stepping onto the patio. Even with the TV I can hear the lapping of waves of the ocean below. I don't know how many nights Justin and I spent out here just talking, drinking—that last one was me—and laughing our asses off. A wave of sadness washes over me like a tsunami as I remember his smiling face sitting across from me. I get at least five of those a day. A smell, a pair of Caribbean blue eyes, hell even just an Armani suit triggers the emotional natural disaster. I have gotten better at hiding when it happens. No more near panic attacks, sharp intakes of breath, and the desire to double over as if punched in the stomach for me. I've found that not having investors believing the head of the company needs a straightjacket is a great motivator to develop a poker face. Only took half a year. I'm a slow learner.

I start on my flavorless chicken—diets *really* suck—as a CBN correspondent reports today's attack. We've made national news. Again. Dobbs comes out with his tray of French onion soup and veal parmesan. My mouth almost waters. I hate being a girl. "Another attack today," he says as he sits. "No casualties this time, thank God."

"I know. Mayor Miracle must be shitting himself. I heard tourism is down fifteen percent this summer. They just got the numbers."

"Not surprising," Dobbs says. "I've lived in this city all my life and things have never been this bad. The newspaper said we were averaging an attack a week."

I chuckle. "And two billion in property damage a month. Everyone was having shit fits at the zoo fundraiser last week about the state upping taxes to pay for it. There goes that jewel encrusted jet Bitsy had her eye on."

Justin would smile but Dobbs just spoons soup into his mouth. "I don't like what's happening to this city. Mr. J.T. must be turning over in his grave. Master Justin too."

If he had a grave. "Things will level out." Or there'll be
nothing left of this city to pick at like these vultures have been
doing. I swear some villain must have put out an ad in *Psychopath
Weekly.* "Come to Galilee Falls. Dad's gone, time to party."
Reaper from Darlington and Boneshaker from fucking England
now permanently call Galilee home, and those are two we know of
for a fact. Ache, Brujah, Boil have all put in appearances this year.
And it's not just supers. Bank robberies, rapes, even murders have
shot up. Superheroes like Geronimo and Olympia are doing their
best, but they're no Justice. He was a symbol. Hell, some even
thought he was a literal God. God's don't plummet to their death
from a hospital rooftop.

"Perhaps the Royal Triumvirate will help," Dobbs says.

"They were probably just passing through," I say, stabbing
my cauliflower. "You know how territorial superheroes are. Justice
only left the city twice to help in others. The Royal's were
probably popping back to repay the favor."

About two and a half years ago, Justice went to
Independence to help banish Emperor Cain after he destroyed the
President's mansion, placed bombs at every national monument,
and kidnapped the First Lady. They got her back, only a museum
was obliterated, and the Emperor is presumed dead. I thought
Justin was in Hawaii with his latest bimbo.

"I hope not," Dobbs says. We eat in silence for a few
seconds before he says, "If only Master Justin were here. He—"

"Well, he's not," I cut in, voice hard. "He's dead." And
I've completely lost my appetite. I set down my fork and stand.
"I'm going for my run."

"Miss Joanna, I'm sorry. I—"

"It's okay," I say, meaning it.

I squeeze his bony shoulder before rushing to the stairs.
The mansion rests on a cliff overlooking the ocean about seventy-
five feet up. Just walking up and down the steps is a work-out.
When I reach the sand, I perform quick stretches before taking off
in a trot to the left. The sun has already set so only a little orange
shades the dark blue and stars twinkling over the sea. The only
way I can stand running is if I have something pretty to look at.
The sand adds extra resistance, so I get more bang for my buck
than the treadmill at work. I used to be able to do a mile and a half

before stopping, but I'm out of practice. Didn't see much point after I left the force. The only times I need to run now are from the limo to the venue when the paparazzi go nuts. Even though it's been a long-ass day, when I pass the house next door I hit my stride. My maudlin thoughts always spur me on, and tonight is no different. Misery has always driven me.

I didn't mean to snap at Dobbs, but he keeps doing that. At least once a week it's, "If only Master Justin was here" or "Master Justin would know what to say or who to call" as if he's gone on vacation and forgot his cell. It'll be a year next month, way too long to be in denial. I lasted a month and a half. I was even convinced I saw him in the park smiling proudly at me once. So I waited for his call. And waited. Waited some more for a sign. A letter. A phone call explaining the whole thing. Never came. I grew angrier and angrier as the days of waiting began to hammer cracks into my wall of denial. Then one day, I lost it. Put a child pornographer in the hospital after pistol-whipping him repeatedly. Broke his jaw in three places, his nose, even his ocular bone. I turned in my badge that day. Justin still didn't come. That's when I finally lost hope. And my mind went tumbling after.

Anger became depression. I couldn't get out of bed, couldn't even sleep without having horrific nightmares, hell even when I was awake. The booze helped a little and a lot of booze helped even more. My boyfriend at the time, Harry, begged me to get help. I refused, he gave me an ultimatum: get help or we were through. I proceeded to go bar hopping for two days then ended up in a hotel with another man. Not my finest hour. Thus ended the close to love story of Harry O'Hara and Joanna Fallon.

Yet even though I embarrassed and cheated on him, my ex is first and foremost a good man. Too damn good. He was going to save me whether I liked it or not. He called the exact right person to come and kick my pathetic ass. Justin's Aunt Lucy flew in from Independence, took one look at me, and said the magic words: "Jesus. Looks like your mother's risen from the grave." One glance in the mirror and I had to agree. I spent thirty days on "vacation" at a private rehab center, slept for three days straight, and came out the other end broken but taped together enough to function. So yes, my name is Joanna and I'm an alcoholic. Almost nine months without a drink and on Step Ten: admit when I'm wrong. Kind of stuck on that one as from birth it has not been my strong suit.

I stop to catch my breath and wipe the sweat from my face. My trip down memory lane has distracted me so I have no idea how far I've gone. Judging from the house above I've done a mile. Yep, there are the lovebirds. A man and woman stand on their balcony holding champagne glasses wrapped around each other. The woman throws her head back and laughs before the man kisses her neck. Their house is more modern than mine, all glass and sharp angles. With the house lit up I can actually make out their features tonight as I pant like a dog. They're both tall, her an inch shorter than him, though he's much bigger width-wise. His hair glows orange against the light, and if I had to guess her short hair is dark brown. I'd also guess they're newlyweds judging from the fact I've seen them making out on that balcony three times this month. They must feel me staring because the man turns my way, says something to the woman, and they both wave. I'm so mortified by my lack of stealth skills, I sprint back the way I came. Maybe I'll start jogging right next time.

Dobbs has cleaned up our aborted dinner and retreated to his domain when I return. I take a quick shower, throw on my pajamas, and debate climbing into bed and watching crap TV all night. The glamorous life of an heiress, right? But there's work to be done. Since I have become an expert multi-tasker, I answer the trillion e-mails on my BlackBerry as I go back downstairs, through the Hall of Pendergasts with all their portraits hanging on the wall, and into the living room again. I press the button under the stone fireplace. It slides to the side.

Justin Pendergast IV wasn't the only one to leave me his legacy. His alter-ego Justice did as well. Uniforms, equipment, weapons, and super-computer hooked into every worldwide law enforcement database, police band, and closed circuit TV in the city. It has programs that analyze trace evidence, faces on CCTV, along with hacking programs so I can get into any computer, plus a whole host of other programs used to catch bad guys. I call her Doris.

I move down the ramp into the dark room. Doris takes up the majority of the space with only a worn leather couch, rack of Justice uniforms in the corner, closet filled with weapons including stuff I never knew existed—the laser gun is fun—and a coffee pot. A literal man cave. There are two rooms that connect here, one with enough lab equipment to give a mad scientist a chubby, and the other a medical clinic/gun range. That's become Joanna's stress reliever room. I've shot a small town's worth of paper men. They had it coming. They're safe tonight though. I flop into the computer chair and start reviewing the log. Doris keeps track of all the emergency calls and is even programmed to recognize and record any suspicious or violent images she finds on CCTV. Hell, even telephone and cell conversations are within her grasp. Big sister is watching.

Most cases are easily handled by the police. Muggings, domestic violence, drug use are noted and archived just in case. With the bigger offenses she sends a message to a special BlackBerry. When I asked Justin why he had two, he said it was a work thing. He'd excuse himself to take the "call" and lock himself in his office. Really he'd use a secret passage, do a quick change into his costume, and zoom off to fight a bad guy. He even had a program to pump his voice into the room as if he was having a phone conversation. There's a speaker in his office at Pendergast Pavilion too. When I accidentally set it off, for a moment, I thought Justin had risen from the dead to lecture me on the Chinese markets. I was a wreck for the rest of the day.

Justice was mostly muscle, a first responder to crimes normal police officers could be hurt in. He wasn't the great detective we thought he was. The man didn't have time to track down every drug dealer and rapist unless they caused maximum damage. Seeing as I'm all of 5'2", now overweight, and prone to panic attacks, I take a different tact. I may not be on the force anymore but once a cop, always a cop. It's in the bones. I have every crime boss, enforcer, sex offender, and known supervillain under some form of surveillance. Every second of my spare time is spent down here reviewing footage, phone calls, and e-mails on my targets. My, or rather confidential informant #794's, tips helped stop a shipment of sex trafficked young girls from further horrors last week. The case against Oleg Casanov is still building, but my tips to the Feds keep making it stronger. And since I was a police officer for twelve years, I know what evidence can be used at trial. I'd give them the recorded conversation about the shipment but since it came from an illegal wiretap they can't use it. I simply guide them in the right direction.

But tonight is all about helping old friends. My old squad, Priority Homicide, caught a triple last night, a drive-by in Diablo's Ward, my old neighborhood. Two dead bangers and one civilian, Dorothea Clarke, grandmother to one of the dead men. They know it was the men's rival gang, the 3-4's, but have no proof or witnesses. Since crime in the Ward is mostly poor bangers killing bangers, and the press could give a shit, CCTV cameras are sparse there. Must be why Justice installed a few of his own, one of which is right around the corner from the crime scene. I pull up the file from that area. Seconds before the shots, a black SUV turns the corner onto the victim's street. The same car speeds away a few seconds later on the next available camera. No other cars turn on that street at the same time. I enhance the license plate, click a button, and Doris automatically starts her magic. Thirty seconds later I have the owner's name, Duquan Harris. Another click and I get his criminal history. Big shock, he's a known 3-4 member. Gotcha. I package the info together and send it to Harry. He's smart enough to know how to make it look legally obtained. C.I. #794 sure is in a lot of places at the right time. I just saved my old friends days of legwork.

I'm reviewing the footage from Oleg's strip club when hurried footsteps on the ramp cause me to swivel around. Dobbs rushes in unnerved. "What is it?" I ask.

"Visitors." I glimpse up at the red light that's supposed to flash when someone's at the gate, but it's still. "They didn't come through the gate."

"Who—"

"Hope we're not disturbing you," a man says as he strolls into sight. My mouth slacks open. "Just popped by to borrow a cup of sugar."

"They insisted, Miss Joanna," Dobbs says.

Of course. Because my life isn't complicated enough.

As if he owned the place, King Tempest leads his compatriots past my apprehensive butler. I scowl at the threesome, but only Lord Nightingale seems to be looking at me. The other two survey the room. "Smaller than I pictured," King Tempest says. "Comfy looking couch." The most famous crime fighting group is in my secret lair commenting on the décor. O-Kay. Tempest strides toward me, extending his gloved hand. "You must be Joanna. Pleased to finally meet you."

He's tall, easily a foot taller than me and big, though not fat. I'll bet those muscles under his costume are all him. Everything but his mouth is covered by a cowl. The only decorations on his costume are the K.T. on his cape, tornado on his chest, and crown with R.T. on his left arm. The other two heroes are less physically formidable but still intimidating. To his right, Lady Liberty stands up straight in her black suit, long blonde hair cascading around her shoulders. She's tall too, near six foot, but thin. The contours on her suit are probably tailored that way. Like the others only her mouth is visible. Right over her small chest in pink are the initials L.L. and in white on her arm is the same crown and R.T. Next to her waits Lord Nightingale. He's an inch or two shorter than her, medium build but how much of that is the dark purple costume I don't know. There's a bird, I assume a nightingale, on his chest and the crown on his arm. For some reason out of all of them he makes me the edgiest. His gaze hasn't left me since he walked in. Studying me. Creep. Wish I could see his eyes under those tinted plastic slits.

I glance at Tempest's hand then up to his hidden eyes. "What do you want?"

The hero pulls his arm away with a chuckle. "We just came to introduce ourselves."

"Why?" I ask, folding my arms across my chest.

Tempest glances at his friends. "Friendly town, huh?" Liberty smiles but Nightingale remains impassive. Tempest turns back around. "We're here to stay. To get this city back in order. To do that, we need your help."

"More accurately, we need that computer," Liberty says. "It's got the whole city wired, right? Cameras, all of it? We need it, and you need to let us use it."

"How the hell did you even know it was here?"

"Justice," Tempest says. "I showed him ours, and he told us about his. He add those additional cameras?"

My back straightens. "How did you know it was *here*? In this house?"

"He told us," Liberty says.

And the hits keep coming. Just when I think I've gotten over the years of betrayal and lies, some assholes show up uninvited, and the feelings come back. "He told you who he was," I say with a scoff. Me, who knows him for twenty years he keeps half of his existence from but spills to three people he knew for a week.

"And we told him," Tempest says. As if that makes it okay.

I glance at Nightingale, whose head is hung a little. Even without seeing his face I know he's feeling sorry for me. This pisses me off even more. "Good for you. Look, I'm too busy right now to play welcome wagon lady. I'll take your request under advisement, okay? You know the way out." I turn around in my chair.

"I don't know why she's making this so difficult," Liberty says behind me.

I scoff and spin around again. "You barge into my home, insult me, and pretty much demand to use my computer. Excuse me if I'm a little bitchy."

Tempest glances back at Liberty, who folds her arms across her chest. "You're right," Tempest says. "We're sorry."

"Thank you. Bye, now."

"Jesus! She's being ridiculous!" Liberty snaps. "We're here to help you! You should be thanking us for uprooting our lives to save this crappy city, not giving us shit!"

"This crappy city doesn't need you to save it, thank you very much. We're fine."

"Not even you can be that thick," Liberty sneers.

My eyes narrow at her. "Just leave."

"Not until you say yes," Liberty says. "You know you will eventually."

"And why the hell would I?"

"Because," Nightingale says, speaking for the first time. The other two stare at him in surprise. "You're a good person. Because you care about this city and the people within it. Because you know we can help. And because…it's what Justin would want. That's why."

Shit. Double shit. A huge part of me wants to kick them the hell out of this house and seal the doors. I want nothing to do with any of this. Of them. I don't want them anywhere near me. The last time I was dragged into the super world I was shot at, beaten, burned, kidnapped, bombed, spent a day in a coma, and watched as my soul mate killed himself to save me. Not looking for a repeat. I've given enough for this city.

But he's right. Hell, they're all right. This city needs them. No one else is offering. I can't really see a downside, at least for Galilee. Fuck, fuck, fuck. Goddamn, being a good person sucks <u>so</u> much.

So in spite of all the reasons why not, the word, "Fine," escapes my lips. And I know I've sealed my fate.

Tempest smiles. "Thank you."

"Whatever," I say. "You'll need the manual and emergency phone. It alerts you to all major crimes." I collect them from the drawer and hand them to Tempest.

Nightingale steps forward and takes them instead. "Thank you," he mutters with a nod before moving away.

"Welcome."

"You've done a good thing," Tempest says.

For who? "Bully for me. Now, if you'll excuse me, I want to finish up what I was doing so I can go to bed. Use the ramp in the corner to get out. It leads down to the beach. I don't want the neighbors to see you."

"Of course," Tempest says. "Team?" He turns to leave and starts walking. Liberty gives me a shiteating grin before following, and Nightingale lowers his head as if embarrassed before trailing behind as well.

I watch as the first two disappear, but Nightingale stops at the exit. He turns around, head still hung and unable to look at me. "Um…have-have a pleasant evening," he says before literally flying away.

"Okay," I mutter. With a sigh, I fall back into my chair and just sit for a minute. "Shit." Just when I think I'm out, they suck me right back in.

At least this time I have nothing left to lose.

CHAPTER TWO

NEW ACQUAINTANCES

I hate this hospital. I hate this fucking hospital *so* much I seriously considered buying it outright, leveling it to the ground and dancing around the ashes. I was kidnapped here. My soul mate died here. Now, at least twice a month, I'm subjected to hours of torture here as a bunch of rich assholes blather on about cutting beds for indigent people and upping costs to make the hospital more profitable. Sadly, along with the billions I inherited, also came several board positions including those for both museums, the zoo, Restoration Society, hospital, and others I can't remember. I prefer my old method of giving back: slapping cuffs on criminals. Feels like I'm working with them now.

As Danforth Mills drones on about a new drug trial, my mind wanders to my new best friends. I was up late last night pulling every clipping, news report, and even police file on the Triumvirate. The computer database was no help. It seems Justin deleted all the files on superheroes. This pissed me off all over again. Even in death he didn't trust me. As if I'd walk up to someone and shout, "Hey, aren't you Olympia?" My manners aren't that bad. So I had to do it the hard way. I yawn from the memories.

They formed about five years ago when King Tempest was just Tempest, Lord Nightingale was The Nightingale. Liberty, always a Lady, was first on the superhero scene a year before, working solo until Nightingale, and then Tempest arrived to steal her glory. They all did okay alone with Liberty defeating Bully, Nightingale recovering priceless paintings from a ring of thieves, and Tempest rescuing an ambassador from a kidnapper. Best I can tell, their paths crossed while they were all tracking down a meth manufacturer whose stuff was poisoning idiotic college students. They stopped the bad men with guns together and decided to team up. So the men crowned themselves nobility and went out to kick ass with the Lady.

Tempest is the leader, a fact the other two don't seem to mind. He's the physically strongest, probably as strong as Justice was, lifting cars as if they were toys. He must be able to heal faster than normal, Nightingale too, because from what I saw in the footage, they'd be dead twelve times over by now otherwise. Not sure about Liberty though. It looks as if that force field of hers goes up the moment there's danger, so nobody can touch her. Lucky bitch. All three can fly too. Must have helped with the bonding.

The similarities end there. Tempest can control the weather, strongly preferring mini-tornados and lightning bolts from the sky to dispatch hoodlums. Liberty's weapon of choice is energy blasts, presumably made from the same matter as her force field. She has a hell of an arm. Nightingale is a little more subtle. He's the best fighter of them, obviously trained in several forms of martial arts. I found myself admiring his flexibility, among other well defined attributes. He's strong too, though nowhere near as Herculean as Tempest, but can bring someone down with one punch. He's also allegedly the brains of the operation. Some people believe he's a telepath, that he can read minds, but when asked, he said, "No." All the strategy, most of the investigating, even new weapons come from him. Maybe he's responsible for my laser gun.

It took them all of two months, and the defeat of Dr. Demented's giant robot, to gain national notoriety. The sheer longevity of their partnership garners press as most superhero leagues last only a few battles before they drive each other nuts and go their separate ways. The Triumvirate soldiers on together, making them the most popular squad in the world. They even have their own pillowcases and action figures. They are good at their jobs. They've saved two presidents, four visiting queens, defeated Emperor Cain three thrice, cleaned up the worst Independence neighborhood, and still have time to visit children's cancer wards and raise money for various charities.

The group dynamic is intriguing too. Tempest does most of the talking when dealing with the press and hostile heiresses. If asked a direct question, the other two will answer, though Nightingale keeps it to monosyllable and appears ready to bolt the first chance he gets. Liberty doesn't have that problem as I learned last night. I think they appointed Tempest as the face of the group because if given the chance, Liberty would run her mouth and get them in trouble. It wouldn't surprise me to find out Tempest was a politian. He's masterful with the press, cracking jokes and flirting with the female reporters. Justice was the same, walking that fine line of serious yet likable. The other two don't seem to mind the spotlight on him. They hang in the back occasionally smiling before flying off side-by-side behind him. Several reporters speculated that Liberty and Nightingale are a couple, though the only proof are pictures of her quickly kissing or hugging him after a battle. There are none of her embracing Tempest, so who knows? I didn't get any of those vibes last night. If anything—

"Joanna?"

I snap out of my thoughts and see the board, all ten members, staring at me with their hands up. "What? Oh," I say, raising my hand for the vote.

"Good," Danforth says. I really hope we didn't just vote to close the free clinic or something. "Then onto the next item on the agenda. The opening of the Rebecca Thornton wing. Joanna?"

"Right," I say, pulling out my notes. "Um, construction was completed last week and the building inspector will be by next Wednesday to sign off. Beds, equipment, medical supplies, etc. is already being set up as I speak. The first of the families pre-selected have been notified and can move in on schedule barring unforeseen complications."

"The press have been calling about it," the Chief of Staff says, none too happy.

"Direct them to Gene Tully in the Pendergast press office," I say. "We still want to keep this thing as low-key as possible, right? Just a few members of the local media?"

"Yes," Danforth says. "I think this hospital has had more than its fair share of the limelight this year."

All eyes glance my way, but I remain impassive. "Good," I say. "Is that all for today? I need to go check on the movers."

"I believe that's it. Meeting adjourned."

Praise the Lord. I toss my notepad in my obscenely expensive Bherkin bag, my stylist and personal shopper Isolde insisted I needed—she was right, it fits everything—and hurry out before people attempt small talk. I loathe small talk. Our Lady of Perpetual Sorrow Hospital was voted second best hospital in the country seven years in a row and is the third busiest. There are a thousand beds, thirty floors, and it's always bustling. She's Galilee's crowning glory next to the Falls across the river. The finest doctors use cutting-edge technology, new procedures, and new drugs inside these walls. The uber-gene was isolated here thirty-five years ago right on the ninth floor. Now its claim to fame is "The place Justice died." God, do I hate this place.

    As I walk to the elevator, the same elevator where I was held at gunpoint by a psychopathic socialite, the staff eye me as I pass. I'm an international celebrity now, I had to get used to it. The pregnant woman in the wheelchair keeps glancing at me in the elevator apprehensively, as if my unluckiness can be spread like a virus. Got used to that too. She's wheeled off on the maternity floor.

    I'm off on good old twenty-six. It's changed a lot since I first saw it almost a year ago while being pulled out of the elevator shaft by the murderous bastard supervillain Alkaline. I always get a chill when I step onto this floor, as if a part of him is still here. Guess he kind of is. We never would have built this place if not for him. If he hadn't raped and murdered Rebecca, Justin never would have thought to build it. Now families who either can't afford months in a hotel or just need to be around for their child, who is getting long term care at the hospital, have a place to stay. I've had crews working around the clock for a year to build this place. Money was no object. Gone is the storage space it once was, replaced with a high-tech dorm with twenty separate, two bedroom one-bath suites, communal living room and kitchen with a doctors and nurses station at the end. The parents can be with their kid 24/7, nurturing them through their illness. At least some good sprang from the whole ordeal.

    Movers, contractors, painters, decorators, and nurses are all hard at work whipping this place into shape as I make my way down to the living room where my assistant extraordinaire Shannon directs traffic while texting. She was Justin's assistant before, and she's the only reason I haven't bankrupt the company yet. She knows all the ins and outs, all the players and their spouse's names too. As always, she's dressed in sensible designer pumps, pencil skirt, with matching vest and white shirt, brown hair in a chignon like mine. I learned to dress like an executive from her, though I try to avoid skirts. My legs are too stout to pull them off.

"Isolde called," Shannon says as I approach. "She needs to move your appointment to four, not three. I told her it was fine."

"Couldn't she just send the clothes?"

"The suits from Paris arrived, and they need to be tailored." She hands me my phone to pull hers out. "Lane also called. The Japanese deal is going through."

"Wonderful. How are things here?" I ask, scrolling through my twenty new e-mails this hour.

"We're having artwork issues. They need your approval on which paintings to buy."

"I could give a shit. Let the decorators decide, that's why they're here. Just nothing depressing or scary." My phone buzzes, and the display pops up. Harry's calling. My stomach used to clench when I saw his name but since Step Nine, make amends, and he forgave me, I'm happy to hear his voice.

Looking back on it we were doomed from the fucking start. Forgetting that he was my boss, I was in love with another man, he was considerably older than me, and the timing sucked, we were just too damn different. We both thought the other would change. He's a hopeless romantic who does all he can to see the good in people. It'd take a memory wipe and personality transplant to make me that way. Just not how I'm built. And besides the job and great sex, we had little in common. He read books, I shot guns. I love to travel, he hasn't left this coast in years. He began mentioning kids, I began mentioning goldfish. But if I'm honest, it really came down to the fact he was too good for me. Way too good. Me cheating and him forgiving me just proves it. For whatever reason some people just have a darkness inside them. It can be tiny and it certainly doesn't make you evil, but those without it can never understand or relate. Harry was all sunshine, and I damn sure didn't want to dim that. He's fine though. About a month after we broke up, he began dating this cute ADA who always had eyes for him. They moved in together last month. I had Shannon send a goldfish.

"Joanna Fallon."

"Jo, it's Harry."

"Hi. How is my favorite ex doing this fine day?" Shannon smirks before walking away. The consummate professional.

The elevator door opens and a strange man in a lab coat steps off, looking around. Probably a doctor who got off on the wrong floor. He's vaguely familiar, but I can't place him.

"Well, thank you," Harry says. "I just wanted to let you know I received another interesting e-mail last night. Informative too."

He and I have had this conversation dozens of times. He'll tell me to stop, threaten to turn me in, say he's worried about me, and in the end thank me. I'm only half paying attention. For some reason it's really bothering me I can't remember who that doctor is. This is why Shannon has to accompany me to events, otherwise I wouldn't know who the hell I was talking to. "Really? I love those types of e-mails. They're usually so helpful."

"It was," Harry says. "Led us right to two murderers. They confessed and everything."

"Then you should thank whoever sent it, sans lecture this time."

"Jo…" and he's off. I pull the phone away from my ear. Who the hell is that guy? He's so busy studying the painting of wavy lines, he doesn't notice the men carrying the ladder. He backs up, lifting up his horn-rimmed glasses in case that helps with the exam, and smacks into the ladder. With Harry droning on I don't hear the workman's words, but the doctor appears embarrassed, cheeks turning red. They turn almost purple when he glances up and notices me staring. His thin mouth drops open and eyes pop behind the glasses. It's damn cute. It's far less cute when more workmen pass with boxes and the still befuddled doctor steps to the side to let them pass. His elbow brushes the painting. It falls off its hook onto the ground.

"Harry, I have to go. You can yell at me later. Say hey to the guys and Bella for me. Bye." I end the call and rush over to the doctor, who turns the painting over, trying to figure out which way is up. "Excuse me. I—"

"I am so sorry," the doctor says, mortified and still spinning the damn painting. "If it is damaged in any way, I will of course pay. I-I know I'm not supposed to be here. I didn't think you'd be here. Not-Not that that excuses me sneaking in, in-in fact it's worse. I—"

"It's okay," I chuckle. I'm used to making people nervous but this is ridiculous.

He hangs his head so he doesn't have to look at me. "I-I'm sorry. I'm not normally so clumsy." I find that hard to believe. Judging from his bushy dark brown hair in dire need of a cut, glasses falling to the end of his straight nose, pasty complexion, wrinkled blue dress shirt and chinos, and scuffed brown penny loafers with actual pennies in them, it wouldn't surprise me if he didn't actually knock down whole buildings on a daily basis. Even when he tries to re-hang the painting, it takes two tries. "I-I'll just go."

He steps away, but I move to block him. "I'm sorry if this is going to sound rude, but…how do I know you? I can't place it. We have met before, right?"

Head hung, he says, "Yes. Um, I-I believe it was about a-a-a year ago. I-I'm Dr. Jonathan Ambrose. I just started here." He holds out his long hand for me to shake, which I do.

I've recently heard the name. If memory serves, I had to approve his hiring and drug study two months ago as a member of the board, but even then the name sounded familiar. Okay, leading neurologist from Independence. Also into infectious diseases and created some retro-virus that saved a million people or something over a decade ago when he was twenty. Youngest person to be nominated for the Nobel Prize in medicine. Since then he developed multiple drugs for Alzheimers, and Parkinsons, then gave away the patents. He's either crazy or rich in his own right. Of course those aren't mutually exclusive. Danforth almost wet his pants when he read that the profits from his multiple sclerosis drug trial would go to the hospital. Potentially billions of dollars if the treatment works. He came here for the trial but also to begin working with our doctors researching gene therapy. But it's not from the hospital that I recognize him from.

He glances up at me over his glasses, and I meet his eyes for an instant. They're dark blue like sapphires. Only one person I've ever met with eyes like that. "Jem!" I say with a smile. "You're Rebecca's friend. We met at the engagement party the night before she…yeah! You asked me to dance a couple times. You were at the memorial service too."

"That-That's right," he says, running his hand nervously through his curly hair.

"Sorry it took me so long to remember. That was a crazy time, the file got lost."

"Understandable."

That night comes back to me, well most of it. Rebecca tried to set us up, saying we were "absolutely perfect" for each other, but at the time I was secretly seeing Harry. When he stood me up, I proceeded to get blotto and spent the night flirting and dancing with the cute but shy doctor in front of me. And he is cute. Not classically handsome by any means, more striking. Medium height, a little on the skinny side with a long face, high cheekbones to die for, and a dimple on his left cheek when he smiles if I recall correctly. I may have touched it that night. Even his ears are adorable, sticking out a little too far. Several times that night I almost kissed him but managed to reign myself in. I wasn't a cheater. Then. I saw him at Rebecca and Justin's funerals, but we didn't speak. "And I'm sorry for my behavior that night, just ditching you like that when you left to get me water. A lot of the night is still fuzzy, so I apologize for anything else inappropriate I did."

"You were fine," he says with a quick smile. "Lo-Lovely even."

I chuckle. "Kind of doubt that. Not really an adjective people use to describe me, especially when I was drinking, but thank you for that lie. It was just a crappy night for me all around." Jem's face falls. "Not because of you! Dancing and talking with you was the highlight of the night."

"I stepped on your feet," he says with a grimace. "A lot."

"That must be one of the things the alcohol erased. Lucky you, huh?" God, I feel like a moron. Change the record, Jo. "So, um, how are you finding our hospital? The board thinks you're the Second Coming, so whatever you want, we'll no doubt give you."

"The facilities, the staff are all wonderful, thank you. I am sure I-I shall be content and productive here."

"Good. Like I said, if you need anything, don't hesitate to ask. Forty virgins, the Crown Jewels, name of a good pizza place, it's all doable. Just give me a call."

"Thank you. I will remember that."

"Joanna!" Shannon shouts down the hall. "We need you!"

Ugh. "I'm sorry, I have to go. It was nice to see you again, Dr. Ambrose."

I'm about to step away when he says, "Jem." When I turn back around, I find him lifting his head, those wonderful eyes meeting mine. "Please, call me Jem."

I smile. "Welcome to Galilee Falls, Jem. See you around." I spin and walk down the hall. Don't know why, but halfway down I glance back and see him stealing glimpses at me too. A lovely tingle wiggles through me from head to toe. Haven't felt that in awhile. It brings a private grin to my face.

"Who was that?" Shannon asks when I reach her.

"An old, new friend."

*

I attempt to force the cute doctor out of my thoughts, which is easier said than done when the rest of the day is spent in boring as hell meetings about contract appendices and profit sharing points. I don't know how Justin didn't stick a pencil in his ear during these things. So my mind wanders to dimples, dancing and doctors.

He's not my usual type. I like my men tough, confident and put together. But it's been over nine months since I got laid, and that last time was beyond awful. Hell, I barely remember it. I'm just bored, depressed, horny and lonely. Never a good combination. The real problem is I have to stay that way for at least three more months, per my sponsor. No relationships for at least a year. Stupid program. Wonder if that counts for men I met before I became sober. I should get my lawyers on that one.

Not that I'm sure Jem's interested in my grandfather clause. Last year was a fucking lifetime ago. He could be married with a baby on the way by now. And I did ditch him without a second thought. Men don't take kindly to that type of thing. He did seem eager to get away from me today, though that could just be the shyness. I remember it took a lot that night to get him to speak a word to me, and then it was about work, the crappy state of the world, or the happy couple. In my drunken haze, I could have mistaken politeness for flirting. I tend to think I'm a sex bomb when plastered. Just another thing I miss about booze.

Okay, this is moot anyway. I learned my lesson from Harry. I don't belong with good, uncomplicated men. I just end up dragging them into the abyss with me. And I don't really have time to date. I wake at six, dress, get to the office by seven, meetings, meetings, meetings usually until eight unless I have a gala or party, which is once every two weeks on average. I spend most weekends at the office, and the rest of my free time is devoted to my side project. I haven't been sailing in weeks. Hell, I don't even have time for a quickie. No cute doctors for me.

I arrive at the mansion at eight after a grueling two hour marketing meeting to find my bland food waiting in the kitchen. Dobbs must have gone to bed early. I scarf the food down right at the counter before going into the living room. A lot of wasted days spent in here watching movies or playing video games with my best friend. Now I just come in here for access to Doris. Tonight is no different. I open the fireplace and step in. The sound of typing echoes up the ramp. Someone's down there. My stomach clenches with fear, and I stop walking. The smart part of my brain knows who it is but the irrational side runs through all the scenarios. Robbers, a villain, even a ghost are possible. Yeah, I'm being ridiculous. I continue down, and sure enough a familiar purple costumed man furiously types on the computer. His back is to me, and if he notices my presence he doesn't let on. "Hello," I say.

He stops typing but doesn't turn around. "Hello," he says before clacking away again.

"Did Dobbs let you in?"

Nightingale doesn't answer for a few seconds, then says, "No."

"I don't know if I'm really comfortable with you guys popping over whenever you damn well please, especially if I'm not home."

More silence, then, "Sorry."

I roll my eyes. Obviously not a conversationalist. "But you're going to do it anyway, aren't you?" I ask, walking over.

"Yes."

I wheel the spare computer chair to his side. He glances at me, then back to the monitor with what looks like an essay on it. "What are you doing?" I ask as I sit.

He quickly looks again. "Updating."

"I have a guy for that." Lizard, great hacker, lousy hygiene.

"I'm better."

I raise an eyebrow. "Finally. A complete sentence. We're making progress." The hero doesn't smile. "So, what have you done to my Doris?"

"I, uh, uploaded the latest facial and speech recognition software, got it access to the Defense Department's mainframe, and currently am adding additional information to the known criminal files from our old system in Independence."

"What about *The Sims*? Can you put that on there too?" I ask with a smile, which is not returned. Okay, I'm trying but he isn't giving me an inch. Fine. "So, how long are you going to be? I need the computer."

"Why?"

"To download porn," I say defensively. "None of your business."

"I have already reviewed the log, recordings, footage, and reports for the day." He glances at me again. "You are very thorough."

I'm very pissed is what I am. "You went through my files?"

"Some. We knew generally who the major criminals in the city were, but we'll review the complete files. I, or one of the others, will come every day to view the day's footage."

"So, in other words, you're cutting me out of the loop," I spit out.

"We may need you in emergency situations, but...we're here now. This isn't your burden anymore."

"My *burden*? Helping my city and keeping people safe isn't a burden. Is that what you consider it?"

The hero hangs his head, I hope from shame. "I-I didn't mean it like that. Of course it isn't. I-I-I just assumed after what transpired last year, and all your sacrifices then and since, you'd desire to be as far from this sort of thing as possible."

"What thing?"

"Violence. Danger. Supers."

"Well, you're being in my house every day kind of makes that hard, huh?" I point out.

"We will go out of our way to make sure nobody links us together. Measures have already been taken. Perhaps it would be best if you frequented this room as little as possible so as to limit our interactions."

I fold my arms across my chest. "Now you're telling me where I can and can't go in my own house?"

"No! No, of course not," he backpedals. "I'm-I'm sorry. I'm articulating this incorrectly."

"Yeah, now I see why you stick to monosyllables."

"I just, I," he says, flustered. He takes a second, lips pursed as he tries to find the correct words. "I—*We're* aware of how close you and Justice were. It is only logical, that due to the circumstances of his death, you would feel partially responsible." My back straightens. "And due to your feelings of culpability, you would locate an avenue to compensate for his loss, i.e. spending hours down here attempting to forestall crimes he would if he were alive."

"So?" I ask, voice hard.

"So, we're here to lift that burden. You don't have to carry this city anymore. You can go out with friends, take trips, even…date. Live your life. As Justin would want it." He turns back to the computer screen. "That's simply what I meant."

"And how the hell would you know what Justin would want for me?"

Once again he's silent, trying to find the words before saying, "He loved you. He'd want you to be happy. And you're not. This could be the first step toward it. Let us do that for you."

I'm speechless. Shame has silenced me. He's trying to help me, and I'm giving him shit for it. "You don't get it. The only times this year I've been even close to happy have all been down in this room. Finding the right footage to take someone down. Helping the police piece together evidence. I almost felt like I was my old self again, for all that's worth," I say with a scoff. "Out there, all that bullshit, it's what makes me nuts. My friends treat me like a China doll, I'm not exactly corporate material, and as for men, hell there's nobody I would inflict myself upon." Nightingale glances at me, and I half smile. "Too broken. Think I always will be. But in here that doesn't matter. Hell, it might actually be a good thing. So you're not cutting me out of this. I'm helping you whether you like it or not. I know this city. I know the players. I have the connections. Nobody but us will know. I want to help. I *need* to help. Don't freeze me out. Besides, it's my house. My computer. I can always just call the cops on you for trespassing. The press would love that, huh? You have no choice."

He sits as still as a statue for seconds, the wheels in his head turning. I wish I could see his eyes under the goggles. Wish I could read his face. Seems unfair he can read mine because I feel him studying it now. Then he turns away. "Fine."

"The others won't mind?"

"They won't care."

"Good," I say with a smile. I scoot the chair over so our arms touch. He doesn't pull away. "So. Show me how to hack into the Defense Department then I'll make us some sandwiches. Sound good?"

"Sounds great," he says after a pause.

"Then let's get started."

And for a brief second, he smiles too.

Chapter three

Dog Days

I get nightmares. A lot. Once a week on the good weeks and three on the bad. I wake up tangled in sweat stained sheets, panting like a dog. It's not always James Ryder tormenting me either, though he makes his fair share of appearances. No, sometimes it's Harry pressing a gun to my head or my mother shoving me off the Falls. Those I can handle. Some deep breaths, few minutes of television, and I'm back to my old self. No, it's the good dreams that ruin my day. The ones where I know it's a dream, that it's going to end, but I don't care because Justin's there and we're walking along the beach, or sailing, or just sitting on the couch talking like we used to. I always sense it coming to an end though. I beg and beg and cry and cry, and he just holds me, caressing and kissing my hair as I cling to him. Then he whispers, "I love you," kisses my lips and vanishes into thin air. It takes me a moment to realize he's gone, that he was never really there, and that I have to wake up now. When the veil of sleep lifts, it's as if the world has dropped out from under me again, and I can't stop crying because I still feel that kiss on my lips.

I can barely get out of bed on those days. My AA sponsor Marlene, a mother of three with her own troubles, has spent many an hour talking the bottle out of my hand after one of those. Hard to reach her when I'm in Tokyo though. Improvising, I woke poor Shannon to watch TV with me. She had to literally push me into the meeting with the telecom executives. Thank God Lane, our CFO, was there because I sure as hell couldn't concentrate. The Justin dreams are growing more frequent, not the once a month like usual, but twice a week for the past two weeks. I don't know if it's because the anniversaries are coming up or because of my new acquatainces. Both judging from the conversations Justin and I have in my dreams. It almost makes me want to sever ties. Almost.

The Triumvirate *is* effective. Been in town two weeks and not only have they arrested Gigantor, stopped Carrion from raising an undead army, and rescued another shipment of sex trafficked children, thus ensuring Oleg Casanov will spend the rest of his life in prison. Nightingale and I cracked that last one just a few hours before I had to leave for Tokyo. I got an anonymous e-mail with the news story and picture of the Triumvirate carrying teenage girls out of a ship container, then another the next day as Feds arrested several key members of the trafficking ring as I stepped off my jet. They also closed down several brothels and a kiddie porn ring. Wished I was there to celebrate with them, that is if they ever celebrate.

They are a serious bunch, especially Nightingale. It takes a lot to get him to talk, let alone smile. He grew friendlier as the days went on, even laughing when I smeared mustard on my nose and didn't know it. The other two only popped by once each and barely acknowledged me. At least they weren't hostile. I can't tell if they dislike me or think I'm inconsequential. Not that I give a shit but for the sake of being comfortable I hope those trafficking busts upgrades me from nuisance to ally in their eyes.

I arrive home from the Galilee airfield at seven in the morning after an eighteen hour flight, fall into my bed, and get to sleep five whole hours before Dobbs wakes me. I'm so exhausted I didn't even dream. I have a luncheon for the Restoration Society at one, and I would cancel but it's my friend Bitsy's event, and she takes it personally when I don't show. She's been surprisingly helpful since I "re-entered society" after Justin's death. She was pretty great, not leaving my side for the first few events and politely telling assholes to shove their comments as they came. I'd known most of the people for twenty years, but was considered an outsider, there solely because Justin needed an escort. Once Ward trash, always Ward trash. Not that it stops them from inviting me so their charity/party/event gets press coverage.

I put on my silk black/white/yellow swirl dress and huge floppy straw hat Isolde selected for this occasion. I'd look pretty damn good if not for the dark circles under my blue eyes. I'm too pale, close to sick looking even which makes my true black hair appear fake. Since it's a luncheon and I'll be sitting the whole time, I put on heels which adds a few inches to my 5"2' frame. I still look and feel like a kid playing dress-up.

Dobbs fills me in on all I've missed in the three days I've been away on the drive to the Historical Society building. I tune out the story about the repairmen in the west wing as we cross over Pendergast Bridge. I drive over this testament to modern ingenuity twice a day but each time the memories flood back. Understandable though. I did try to kill myself on this bridge twenty-one years ago after my father was murdered. If that wasn't enough, that same night I met Justin and fell head over heels in love with him. He saved my life in so many ways. It's actually good to drive over this thing. Reminds me of why I go to these charity luncheons with those vapid women who thumb their surgically altered noses at me. It's what he'd do. It's hard, I hate it, but if I can help even one person, then it's all worth it. Just wish I didn't have to wear a damn dress and heels to do it.

I'm late as usual, so most of the women are already in the banquet hall for cocktails. Another problem with these things is the alcohol. My mouth waters at the sight of those Bloody Mary's and Mimosas. I move to one of the waiters carrying food. No wonder I've gotten so plump. Okay, quick appearance then leave. There are about twenty to thirty women here, all with ornate hats every color of the rainbow and enough diamonds to fill a conflict mine, which they all probably did at one time. A literal ray of light shines through the skylight onto Brittney "Bitsy" Armstrong's rose colored hat. Like almost every other woman here she's thin, tan, with straight brown hair and tucked everything. She holds court with a few women, only one of whom I don't know. Bitsy spots me scarfing down two cucumber sandwiches in the corner. Damn. She excuses herself and walks over, double kissing my cheeks. "You came!"

"Of course," I say.

Bitsy links her arm through mine and starts leading me back to her friends. "There is someone here you *absolutely* have to meet. She's a riot."

Lorna, Samantha, Rachel and Helena surround a tall woman dressed in a low-cut, bright red dress with cherries on it and matching pillbox hat. Edgy for this crowd. She's gorgeous with perfect tan skin, glossy dark brown hair cut in a pageboy, high cheekbones, and big brown doe eyes. I know her from somewhere I can't place. The other women paste fake smiles on, but the stranger's seems genuine. "Hello, all," I say.

"Joanna," Lorna says, "good to see you."

"Joanna, this is Alexia," Bitsy says of the stranger. "You know Alexia, the model. She's married to Brendan Darby, the new Galilee Angel's running back. Lexie, this is my good friend Joanna Fallon. She's head of Pendergast Industries."

"Delighted to meet you," Lexie says with a nod.

"Likewise. I love your dress."

"Thanks. Calvin made it especially with me in mind," she says, preening.

"He is such a sweet man," Samantha says as if she bore his children.

All the women are practically salivating having a real celebrity in their midst not just the usual socialites and business types like me. A supermodel is one step away from a movie star. This poor woman will be inundated with invitations to every event in town and a million calls for lunch. Good luck to her. "How do you like our fair city so far?" I ask.

"It's certainly friendly," she says with smiles all around.

"Friendliest city in the world," Lorna says, beaming.

My eyes roll involuntarily, and Lexie smirks. "Seems that way," she says.

"So you moved here because of your husband?" I ask.

She sips her mimosa. "Among other reasons."

"Brendan was with the Independence Eagles," Bitsy says to me before turning back to Lexie. "Joanna here doesn't follow football."

"Well, I won't hold that against her. I barely follow it too. I'm not big on violence."

"Amen to that," I say. The women tense up. They do that a lot around me.

Bitsy was trained from the womb for just this situation. Ever the hostess, she says, "You two have something else in common. Lexie, didn't you move into Grady Levine's house? She's your neighbor, Joanna."

She's one of the lovebirds then. "Really?"

"You know I think I've seen you running the shore," Lexie says. "You always look so determined when you run."

"And you always look very cozy with your husband," I say.

"You know how it is when you can't keep your hands off someone," she says, blushing. Me and the other women don't say a word. She smiles again. "Or not." Lexie clears her throat. "Will you all please excuse me? I have to powder my nose."

"I'll show you where it is," I say, eager to leave.

I lead the model away from the girls. "I don't really have to go," Lexie says.

"I figured. They can be a bit much all together like that."

"Are they better individually?"

"Not really," I say with a smile.

"I was just afraid I was going to fall asleep. I hate inane talk about Botox and boarding schools. I get enough of that at photo shoots." We make our way to the hallway where the bathrooms are and socialites are not. Lexie sighs in relief as she leans against the wall and closes her eyes. "This is soooo much better. I hate these things. You need a lobotomy to get through them."

"Then why'd you come?"

"Same as you, probably. Support a good cause, network, meet new people, blah blah blah. I'm setting up a charity for battered women, building new shelters. Can't invite people to events and get their cash if I don't know them. Such is the price of being a decent human being."

"Well, count me in. I've seen firsthand how important shelters are."

She pulls out gum from her cherry purse and offers me a stick, which I take. "Yeah, you were a cop, right? Do you miss it?"

"When I have time. You miss Independence?"

"When I have time," she says with a smug smile. "I threw a hissy fit when Bren told me he wanted to move here. I was born and raised in Independence. All my friends, my family, my haunts, they're all there. I knew that city inside and out. And, I mean no offense by this, then to move to a war zone without a decent fashion scene…it's been an adjustment."

"The crime's not really as bad as the news would have you believe. Most ordinary citizens never come across a villain in their lives."

"Really?"

"Yeah," I say with a reassuring smile. "You're perfectly safe."

The sound of shattering glass and screaming women jolts me so bad I swallow my gum. Oh shit. Not good. The women continue wailing as if set on fire as Lexie and I round the corner of the hallway. Double shit. Four men in black tactical suits toting automatic weapons and one familiar woman rappel through the broken skylight while a helicopter hovers above. Triple shit.

Fucking KitKat. Wonderful. She's low on the villain food chain with no real powers to speak of. Mostly a thief but a damn good one, breaking into jewelry stores and museums. $500,000 this year alone. Her real claim to fame is being voted sexiest villain three years in a row. Easy to see why with a brown bustier and tight pants with claw marks across them encasing a curvy figure. Her orange hair hangs loose, obstructing the harlequin mask. The guests shriek and run around almost in circles out of blind terror. I'm so shocked I can barely process the whole scene. One of the henchmen lands a foot from Bitsy. She takes one look at the huge gun and faints dead away, head thumping hard on the floor.

Without thinking, and let's face it I rarely do, I dash over to my friend, just one of the many scurrying around in panic. The men move to the doors to block people from escaping as KitKat circles the room with a smile on her ruby red lips. I reach Bitsy and fall to my knees beside her. There's blood spewing from where she hit her head. I put pressure on it.

"Good afternoon, ladies," KitKat shouts over the mayhem. "Sorry to crash in. I know it's bad manners, but so is screaming, so *shut up!*" The henchmen at the main door points his gun at the ceiling and lets loose a barrage of bullets overhead. Everyone covers their ears and cowers, myself included. For a flash, I'm back on the hospital roof, bullets whizzing by my head as Alkaline's goons try to blow my brains out. The room falls silent except for a few whimpers. I'm trying my damndest to stop trembling and calm my ragged breath. *Not now.* Don't you dare fall apart now, Jo. "Good! Now, if you'd all be so kind as to hand your jewelry and purses to my friends here, I'd be much obliged."

Dear God I hope Lexie is calling the police. As we all remove our trinkets with quaking hands, the men and KitKat quickly circle the room collecting them. Helena has trouble getting her five-carat emerald ring off, sobbing as she tugs on it. When the man reaches her, she's near hysterics. "It won't come off!" she cries.

He points the gun right at her forehead. "Get it off now!"

"I-I can't," she whimpers.

The man presses the barrel to her flesh. "Now!" he roars.

"Leave her alone!" someone with my voice shouts. My mouth closes, and I realize it was me. Oh, fuck.

All eyes, including KitKat's, swivel toward me. She smiles and saunters over to me, pistol in hand. "Well, well, well, look what the Kat's caught. Joanna fucking Fallon. This is my lucky day."

I can't take my eyes off the gun pointed a foot from my heart. "Just take the jewels and go. There's no need to scare or hurt anyone," I manage to say with authority. Inside I'm about to join Bitsy on the floor.

"Gee, thanks for the advice," she says before studying me for a second. "You know the pictures on the news didn't do you any justice." She giggles. "Get it? Justice? Anyway, I just wanted to say thanks for getting him killed. I've made more money in the past few months than the whole two years before. It was real swell of you."

"Go to hell."

She clucks her tongue. "Boys, guess who just volunteered to be our hostage? This woman just keeps on giving."

"Done ma'am," says one of the henchmen. He hikes his pouch over his shoulder. Larceny completed, the others return to the rappel ropes.

KitKat tilts her head to grin down at me. "Ready to go, JoJo? Get up." She grabs my arm, but I yank it away with a sneer. I can stand by myself. "Hope you're not afraid of heights."

"I'm not," a woman says above.

All eyes move up to the source. Hovering in what's left of the jagged skylight is Lady Liberty with a huge smirk, blonde hair and cape flapping from the nearby helicopter. I will never say another bad word about her again. The bad guys, including KitKat, all gape at her for a second. I don't waste the opportunity. As I was trained at the academy, with one fluid movement, I grab the barrel of her gun, step to the side, yank it toward me so hard it breaks her finger, tilt her wrist down, and commandeer the gun. She yelps in pain and surprise. Still got it.

At the same time, Liberty swoops down like a hawk toward the now frightened mice. The henchmen raise their guns as she rockets toward them. By the time I have the gun, the men open fire. All the ladies scream in panic, some ducking down, but I tune this out. I point the gun at the villain while sweeping her legs out from underneath her. In shock, she remains on the floor, staring up at me as spent slugs rain down on us. The bullets hit Liberty's force-field and cascade down like copper hail. Oblivious, the hero glides around the room punching, kicking, and generally beating the shit out of four hulking motherfuckers with guns. Two pounce at the same time but with a swift kick backwards and glittering energy blast forward, both topple like dominos. Without missing a beat, she dispatches the last one with a roundhouse to the jaw. He crumples to the floor unconscious like the others. It's all over in about ten seconds. Girl power.

Panting from the effort and still in battle stance with fists raised, she surveys the room for more threats. She stops on me, meeting my eyes. "That all of them?"

"Guy in the helicopter," I say.

"I'll get him. Police are on the way." She glances down at KitKat. "Looks like you can handle the rest." She smiles at me. "Good job." And as fast as she came, she's gone.

A few seconds later the ropes fall and the helicopter flies away so we can hear the sirens in the distance. The other women rise, all but KitKat who glares up at me. I grin. "Bitch, you crashed the wrong fucking party."

*

I insisted on riding to the hospital with the still sobbing Bitsy. The paramedics revived her with smelling salts but advised she should go get checked for a concussion. All in all it could have been a hell of a lot worse. A few other guests were treated for minor cuts and bruises. When the ambulance was pulling away I saw a medic splinting KitKat's finger in the back of a police cruiser. That brought a small smile to my face.

The emergency room at Our Lady is quiet when we arrive, so we're brought right into an exam room. "Get Dr. Ambrose," I order the intern who begins looking my friend over. Only the best for my friend. Bitsy threw up twice in the ambulance, so I'm certain she has a concussion. Last year made me quite the expert. About ten minutes later, and a million assurances nobody will hold the robbery against her since it was her party, the good doctor with nurse in tow arrives. I'm embarrassed to admit my stomach flutters when he steps in. He glances up from Bitsy's chart, glasses perched on the end of his nose, and his mouth opens a little in surprise when he sees me. It takes a second for him to remember himself. His mouth sets into a firm, straight line. "Mrs. Armstrong?" he asks, all business.

I pat her hand. "I'll let Dr. Ambrose examine you." I stand. "I'll be just outside."

With a smile her way, I walk to the door. Jem doesn't glimpse up as I pass. My cell has been buzzing non-stop since we left, so I go to the waiting area and plop down in one of the chairs. On the TV above a reporter recaps the "hostage situation at the Restoration Society luncheon just minutes ago." I give it half an hour before my name crops up and I'm inundated with phone calls from reporters. My cousin Veronica, one of said bottom feeders though I never hold that against her, has already tried per my call history. Dobbs, Gene Tully my press guy, my old partner Cam, and Harry have all left voice messages. As I'm texting Dobbs to come get me, Thayer Armstrong, Bitsy's husband, rushes into the lounge. He spots me and hurries over. "I got your message. How is she? Is she okay?"

"Fine. They're examining her now." As if on cue, Jem strides into the waiting area with his head up for once. "Thayer Armstrong, this is Je—I mean, Dr. Ambrose. Thayer is Bitsy's husband."

"Your wife is resting at the moment. I suspect she has a concussion, but we'll need a CAT scan to confirm. She's coherent, up and talking, and that's a very good sign, but a head wound can be tricky. Should the scan show swelling, we'll want to keep her for a few days to monitor her. Regardless, she'll need to stay overnight for observation."

"Can I see her?" Thayer asks.

"Of course. She's in exam two. We'll collect her for the scan shortly."

"Thank you, doctor," Thayer says before walking away to find his wife. If I didn't know the man went through mistresses like socks, I'd almost believe he loved her.

"So, she'll be okay?" I ask.

"Yes, I believe so." He glances down at the blood on my dress. "Were you injured?"

"Oh, no, it's Bitsy's blood. I'm fine."

"And are you, I mean, you just experienced another trauma. Do you need, are you," he stammers, "would you like me to recommend—"

"I'm fine," I assure him. "No psychiatrists. I'll be fine. Just another day in Galilee Falls. It's—"

The sound of a gunshot stops my words and my breath. My whole body locks up like Ft. Knox. For an instant, the hospital vanishes. I'm stuck in a black subway tunnel running for my life as two men shoot at me. The bullets whizzing past me, my sore body pushed to the limit, and even the gravel under my bare, bleeding feet overwhelm me. A man says my name, but his touch pulls me from hell. I'm back at the hospital, shaking uncontrollably as Jem's concerned eyes study me. I can't breathe. No matter how hard I try, no air will enter. This makes me panic even more. I'm gonna die. I don't want to die. Without a word, the doctor grasps my hand and leads me past the nurse picking up the metal tray with instruments she dropped. We enter an exam room. Jem shuts the door before positioning me in a chair in the corner.

He kneels in front of me, dark blue eyes meeting my tear-filled ones. "Joanna, listen to me. Listen to my voice. Listen to my voice. You are safe. This is a safe place. You are safe. No one is going to hurt you here, I swear it to you, but you need to breathe." Jem places my hand on his chest, then covers mine with his. "Breathe. Follow my lead." His chest moves up and down as he takes a deep breath. Then again. I'm beginning to see spots now. "Stay with me, Joanna. I am right here with you. I'm not going anywhere. Breathe. You can do it, Joanna. Just breathe. *Breathe*," he orders through gritted teeth. I gasp as I expel the air I was holding. Tears trickle onto my cheeks. Jem smiles, making his eyes almost twinkle. He curls his fingers in mine to make a fist. "Good.

Excellent. See? It's easy. You're doing brilliantly. Keep going."
For about thirty seconds I match him breath for breath, my eyes
never leaving his. The trembling lessens with each pant. I can even
wipe the tears away. "You're doing great," he says with another
smile. Those smiles calm me more than the deep breaths.

A minute later I can breathe without having to force it. I
can even talk. "I'm okay," I whisper. I don't really want to but I
pull my hand away from his chest. "Thank you."

"How often do you have panic attacks?"

"Whenever some psychopath points a gun at me," I chuckle
as I wipe more falling tears away. "Um, they used to be more
frequent. Loud noises, a man who resembled Alkaline, looking
down from a height would trigger one, but it's been four months
since the last one. My old therapist wanted to put me on meds, but
I'm an alcoholic." I chuckle again, "Pills are a gateway. I'm not
even supposed to have aspirin." I gaze down. "I was on Prozac
years ago but it made my thinking fuzzy. God, this is so
embarrassing."

"Don't be embarrassed," he says. "It happens to the best of
us."

I look up again to his sympathetic smile. "You have panic
attacks too?"

He nods. "Not for years now, but I did."

"Why? What happened?" His face falls a little, and I regret
the question. I look away. "Sorry. Sorry. It's none of my business."

"No, it's…my fiancée was murdered. I was the one who
found her." I glance up at him in shock. "And the guilt,
the…unfairness of it all, swallowed me into the abyss. I know how
difficult it is to come back from something like that. For a year I
could barely eat, I couldn't sleep. I felt so…empty. Alone.
Everyone tried to help, but…" He shrugs. "They just couldn't
know what it felt like. They couldn't understand. So whatever you
feel, whatever you do to cope, it's normal. Never be embarrassed
about being human. Especially around me."

"When does it start getting better?"

"When you allow yourself to really feel it. To accept it."

"Accept what?"

"That…the life you had before is over. That things will
never be the same. That for better or for worse, *you're* not the

same. Where you choose to go from there is entirely up to you. You can either let the pain, the guilt, become your only friend. Your prison. Or you can let it teach you, perhaps even make you stronger in some ways." He shakes his head. "But I won't lie to you, it's always there under the surface. The darkness. It's a part of you. Forever."

Before I can stop myself, I tentatively reach across and squeeze his hand. "I'm sorry."

He squeezes back. "*I'm* sorry."

I meet his eyes, searching deep to confirm my suspicion. I find it. That same haunted look I always see in mine. Eyes that have gazed into that abyss and seen it staring back. He's as broken as I am. Kindred spirits. We gaze at each other for a few seconds, not blinking or even breathing. This is a rare find, and we both know it. "Jem—"

The door opens, and I yank my hand away. A nurse pokes her head in. "Mrs. Armstrong is ready to go to radiology."

Jem leaps up like a jack-in-the-box, running his hand through his unruly hair. "Good, um, yes, um, thank you." The nurse glances at me, then at him, and shuts the door. "Um, I-I-I had best get back in there. Ar-Are you alright? Would-Would you like me to page a psychiatrist or write you a scrip for Valium or, no you can't take pills. Forgot that. I-I suppose I could—"

"I'm fine now. Thank you."

He nods. "Yes. Right. Sure. Um, I-I had better…" he gestures to the door, and smiles nervously. "Ha-Have a nice day." And he walks out.

I don't move for a minute. I can't. I'm completely dazed by what just transpired. Not that I can exactly explain what just happened. I just know the last time I felt like this I was twelve and standing on Pendergast Bridge, staring at the boy who would become the most important person in my life. My body tingling from my soul out from the recognition that nothing, *nothing* would ever be the same for me again. And it is…brilliant. Exciting. Miraculous.

And more damn terrifying than a million guns held by a million villains pointed at me.

*

I give my statement to one of the officers accompanying the henchmen to the hospital and get the hell out of there as quick as I can. Dobbs knows me well enough to not ask a lot of questions on the drive home. I change out of my bloody dress into jeans and black shirt, grab some chips and candy from the pantry, and begin work on my new project: Dr. Jonathan Fucking Ambrose, MD, Ph.D.

I know it's kind of stalker-ish to have Doris run a database search on a guy I like, but I will refrain from driving by his building ten times a day or rooting through his trash. Maybe. I locate his full name, Jonathan Greene Ambrose, date of birth, and social security number from the hospital records and plug them in. It'll take Doris about ten minutes to collate, so I go into the living room for better reception to return calls. Harry's cell goes to voice mail, so I leave a message. Same with Cam and V. Everyone's busy. I do speak to my head of PR and review the press release about to go out. The computer is done by the time I am. Close to two hundred documents found. This is going to take awhile.

Let's see. Born just outside New Urbana. Parents deceased. I pull up a picture of them at a charity event. Ugh. Both are serious and haughty, not even smiling it for the camera. I know their type: thinks they're better than everyone. It's as if they're judging me even in this photo. Father, Christian Ambrose, was heir to the Stonehouse Pharmaceuticals fortune. He was a doctor too, a geneticist, wow one on the team that isolated the uber-gene that causes people to have superpowers. It seems genius runs in the family. There's not a lot on Christian or his wife Eloise except a marriage announcement and a few sightings at charity events. The article that catches my eye is the one about the house, or really mansion fire when Jem was sixteen. Killed both parents. The article mentions a brother, Jordan, but it's the only time. Maybe he died too. And there's no engagement announcement either. In fact there's precious little about Jem's personal life anywhere. A few mentions on the New Urbana or Independence society pages but otherwise all the files are academic or professional. He started college at age fourteen, developed the retrovirus before he graduated med school at age twenty, has a trillion awards, has lectured all over the world, was one on Independence's bachelors of the year twice, and has an IQ of 198. I fall back in my seat with a sigh. Great. I sure can pick them. Perfect. He's fucking perfect. And probably still in love with his dead fiancée.

"Hello."

Shit. I spin around to find Lady Liberty smiling and strutting toward me. I was so deep in thought I didn't hear her come in. "Why are you looking up Jonathan Ambrose?"

"I-I," I stammer, clicking out of the file, "we hired him at the hospital. Just making sure, you know it wasn't a mistake."

Her eyes narrow. "That's it?"

"Why else would I waste my time on…" I chuckle nervously. "Never mind. Did—Do you need to use the computer or—"

"No. I just wanted to check in on you. It was intense today."

"I've been in worse."

"I'm aware. Still, most people would have crumbled. You handled yourself well in there. I was impressed."

"Thank you. I'm just glad you showed up when you did."

"Thank whoever called 911." She looks me over. "Well, if you're not a basket case, I have a city to patrol. Never a dull moment here, huh?" She smirks. "I'll let you get back to your side project. *Ciao*." She gives me a two finger salute and begins to walk away. When she reaches the exit, she stops and turns around. "You know, I just decided something. Nightingale was right about you. You are going to be good for us. I am officially going to start liking you, Joanna Fallon." She smiles brightly. "Welcome to the family." She winks, turns on her heel, and flies away.

"O-kay," I say to myself as I turn back to the computer.

The family. The violent, dysfunctional, superhuman family. Great. Why do I suddenly feel like smashing this computer, blowing up this room, and running as far from the city as I can? I don't want this. I don't want people pointing guns at me anymore. I don't want to look at disgusting photos of human degradation. I want…

I re-open the file on Jem with a sigh. But that's my life. Was the moment my father died. Jem's right. I have to accept that.

I live deep in the abyss, it's part of me, and it sure as hell is not a place I would ever afflict upon him.

I delete his file.

CHAPTER FOUR

NEW FRIENDS

Running fucking sucks. I hate running. I hate sweating, I hate not being able to breathe, I hate my legs aching. It's ruined the beach for me. I'm supposed to get a rush or thrill at some point, but maybe I have no endorphins. Sure would explain a few things. The only reason I'm enduring this now is I was going batshit in that house. Couldn't even wait until night to run away. I've had constant phone calls from reporters for two days now, both at home and work. Once again in the eyes of the public, I'm a hero. Bitsy even went on television claiming she'd be dead if it wasn't for my intervention. I could handle the attention, even the paparazzi at my gate, but not one little message from Jem. He phoned yesterday, befuddled as usual, to check on me. I felt as if I were back in high school, listening to the message a dozen times to find hidden meaning in every pause. I finally deleted it without calling him back, then obsessed over that decision too. Hence the running. Physical torture beats the mental kind any day of the week.

As I'm running past my usual stopping place, I hear a woman shout, "Joanna!" from above. The female lovebird waves from her perch, and I stop to wave back. Really it's to catch my breath. I can't seem to get past the mile mark without falling face first into the sand. Lexie signals me up and shouts, "Come on!" What the hell? Like my house, hers has a million steps, and I'm about dead when I reach her patio. She greets me with a bottle of water and a smile fit for a supermodel. "Thought you might be thirsty."

I gulp down the water. "Thanks."

"Come on in, hero. Meet the husband."

Their home is a post-modern masterpiece, all angles, white walls, and glass. It's a lot less depressing than mine. Maybe I should knock out my roof and add skylights. I won't though. Even after almost a year there, the mansion doesn't feel like mine. I couldn't even re-do Justin's bedroom and I sleep there every night. Hell, I still think of it as Justin's bedroom.

A man, I presume the husband, lounges on a huge black leather couch immersed in Sports Central re-caps. He's an attractive man if you like bohunks. His red hair is longish, down to his shoulders, and wavy with muscles bulging through his white t-shirt and blue jeans. I can see why the Angels shelled out millions for him. "Babe, we have company," Lexie says.

"Just a sec. I want to see if U-Urbana won against Lake City."

Lexie rolls her eyes. "You'll have to forgive my husband. They didn't teach him manners in the cave where he was born." She walks around to the couch, snatches the remote from the armrest, and shuts off the TV.

"Hey!" Brendan says.

"We have a legitimate hero in our home and all you care about are football scores!"

"What?" He turns around, and when he spots me, his mouth opens a little. "Oh, shit. Sorry," he says, standing.

"No worries."

"Joanna, Brendan. Brendan, Joanna," Lexie says.

He walks over to shake my hand. I'm a dwarf beside him. "Nice to meet you," he says. "Lexie's been sitting outside for hours waiting for you to show up."

"I was working on my tan, thank you very much," Lexie says.

"Yeah, right. I told you to just call." He returns his attention to me. "She's very impressed by you."

"Why?" I ask.

"You saved all those women," she says, rounding the couch to reach us. "I mean, I didn't see it or anything because I was cowering in the bathroom, but I heard all about it!"

"I really didn't do anything," I say. "It was mostly Lady Liberty. I just disarmed KitKat."

"Even still. You ran into that room to help your friend. That's huge. That alone makes you a hero."

"Or a moron," I counter.

"You should know there's nothing you can say to change her mind," Brendan says, wrapping his arm around his wife's tiny waist. "Once she's made it up, you're doomed."

"Doomed you, babe," she says with a smile. He leans in to give her cheek a peck. If they start making out again I am so out of here. She looks at me. "Sorry. We're shameless."

"It's okay."

"Bren, can you go get that fruit salad in the fridge? I'm starving."

"Be right back," he says before leaving.

Lexie grabs my hand and yanks me toward the couch. "Sorry, I'm totally kidnapping you right now. I am *dying* for girl talk, and you are the only person in this godforsaken city I even remotely like." We sit on the couch. "So, new best friend, what on earth possessed you to run into that room the other day? I mean, I know a little about your history, but still. You must really like that Bitsy woman."

"I guess. I didn't really think about it."

"So you're just one of those insanely brave people who run into burning buildings to save people. I so admire that."

I sip my water. "Well, you got the insane part right at least."

She falls back in the sofa. "You're being modest. Admit it, you rule. Hell, if half the crap I heard you went through last year is true, I'm shocked you're not in a padded cell. Kidnapped twice, getting shot at, watching your best friend die, that's like a lot." She licks her lips. "I knew him, you know. Justin. We met him at a few parties through the years. He was quite a guy."

"Yes," I say, gazing down.

I drink my water. I know what the next question is. "Did you know?" I always say, "How could I not?" and excuse myself.

Instead, she asks, "Are you still in love with him?" I almost choke on the water, coughing it all up onto my shirt. Lexie gasps and reaches across to get me a tissue. "Oh, crap. I am so sorry! Me and my damn mouth! Brendan's always telling me I have no filter. It's just that someone told me you were crazy in love with him for decades. I totally get why, he was a major babe. I can't even imagine what that must have been like for you. I guess you'll always love him, huh?"

I have no idea what to say. "I-I suppose."

"I get that. If something happened to Brendan, I'd never get over it. Widow's weeds for life. And I look dreadful in black."

"Are my ears burning?" Brendan asks as he walks in. He has two bowls of cut up fruit and forks. "You surviving the Spanish Inquisition there, Jo?"

"She hasn't strangled me yet, so that's a good sign."

He kisses the top of Lexie's head. "It's early yet, babe."

"Oh, go away."

"I live to serve." He kisses her again. "Nice to meet you, Jo. I have a feeling we'll be seeing a lot more of each other. Scream if you need back-up."

"Pretty sure she can take me, babe." We watch as he walks out. "Hot, isn't he? You can bounce a quarter off his ass. Literally."

O-kay. I clear my throat. "So, how long have you two been married?"

"A little over three years. We were friends for about a year, lovers for another after that, then made it official. I mean, we drive each other nuts, but that's part of the fun."

"You seem very much in love," I say, eating a piece of cantaloupe.

"Love of my life. No question." She shifts on the couch. "So, what about you? Your heart healed enough to let someone in yet? Got your eye on anyone?"

I gaze down at the fruit. "No. Not really."

She examines me, then laughs. "You are so lying! I can tell. My bullcrap detector is never wrong. Drives Brendan nuts. So, who is he? Is he handsome? Is he a playboy? Lawyer? Maybe a doctor?" My grip on the fork tightens. "Oh, a doctor! Nice. So, what's his name? Is he cute? Have you gone on a date yet?"

I glance up, more than a little uncomfortable and showing it. "There's no one. Really. My last relationship ended badly, and I am absolutely not in a place to jump into another one."

"Well, love has its own timetable. When the right guy comes along, it doesn't matter if you're busy, emotionally ready, or even looking, everything just falls into place. Can't fight fate, new best friend. I speak from experience. So, what's his name?"

"There's no one," I insist.

She pouts. "Fine. We obviously need a spa day or two to solidify this friendship before you share all your dirty little secrets." She smiles. "But I will get it out of you," she says, biting the watermelon and winking. "Then onto more neutral topics. Are you going to Rachel Mills' twenties party and *who* are you wearing?"

*

I return home an hour later with an appointment at a spa and another to go shopping for party dresses with my second new best friend. The odd thing is I don't mind. There's something about her I actually like, maybe her honesty. She's not fake, not playing games. It's refreshing, especially within the society set. I'm cautiously optimistic. At the very least there'll be someone at parties who doesn't look down at me.

I shower, change into jeans and camouflage top, braid my hair, and make my way to the command center. I once timed how long it took to get there from Justin's bedroom, and it came to four minutes. Seventeen thousand square feet. This house is too damn big. I really fucking hate it here, I really do. Besides the size, I'd swear the former Pendergasts are floating around, judging me, pissed to have an interloper in charge of their legacy. I should move into a townhouse or penthouse and turn this place over to the historical society for tours or just shut it up. Doris can be moved and set-up someplace more convenient. I scoff. Yeah, that's going to happen. Maybe in ten years I can let go. Until then…at least I get some exercise. And it's not so lonely anymore with my regular guests popping in all the time.

Lord Nightingale, in full regalia, is hard at work with Doris when I walk in. Wouldn't they be more comfortable in jeans and t-shirts? Wonder if they'll ever slip up and let me in on their secret identities. Doubt it. Justin kept it from me for twenty years and would have kept it for twenty more if a teenager hadn't let the cat out of the bag. Bastard. Both of them. "Howdy, stranger," I say as I stroll down.

The hero spins in the chair to face me. "Hello."

"Long time no see. Miss me?"

"Um, I-I-I suppose," he says, a little flustered. I seem to have that effect on people lately.

I lower myself into the chair beside him, and he tenses as he always does when I'm within two feet of him. "Good work on Casanov. I heard they added racketeering and facilitation of rape to the charges. Could we be any better at this? I think not."

"This is your victory more than mine. You did the majority of the work. We simply finished what you started."

"Well, I am so clearly awesome. Can't argue with that."

I think he smiles, but it's too quick to be sure. "And how-how are you doing? Liberty informed me what transpired a few days ago. You weren't physically injured?"

"Nope, not a scratch."

"And mentally?"

I shrug. "I had a massive breakdown in the hospital, but a fri—*someone* helped me through it. Nothing since then."

"Good." He pauses. "What you did was very brave. You're to be commended."

"Praise from Cesar. I'm flattered. Maybe I can get the club ring now," I say, stretching in my chair. His eyes dart to my pressed out chest then quickly spins to face the monitor. I'll let this objectification slide. "So. We took down a major crime boss. Let's not let the moss grow. What next, handsome?"

"I'm, um…" he shakes his head to clear it. My boobs are *that* great. "A large quantity of C-4, Semtex, and gelatin were stolen from a military base fifty miles from the city last night. What's worrisome is this is the second such theft in as many days. Both times they drove onto the base using fake IDs, incapacitated the soldiers on watch with one death, then drove off with the ordinance. The sketches the surviving soldiers provided of the culprits are generic at best. No one was really paying attention."

"Our tax dollars at work," I say. "How much did these guys get?"

"Enough to level several buildings. Best case scenario, they package it off and sell it black market."

"Worst, this wasn't for the money and whoever did it has a plan," I finish. "A fanatic with a grudge. Yikes."

"Yes. Yikes. The problem is with no fingerprints, unobservant witnesses, and no prior crimes with the same M.O. I am at a loss how to proceed. Tempest examined the scene but found nothing of use. It is a quandary."

I raise an eyebrow. "Or you've been holed up down here in the dark for hours, and your brain is fried. Scoot over." I bridge the gap between us, and he moves so the arms of our chairs touch. I start accessing the databases as he watches, still tense beside me. Don't know if I should take that personally. "It's going to be a pain in the ass to go through, but I am going to get you a list of all the black market explosives sellers and buyers within seventy-five miles." I print the page before going to the next. "I am also printing you a list of bomb makers and criminals known to have used ordinance in their crimes." I press a few buttons and out pops the list. "Done. Now, just because I like you and am super nice, I am going to get us some lunch and help you locate these bastards. Sound good, your Lordship?" I stand up. "You take a break. Go outside, fly around, do yoga on the beach, just get out of here for fifteen minutes. You need it."

Because I'm feeling particularly generous today, and we're going to be down here for hours, I assemble a feast. Salad, turkey on wheat sandwiches, V-8 juice, and chips which I will do my damndest to resist. He's still gone when I return. I do love a man who listens to reason. I switch on the radio to the classic rock station, set up the remote laptop so we can both access the computer at the same time, sit down with my sandwich, and start culling the lists. My partner in anti-crime returns a few minutes later to resume his post. I learned in the week we were compiling the Casanov case he doesn't like to talk while working, so we do our separate assignments side-by-side. He's not the most sociable of people. Probably why we get along so well.

As we reach hour two, I have the locations on seventy-five percent of my scumbags and strained eyes from staring at this monitor. At least the tedium is broken by my new favorite game: count the times the hero glances at me when he thinks I'm not looking. Fifteen times in two hours. I don't know whether to be flattered or creeped out. Wonder if he does the same thing with Liberty. In my limited experience observing them together, I've come to the conclusion they aren't a couple. There's no touching, no tenderness of voice, nothing to indicate they bump uglies. And if he has a girlfriend, she's very understanding considering he probably has a day-job then spends hours either here or on patrol. No, he doesn't have a girlfriend. It's been a long time since he has judging from his reaction to me. Poor guy. All work and no play. No way to live.

It's my turn to glance. He rubs his neck and grimaces in pain. "Super-healing on the fritz?" I ask.

"What? Oh, no. I've just been hunched over for so long it finally caught up with me. I'm fine."

We continue working for a few minutes, and the rubs continue. After the tenth time, I throw my pen down. "You're driving me fucking nuts. Would an aspirin help?"

"No. My body metabolizes them too rapidly. Multiple Vicodin or Oxycotin might."

"Well, we're out." I came home from rehab and found all the pills and booze gone.

"I'll be fine," he says as he turns his head toward me, followed by a quick intake of breath.

I push the chair away from the desk. "Oh, for fuck's sake," I mutter as I stand.

"What-What are you—" he asks as I walk over.

"Turn around. I'm good at this." He hesitates but obeys. "Where does it hurt?"

"Um, um, the bo-bottom of my neck and shoulders. Are you—" My hands slipping onto his shoulders makes the hero jolt. Yeah, it's been awhile since he's gotten laid. "You don't—"

"Shut up," I say, kneading his shoulders. "I used to do this for Justin all the time, so don't read anything into it. It's either this or I smash my laptop over your head in frustration. So relax. You're as tense as a man facing execution." I dig my thumbs into the base of his neck, moving in a circular motion. I used to do this for Harry too. He'd take off his shirt, I'd pull out the baby oil, and work out his kinks. The massage usually only lasted a minute or two before he pounced. God I miss those nights. Lust ripples through me at the memory of our oily couplings. Nightingale's not the only one who needs to get laid. "Feel good?" Nightingale nods. I'm coming up on my old record, eleven months. It's unnatural. I mean, the program says I shouldn't start a *relationship*. A one night stand isn't a relationship. It's…stress relief. They advocate *that*. It'd be a mercy on both ends. Gazing down at Nightingale with his pink lips relaxed and smooth breathing, I have the strongest urge to spin this chair around, rip off the lower part of his costume, climb on top of him, and screw his brains out right in that chair. I'd leave the mask on. Be kind of thrilling to fuck a guy without knowing who he really is. My hands slowly move from his shoulders to his collarbone and the start of his pecs, rubbing up and down. "Bet this feels even better," I whisper duskily. His head tilts back to see my face. I smile seductively, but that smile falls when I meet his eyes behind the plastic coverings. I gasp a little in surprise. Fuck.

"Well, well, well. Isn't this cozy?" Liberty says behind me.

As if he were radioactive, I yank my arms away. Double fuck.

Nightingale and I spin around to see both Liberty and Tempest standing by the beach door smirking. "Do you want us to some back later?" Tempest asks.

"I-I-I had a crick in my neck," Nightingale says.

"Of course you did," Liberty says in an insinuating tone.

"Really, *nothing* is going on," I insist.

Liberty's about to open her mouth again, but Tempest waves his hand and says, "We believe you. We just came for an update on the robberies."

"Of-Of course," he sputters, moving as far from me as possible. All business, Nightingale reviews our progress.

"Good job you two," says Tempest. "Liberty and I will begin interrogating the people on the lists. See what intel, if any, the scumbags can give us. We'll take it from here. Nightingale, go home and get some rest. You look like hell. I'll be in contact."

Why do I get the sense I've been dismissed in my own house. If I didn't want to get the hell out of this fucking room I'd throw a hissy fit. Instead, I say, "Thank you," and start walking toward the ramp. "Good luck." Nightingale keeps his eyes on the floor as I walk out, but Liberty isn't as bashful. With a proud smile, she gives me a quick thumbs up. I cannot get out of here fast enough. I don't feel safe until I close my bedroom door, whacking my head against it in frustration.

Brilliant.

Wonderful.

Perfect.

I let out a long, deep sigh. Why can't anything ever just be fucking simple?

Chapter Five

Roaring Twenties

Ever since third-generation real estate mogul Danforth Mills married his considerably younger third wife Rachel, daughter of his old business partner, he became less known for his business savvy and more for his over-the-top parties. Millions wasted on fire breathers, a chocolate fountain as tall as a house and pop stars serenading his young bride. Don't know how they'll be able to top the circus themed soirée this summer with the entire troupe from *Cirque de Marquee* meandering around and contorting right in front of you. Ugh.

At least I get to wear classier clothes this time. The 1920s was an impressive era fashion wise. Lexie and I figured all the other women would be decked out as flappers, which my stylist Isolde confirmed, so we went different routes. Lexie's more dapper than her husband in a tuxedo a la Greta Garbo, complete with top hat. We do match in the make-up department with bright red lipstick and dramatic eyes. Even dressed as a man she's prettier than me.

I decided to go simple yet elegant with a sleeveless black satin couture dress with an asymmetrical, layered hemline. Lexie thought it was too plain and insisted crystals be added. She actually put my whole look together with great detail, including the peacock feather on my headband, even bossing her hairdresser around while he worked on me. Don't know why she cares so much, but I was happy to have her take over. Beauty rituals are not my wheelhouse.

"We're just making an appearance, right?" Brendan asks.

Lexie rolls her eyes. "You TiVo'ed the game. It'll be there." We, really Lexie, insisted we ride in the limo together. Built in excuse, blame the other person when we leave in half an hour. Devious mind, I like that in my friends.

"It's not just the game. I have practice early tomorrow, among other things."

"Sweetie darling, I love you to bits, but you really need to stop complaining. This is your debut into society. You don't want everyone to think you're some uncouth, ungrateful anti-social jerk do you?"

"Yeah, that position is filled, thank you very much," I say with a smirk.

Lexie playfully smacks my arm as Brendan and I chuckle. The limo door opens, and the flashbulbs begin popping outside. Brendan climbs out first, then helps Lexie and me out. There are about a dozen paparazzi and entertainment news outlets behind the barrier shouting questions and snapping pictures outside the Austen Castle entrance. They shout for us to pose, which Lexie does like the pro she is. Brendan holds his wife, smiling and kissing her cheek with pride. I walk on. The camera loves me about as much as I love it.

Austen Castle is an old mansion, even older than mine, with a turret, ten acres of gorgeous gardens and even a labyrinth. The city purchased it when the owner killed himself in the crash of 1929. I wonder if the Mills appreciate the irony of holding their twenties party here. Probably not. I've been here over a dozen times for parties through the years with Justin, so I don't dawdle awing over the paintings and sculptures. Seen one naked chick on a fainting couch, you've seen them all. I wait for the Darby's by one such painting, instead observing the high end party people. There are a few women dressed in my style, and even one or two dressed like Lexie—she's going to hate that—but most are in elaborate flapper dresses with cigarette holders sans cigarettes. The majority of men are dressed either as gangsters with fake Tommy guns or in seersucker with straw hats. Down the hall in the ballroom jazz music booms. It's damn catchy. A few flappers grin as they pass me, then whisper to their date when their backs are to me as if I've vanished into thin air. I pull up my wrap, making sure it covers the burn on my arm. Half an hour. I can do half an hour.

A minute or two later, my dates finally stroll in. Even in this glamorous crowd, you notice them. "We thought you ditched us!" Lexie says.

"I try not to talk to the press if I can help it," I say.

"Wish that trait would rub off on her," Brendan says.

"Light of my life, we are celebrities. It's expected of us." She shakes her head. "Anyway, duty done. Let's get in there and party." She links arms with us. "I need some hooch."

The ballroom is packed with the two hundred plus guests milling around, chatting, swilling champagne, eating hor'dervs, or dancing the Charleston over by the twenty-one piece band. Blown up movie posters and fashion magazines from the era line the walls. The lights are dim to give it a speakeasy feel I guess. It just makes me claustrophobic. "I need a beer," Brendan says.

We worm our way to the huge bar. I order my usual ginger ale before we locate an empty table to sit at. I spot my CFO Lane and his wife Heidi and wave. I do the same with Clinton Bell and his fiancée Gwen, who glares at me then pulls him away. He's had a crush on me for years. "So, you want me to introduce you to people or—"

"Rule one of popularity: never go to them, let them come to you," Lexie says, sipping her martini. "Give it a minute."

Not even a minute. Thirty seconds later, Rachel drags Danforth to us. Dan and I nod at each other. "Oh, my God! You came. Danny, this is Alexia, the supermodel. We met at Bitsy's ghastly party. And this must be your husband Brendan. We actually flew to Los Sangre to watch you play last week. Box seats, of course. You're like a tank. We're so lucky to have you on our team."

"Thank you," Brendan says.

Rachel lowers herself beside Lexie, eyes wide with excitement. "I'm so honored you came. Really. I was scared the last party you attended would sour you to the Galilee social scene. I don't know about you, but I was scared out of my wits! I'm not used to that sort of thing, unlike some," she says, glancing at me. I swear I could save a busload of children and nuns, and these people would still thumb their noses at me. "We had to take a trip to St. Barth's just to calm my nerves. My analyst thinks I might be suffering from PTSD. Are you?"

"I missed most of the fun," Lexie says. "I heard the shots and ran for the hills."

"How smart of you," Rachel says, touching Lexie's hand. "Wish I could have. My entire life flashed before my eyes."

"How dull for you," I mutter into my glass. She doesn't hear but Brendan smiles. "Have you seen Bitsy? Is she here?"

Rachel acknowledges me for the first time. "I invited her, of course, but I can't imagine she'd show her face here. Not after what happened."

"Rachel, she didn't invite KitKat there. It wasn't her fault."

"I'm sorry, but how do we know that? I mean, none of us suspected Grace Pickering of being in cahoots with Alkaline, but she was. And I heard Thayer lost millions when the deal with those Germans fell through. They're desperate for money."

"And I heard you had vaginal rejuvenation surgery." Everyone gasps. "Doesn't make me think you wore the thing out."

"How-I-I—" she stammers before standing. "You trash!" She grabs her husband and scurries away.

Lexie, being much more of a lady than I, waits until Rachel's out of earshot before bursting into laughter. Brendan and I chuckle right along with her. "That was freaking brilliant!" she says as she raises her drink. We all clink glasses.

Brendan spots one of his teammates, and insists we go over to chat. As Lexie checks her cell for the fifth time in half an hour, I spot a business associate I'm flying to Independence with in two weeks, and I excuse myself. I mainly come to this crap to network and "foster relations" as Justin called it. I watched him do it for so many years when it was my turn, I was practically a pro. About ten minutes into the discussion, all thoughts of health care reform flee my brain when I spy my ex-boyfriend twirling his new lady love on the dance floor. My mouth dries up.

I've seen Harry in person only a handful of times, but never with my replacement. He picked a good one. Bella Harding is cute with shoulder length blonde hair, big brown eyes, tan skin and curvy figure tonight in a pink flapper dress. She's also more age appropriate, early forties, but doesn't look it. I worked with her on a few cases. She's a good prosecutor. Very detail oriented. I must be staring because when the song stops, Harry zeroes in on me. He looks damn fine tonight in a dark three piece suit, spats, wire rimmed glasses, and fedora covering his brown hair. Shit, now I'm going to have to say hello. Where's a supervillain when you need one?

We meet halfway, smiling awkwardly when we stop. "Well, fancy meeting you here," I say.

"I'm friends with Rachel's mother," Bella says. "Nice to see you again, Joanna."

"Yeah, the last time was on the Fontanesca case three years ago? You kicked their asses."

"I had good evidence," Bella says with a smile.

Pleasantries over, it's awkward silence time. Harry breaks it after five seconds. "You look lovely tonight."

"Really?" I ask, examining myself. "Thank you. I had a supermodel makeover. Literally. I'm a work in progress." I immediately regret the words. He knows this better than anyone. I clear my throat. "You both look nice too. Very authentic. Though you should fix his tie, Bella. It's crooked."

"Oh," she says, adjusting it. "Thank you."

"No prob. Well, you two have fun. My dates need a save from Sparkle Cohen. It was nice to see you. *Both* of you. I mean that."

"Thank you," Bella says, taking Harry's arm.

"Excuse me." I hustle away as fast as I can without being obvious, my smile falling with each step. I can't help it, I have to look back. Yep, bad idea. Harry pulls away from their kiss, caressing Bella's cheek as she smiles. God, they look so fucking in love. I'm glad, I *really* am, but I just wasn't ready for this, seeing how well they fit together. He's completely moved on. That realization stings more than a little.

Sparkle Cohen has been covering the Galilee social scene probably since the 1920s. Tonight she's in a huge white fur coat with her matching hair wavy in the style. "So, which is better? Galilee or Independence?" she asks Lexie.

"Guys, are you ready to go yet?" I ask.

"Hello, Joanna," Sparkle says.

"Sparkle. So, are you? I'm all partied out."

"I guess. We—" Brendan starts.

"No!" Lexie practically shouts. "Not yet." She checks her phone again and smiles brightly before returning the phone to her pants. "We-We haven't danced! We can't leave without dancing. Just a few more minutes, okay?"

"Fine. You enjoy your dance. I'm gonna get some air, okay?"

"Perfect! Sounds great. Air is awesome. Go get some. Go!" she says, shooing me away.

I raise an eyebrow. Okay. Whatever. I move through the open doors onto the veranda. More guests mill around chatting as sparklers flicker along the railing. I keep walking down the stone steps into the garden. Need some alone time. Even at night the garden is glorious with pristine hedges of holly. I continue down the pebble path until the music grows faint and I'm surrounded by a broken circle of flowers and hedges. With a sigh, I rest on the stone bench in the middle of the semi-circle with my back to the castle. A few people scamper around me like wood nymphs on their way from the labyrinth at the end of the path. Justin's old college friend Sam Martin and his wife nod as they pass. When they're gone, I take a deep breath. I seriously hate parties. After this one I'm on sabbatical. None until next year. Catty comments, watching ex-boyfriends suck face, booze all around is not my idea of a good time.

A stiff breeze blows, and I pull my wrap tighter. Wish I had gone the tux route too. I mean, she made me look beautiful, but no sleeves is—

"Are you cold?" a familiar voice asks behind me.

My heart thumps hard against my ribcage, and I spin around. Jem stands ten feet away looking breathtakingly good. His usually wild hair is parted to the side and slicked in waves. No glasses tonight either, so I can see that his curling eyelashes make his eyes pop, and he wears that tux better than anyone here. As I take him in I realize my mouth is slacked open, I snap it shut. He doesn't notice my reaction. He steps toward me as he slips off his coat. "Here," he says, holding it out.

I remove my thin wrap, and he glances at my scarred arm before I slip the coat on. "Thanks." It's really warm and smells like him, aftershave and antiseptic from the hospital. Better even than Old Spice.

"I-I saw you come out here," he says, self-conscious once again. "I-I just wanted to see if you were alright. I can leave if you want to be alone."

What a thought. "No, it's fine. I was just…I don't like parties. Never have."

"I-I don't like them either," he says, sitting at the far end of the bench. "I don't enjoy being out of my element. If-If I can help it. I-I have a hard time connecting with people. I-I never mastered small talk or any of the other social arts. I avoid social occasions as much as possible. I-I was tested for Aspergers when I was a child but didn't fit the criteria. The doctors finally threw up their hands and deduced my anti-social tendencies were due to my abnormal IQ, whi-which is a valid conclusion. And I…have no idea why I just told you all of that," he says with a chuckle.

"It's okay. If it makes you feel any better, I don't have the excuse of being a genius. I'm just a bitch," I say with a smile.

He doesn't smile back. "I don't think you're a…bitch."

"Give it time." He looks at me with pity. I pull the coat tighter around me. "So if you hate parties, why come to this one? Didn't want to snub the head of the hospital board?"

"That was one consideration, yes. At my last hospital I was considered less than a team player. Multiple personnel from the hospital are here whom I should foster positive relations with, if not for friendship purposes than for professional ones. This is as good a setting as any." He pauses. "You're the only person in this city I even remotely know."

"And I already like you, so you're wasting your time," I say with a smirk. His expression turns grave, and even in the dark I can see him blush. "So, why aren't you in there playing well with others?"

"I saw you come out here and wanted to check on you. You didn't return my call."

"I was embarrassed. I don't usually let people see me like that."

He's quiet for a second, then says, "You never have to be embarrassed around me."

I half smile. "Thanks." Time to change the subject before the weight of my crush crushes me. "You look very nice tonight."

He studies himself. "I suppose. Someone suggested I cut my hair, have a tuxedo fitted, and to wear my contacts tonight."

"Lot of that going around. My friend made me over too. Took hours."

"Well, it-it was worth it. You look ravishing." I raise an eyebrow, and his eyes double in size. "I-I-I-I didn't mean, I mean, I'm not going to *ravish* you. That, I mean—"

"I know what you meant. Thank you," I say with a chuckle. We're saved by a giggly Rose Franklin and a man who is not her husband as they run up the path from the labyrinth. They're oblivious to us because the man tosses Rose against the hedge and proceeds to feel her up not fifteen feet from us. As if this night couldn't get any more awkward. "Hi, Rose!" I say loudly.

With a gasp, she pushes the man away. "Oh! Joanna! I was just..." No lie comes. Instead, she grabs the man's hand and pulls him toward the castle.

"Say hi to your husband," I call as she flees.

"I know that man," Jem says. "He works in oncology."

"Well, now you can blackmail him into being your friend. See? Aren't you glad you came now?"

He smiles at that one, and I throw one back at him. Then we sit in silence just smiling for a few seconds. "Do-Do you want to go back inside? We—"

"Not yet, but you can—"

"No," he says, shaking his head. "I-I'm perfect here." Another couple come running down the path giggling and splashing their hooch on the gravel. "Well, maybe not *here*."

I stand. "Come on. I know where we can go."

He follows me toward the labyrinth. We stand side-by-side as he studies the plaque with a map of the circular labyrinth, all curlicues to the center. "Oh. It's a full recreation of the labyrinth built by Daedalus for King Minos of Crete to hold the Minotaur. Fascinating."

"I love getting lost in this thing," I say.

"Actually, that is a common misconception. It is, in truth, impossible to get lost in," he instructs me. "As you can see, it's unicursal. Unlike a maze, there is no complex branching. It's a simple path. One path. There is only one choice to be made: whether to enter or not."

I step to the entrance. "I know my choice." I walk inside. The hedges are about twelve feet tall with gravel underneath and lights every few feet. Imposing.

Jem runs to catch me. "If this is a true recreation, then it truly is a work of art," he says excitedly. "You know these have been around for a millennia. They were used by almost every civilization in group ritual or private meditation."

"Meditation?"

"Well, consider it. You're twisting, turning, attempting to find the center, the way out, but the way in *is* the way out. The path may be long, you may believe you're lost, but no matter what you are always on the correct course. There are no wrong choices because the path is already set for you."

"Like fate."

"*Exactly* like fate. It's a physical embodiment of a pilgrimage toward salvation. It's confusing, frightening, and as long as you don't let that fear paralyze you, in the end you will always reach your destination. As Socrates said, 'We thought we were at a finish but our way bent round and we found ourselves back at the beginning, and just as far from that which we were seeking at first.'" He notices me staring and turns sheepish again. "I'm sorry, I'm always doing that. Boring people with random facts. My brother called me, 'Mr. Know-It-All.'"

"You weren't boring me. Quite the opposite. I was just thinking I should bring some people from A.A. here. A lot of the tenants are the same."

"Which, if I may ask, step are you on?"

"I waffle between ten and eleven. Eleven has a lot of God talk but to me it means what this place does. Accept what's happened and move on. Some days are better than others."

"How do you mean?" Jem asks.

"Well, I just saw my ex-boyfriend sucking face with his new amazing girlfriend. Part of me felt like cringing, but the other is really happy they're together. He deserves happiness. Our breaking up was a hundred percent my fault. I wanted to push him away and did the one thing I knew would do that. He's such a good guy. I mean, when I was in rehab, he actually came to one of the group sessions. He didn't have to do that. He should have wanted me rotting in some gutter, and it made me realize I never believed I was good enough for him. I thought I had to save him from me, but in reality it was to save me from him. I had to end it before it got too deep. He never could really understand me. That I'd always feel less than around him. So I just have to accept that and move on. I still feel like a shitty person for wishing he'd join the priesthood. Or at least wait until I get a boyfriend that trumps his gorgeous D.A. girlfriend. Does that make me a bad person?"

"That makes you human," Jem says. "I observe happy couples and get so… jealous it almost cripples me. Why is it so easy for them but so difficult for me? I am aware how odd I am. I-I-I have difficulty connecting with other people. It's difficult being smarter than everyone else. People don't like it. But what am I lacking that makes me so—"

"Unlovable?" I finish. "You're preaching to the choir. Try being in love with your best friend and asking yourself that very question every time you're around him. 'Why not me?'"

His eyes narrow. "You-You were in love with Justin?"

"Since the moment I laid eyes on him. He didn't know until the end. You know, I only hooked up with Harry because he got engaged to Rebecca." I roll my eyes. "God, was I jealous of her. I used to imagine the million ways I'd frame her for a crime. Coke in her locker, thousands owed in parking tickets. And the fucked up thing was, deep down, I genuinely liked her. She was an amazing Mom and doctor, and she made Justin *so* happy. She gave him the best months of his life. I wish I could have thanked her for that." A couple passes us going the opposite way, and we nod. We've reached the center and keep walking.

"She liked you too. I believe her exact words were, 'I've never met someone so fierce, so loyal, so determined.' She built you up to such epic proportions when it came time to meet you I was exceedingly nervous. She all but had to thrust me across the room to ask you to dance."

I chuckle. "Let's make a deal. If I shouldn't be embarrassed around you, then you shouldn't be nervous around me. Fair?"

He nods. "Fair."

"Good." We stroll in silence for a few moments, arms brushing against one another. "So," I finally say, "you probably told me this already, but how did you and Rebecca meet? The hospital?"

His mouth tightens. "Um, through my fiancée, Uma. They were best friends in medical school. We lost touch after Uma's death, but when Rebecca finished her internship I helped her get a fellowship at my hospital in Independence. She was…a true friend."

"How long ago did your fiancée die?"

"Almost eight years. We, um, met while she was an assistant in one of my labs. She was brilliant, had an uncanny knack for the work. She used to joke no disease was safe with the two of us on its trail," he says with a beaming smile.

I can't help but smile too. "So who chased who?"

"All her. She was one of my students, so when the thought crossed my mind, or she made an overture, I ignored it."

"Until you couldn't."

"Yes. She had to change labs, but it was worth it. We dated a year before I proposed. She was murdered a little over a month later."

My mouth drops open. "Jesus Christ, I'm so sorry. Hell." We take as few more steps. "What, I mean, did they catch the guy?"

"No."

We keep going, and I glance at him a few times but he stares straight ahead. I can't stand the silence after ten seconds. "When I was twelve, my father was shot to death in his taxi cab. They never caught the guy either. A week later, I tried to kill myself." I gaze down. "I was about to jump off Pendergast Bridge when Justin pulled up and spent an hour in the freezing cold talking me down. He saved my life, but…" I shake my head. "I don't think you ever come back from something like that. Not intact. It changes you, infects you with its…darkness. The world dims a little, and it's like only you can see it. Justin was afflicted too, that's why we got along so well. Two orphans with nothing and no one but each other. My constant."

"You're still in love with him."

"Probably about as much as you're still in love with your fiancée. Just because they're gone doesn't mean they take the love with them. He was my soul mate. As long as I breathe he's in here with me, and I am doing my damndest to remember that. I lost sight of that in the darkness for awhile, and I won't let that happen again."

There's only the sound of our footsteps for seconds until he says, "You're right. About the dimming. Your entire perception of life shifts when true evil touches your life. When Uma died, I just fled. I didn't tell anyone where or even that I was going. I packed a bag and took the first flight away. I spent some months in India because it was where I felt closest to her. She was from there. My lost year where all I did was walk, meditate, and do whatever I could to regain that light back by answering the fundamental question of life. *Why?*"

"You find the answer?"

"Of course not. Because there is no answer." His eyes move down. "All I do know is that as wretched as it was, her death was part of my path. It set in motion the rest of my life. If she hadn't died I never would have…gone on to do all I have. 'It is always darkest before the dawn.'" We step out of the labyrinth. With a proud smile, he says, "See? Trust. Just follow the path, and you will find yourself right where you are supposed to be."

"I believe you," I say with a matching smile.

We just stand there grinning like idiots with only a foot between us. Then our eyes meet, and the smiles stretch as long as the equator. I feel it again, that spark of recognition, and damned if it doesn't make me feel close to happy. And scared shitless. The air, the night, the world grows still and silent as if the universe has ground to a halt. Judging from the way he's gazing at me, whatever this is I'm not alone in its glow. Oh…hell.

The spell is broken a second later when a waiter rushes over to us. "Excuse me, are you Miss Fallon?"

Thank the Lord. "Yes. Why?"

He pulls out a piece of paper. "A woman in a tuxedo told me to give this to you."

"Thank you." I open the note to read it. *Dearest, we had to leave. Brendan got sick and we couldn't find you. Please don't be mad. Will make it up to you._Ciao, Lexie.* "Shit."

"What?" Jem asks.

"My friends ditched me. I don't have a ride home."

"Oh." He pauses. "Well, I-I can drive you home. It's not a problem."

"Are you sure?"

"Absolutely," he says with another grin. "I insist. It's not every night I get to rescue a damsel in distress."

I bite my lower lip. Bad idea, Jo. Very bad idea. "Okay, then. Thank you." I am a damn moron sometimes. I take off his coat and hand it back. "Well, since you're doing me a favor, I'll return it. We won't leave here tonight until you've impressed three work colleagues and are on the path to friendship or at least lunch with them."

"I-I don't know if that's—"

I hold out my arm for him to take. "I insist. You need friends, and I intend to get them for you. Remember I'm fierce, loyal, and determined. You don't stand a chance in this fight."

He glimpses at my arm, and after a moment's hesitation he locks his arm in mine. "I believe you."

"Smart man."

*

We pull up to my mansion two hours, two dances, and one lunch date with a group of colleagues later in his dark green 1957 Porsche 356 Speedster A classic convertible. He takes care of his car, it may as well have just rolled off the factory floor. I appreciate that in a man. Two years ago I would have screwed him just because of it.

The gate parts after I enter the code I provide without hesitation, and he rolls up to my door yet doesn't turn off the engine. We sit in silence, neither moving or looking at the other. Haven't done this is awhile, an awkward end of a date. Not that that's what tonight was. A date. Whatever it was, I sure as hell don't want it to end, but know if I invite him inside disaster will ensue. He'll expect something that cannot happen at this point and probably hate me for it. Shit.

"I had a great time tonight," I say.

"As did I."

Get out of the damn car, Joanna. "Well then," I say, pulling on the handle, "thank you for the ride. Good night." I step out of the car and shut the door. There. Good. The car begins to drive away, but I realize I haven't released the door handle. Double shit. "Wait!" The car comes to a quick stop as Jem slams on the brakes. I throw open the door and jump in again. "Okay, here's the thing," I begin. "I want to invite you in. I *really* do. I've enjoyed tonight more than you know, but if you come inside I need you to know *nothing* can happen. I just, I can't handle anything but friendship right now, and even that is iffy. I'm sorry. If you're not okay with that, I completely understand." My brow furrows at a horrible thought. "Unless I was misreading the entire situation, and you just want to be friends. If that's the case, then please forget this entire, horrible, embarrassing tirade. Either way, would you like to come in and watch a movie with me and just…hang out?"

His open mouth snaps shut. "Um, I'd like that. Yes."

I breathe a literal sigh of relief. "Great. Good. Lovely. Come on."

Hallelujah. Jem shuts off the car, and we get out. The mansion is dark and especially creepy now. I kick off my heels at the door then turn on a light. "Did you ever get the tour?"

"Um, no," he says, glancing around the foyer with all its priceless vases and paintings.

"Mind if I do it later? If I don't get out of this dress soon, I'm going to rip it off." Mental head slap as he blushes. *Good start, Jo.* "Uh, why don't you get us something to eat? The kitchen is through the left hall, second door on the right. Give me five minutes." I pick up my shoes and bound up the stairs. When I reach my room, I all but tear off my dress, Spanx, uncomfortable yet sexy bra, and pantyhose. I replace them with black sweatpants, shirt, and blue hoodie before fixing my hair and gargling with mouthwash just in case my willpower fails. When I return to the kitchen, Jem is muttering to himself as he opens and closes cabinets. "I'm back. Need help?"

"I can't find your popcorn maker," he says with a scowl. "How many cabinets do you *have*?"

"Too many," I scoff. "And the popcorn maker is in the living room. We just need to do the butter in here." I pull out the tub and a mug, putting them in the microwave.

"How large is this house?" Jem asks.

"Seventeen thousand square feet. I've been coming over here for twenty years, and I don't think I've been in all the rooms. People think it's haunted too. Bitsy swears she saw a woman in Victorian dress in the second floor hallway. At least I'm never alone, huh?"

"Is that why you stay here? Because you think—" He shakes his head. "Never mind."

Mercifully the microwave dings, and I remove the cup. "You sound like my cousin Veronica. She's convinced I walk around in Justin's clothes talking to his ghost. But that's only on Wednesdays," I say with a smile. He grins back. "No, I stay here because this is the closest place to a home I've ever had. Some of my happiest memories occurred right here. It was literally my safe haven. When my mom was on a bender or feeling especially evil, I could come here, stuff my face with popcorn, and spend time with my best friend until I was strong enough to face that apartment again."

"I'm sorry," he says with a pitying look.

"Yeah, well, she's dead and burning in hell now. All's well, yada yada. Come on, it's movie time." I lead him out of the kitchen to the living room. As we pass through the Hall of Pendergast, he slows to examine the portraits. "It's the family dating back to the founding of the city. They creep me out. Feels like they're watching me, disapproving that an interloper is in charge of their legacy. One from the lower classes no less. I know I'm projecting but…" I shrug. "I was thinking of commissioning one of Justin with Rebecca and Daisy just so there's a few friendly faces up there. I know they weren't technically Pendergasts, but they would have been."

"I think she would have liked that," Jem says.

"Yeah." I pause. "Onwards." I flip on the living room lights. As he looks around, I start the popcorn. "You can choose the movie."

By the time the popcorn starts popping, he picks one out with a grin. "*Excalibur*."

"Don't think I've seen it."

"Arthur and the Knights of the Round Table. I was obsessed with the legend as a child. My brother and I used to go on quests for hours, slaying evil sorceresses and other threats to our kingdom. He was Arthur, and I Lancelot, or Merlin depending of which part we were re-creating." He chuckles. "We-We even chucked one of Father's swords in the pond and swam under to retrieve it." His smile wavers. "I won and Jordan didn't speak to me for days. I hadn't stayed historically accurate." The smile's completely gone now. "Anyway, will this do?"

"Sounds perfect."

He slides in the movie before sitting on the couch. I shut off the lights and join him with our popcorn and water just as the movie begins. The music swells, and we smile at each other. I haven't hung out with anyone in over a year. We watch for awhile in silence until…the sex scene. We glance at each other, and I hold in my chuckles. Guess he forgot about this part. A minute later, when everyone is fully clothed again, there's still tension in the air so Jem clears his throat. "This-This film is one of the few that stayed true to the most popular telling of the legend. It-It evolved through the years, as all folklore does. In the original versions, there was no Camelot, Lancelot, or even Guinevere."

"I'll bet you know every telling from every book," I say with a smirk.

His face contorts in shame. "Yes. I have a photographic memory."

"Why on earth would you be embarrassed by that? Especially around me." I sit up straight. "In fact, I just realized you know almost every mortifying fact about me, but I know none about you." I flop back on the couch. "I want to know three embarrassing things equal to rehab, in love with my best friend and suicide. If you can. I dare you. Top those."

Jem glances at me, and I raise an eyebrow. He takes a second to gain courage, and then says, "My parents never loved me." My eyebrows drop. "We were…adopted. Father thrust us upon Mother, but even he never treated us as children. I was raised by nannies and tutors, subjected to psychiatrists, doctors, and trainers to make us the best we could possibly be. We barely left the compound, rarely associated with other children. We were treated more as experiments than children. I didn't go to proper school until I was thirteen when I began college. I was so frightened there among…people, I barely uttered a word the entire first year. Does that count?"

"Hell, yes. I-I'm so sorry."

"As you said before, 'Alls well, yada yada.' They're dead now."

"Did you ever try to find your birth parents?"

"All the records were destroyed in the fire. That's how they died. I was away at college at the time. Jordan drove up to tell me, then he vanished for awhile."

"Why?"

"He said he wanted to 'discover who he really was,'" he says with disdain. "I refused to go with him. He took it badly."

"You were in college, you couldn't just drop everything."

"That's what I said, but once he gets his mind set to something…" He shakes his head.

"Do you keep in contact with him?"

"We…see each other on occasion. I have no idea where he is right now, what he's up to," Jem says grimly.

"That bothers you."

"More than you can imagine." He disappears into his head, and judging from his expression, it's not a good journey. He snaps out of it with a half smile. "Anyway. Can that be number two?"

"I'll count it. So, what's number three?"

His gaze returns to the TV with a frown. He hangs his head for a moment. "Well, um," he clears his throat, "I…as you may have noticed…" He scowls, "I've only ever had one girlfriend. My-My fiancée. I-I-I never learned flirting or other social graces. Women tend to think I'm odd, and there were…other considerations. And since Uma, I suppose before her even, I've been so focused on my work it didn't seem that important."

"Save millions of people's lives or go on a coffee date. I can understand that."

"You can?" he asks as if a weight has lifted.

"Yeah. I mean, I was all about my career. Still am I guess. Whenever I was sitting across from some man droning on about golf, I wished I was back at the precinct or running down a lead. It's what made me happy, not…you know. I mean, it felt physically good when it was happening but hollow. There are more than a few encounters I wish I could take back. No, realizing what's important to you and doing it, despite what others think, is admirable. Just so long as when the real thing comes along, you don't bury your head in the sand from fear." I shrug. "So, do I know all your secrets now? Nothing else you want to tell me?"

"I…no. That's all."

"Then I win. I've had a far more embarrassing life than you. You never have to be nervous around me again."

"I...okay."

I yawn. "Good." I turn back to the movie and snuggle on the armrest before pulling my legs onto the couch. "Then I do believe this is the beginning of a beautiful friendship, Dr. Ambrose." I close my eyes. Damn, am I tired. I yawn again and stretch out my legs so my feet touch his thigh.

I feel the warmth of his hand hovering over my bare foot for a few seconds before he hesitantly rests it there. "Friends."

I fall asleep minutes later enjoying the feel of him against my skin. It's enough. For now.

CHAPTER SIX

INDEPENDENT WOMAN

A person would think that those who can afford a thirty dollar salad would have manners, but I guess money can't buy you class. Even hundreds of miles from home and people still feel the need to point me out to their dining companions. A man I recognize as a Senator stares with impunity. Not even my glare stops his rude behavior. It's been a fucking year, I should be yesterday's news by now. Nope, still a circus freak.

Lucy's late. I figured if I was in Independence, her new homestead, I should take her out to lunch. A pittance for basically saving my life, but it's a start. Last time I saw her was just after I got out of rehab. She and Dobbs picked me up, drove me home, and she stuck around for two days just to make sure I settled back in. Hell she even attended my first AA meeting on the outside with me. Lucy may look down on me, she may not approve, hell I'm not even sure she likes me, but that woman was more of a mother to me than Maeve ever was.

My phone buzzes and I check it, smiling when I see who it's from. Jem's text reads, "*How's it going?*" At lunch yesterday I mentioned how nervous I was about this lunch. He's so sweet for checking on me. I type back, "*Not here yet. Fine. Will call later.*" As I put the phone away, I spot a familiar face.

Lucy Helms has barely changed since I first saw her poking her head out of that limo, telling her nephew to get back in and leave me to die on that bridge. She was just worried I'd take him over with me. She's still stick thin, with a sharp nose, cheekbones, and brown eyes. Her more salt than pepper hair is shorn in a pixie cut. She doesn't smile when she sees me. "Hello, Lucy."

The maître pulls out her chair, and she sits. "Joanna."

"Thank you for meeting me. You look great."

"As do you. Much improved."

"Thank you. I feel good."

We order drinks and lunch, and the waiter leaves.

"So, how did the meeting with Sen. Dumphy go? Will he propose the amendment?"

"Yes. We were very persuasive. The Ward and areas like it could use more free clinics, that's for sure."

She stares at me for a second. "You have become quite the deft power player, Joanna."

I shrug. "A lot of it's common sense and hiring the right people. Half the time I just wing it. I don't know what the hell Justin was thinking giving me the company."

"He thought you were up to the task. Someone had to carry the torch, and he knew you'd rather die than let it extinguish."

I gaze down. "I almost did."

"But you licked your wounds, picked yourself up, and kept carrying on. Have you stumbled since?"

"No."

"Then it's over. No use beating yourself up about it. It's wasted energy."

She always cuts to the quick. I like that in a person. We sit across from each other in silence for a few seconds before I work up the courage to say, "I know I told you this already, but…thank you. For kicking my ass, for taking me to that place, for putting up with that therapy session, all of it. You didn't have to—"

"Of course I did," she cuts in, sounding offended. "I've invested too much time and energy in you to let you drink it all away during some pity party. Besides…we're family. He would never forgive me if I let something happen to you."

We let those words hang between us like a hangman's noose. I gaze down again, and she glances around the room anywhere but at me. "It'll be a year next week," I say.

"I know."

"Mayor Miracle organized a rally in the park. They're unveiling a statue, and I'm supposed to give a speech," I say, rolling my eyes. "I don't have a clue what to say. 'Look how much the town has gone to hell since he sacrificed himself for me. Sorry, my bad?'"

Her thin lips purse with disapproval. "If this lunch is going to turn maudlin, I'm leaving. I don't want to hear about your misplaced shame. He loved you. He did what he had to to protect you. And I doubt if he was presented the situation over again, he would make a different choice."

The waiter returns with our salads and leaves. Like a chastised child, I pout and pick at my food. "I keep dreaming about him."

She stops eating. "And I definitely don't want to hear about *that*."

My eyes narrow. "Nothing sexual. We just talk. He always seems so…happy. He says he's proud of me a lot." I set my fork down. "Jesus Christ, even when he's dead I need his approval. How fucked up is that?"

"He may not have always liked your choices, but he was always proud of you. Even now. As am I."

"Thank you," I say, humbled.

She clears her throat. "Now, may we please change the topic? This lunch has become far too gloomy for comfort. What else have you been up to besides communing with the dead?"

I fill her in on the latest business deals, gossip and scandals in Galilee. That last one takes awhile. She tells me about her volunteer work at the National Museum and new girlfriend, Amelia. "Ernest Miracle must be kissing the Triumvirate's feet for arriving two months before the election," Lucy says. "I heard that crime went down two percent in a month."

"That's what the paper says."

"I heard what happened at the Historical Society."

"Yeah, thank God Liberty showed up when she did," I say.

"So you approve of supers now? My, what a difference a year makes."

I start picking at my food. "Actually, I'm, uh…working with them."

Her fork stops midway to her lips. "I'm sorry?"

"They just appeared one night wanting to use the computer. Justin must have told them where to find it. I offered to help, and after some persuasion, they agreed."

"Is that wise? After what happened last year?"

"I don't go out in the field with them. I'm not out there beating up Hexen. I sit in front of a computer in an underground office and compile data. It's what Justin would want."

"The hell it is! He would want you to be safe. Out in the world living your life, not trapped in a bunker performing illegal searches for people who put a target on your back."

"Well, at least this time I know I'm in league with a hero."

There's that look I've missed. That "why do I associate myself with riff-raff" gaze she doled out to me like a toothbrush at Halloween. "Fine. It's your life. Just be careful."

"Like a virgin at an orgy," I say, toasting her with my water. There's that look again. "So, did Justin ever mention anything about them that might be useful?"

"He rarely mentioned that side of his life to me. I wanted no part of it, for obvious reasons you should well remember." She sips her water. "I do know they were effective at their jobs. When Independence realized they left, there was an outcry. And I don't want to carry on with this discussion. I've had enough superhero discussions for a lifetime." She dabs the side of her mouth with a napkin. "So, besides your little side project, anything else you care to tell me? Are you seeing anyone?"

"No-Not really," I stutter. "I made some new friends. Remember Jem Ambrose, Rebecca's friend? I think you met him."

Her mouth purses with disapproval. "I know the name."

"Well, we've been having lunch." Every other day for the past two weeks. I keep finding reasons for showing up at the hospital. God bless the recovery wing. Not to mention the late night phone calls into the wee hours. "And we went hiking to the Falls. He didn't know anyone else in town, so I took him under my wing. Figured I owed it to Rebecca."

She studies my face, and I wish I could hide in a closet. "You're blushing, Joanna."

Oh, fuck. I hate being pale. "We're just friends. Really. He's just, uh, I can talk to him. About almost anything. He's...easy to be around, and really smart, and sweet, and awkward and I don't know." I chuckle. "And he's *so* screwed up. He has no idea how amazing he really is. It's fucking wonderful. I don't feel like a freak around him. But there's this strength in him too." I shake my head. "When we're together, it's just natural. Like when I was around...you know, minus the constant need to impress," I say, looking away

"He sounds wonderful," Lucy says.

"He is! That's the problem. I…like him. A lot. But I don't know if I can trust him. And I want to, I may even, which scares the fuck out of me. Plus, you and I both know I'll find some way to screw it up, especially if we start dating." I groan. "Ugh, I hate this. I sound like a fucking girl."

"Can't have that," Lucy says with a smirk. "You need to stop worrying, Joanna. If it's meant to be, everything will fall into place."

"You sound like my friend Lexie."

"Another friend? Aren't you popular."

"She and her husband moved from Independence too. They…" Holy shit. My mouth falls like my stomach, but I snap it shut with a chuckle. "They're good people." I chug my water.

"It sounds like you're doing well." She signals the waiter for the check.

"You too."

I pay for lunch, and we step outside onto the busy Independence streets. The white Presidential Monument arches tall above the city with the flag whipping in the wind. Makes me feel almost patriotic. The restaurant doorman hails a cab, and my driver pulls up as well. "Take care of yourself, Joanna." Lucy gives me a stiff hug before climbing into the cab.

I wait until it's out of sight before sliding into my town car. What a difference a year makes. I do believe that woman officially likes me. "Airport, please."

The driver starts moving as I pull out my cell. We round the corner. Gone an hour and I have seven messages, all work, but my mind isn't on them. We stop at a light. I can't believe I didn't see—

The sound of sirens, automatic gunfire and crashing cars jolts me from my thoughts. The intersection in front of us flips from calm to crazy in a second flat. The cars passing through gun their engines to get out of the way, of what I don't know. Nothing good, that's for damn sure. The gunfire booms louder with each passing millisecond. My mouth dries up and body goes on high alert. Fuck. I blink and an armored truck with three men, one hanging out the passenger window and two in the back, firing Uzis zooms into view with only one bullet riddled police car chasing it. A few cars in front of the truck veer to a stop as their driver's panic. The few cars behind the truck swerve out of the bullet path, one crashing into the glass window of a bakery. Right as the truck passes into our intersection, the tenacious police officers lose the battle. A bullet hits the latch and the hood of the car flies up, blocking their line of sight. The officer loses control and swerves in our direction. Instinct takes over. I scream, "Get down!" at my driver as I duck. I've barely stopped moving when glass rains down over me as a barrage of bullets meant for the cruiser pepper the town car. The carnage is over as soon as it started. I open my eyes and see the plumes of smoke wafting out of the upholstery where the bullets lodged in the driver's headrest. "You okay?" I ask the driver.

"Oh, Jesus, oh, Jesus," he mutters. He's fine.

Another crash, louder this time, makes me sit up. The armored truck is out of sight and the bystanders in cars and on the street slowly rise from the pavement. A construction worker helps the police out of their overturned car ten feet to my left. The gunfire stops a second later, and I let out the breath I was holding. I think it's—*nope.*

The gunfire begins again, moving closer. Time progresses slowly. The few people still on the street sprint inside for cover. My driver starts praying again and ducks down as a man in full tactical SWAT gear and balaclava lays covering fire behind himself as he rounds the corner. Coming right for us.

I don't think. I just do. My hand reaches inside my purse, pulling out the Taser and pearl handled .22 I carry for just such emergencies. I have to time this just right. I peek through my shattered side window. With the gun now in my waistband and Taser in hand, as the shooter runs beside the front passenger door, I throw mine open with all my might. It hits home. He smashes right into the door, chest and legs first. Dazed, he drops the Uzi and falls to the cement with a groan. The moment he wipes out, I zap his leg with the Taser. His body convulses, then grows still when I release the button. I know from experience how scrambled the bastard's brain is now. Good.

On shaky everything, I manage to climb out of the car, training the .22 on the stunned man. The Uzi has skidded out of reach but not the Glock on his belt. Breathing heavily, I crouch down and retrieve it, throwing the .22 into the town car. I keep the

Glock on him as I Taser him again. I'll just keep zapping until the cavalry arrives.

"Holy shit." My gaze whips up toward the man who steps out of the store in front of me. More people follow him. That's when I realize the gunfire around the corner has stopped.

"Everyone get back ins—"

Quick movement to my right startles me enough to turn the gun that way. As if materializing from thin air, a tall man in a black and white costume with "WN" on his broad chest appears. My gun is trained right on his completely masked face where only the eyes are visible. They lock on mine, and he's suddenly breathing as heavily as I am, gasping even. The man raises his hands in surrender. "Please lower your weapon," he whispers for some reason. "I'm one of the good guys." That voice literally sends a chill down my spine as if someone walked over my grave. Why—

"Lower your weapon," another man shouts. I glance left to find a bleeding police officer approaching, pistol right on me.

I toss the Glock near the Uzi. "You guys are welcome," I say cattily.

The, I'm assuming, hero lowers his hands as the officer steps beside me. "Got this?" the hero asks in that same low tone that can barely be heard over the oncoming sirens.

"Yes, sir," the officer says, pulling out his cuffs.

The hero nods, then looks back at me, eyes burring on my face. He stares but when I try to meet his eyes, he gazes down. "I…" His mask moves where his mouth should be but no more noise comes out. Instead he grabs me by the shoulders hard enough to hurt, giving me one quick shake. "*Never* do that again." He releases me, and disappears as fast as he came.

I roll my eyes. Sometimes I really hate superheroes.

*

Better late than never. I return home five hours later than planned what with giving my statement, accompanying my driver to the hospital after he went into shock, followed by a traffic jam to the airport. I'm glad I broke that bastard's nose for all the trouble he and his friends caused me. On the plane I was waiting for the panic attack, or at least cathartic crying jag, but neither reared their ugly heads. Instead I fell asleep until Shannon woke me when we landed. Both she and Dobbs knew better than to ask questions. We drop Shannon off at her apartment and drive home listening to the news. The robbery didn't go national, and I can only pray my name doesn't get leaked or it will. I don't want certain people to worry. When we walk into the mansion, without a word Dobbs and I go our separate ways. I can tell he's worried, but I don't want to talk about it. Ever.

I strip off my clothes—even now shards of glass tumble out—and climb into the scalding shower until I prune. I feel nothing. I heard four police officers were injured, two civilians were shot, but no fatalities. My driver, who I learned is named Luis after we spent an hour in the hospital waiting room, is now at home with his wife and babies, no doubt hugging them tight. Lucky bastard in every damn sense. I towel off, throw on pajamas, and slide into bed. Okay, really I stare at the phone on my nightstand, buzzing with nervous energy like I'm about to supernova. I lose track of how long I do this, willing it to ring or for me to pick it up and dial.

I sent him a text at the hospital that lunch went well, that I was looking forward to our sailing lesson tomorrow, and nothing else. He's probably at home now, reviewing gene therapy studies for his next project. His eyes light up when he talks about the research. I could call or just show up at his apartment. No, that's the exact wrong thing to do at least for me. I know what will happen, and it can't. I stop the torture by fleeing the temptation. Works with the booze.

Oh, of course. I have guests. Tonight both Nightingale and Liberty sit at the computer. Perfect. We're still tracking down the explosives with little success. That success being the criminals in town are quaking in their boots after getting paid a visit or ass-beating from the Triumvirate. Both heroes look my way as I walk down. Since the backrub debacle Nightingale and I have been quietly working side-by-side with no mention of anything not pertaining to the work. I just adore an awkward office environment.

Liberty pivots around first, mouth open in surprise, while her companion spins back the way he was, away from me. Not a happy camper. "There you are," she says, standing. "We were worried. Are you okay?"

"Why?" I ask.

"Why do you think? We heard what happened."

Of course they did. "How?"

"We have connections," Nightingale says with a hint of anger.

"Did you really Taser a guy in the balls?" Liberty asks with a mischievous smile.

"Just the leg and shoulder."

"Too bad." She scans me like an MRI machine. "Well, you look intact. How are you feeling?"

"Fine," I say, scanning her too. Wish I could see her eyes.

"It's always a trip, huh? Getting shot at?"

"If you say so."

Liberty's mouth purses. "Fine, don't give us details." She glances at her colleague. "See what *you* can get out of her. I'm going on patrol." She spins on her heel and walks away.

"*Ciao*," I say.

"*Ciao*," she says before lifting off the ground and flying down the passage.

A small smile crosses my face, but I drop it before gazing at Nightingale, who is still blanking me. I sit in the spare chair next to him. "What are we working on tonight?"

"Nothing," he says. "Reviewing files."

"Any news on the explosives? We know they haven't been sold in Galilee so maybe we expand to Pacific City or—"

"We've hit a wall," he says, voice hard. "The government's on it."

"So, we're giving up? What if—"

He turns to me. "We're you even going to tell m—*us* about the shoot-out?"

My mouth snaps shut. "Why? I'm fine. Shit happens."

"You were shot at. You risked your life for nothing. What were you thinking?"

"That a dangerous man was getting away, and that I could stop him."

"It was idiotic," he says. "You could have been killed. Don't you care?"

"I…" I can't seem to find the right words. "I reacted. I did what I had to."

"That's the point. *You* don't have to. White Night had the situation well under control."

"Not from where I was sitting. In my bullet riddled car, I might add. You weren't there. The man who shot at me was getting away. I could stop him. I did. You of all people should know what that's like. So unless you're hanging up your cape: pot, kettle, black your Lordship."

This shuts him up. He sits there breathing heavily and staring. After a few seconds, he hangs his head and says, "I just don't want anything to happen to you. You're…a friend." He clears his throat and returns to Doris. "I-I assume you won't be that foolhardy again. There are too many people who depend on you. Employees, family, whatnot. You had an ordeal today. You must still be in shock. You should speak to someone."

"I'll be fine. It wasn't like the KitKat incident. I wasn't the target."

"Still. There must be someone more…suitable for you to talk to. A person you're more at ease with."

"I'm not calling anyone. There's no need. Look, stop worrying. I'm really okay. What I need right now is to work." I turn to the computer screen. "So, if they didn't sell the explosives, then we're looking for a terrorist group or possibly a villain. There are a few villains we couldn't find in the city, but maybe it wasn't one of our regulars. Or the locations of the bases were incidental. Galilee won't be the target. The base had the laxest security or an inside man."

"Everyone was cleared. We've hit a wall. We really have done all we can. It's time to move on."

"So we're just giving up?"

"We'll keep our ears to the ground and eyes open. Nothing else to do."

"I don't like giving up," I say.

"I know," he says, glimpsing my way. "Nor do I. We just…have no choice. Accept what we cannot change, correct?"

I raise an eyebrow. "Been to many A.A. meetings, have we?"

"Have you been to one recently?"

"I'm not going to get plastered because some asshole sprayed bullets at me."

"If you say so," he says in a small voice. The temperature in the room feels like it's gone down twenty degrees, the chill emanating from my companion.

"I do say. And it's none of your damn business anyway."

"Fine." It lowers another ten degrees.

"Good. So, what should we do in the meantime?"

He pauses before swallowing as if he's tasted something sour. "We're trying to track Boneshaker. One of the men we spoke to about the explosives said he was approached last week by Mr. Percy about a potential job at the Botanical Gardens. We're keeping an eye on it. Then there's the garden variety crime. Tempest is pursuing a family annihilator, as is your old squad. All is well in hand." He stands. "I'm done here, it's all yours. Enjoy your evening, Miss Fallon." He steps away, mouth set straight in anger.

It infects me. "Excuse me, are *you* mad at *me*?"

"Of course not," he says sharply, killing those words.

I roll my eyes. "Jesus Christ, what the hell do you want from me, man?" I leap up and stalk toward him. "You want me to bear my soul to you? Share my innermost thoughts and fears? You want me to trust you?" I ask with a laugh. I try to meet his eyes but his head swivels to deflect. "You won't even look me in the eye. You don't even have the balls to tell me who you really are. Until you do, you're just another masked vigilante who uses my computer, and I occasionally have a sandwich with. You're keeping me on the outside, and though I do know and respect why, it makes trust hard. It's a two way fucking street, and you're still on the highway."

"And you're not?" he asks, voice hard. "Have you told anyone what you do in here?"

"Those who need to know do."

"And you don't trust the others to understand."

"Don't you turn this around on me! I'm not the one…" I snap my mouth shut. "You know what? I'm done with this conversation. *Done*."

"Fine. As am I."

"Good!"

"Fine!" He lifts off the ground and flies away, taking the last word with him.

Of all the...*he* has the nerve to...fuck him! He should thank me for keeping my trap shut not giving me shit. I swear all superheroes are nuts. Certifiable.

I'm done. I'm spent. I need out of this fucking room. I've done enough for the betterment of humanity today. I shut off the lights and stomp up to the house, fuming. First I get chastised, again, for helping then I'm made to feel like shit for not shouting from the rooftops that I'm in league with heroes? I don't tell anyone to keep my ass safe, same as him. Until he rips that mask off, he just needs to keep his fucking mouth shut about trusting people.

After brushing my teeth, I turn off the lights and get into bed again. No matter how hard I try, and I do try, my mind races a trillion miles an hour. Images from the day are replayed until I'm curled in the fetal position hugging my legs. Guess I'm not as strong as I thought. It just took awhile to sink in. I was shot at today. If I hadn't ducked when I did my brains would be splattered inside that car like a macabre painting. I've had front row seats to that horror show before. Fuck it. I open my eyes and turn on the TV, hoping the noise will drown out my thoughts.

After fifteen minutes, I give up that dream as well. God, being sober sucks. If this were a year ago I'd be pouring Bourbon, popping a pill, or driving over to Harry's so he could screw the demons away. A year before that I'd call Justin and we'd talk or meet for late night pancakes at Nell's Diner. Now I know why he was always in the city at night when I needed him. I just thought he was working late. Suppose he was.

Fucking superheroes. He could have told me. He *should* have told me. Even now a large part of me hasn't forgiven him for all the lies. I know the reasons in my head, but that doesn't mean the wound in my heart isn't still tender. How the hell are you supposed to trust a person who won't share such an important part of their life with you? A part of themselves? How can you even begin to build on that? No idea, but boy do I want to.

Chapter Seven

Guardian Angel

Of course I'm awakened all of two hours after I fall asleep by the ringing phone next to my head. So much for Jem, me, a beach, and nothing but a towel. This had better be life or death or heads will roll.

"Hello?"

"It's Tempest. We need you down at command."

"What—" He hangs up. "Fuck."

I toss on my robe and hustle downstairs. I expect to find the threesome in the command center, but the lights are off. Static from the radio fills the room, followed by Tempest's voice saying, "Guardian, come in. Repeat, Guardian come in. This is K.T., come in, over." I think I'm supposed to be Guardian? I've never used the comms unit on Doris, so it takes me a second to find the right button and headset. "Repeat, Guardian—"

"Um, Guardian here," I say into the headset.

"Good to have you, Guardian," Tempest says. "Sorry to wake you. We need an extra set of eyes to cover our six. We've located Boneshaker at the club Noir, but we have an estimated eleven accomplices with guns here. We're wirelessly patching into his security system now."

"I don't know how to get that signal. I've never done this before."

I hear a man, I think Nightingale, talking in the background then Liberty saying, "Jesus, *you* tell her," followed by static. I think I lost the connection. Shit! Where the hell is that manual? As I rifle through the drawer the static ends, and Nightingale says, "Guardian, come in. Here's how to do it." He gives me step-by-step instructions, which I manage to screw up more than once. I hate technology. Nothing is ever simple. All that matters is eventually the feed pops up on the monitors. We're in business.

I count twelve cameras in the main room where waitresses and cleaning people sweep up booths and the dance floor. I've been to Noir. It's all blue neon lights and black walls. Looks dull in black and white with the house lights on. Another camera captures the hallway where more waitresses and beefy men with sidearm's walk to and fro. Yeah, that's not standard equipment for club bouncers. What really catches my eye is the screen where the cameras overlook a stairwell where two more guards stand outside a door.

"What do you see, Guardian?" Tempest asks.

"I count seventeen possible civilians, most in the main club with four or five in a hallway or storage areas. This is unconfirmed, but my best estimate is ten henchmen in the same areas and all carrying side arms. Hallway appears about fifty feet long with four doors along it."

"What about Ramsey?" Tempest asks. Timothy Ramsey, A.K.A. Boneshaker, is infamous in Europe for crumbling whole villages and castles, including ones with sitting royalty inside them just trying to enjoy Christmas dinner. Since he's been in town, he's only robbed a bank, but last week sent a letter to the papers promising "a bloody big show" when we least expect it. He'll be kicking himself for waiting so damn long to keep that promise in about ten minutes time.

"Not visible, but best guess is he's down in the basement. There are two armed guards standing watch there. Unknown how many people are inside the room."

"Okay, guys," Tempest says, "take positions. Keep the comms channel open but the chatter to a minimum. Only break silence when absolutely necessary."

"Affirmative," I say.

"Positions," Tempest says. "Good hunting, people."

I can imagine the three of them on a cold club rooftop huddled together, nodding at each other before flying silently to the entrances. They've done this hundreds of times but still must be nervous. Lord knows I was before every bust. Hell, my leg is spastic right now from the anticipation, and I'm miles away safe as houses.

I hear the sound of wind whooshing over my headphones as they fly followed by dead silence. "Okay, Night," Tempest says, "the alarm."

The screech of the alarm is faint over the headset. Showtime. On the monitors, the people inside the club jolt and glance up at the sound just as water starts falling from the sprinklers. The civilians seem frightened but the men with guns immediately go on guard, tensing up and moving their hands nearer to their guns. The smarter people start running for the exits but some are too stunned to move. The three henchmen in the back hallway grab their guns from the holsters while running toward the basement door. One of the guards by the mystery door pokes his head into the room then disappears inside as the hallway goons arrive to take over sentry duty. Boneshaker is so in there. I feel it in my…well bones.

Thirty nail biting seconds pass as I watch all this. What the hell are they waiting for? "Guardian, civilians clear?" Tempest finally asks.

"Majority. Most bogies are in the back hallway."

"Then go-time people."

BOOM!

An explosion over my radio almost shatters my eardrums while on the monitor the roof caves onto the wet dance floor. Everyone inside jerks from the shock. The few people still inside leap away from the falling debris, some skidding in the water on their stomachs like otters. The henchmen in the hallway run toward the main room, guns up. Only three remain in the back. I hold my breath as Liberty, force field almost shimmering on my black and white monitor, zooms down from the hole. She throws two glowing orbs at the nearest men before they can get shots off. Nightingale glides in behind her, dodging and weaving the bullets coming his way. Like a bird of prey, he picks up one of the men by the collar only to toss him into a wall. Over the gunfire and still falling water I hear as the body hits, bones cracking. I grimace.

As bullets bounce off Liberty's force field, and she zaps the offenders with energy blasts, Nightingale touches down between two men. With a few swift moves he disables them with strategic kicks and blows worthy of a kung fu master. Upper cut, roundhouse kick, yet he's so graceful, like a killer ballet dancer, I can't help but be impressed. When another man lunges at him from behind, I shout, "Night, six," and he immediately kicks behind, hitting the man in the stomach. The man crumbles.

"Thank you," he mutters.

"Guardian, hallway?" Tempest asks.

I was so engrossed in the fight I forgot about him. I check the monitor. "Three, with one inside the office."

Before I utter the last word, the door at the end of the hallway falls from its hinges, and Tempest appears on the other side with his leg raised. The two henchmen down the hall open fire, but Tempest spins out of sight to take cover outside. Guns raised, a second later the men advance with caution. Just as they reach the door, there's more crashing sounds over my comms as Tempest busts through the roof fist first behind the men. His feet don't even touch the ground as mid-air he turns at a right angle, flying at the goons, arms outstretched in a straight line. He smashes into the men before banging them into either side of the wall, knocking them out. I think I can hear bones break. Tempest lands beside the prostrate henchmen. "Team, status?" he asks.

I glance at the dance floor feed. Nightingale stands over a bleeding man, giving him a swift punch to the face. "Last bogie down," Liberty says.

"Hallway," Tempest orders. The others sprint toward the back as Tempest saunters down the hall. The last guard by the basement door visibly shakes. I would too. The Triumvirate congregate on either side of the stairwell. "Hey, you with the gun," Tempest calls. The guard trembles even harder. "You have a choice to make, sir. Throw us your gun then follow it up here, or we'll break all your fingers prying it from your hand. You have five seconds to decide." Without a moment's hesitation, the man tosses the gun then runs up the stairs fleeing to the open door down the hall. Smart minion.

Tempest is the first down the stairs with Liberty at his heels and Nightingale close behind. The surveillance camera begins to quake, then I hear rumbling over the comms. It starts out light as if the wind were blowing, but by the time they reach the door, the entire building is swaying and crackling, including the narrow passage the team's in. Earthquake. Boneshaker, you bastard. The security cameras and plaster from the roof and walls shed to the ground. I've lost the feed from five, no six cameras. The one in the passage jerks so much I can barely make out Tempest kicking the basement door in. Immediately gunfire and shouting begin, but I can't make out the words. The last image I get before the camera dies is Nightingale's body jerking as multiple bullets burrow into the chest from what sounds like an Uzi, then a high-pitch shriek as a bullet hits his comms unit.

"No!" I scream as I leap out of my seat.

"Night is down," Tempest shouts over the gunfire.

"They're getting away," Liberty says. "I'm going—"

"Lib, wait—"

Then nothing but static.

Oh, shit.

Oh, shit.

What the hell am I supposed to do? What should I do?

I stand trembling as the adrenaline overloads my system for the second time in twelve hours. Bile rises into my throat, but I choke it down. I can barely breathe. I can't think. Should I call the police? They're on their way already because of the alarm. Should I get into my car and drive over there? That's what I want to do. *Bad.* But it'd take fifteen minutes and by then the police, fire, and EMTs will be there, and I'd be in their way. Fuck. *Fuck!* There's nothing I can do. Nothing. I'm useless. "Useless!" I shout while kicking the chair. It skids until it hits the wall and topples. Useless.

I pace around the room, breathing heavily but not getting any air in for a few seconds. I shake my hands to expel some of the energy, which helps for whatever reason before grabbing the other chair to sit. I press the comms button, and the static stops. "Team, come in." Static. "Team, this is Guardian. Please respond." Nothing. I pull up the CCTV footage from the nearest camera down the street from Noir. Shit. Not helpful to my peace of mind. I'm watching a damn disaster movie.

The club is a wreck with parts of the brick walls and roof crumbling into bread crumbs while firemen and police brave entering the toppling structure. Another truck and ambulance stop in front, with two more police cruisers behind. I watch on one of the few remaining security cameras inside as the firemen search the debris and police tend to the still unconscious and cuffed henchmen. "Team, come in."

Static.

They can't be dead. This was nothing to them. They've taken down giant robots and stopped a fucking nuclear bomb. A few men with guns and a villain is a cakewalk. He just…I'm sure he's been shot a dozen times before and walked away without a scratch. Tonight will be no different. It has to be because I can't have just watched another person I care about die in front of my eyes. I hate this. I hate this so fucking much. "Team, come in!" I don't do helpless well. I couldn't do anything then, and I can't now. There has to be something I can do if I just think. Think! "Come in, please. Please, come on," I whisper to myself. I'm losing it. I can't do this again. He—

"Guardian, do you copy?" Tempest asks over the radio.

If I wasn't sitting I guarantee my ass would be splayed on the floor by now. Thank God. Thank you, God. I let out a ragged whimper and wipe the tears from my eyes before saying, "I'm here."

"Status report. We've apprehended Boneshaker and are en route to the nearest police precinct. He's unconscious."

"Are you okay?"

"Well, we need showers after chasing him through a tunnel into the sewer but otherwise perfect. Status on Nightingale?"

Shit. Motherfucking, goddamn, shitting shit. "Um, unknown. He-He was shot in the chest before the feed cut out," I say, voice quaking.

"Nothing on comms?" Tempest asks.

"No."

"I'm sure he's fine," Tempest says, calm as can be. "Lib, go back and check on him."

"Roger," she says.

"I'm at the precinct now. Good job tonight. Couldn't have done it without you. Tempest, over and out."

Now instead of static, there's nothing but silence. Bastard cut the connection. I fall back into the chair, mouth open in shock. That's it? That's all I get? I watched them…I thought they…they…I rip off the headset and stare at the security feed from down the street. He hasn't come out yet. What if he's buried under a literal ton of rubble, and they don't know he's there or can't get to him in time? I watch as EMTs check on the battered henchmen under the attentive eye of the police. I watch as a small crowd gathers outside while more police and ambulances arrive. I don't see Liberty arrive. I don't see Nightingale walk out on his own. I pull my legs to my chest and hug them. Come on…

Some time passes as I just stare. Numb. Detectives, then press show up outside the club. The less hurt henchmen are carted away in squad cars and others leave in ambulances. Detectives mill around, attempting to piece together what happened. Eventually they disappear into the hallway. If he was injured, they would have wheeled him out by now. If he were dead, they'd leave him for CSI to work on. When CSI arrives I hug my legs tighter, resting my head on my knees. Come on, you bastard. *Come on.* Don't you do this to me. This is…I can't…I just sat here and watched as he—

"Are you alright?"

My head jerks up. A muck covered Liberty and dusty Nightingale stand at the entrance staring at me. "Yeah, you feel sick or something?" Liberty asks.

Fresh tears I've been holding back spring out. He's alive. He came back. Oh, thank you God. Thank you. "I—" is all I can get out. I can't let them see me cry. I wipe my eyes and start playing with the computer. "I'm fine. Tired," I say, voice shaking.

"We were pretty awesome tonight, huh?" Liberty says. "Could have done without the trip to sewerville though. Can't wait to see the playback."

"Right," I say.

"Oh, you don't have to pull it up tonight. We'll review it later. Just wanted to check on you. You sounded freaked over the comms."

"I'm fine," I say, still not looking at them. Go away tears. Fuck off.

There's silence for some seconds, and out of the corner of my eye I spy Liberty mouthing something to Nightingale while nudging him with her elbow. He scowls and shakes his head. "Anyway," Liberty says cheerfully, "I am in dire need of ten showers. I'll leave you two to wrap things up if you don't mind. Thanks for all your help tonight. Ciao!" she calls, flying away.

I half expect Nightingale to follow suit, but he doesn't move from the passage. He glances at the exit, at me, at the exit again, not sure what to do next. When he decides, he clears his throat and moves toward me. "We, um, just need to add a few notes to the Boneshaker file." He brushes past me to pick up the overturned chair. "Write an incident report and whatnot." He sits in the chair far enough away from me to realize he's uncomfortable. "If-If you're too tired I can—"

"I'm fine," I snap. "Just tell me what to do."

He's quiet for a few seconds, then says, "Are you still angry at me for—"

My mouth drops open, and my gaze whips over to him. "Am I *angry* at you? I-I-I'm pissed to fuck!" I leap up, eyes bugging out of my head I'm sure. "You assholes woke me up in the middle of the night to have me watch as-as-as you were shot at, then buried in rubble by a fucking psychopath! I-I had to sit here, in this fucking room miles away as you took half a dozen bullets to the chest right in front of my goddamn eyes! I thought you were..." I snap my mouth shut, turning away from him. "Do you have any idea what it's like to watch someone you care about die and not be able to stop it? Because I have firsthand experience, and it's..." Shit, I can't stop the stupid damn tears this time. I violently wipe the offenders away.

More silence, then, "You care about me?"

I spin around, mouth flopped open again. "Of course I fucking care about you, you asshole! Jesus Christ! We had one stupid tiff! That's what friends do. We fight, we talk, we make up. What we don't fucking do is let our friend think we're dead even for a second!"

"I thought...I didn't think...it didn't even occur to me. I'm sorry."

"Well, you damn well should be!" With a sniffle, I wipe my eyes a final time. "Just...don't do it again. Try not to get shot. Period. If something happened to you...I'd fucking kill you."

"I feel the same way."

"Good. Then we're in agreement. Nothing will happen to either of us."

A smile crosses his lips. "I can live with that."

I return it. "You better." I scoff and sit again, shaking my head at the ridiculousness of...everything. "What a fucking day. I get shot at, you get shot. Hell, maybe I am cursed."

"*I'm* the one who was actually shot," he counters. "If anyone is cursed..."

I glance at his chest. "Does it hurt?"

"My ribs itch like mad, but that means they're healing. I'll be fine by tomorrow."

"Is there anything I can do?"

"No, but thank you," he says with a quick smile.

I smile back. "Well, if it makes you feel better, you were fucking brilliant tonight. That backwards kick you did, that was pretty bad-ass," I chuckle.

"Thank you for informing me about him."

I shrug. "Well friends don't let friends get shot in the back. It's part of the code."

"I…consider you a friend as well." He hangs his head a little again. "And I do trust you. I would tell you who I am, I swear I would, but the others aren't ready yet. I cannot go against their wishes. They…they're all I've had for a long time."

"They're family," I say.

"Yes, I suppose they are." He pauses to clear his throat. "So please don't take it personally."

I pause, working up the courage to ask, "You would tell me? Honestly?"

"On my life."

And I believe him. "Good."

We sit just half smiling at each other for awhile. I drop the smile, and before I can stop myself I reach across and squeeze his gloved hand. He squeezes back before I pull away and rise. That's enough for tonight. "I'm exhausted. I'm sure you are too. We can do the paperwork later."

"No, it won't take too long. I'll do it. You go to bed."

"You sure? I can keep you company."

"No, you've done enough for me tonight. Get some sleep."

I pat and rub his shoulder. "You too." I walk up the ramp, glancing at him to see if he's watching me. He is. "Goodnight, your Lordship," I purr with a cheeky grin.

"Goodnight, Joanna."

Something about the way he says those words makes me warm all over. The feeling doesn't wane as I go upstairs and climb back into bed. Two bad men behind bars, one friendship salvaged, and federal funding for seven free clinics. Not bad for a day's work. I close my eyes.

Maybe tomorrow I'll crack world peace. My partner can help.

CHAPTER EIGHT

PRACTICALLY PERFECT

It's a beautiful day, the last for this week per the weather report, so I intend to take full advantage. World peace can wait. At eleven, after breakfast in bed thanks to the best butler in the world, I saunter my usual route down the beach. I'd run but I'll get enough exercise on my sailboat later. There are just one or two things I have to take care of while Dobbs packs my picnic basket.

A work crew on the beach sets up tables and chairs under a tent while Lexie, dressed in a pink velour track suit with huge sunglasses and coffee tumbler, directs traffic. A late night was had by all. "No, I said eight chairs per table! Twice! Jesus," she mutters.

"Hi," I say. "Hope I'm not interrupting."

"Oh, hello. No just getting ready for the fundraiser. It's such a pain in the ass." She sips her tumbler. "Shit, I'm out. I am not making it though this day without twelve cups of coffee. Come on up. You can help me scream at the cleaners."

I follow her up the stairs, which more than makes up for my not running, while she takes the mountain in stride. I'm gasping while she whistles. Unfair. The cleaners scrub and vacuum the house in preparation for her fundraiser tonight as others decorate with freesias and unlit candles. She gives orders as we pass into the kitchen, filled with stainless steel everything. Brendan, dressed in a green Independence Eagles jersey and shorts stands, at the counter eating cereal as caterers stack up crates of food. "Look who popped by," Lexie says as we enter.

"Hey, Jo," Brendan says with his mouth full.

"Classy, darling," Lexie scolds. She pours us coffee. "Bren, coffee?"

"Thanks babe," he says.

"Like morons we were out all night after the game. Keep forgetting we're not as young as we used to be," Lexie says.

"That's for damn sure," Brendan says.

"What were you guys up to?" I ask.

She passes around the cups. "Club hopping with a few teammates and wives. My legs are killing me from all the dancing," Lexie says. "At least we weren't at the other one that exploded or whatever. This city," she says, shaking her head. "And now I have this fundraiser today."

"That's actually why I stopped by. I'm not going to make it tonight, I'm sorry. I'm not just up to it. It's been a long couple of days, and my ability to bullshit and schmooze is impaired. I'm sorry."

"You have to come! You're the only person in town I like!" Lexie says.

"Hey," Brendan says.

She scowls at him. "Oh, you don't count. You're my husband."

"Thanks, babe."

I pull out the check from my pocket. "I'm really sorry. Here, for the shelter."

She takes it. "Well, forty grand *begins* to make up for your abandonment, I guess."

"Um, who ditched who at the Mills' party? We're square now."

"I told you we only did that because you looked so cozy with your doctor out there. I knew he'd take *very* good care of you. And by the way, it worked so you're welcome." She leans on the counter. "So, how *are* things going with the good doctor? I haven't spoken to you in days. I'm dying for the next chapter in the saga."

Brendan picks up his mug and walks over to the sink. "And I'm taking that as my cue to leave. See you around, Jo." I wave as he walks out.

"Girl talk gives him indigestion," Lexie says. "So. Tell me! What is going on? Has he kissed you yet?"

"No. I told you, we're just friends."

"Right. Sure. I totally believe you," she says in a monotone. "That's why you get all goofy smiley when you talk about him."

"I do not."

"You so do. It's beyond cute. So, it's been two weeks, and you've seen him almost every day, have you even held hands yet? Called him in the middle of the night just to hear his voice?"

My cheeks flare up in embarrassment. "I had a bad day and couldn't sleep." Twice.

"And he was the only succor you could find," she says dramatically. "*Tres* romantic. You're totally falling for him. And why not? He sounds like a fantastic guy. Sweet, smart, interesting, and crazy about you. Cute too, in a nutty professor sort of way. You could do a hell of a lot worse."

"I know," I say, playing with my mug.

She sips her coffee. "Just one piece of advice: be careful."

"Why?"

"I knew a guy like him once. Shy, been through hell, just makes it hard to let people in. But once someone's in, they're in forever. Just don't do anything until you're a thousand percent certain you're ready to give as good as you get. That's all." She sips her coffee. "Anyway, traitor, I have a trillion things to do today. Lexie's wisdom shop is closed. Time for me to kick your butt out. Come on."

As she leads me back to the beach, past the lounging Brendan who winks at me, I tell her the best people to hit up for donations. Guilt assuaged, I wave good-bye and walk home, a knowing smile on my face when I turn my back to her. No doubt now. I chuckle and shake my head at the absurdity of it all.

Traffic isn't bad until I enter the city where kamikaze pedestrians and taxi drivers do their damndest to give me a heart attack. Jem lives in the center of town in Parkscale, the ritzy part of the city with Stan Lee Park just around the corner. Jem's building is one of our newest and biggest, forty-five stories high and most of it blue glass built on top of the old building which was demolished after a fight between Justice and Shrieker. Most new buildings have similar history. The doorman phones Jem's apartment. This place still smells of paint and carpet glue. It takes awhile, but eventually I'm allowed up to his penthouse. I knock, then hear a thwack and grumbling inside before the door opens.

"Hello," Jem says, rubbing his shin. God is he too cute for words dressed in a dark blue robe over striped pajamas, wild hair and toothpaste in the left corner of his mouth. I have the strongest urge to lick it off. "This is a surprise."

"It shouldn't be. We're supposed to go sailing today, remember?"

"We are?"

"Yeah. Remember I said I was thinking of going, and you said you always wanted to learn, and I said, 'Well, why don't we start your lessons Sunday,' then you asked, 'Can it be Saturday?' I shrugged, and you said, 'I'd love to. You are the kindest, most generous friend I've ever had. Monuments should be constructed in your image.' Remember all that?"

He grins and the dimple appears. Dear God, puppies aren't even this adorable. "I do now."

"So, you gonna let me in?"

"Right," he says, shaking his head. "Right. Come in."

His apartment isn't how I imagined it. I expected something smaller with a little more personality. All the walls are stark white, as are the venetian blinds that cover a whole wall. The hardwood floors still glint with wax from the sunshine radiating through the skylights above. The only decorations are four large overstuffed bookcases, telescope, aquamarine and white couch, glass coffee table and television. A few paintings still in bubble wrap lean against the wall and fireplace. I hold the handrail as I walk down the two steps in the living room. "It's…big. Definitely has potential. Maybe paint a few walls, throw down some rugs." I look up at the blue sky. "I love the skylights and cathedral ceilings. You can sit by the fire and gaze up at the stars."

"That's exactly why I moved in. That and the view. Hold on." He walks over to the fireplace and grabs the remote from the mantle. When he presses the button, the blinds rise, revealing buildings of various heights below and the red, yellow, and orange of the park's trees. "It's even better at night with the buildings illuminated."

"It's beautiful."

"Yes," he says, staring out with a contented smile. He glances at me, and I smile back. "I need to shower before we leave."

"Take your time."

Jem gives me another quick smile before disappearing into the hallway. I hear the door shut before I start my snooping. I begin in the kitchen to make us coffee. It's small with a stainless steel island in the middle of the room and faux wood counters with only a microwave and coffeepot on them. In the fridge I find rotting Chinese take-out boxes, milk, olives, peanut butter, and two slices of bread. Looks like my old fridge. With the coffee percolating, I move on.

The guest bathroom doesn't even have toilet paper in the dispenser. Wonder if I'm the first guest he's had. The master bedroom door is closed, but the other two bedroom doors aren't. The first is a study with more overflowing bookcases, a file cabinet, and large desk covered in journals, loose papers, and files stacked inches high. I read one of the stray papers but don't understand a word of it. Medical jargon. The last room proves more interesting. As I enter, I notice a shadowy figure in the corner. I quickly flick on the light. An attack dummy, just a torso and head of a fake man. He looks worn, as does the punching bag hanging from the ceiling held together by duct tape and fraying fibers. Well used. The floor is covered with blue mats like those found in a dojo. Huh. I shut off the light.

The coffee is done by the end of the tour. I still hear the shower running, so I quietly sneak into his bedroom with his cup. Okay, I'm shameless, but I am dying to see inside. Like the rest of the apartment it's sparely furnished with only an antique armoire, double bed with plain wood headboard, nightstand, and TV on a dresser. The bed is unmade with soft white sheets and a dark purple comforter. The shower turns off in the adjoining bathroom, and I quickly flee.

I have anywhere between ten minutes and an hour before he comes out depending on his beauty ritual, so I continue my investigation in the living room. First stop is the telescope, which I'm glad to find is pointed at the sky and not at a woman's bedroom. The bookcases mostly have biographies of political figures, non-fiction on wars, medical breakthroughs, spies, political policies, true crime, a lot on forensic investigating and profiling, and a few mysteries thrown in for flavor. What really captures my attention is the shoebox on the top of the corner bookcase. It's calling to me like a Siren. I crash into the rocks.

Jackpot.

Inside are photos, ticket stubs, even jewelry. A ring, a solitaire diamond on a gold band. There's an inscription inside, "J.A./U.G." with the infinity symbol between the initials. An engagement ring. I put it back and take out the photo on the top.

I've seen it before. I recognize it from Rebecca's mantle amid other family photos. She and a beautiful Indian woman have their cheeks pressed against each other making kissy faces for the camera. The next one in the box has Jem and the same woman, I presume Uma, sitting under a tree each reading a book while holding hands. Uma holding up her engagement ring to the camera as Rebecca hugs Jem in the background of a bar. There are a few more snapshots of their romance like the couple at her parents' house, Uma curled up on a couch asleep, them playing darts. In every shot they're serenely happy, glowing even. Is it wrong to be jealous of a dead woman I've never met? Probably.

Her obituary is halfway through the box. I've already read the murder book thanks to Doris. Uma Gupta was declared brain dead after a single gunshot wound to the head during an apparent home invasion. Per the file, Jem was the one who discovered her in their apartment, lying in a pool of blood. I saw the crime scene photos, it was pretty gruesome. They took her off life support the next day. She was twenty-three years old. They never found the shooter.

The next batch of photos are older and more worn. The first is a wedding photo of two unsmiling young people I recognize as Jem's parents. Can't even muster a smile on the supposed happiest day of their lives. I know he told me he was adopted, but Christian Ambrose has the same hair and killer cheekbones as Jem. Maybe he was the product of an affair and was just told he was adopted. Wealthy people are assholes like that. The next photo is of an older woman with her white hair in a bun reading to two small children by a pond. One of the boys has his back to the camera but the other has to be Jem. Same dimple. He smiles even bigger while hula-hooping in his dark bedroom beside a desk stacked high with books. The next is at Christmas. Jem, wearing a crown and with a silver sword by his side, stares intensely at the camera with almost hatred. His Camelot phase. Wait, didn't Jem say his—

The sound of an opening door startles me. I toss everything back in the box and shove it up on the shelf as Jem steps out. He's dressed in brown boat shoes, pressed khaki pants, and royal blue fleece shirt. Gone is the toothpaste, only to be replaced by shaving cream on his earlobe. "I was just, uh, looking at your books. You have a lot."

"You can borrow one if you want."

I step away from the bookcase. "I'm not much of a reader. But, uh, I like your workout room. How long have you been boxing?"

"I've dabbled through the years," he says, sipping his coffee.

"Nothing like beating the crap out of something to relieve stress, huh? I go shooting."

He quickly touches his chest. "I'm not a big fan of guns." He takes another swig of coffee. "I'm ready if you are. Am I dressed appropriately?"

"Might want to change one thing. Hold on." I grab a tissue, and his eyes follow me as I approach. His head moves away as I reach for him. "Stop it. I'm not going to bite." I wipe the white foam from his ear as he stares at me. Damn, even his eyes are tense. "There. Now you're perfect." I smile and meet those strained eyes. He's studying me again, and my smile drops. The fluttering in my stomach makes me step away. I've found that when I get the urge to pounce the best thing to do is flee. "Come on. Daylight's wasting."

Hope I don't have to jump into the ocean today.

*

My forty-foot cruising sailboat *The Athena* has become my refuge since Justin's death. It's the only place I can go where no one will find me, and that I can be well and truly alone. The middle of the sea is awesome like that. I learned to sail with Justin in our late teens, and at least once a month we took her out. Well, until he met Rebecca. There's something about riding along the open water with no one around for miles that is so freeing. You're relying on yourself and Mother Nature to reach your destination. I can get behind that simplicity.

As I'm sure he does all things, Jem picks up the machinations of the boat quickly. He only fouled the preventer shroud once. It took me months to get that right. Of course I never tripped on the ropes twice like the good doctor. He caught himself before he fell overboard but damn near gave me a heart attack anyway. I even taught him to steer and navigate. For the most part we don't talk, which is nice. It's hard to find people I'm comfortable just *being* with, where we don't have to fill every moment with chatter. Where it's just easy. There isn't enough easy in this life.

I stay on the bridge steering while he sits at the bow taking all the beauty of the ocean and sky in. Occasionally he feels me staring, pivots around, and presents me a tranquil smile before turning back. Think I just found my first mate.

When we're halfway back to port, I decide to drop anchor and serve dinner. It's my favorite time of the day, twilight, where the moon and sun share the sky, blending their darkness and light, creating deep oranges, purples, and blues. I join Jem on the bow where he arranges our feast on the blanket. We had sandwiches for lunch but dinner is a little more formal with Caesar salad, chilled salmon, sparkling cider, and cheesecake for desert. He mentioned it's his favorite. Dobbs even put a candle and holder for the centerpiece, not that I light it. This is already the most romantic non-date I've ever had, no need to add to the atmosphere. I pour the cider then hand Jem the plastic flute. "To serenity, beauty, and good company," I toast. He taps my cup with a nod and we drink. I devour my salad as he yawns for the fifth time in half the minutes. "Getting tired? I can make more coffee."

"No, I'm fine," he says still yawning. "Sorry. I didn't get home until three last night." He turns away toward the horizon. "One of my patients on the drug protocol was admitted last night. He's fine, though."

"That's good," I say with my own yawn. "Look, you've got me doing it now too."

He looks back at me with a grin. "What about you? Tired?"

"Yeah. I had a work emergency come up too that took some time. I had to go into the office and…" I meet his eyes, and the rest of the lie vanishes from my head. The sincerity in those pools of dark blue sort of infects me. "No, I'm not doing this."

"What?"

"I was going to lie to you," I say with an awkward smile. "I don't want to do that. I don't want any major secrets between us, they just poison the relationship. Justin never told me about Justice, and it almost destroyed us. That's not gonna happen here. So…for the past month and a half, I've been working with the

Royal Triumvirate. I just do research, I'm not in the line of fire or anything."

"Oh," he says, glimpsing away again.

"Like I said, it's a part of my life, and I felt that you should know."

"Well, thank you for trusting me with your secret," he says sadly.

"You're welcome." I pause to find the right words. "And you can trust me with yours, whatever they may be."

He simply stares in the direction of the setting sun. "I know."

We sit in silence for a few seconds as the boat gently rocks. "I have another confession to make," I finally say.

"Another one?" he asks with a raised eyebrow.

"Last one, I promise," I say with a half smile. "When you were in the shower I snooped around. I couldn't help myself, I'm sorry."

"I know. Well, I assumed. Discover anything of interest?"

"Few dead bodies, your porn collection, women's underwear in your size, the usual," I say, which garners another dimpled smile. "No, just books and photos."

"The ones in the shoebox?"

"Yeah." I pause. "You were a cute kid. I really liked the one of you and your brother with the nanny by the pond. You seemed so happy."

"That was Nanny Lynn. She was our favorite governess, mostly because she'd sneak us candy and let us watch television with her. I still record that soap opera. Uma used to laugh when Rebecca and I discussed the characters and ridiculous storylines."

"You weren't allowed candy or TV?"

"Only educational shows. Father was convinced the brain could only hold so much information, therefore he didn't want us filling our heads with trivialities. And sugar made us hyperactive and unable to concentrate. Lynn was with us three years before Jordan let our extra-curriculars be known. She was fired on the spot."

"Holy shit, I'm sorry." I scoff. "And I thought my childhood was fucked up."

"It wasn't all bad."

"At least you had your brother, right?"

He turns away again. "Yeah."

"You don't talk about him very much," I observe. "Did you have a falling out or something?"

"Or something." He pauses. "He didn't approve of my marrying Uma."

"Why? Because she was Indian?"

"No, because he was jealous. All we had was one another, then he turned his back and I had someone else. After her death, the few times we've seen each other, we're…combative at best." He glances back at me. "If you don't mind, I don't wish to talk about this anymore."

"Of course. Sorry."

"Nothing to be sorry about. It's perfectly natural to be curious. He's just not worthy of our time."

I have a trillion other questions but refrain. "Okay."

We sit across from one another and pick at our food in uncomfortable silence. After about fifteen seconds, he tosses his fork down with a sigh. "You have to understand, the conditions of our childhood were intolerable. We were isolated, constantly made to believe we had to be perfect, pushed to our limits, it was tantamount to torture and lasted the whole of our childhood. Our only refuges were our imaginations and one another. Us against the world, but it wasn't the real world. When we finally ventured out, left our microcosms, he floundered and attempted to take me under with him. I didn't much enjoy college, but I loved what I was studying and knew all would be worthwhile in the end. That was my first betrayal, not dropping out with him. Afterwards, I didn't see him for years. There was the odd phone call or postcard, but nothing substantial until our parent's funeral. We reconnected but he was traveling the world, doing God knows what, and I was in college. We spent summers and holidays together, phoned at least once a week, but I sensed he desired more. It was working until I met Uma. Then the snide comments became outright rudeness and open hostility. He vanished again after a huge fight. A few months later, he reappeared after hearing of our engagement, acting as if nothing had happened, all smiles and apologies. He was brilliant after she died and seemed genuinely sorry for my loss. I soon learned it was all an act."

I pause before asking, "He killed her, didn't he?"

"Yes. Not that I can prove it. Nor can I prove he set the fire that killed our parents. My brother is far too clever for that. I had investigators try to track him down even to this day, but if he doesn't wish to be found, he won't be." For the first time he gazes at me, mouth set straight. "Now you know."

"I'd tell you the guilt you feel is wrong, that she didn't die because of you, but then I'd be a huge fucking hypocrite. Not to mention a liar. If you hadn't come into her life, she might still be alive. That is just a hard fact. But it still wasn't your fault. I don't blame Justin for what James Ryder did to me anymore than Uma would blame you. And given the choice even now, of never meeting him or having to go through all I did, I'd chose him every fucking time without hesitation. Some people are just worth it." He stares at me and I half smile before looking away. His gaze doesn't leave my face, but I can't bear to see him for fear of breaking my shaky resolve. The silence is unbearable too. "The sun's gone. I guess we should be heading back soon."

"I suppose," he says.

I sigh. "God, I love this boat. Justin and I used to make sure we took her out once a month. Just the two of us. No distractions, no worries."

"I can see why you like it."

"Yeah. The tradition kind of ebbed away when Rebecca came onto the scene, though. You know the moment I knew he was officially gone was the second time he cancelled on me in as many months. The knife twisted when he let it slip he took her out here to propose. Probably in this very spot. I mean, it was bad enough he proposed, but to do it on *our* boat just cut to my heart. Betrayal on top of betrayal." I scoff. "How little did I know, huh?"

Jem's silent for a second, then, "I'm sure he had his reasons to keep that from you. It wasn't done to hurt you."

"I know the reasons. I do. Hell, I even sort of forgave him. Well, as much as you can forgive twenty years of lies. It still…" I bite my lip to stop the oncoming rant. "Sorry. Just being here, the anniversary in a few days, working with superheroes, and being with you just dredges it all up."

"Why being with me?" he asks, finally looking my way.

I half smile. "I don't know. You remind me of him. You're both dependable, kind, strong, smart, easy to be around. Practically perfect in every way."

"I'm not perfect, Joanna. And neither was he," he says with an undercurrent of anger.

"I know that. Now. Until Ryder, hell, I thought he was God. He could do no wrong. Everyone said I had a blind-spot when it came to him, and it wasn't until that blind-spot almost got me killed that I finally woke the fuck up," I say, almost chuckling. "I mean, he was vain. *So* vain. He'd spend an hour in front of the mirror getting his hair just so. Everything had to be perfect. If I left my jacket on the couch or God forbid forgot to use a coaster, I got a lecture. He was such a know-it-all too. Always telling me how to dress, to talk, hell even to eat. He meant well but it could be so grating. He was such a control freak. And he could be so fucking inconsiderate! I mean, I get all the cancelled appointments now, but sometimes he'd expect me to just drop what I was doing to meet him at some party or work event so he wouldn't have to be alone after some model cancelled on him. And the fucked up thing is, I always went! I skipped drinks with other cops or dinner with my own family to be his wingman. Then the few times I couldn't, because I was working, he'd be cold the next time I saw him. And there was very little give and take. We always did what he wanted, and I just learned to like it.

"Then, to top it all off, when he met Rebecca, he dropped me. The only times I got to see him, she was there. And then, once again, he expected me to stop my life to go to Daisy's ballet recital or Rebecca's tea and scones party. And once again I went because I thought maybe one day he'd open his eyes and see that I was the one who was always there for him. That I was the only one worthy of his love. I was such a fucking idiot. But…even in spite of all that he was my best friend. And I loved him with my all. But he's gone. I just need to finally and completely lay him to rest. To move on." I look into Jem's solemn eyes. "Is that even possible?"

Those sapphire eyes bore into mine as he says, "*God, I hope so.*"

Despite the increasing cold it's as if my entire body is alight with heat. Only twice before have I felt like this, once with Harry and the other with Justin, but those were flickers compared to this volcano. Every one of my cells is begging me to move toward him, to press my lips to his and just give into whatever this sensation is, but I fight them. It isn't time yet. I just don't know how much longer I can hold out.

Jem's eyes fill with sadness, and his face falls. I can't stand to see him in pain, especially when I'm the cause. I pull my legs up to my chest, hugging my knees and gaze up at the moon. "I'll take us back in a minute."

"Fine," he almost whispers. We both stare up at the night sky in silence, misery filling the space between us. "I'm not Justin, Joanna."

"I know," I say after a pause. I stretch my legs out and set my hands on the deck for support. After only a moment's hesitation, I move my hand on top of Jem's, entwining my fingers in his. He lets me. "I *know.*"

CHAPTER NINE

DEATH ECHO

I can make it through this day. I can. It is a day like any other. The sun rises, people go to work, they go home and the sun sets. Nothing extraordinary about it. Yeah, well, that's what I thought exactly a year ago today, and by the end of that day I'd been held hostage, shot at, killed a man, and watched as my best friend plummeted to his death to save me from the same fate. One never knows what is just around the corner.

Mayor Miracle arranged the memorial event in Stan Lee Park at three, where he'll unveil the new Fountain of Justice. I approved the design—the scales of justice pouring water with the names of the three heroes who donned the symbol. Justin would have liked it. An estimated thousand people, and who knows how many members of the press will be in attendance despite the rain. I got roped into making a speech, which my speechwriter handed to me as I hurried out of the office.

So far the day has been fine. Got enough sleep, went to work early, harangued the Senator about the healthcare bill, had lunch with Lane and a few other executives, and am now sitting in a police escorted town car on my way to the park. Please let the dry fish at lunch be the worst of the day. I'm dropped off at the Southside and led through the barricades toward the stage while a few tourists and paparazzi snap pictures. I ignore them. The nerves I always get before public speaking began in the car but get worse as I wait in the tent with interns and assistant event planners from city hall running around and screaming into their walkie talkies. My only goal is not to have a panic attack on stage. If I can do that, the day is a success.

Someone taps me on the shoulder, and I turn to find my cousin Veronica standing beside me. We look a lot alike, same height and build, but her curly hair is tawny and her eyes are brown. She sits next to me with a sigh. "You know, my editor was ecstatic when he found out I was the only reporter in town with backstage access to this thing."

"You're welcome," I say.

"*But* so far the only newsworthy thing is that all the interns Mayor Miracle hired are far too gorgeous to just be fetching him coffee. Does the man get them from a modeling agency?"

"There's your Pulitzer right there: discrimination in city hall, only the pretty may apply. Might actually be worth looking into," I offer.

"I just may." She pulls out her recorder and shoves it in my face. "Quote me, cuz."

"I'm honored to be here celebrating the life and good deeds of my friend, Justin Pendergast IV. He, his father, and grandfather deserve this memorial for all they did for this city. I only hope that when people walk past it, they not only remember the men, but also what they stood for."

"And how are you personally feeling today?"

"Of course this is a difficult day, but it is a day of remembrance. I choose to remember the good, which far outweighs the bad."

She stops the recorder. "You've gotten more eloquent since you hired people to tell you what to say." She stuffs the recorder in her coat. "Off the record, how are you?"

"So far, so good. No crying jags, no flashbacks, no impulses to reach for a bottle. I'm good."

"And where's your boyfriend?" she asks in sing-song.

"Shut up, he's not my boyfriend. He is a boy who is my friend."

"*Right.* So where is your platonic male friend who you spend hours on the phone with between romantic sunset cruises?"

I just had to tell her about that. "He has a job. And important meetings today."

"Too bad. I really wanted to meet Dr. Love."

"Don't call him that. Jesus, what are you? Twelve?"

She chuckles. "What? I never got to tease you about boys, except Justin but that got old after the first ten years," she says, rolling her eyes. "And I missed my chance when you were with O'Hara because you didn't tell me, which I have not forgiven you for by the way."

"Gee, wonder why I didn't tell you."

She playfully punches my arm. "Oh, come on. I want to meet him. See if he's good enough for my baby cuz. Dad—"

All the chatter stops, and there are a few audible gasps when three familiar masked vigilantes waltz into the tent. We all knew they were coming, but as most people have never been this close to superheroes, I understand their reaction. V practically begins panting at the prospect of getting face time with them. "Good afternoon," Tempest says to everyone.

Nobody moves or says a word. I roll my eyes, tug on V's jacket, and we stand. "Hi," I say, walking over to them. "I'm Joanna Fallon. Thanks for being here today."

Tempest shakes my hand. "Our pleasure. It's nice to meet you."

I glance at Liberty. "I don't know if you remember me, but—"

"Believe me, you are hard to forget Ms. Fallon," Liberty says. "Glad to see you're doing well."

"Thank you." V lightly hits me with her foot. "Um, this is Veronica Lilley with the *Galilee Gazette*."

"We've read some of your articles. They're very good," Tempest says.

"Good enough to grant me an interview?"

"We'll consider it," Tempest says.

I meet Nightingale's eyes, then signal over to the catering area. "Will you excuse me? I need coffee." I walk away toward the food to let V sell them on an interview. At the table, I pick up a glazed donut and start picking it apart. Sadly I'm never too nervous to eat.

On my second donut, when the last of my fellow munchers leave and the coast is clear, Nightingale steps beside me and picks up a coffee cup. "How are you?" he asks quietly.

"Holding it together," I say, stuffing my face. "Thanks for being here today. It means a lot."

"Of course. I know how hard this is for you. I—*we're* here for you. Always."

I flash him a smile. "Thank you."

For once Mayor Miracle is a welcome sight. He rushes into the tent with his security team close behind. Immediately, he zeroes in on the heroes. They are the ones who are going to get him national attention, not a fountain. "Oh my goodness, it is an honor to meet you," he says, shaking Tempest's hand. "Truly an honor. Thank you for agreeing to be here."

"Justice was a friend," Tempest says. "So, who speaks first?"

"The mayor, then you, then Miss Fallon who will unveil the fountain," the event planner says. "We should take our place. It's time."

"Okay," Miracle says. "Let's get out there before it starts pouring again."

I have enough time to touch-up my makeup and brush my hair before the planner makes us line up. I'm right behind Nightingale, who stares straight ahead. A few seconds before our cue his hand moves toward me, palm up. After making sure no one is watching, I entwine my fingers with his and squeeze. We pull apart before walking to the stage. Damned if I don't feel better.

The crowd goes batshit as the heroes step onstage, waving to their fans. It's stopped raining so there are easily a thousand people filling the grassy field and paths. Some hold up signs with "We miss U Justice" or "Make me your Queen, King Tempest." The mayor moves to the podium, and the rest of us sit in the chairs behind him.

On the jumbotrons scattered around the park pictures of Justin, his father, grandfather, and their alter-ego Justice fill the screen. J.R., Justin's grandfather and the first Justice, cutting a ribbon on the new wing of the museum, followed by Justice's first ever fight with Freak, the brawl that made him a superstar. Then J.T., Justin's dad, with Tessa, his mother, at some charity gala followed by Justice running out of a burning building with a woman in his arms. Justin pops up next standing on a familiar stage in a tux speaking to a crowd. It's the last photo of him ever taken at the recovery wing fundraiser exactly a year ago today. I remember that exact moment as clear as if it were happening right now. That proud smile, now a story tall, was all for me. The first pang of the day hits strong enough I sharply intake air. No more looking at pictures for me.

I sit ramrod straight and expressionless as Miracle begins his speech, which is a variation of the one he gave last year at the memorial service. He was the city's savior. We owe him a debt of gratitude. His death was tragic. We'll never forget him. It's all so trite I want to stick pencils in my ears to stop the noise. As I'm a glutton for punishment, I glance back at the jumbotron five minutes into the speech. Justice escorts James Ryder, A.K.A. Alkaline, onto the street. His greatest triumph. Little did he know that act would sign not only his death warrant but those of the two people he loved most in the universe. Ryder's handsome face appears almost smug during the perp walk. He had that same expression exactly a year ago on the hospital rooftop as I pointed a shotgun in his face right before he realized I wasn't pulling the trigger. There isn't a day I don't regret that decision. Right now he's in the bowels of Xavier Prison in a nice version of The Hole. He receives no visitors, no letters, one hour of exercise a week with shower afterwards, and from the reports I receive from my spies, he spends most of his day asleep from the tranquilizers or pacing his cell. A living hell. But just the fact he draws breath when Justin, Rebecca, and Daisy don't enrages me so much I want to punch someone. And have.

Miracle finally shuts up and introduces the Triumvirate. The noise level ratchets up to eleven. Tempest steps up to the podium with the other two taking their usual positions behind him. They wave to the crowd and the screams rise up another notch. I'm almost deaf now. Thank you fan girls of Galilee. "What a warm welcome! Thank you," Tempest says. The crowd settles a few seconds later. "We are so honored to be here today. It's humbling to see so many of you here to celebrate such a great man." More applause and a few screams of love boom from the audience. "We're not really big on speeches, so I'll keep this short. We only worked with Justice once a few years back, but that man sure could make an impression. We were astounded not only by his professionalism but also his compassion. This wasn't a game to him. It wasn't about thrill seeking or glory as it is for some." He pauses, "Present company included." The crowd chuckles, as does Tempest. "No, he was a true believer. A believer in the betterment of humanity. That it is all our duties to help our fellow man, or woman, if we are capable. It's not always easy, or fun, but it's the only way we can really survive. Live together or die alone. Justin Pendergast believed in that principal, and he was willing to sacrifice his life for it. But he did not die alone, as all of you here prove. We're proud to have called him a friend and to continue the work he began. As should all of you be. He was a good man, one of the best, and he will never be forgotten. Thank you."

And the audience goes wild. Screams, applause, whistles loud enough to burst eardrums. Great, I have to follow that like Mort Stilson and his polka band after Elvis rocked the house. The trio smile at me as they sit. I'm too nervous to smile back. That damn Tempest and Miracle pretty much covered all I was going to say. The show must go on though. I force myself to stand and make my way to the podium. I hate public speaking on a good day, and today ain't one of those. My breath is ragged and hands shake as I pull out my now useless speech. *I can do this.*

I scan the crowd. He's nowhere to be found. Last year I thought I saw him with that same proud smile on his face, and it helped me get through the speech. So I glance back at Nightingale, who gives me an encouraging smile. It'll have to do. I turn back. Mouth, take it away.

"I, um," I clear my throat, "yeah, pretty much everything I wanted to say was said already. Justin Pendergast was a great man, one of the best, and we miss him. End of story. So instead, I'll take this time to thank the Triumvirate for not only coming today, but for all they've done since adopting our city. This past year," I scoff, "has been a tough one to say the least. Our crime rate skyrocketed, our economy suffered, hell people were afraid to leave their homes. One man dies and the whole world goes to hell. I don't know if it's just human nature or what, but…shame on us for letting that happen."

The audience murmurs, but I continue on. "It should be up to each and every one of us to make sure that doesn't happen, not just those with the misfortune of having been born special. Justice loved this city, he loved its citizens, he believed in all of you, and he gave his life for that belief. He martyred himself, they all did, in part to make this world a better place. And every time we bully someone, ignore another's pain because it's easier, or turn a blind eye, we are spitting on that sacrifice." Okay, I know I need to shut up but my mouth won't stop moving. "I'm just as guilty as the rest of you. Really it was me he died for. He killed himself to save *me*. And what did I do? I self-destructed. Ended up hurting all the people who cared about me. I almost squandered the gift he gave me. I almost let that sacrifice be in vain. I almost let the evil he was fighting win. I won't let that happen again." I shake my head and scoff. "And hell, if I can do it, so can you. Start small. Volunteer somewhere. Give money to charity. If you see someone being picked on, speak out. And whenever you pass this fountain, remember these words: 'The only way for evil to triumph is for good men to do nothing.' Live by them. Be someone's hero. Because this world sure as hell needs some. Thank you."

There's scattered applause from the stunned peanut gallery until the three heroes behind me rise to give me a standing ovation. Their enthusiasm gets the rest clapping too, though not as enthusiastically as my friends. I half smile at my cheering section as I walk over to the ribbon holding up the sheet on the fountain. The mayor barely has time to stand as I unceremoniously grab the stupid big scissors and cut the ribbon. I'm supposed to pose, but I need to get the hell out of here before I really lose it. The sheet falls, revealing the light gray slate fountain of scales. I shove the scissors back at Miracle before fleeing the stage. Think I just lost some popularity points.

Everyone backstage gawks as I walk in, not that I give a shit. I have to get away from here. Fast. Where the hell is my purse? "Hey, are you okay?" V asks, following behind me.

"I can't find my purse," I say, checking by the food.

"It's over here," she says, pointing to the chairs.

Thank God. "Thanks." I pick it up.

"Jo, are you sure you're okay? What you said was—"

"I know. It just, it needed to be said. If the truth makes me unpopular then I'm willing to make that sacrifice. And you can quote me on that."

"Here, here," Liberty cheers as she comes backstage. "That was bad-ass, JoJo. Kudos. And you can quote me on that too, reporter girl."

The gang's all here. I glance at the livid mayor, impassive Tempest, and concerned Nightingale. "What in the hell was—" Miracle says.

"Leave her alone," Nightingale orders, voice hard as titanium. Miracle's mouth snaps shut for the first time ever. Nightingale takes a step toward me. "Miss Fallon, are you alright?"

"Fine. I just have to get back to work. Excuse me."

I turn away from prying eyes and haul ass. When I step outside, the dispersing crowd eyes me with apprehension. Great, guess that could have gone better. At least I didn't have a panic attack, just verbal diarrhea. Yeah, much better. People love being made to feel like shit. I stride as fast as my high heels can take me out of the park, joining the anonymous people on the city sidewalks. I'm going to wander until I find the cork to the bottle of my emotions again.

That is if there are enough miles on the planet.

*

My aching feet know where I need to go. After about half a mile, I kick off my heels and pad barefoot along the river walk. The wet pavement does feel wonderful against my feet. Carefree college students and others jog past me without a glance. Just another normal person out and about on a normal day. I guess I knew where I was going when I left the tent. I've been putting this off for a year. I've been tempted a few times, even pushed the elevator button, but chickened out when the doors opened. Probably going to do the same today, but I am damn well going to try.

Just not alone.

I walk into the hospital, past the volunteer receptionists who know me to the elevators. Jem's office is on the fifteenth floor with the other neurologists. A few nurses glance at me and my now black bare feet, but I ignore them. Miranda, assistant to Jem and two others, grins as I approach. "Hello, Miss Fallon. Dr. Ambrose isn't here at the moment."

Of course not. "Do you know when he's expected back?"

"No, sorry. I can tell him you stopped by."

"No, that's okay. Thank you."

I trudge to the elevators in a haze. I don't know if I could or really should do this alone. Right now everything within me is disconnected, including the wiring inside my brain. Nothing seems real, nothing's substantial as if I'm a ghost haunting this realm. The last time I experienced this was before my last binge. I wanted the nothingness to remain so I drank for three days to make sure it would. Okay, I need to find a meeting. I resolve right now to not even look at alcohol for the rest of the day. I'll attend a dozen meetings if I have to. But first this. I *have* to do this. With or without Jem.

I ride the elevator up and down for a few minutes, standing in the back corner like a wallflower. Pregnant women, nurses, visitors, parties in wheelchairs all enter and leave. None go to my floor. I was hoping fate would intervene, but she must be busy. Hell, is she was in front of me, I'd punch the bitch in the face for all the literal grief she's determined is my lot in life. When the last person, a doctor I vaguely recognize, steps off on the eighth floor the elevator remains still. It won't move unless someone presses the button. I wait fifteen seconds for someone to save me from this, but no joy. Moment of truth. I take a deep breath and step forward to press the button for the roof.

The doors open a few tense seconds later, and I'm there. I think I may throw up.

It's windy, expanding my chills exponentially. I tug my coat closer. This was a stupid idea. What the hell was I thinking? The doors begin to close but my arm, acting on its own, blocks it. My legs have joined the revolt because they move me onto the concrete roof. I'm here. I did it. And it's exactly as I remember it. Raised helipad with a ramp. Stairwell door with a light above it. Huge silver air conditioning vents and other large machines. Chain link fence at an angle around the perimeter of the ledge strong enough to hold one but not two people. My nightmare landscape. The scene of the final battle between two godlike men hell bent on destroying each other with me caught in the middle.

It looks so...normal.

My legs propel me forward, but my brain is a few seconds behind. The stairwell door looks the same, undamaged, but if examined closely there are a few dents in the metal door and in the wall beside patches in lighter colors. Bullet holes from when Alkaline's goons shot at me. Missed blowing my brains out by a few centimeters. When I came back out with Justin, I shot right on back. Got a goon right between the eyes. The second man I've ever killed, and I pray the last. Though I had no choice either time sometimes guilt overwhelms me. No matter the justification, I've still taken lives. It's a heavy burden no matter the circumstances. I don't linger here.

I pass by the air ducts where I had a showdown with a woman I thought I'd known for two decades. She'll be spending the next two in prison, longer if I have anything to say about it. Can't wait for her first parole hearing. She let a monster out of his cage all in the name of love, then stood by as he raped and murdered two innocent women and a child. That bitch will never be free as long as I draw breath.

Finally, I round the corner of the helipad where the worst of it occurred. The concrete on the ground is uneven as if riddled with anthills, the only sign of "the epic battle" as it's called. There are small patches where Alkaline dripped acid and bigger ones the size of fists and torsos where Justice got in a few licks. By the time I was done with Grace, both men's faces resembled raw hamburger and their bodies were caked in blood. The second most gruesome sight I've seen.

The chain link where I dangled thirty floors up is much shinier than the rest. Look to the left or right and it's gray and red from rust, but the replacement is silver. I must not be the only one who spotted this because there are a few bouquets of flowers and cards resting against this spot. There's even a candle extinguished from the rain. I heard the janitor comes up here to remove the makeshift memorial that pops up every day. They keep trying to erase what happened here, but they can't. Not all the way. I pull out some matches and re-light the candle.

It was night last time I was up here. As I held onto that fence for dear life in a fucking cocktail dress, all I could see was darkness below. Before I can stop myself, I walk to the edge and peer down. The Andalucía River is nothing but a dark line as thick as a piece of tape. An abyss if there ever was one. Across the river, the Falls, white water over black onyx, continues its never-ending cycle. It's beautiful. I hope as he fell Justin got to see this majesty of nature one last time.

I close my eyes. Our last moments together occurred right here. Alkaline stood where I am now, grinning down at us with triumph as the fence continued to rip apart one link at a time. Justin, once Adonis revisited, held on with only one hand above me beaten, burned, Broken. He gazed down at me, peace filling his face, sending terror to mine. The moment my eyes met his, I knew. I knew his heart as I knew mine. Always had. *I love you.* His last words were, "I love you." To me. I didn't have to say them back before he let go. I felt his body fall beside me and did nothing.

His last words were, "I love you."

"Joanna?"

My tear filled eyes fly open, and I spin around. Jem stands a few feet away, concern radiating from his every pore. His hair is a mess, wild and his clothes rumpled. No glasses either. He came in a hurry. Not like him to forget the details. "Joanna, please get away from there. It's dangerous."

I turn back to the abyss. "I was just thinking. About last words."

"Last words?"

"Yeah. I read the most common are, 'Oh, shit' or 'Oh, God.' Justin's were, 'I love you.' He looked me square in the eyes and told me he loved me. He'd said it in passing a few times, the usual, 'You're my friend, I love you,' type of thing, but deep down I never really believed him. If he loved me then he should *love* me, you know? Like I did him. But at that moment, his last moment, I finally became a believer. Because that's what love is, right? Putting someone before yourself? For twenty years he loved me, and I think I just now realized he loved me a hell of a lot more than I loved him. If I even really did love him. Maybe I'm just not capable of it. Two people were on that fence, and the *thought* of letting go never even crossed my mind. Not even for a millisecond. But it crossed his. Because he was good, and strong, and capable of the biggest love of all. And he's dead. And I'm here. It should have been me."

"No," Jem says forcefully. All of a sudden he's next to me, grabbing and turning me toward him. "*No.*"

"Anyway you look at it, his life was worth more than mine. I die, a few people are sad for awhile, but they move on. He dies, the whole city implodes." I wipe a tear off my cheek. "Who the hell am I? I'm nothing. A traumatized alcoholic who ruins everything and everyone she comes into contact with."

"That's not true."

"It is. I hurt *everyone* I care about. Justin, Harry, Lucy. I make everything worse. I mean, why the hell would God let me live when such better people die? Rebecca, Daisy, my dad, Justin. It-It-It doesn't make sense."

"No, it doesn't. That's why it's the eternal question: why him and not me? Why does a murderer go free while an innocent man is convicted? Why does my brother draw breath but Uma doesn't? There is no answer, Joanna. I've searched for it all my life and haven't found a clue. And believe me when I say if you let that question take over your life, it can nearly destroy you. Pursuing that question allows guilt to guide your life, and that is no way to live it." He closes his eyes. "*Believe me.*" He opens his beautiful eyes again, looking square in mine. They're brimming with sadness and hope. "You-You turn around and survey your life, your goals, and you don't recognize them. Or yourself. But you continue looking because the quest is all you have. And you're alone. *So* alone for so long with only that guilt to drive you that when someone wonderful comes along, so wonderful you actually begin to imagine another life for yourself full of love and joy, it rocks you to your core. You've seen the dawn after a million starless nights, and it's *beautiful*, but you're afraid it's just an illusion. That it'll be taken from you, or that you never really saw it, and you're alone again once more with that ache. I don't want that for you. Justin wouldn't either. You survived. You're alive. *So live.*"

I can't hold back a moment longer. I fling myself against him, wrapping my arms around his torso in a hug. His limbs envelop me as I finally allow myself to burst into tears right against his pulsing heart. It beats so fast and strong against my cheek. Our limbs melding, his warm body feeding my cold one, his smell of stale sweat mixed with faint cologne, all of it bliss.

We remain like this for one perfect second before I sense him gazing down at me. I pull apart to look up but don't dare meet his eyes. His hands move to my cheeks, cradling my face. His thumbs wipe my still falling tears, and I place my hands over his. "Please tell me I'm not crazy," he whispers desperately. "Please tell me I'm not imagining this. Please tell me you feel this too. *Please.*"

I want to speak, but the words won't come out. Everything becomes real when you say it out loud. Somehow I find the courage to gaze into his eyes, the sadness brimming in them shifts to awe and something else that scares me to fucking death. I leap away. "I-I have to go. I-I can't…I'm sorry. Bye."

Like the fucking coward I am, I sprint off that rooftop as fast as I can, down the stairwell, and out of the hospital before all my resolve fades. I can't take much more of this. I can't keep this up. He just needs to…no. I stop at the edge of the dark river to catch my breath. No more. This needs to end one way or another. I'm done.

I quit.

*

After two AA meetings, where I just sit in the back listening to stories a hell of a lot worse than mine, I have the cab driver take me to the marina. It's raining pretty bad, and the radio warns of thunderstorms, but I could give a shit. I'd go home but in retrospect I don't really have one. That mansion isn't mine. There's nothing in there I earned or even really want. The ghosts in that place are too much for me to handle tonight.

I'm soaked just walking to the *The Athena*. I grab my raincoat and sneakers from the galley, untie her and sail the fuck out of town. The waves are high and angry tonight, I have little visibility, the wind pelts rain droplets against my cheeks as if shot from a BB gun, but I figure I'm the only person crazy enough to be out tonight. Besides, I love it when it's wild and crazy like this. Me against Mother Nature. I push the throttle down as far as I can, and we leap over the waves before coming crashing down to earth with a teeth rattling thud. I have no idea which way I'm going, but I keep at it. Can't get lost if you don't have a destination.

The storm worsens as I get farther out to sea. Maybe I'll just keep going until I reach some deserted island or Fiji. I was supposed to go there with Harry but we never made it. Twice. Will this time. I'll live in a hut by the shore. Fish for my dinner and grow my own vegetables. I can just vanish. Live a simple life. Start over.

About two miles from port my body is as numb as the rest of me. My fingers ache something fierce from the cold and clutching the wheel for dear life. Chattering teeth and shivers soon follow. Fuck. Fiji's going to have to wait. I have no choice but to drop anchor so I can warm up. Fiji would be no fun with pneumonia. The boat pitches and sways, knocking me against the rope railing as I make my way below deck. I accumulate more bruises through the galley, hallway with the head and shower, into the bedroom. There are clothes in the dresser. Justin's sweats should fit.

As I'm pulling out the pants from the drawer something rustles underneath, it's a folded piece of pink paper. I open it. It's a crayon drawing of three people on a boat: man, woman, and little girl. Underneath Rebecca wrote, "Daddy Justin, Mommy, and Me."

Motherfucker.

I just stare at that damn picture, my mind churning as fiercely as the ocean below. They'd be married now. Sleeping in the bed I now inhabit. Daisy might be at one of her dance recitals as her parents watched proudly from the audience. Justin and Rebecca would be on such a high they'd go home, put the cherub to bed, and decide it was time to start on a sibling for Daisy. I'd be at a crime scene with my old partner Cam then home to my old apartment. Harry and I would have probably broken up by now, stemming from the night of Justin's engagement party when I went off on him for a misunderstanding. We would have found our way to being friends, though. Then, on the weekend, the Pendergasts and I would come together on this boat for a day of fishing, beer and laughs. Rebecca might have invited her friend Jem to the celebration. She'd been trying to get us together for months before we actually met, and that imaginary night he would have finally worked up the courage to kiss me. At least that's how I would have liked it to be. That's the way it *should* have been.

I crumple the picture, tossing it to the floor. This fucking room. This fucking boat. He's everywhere. Haunting me. I throw the sweats that reek of his aftershave as if they were coated with poison across the room. I can't breathe in here. I have to get out. When I reach the deck, nothing improves. I can practically see him at the wheel winking at me. I make my way to the bow and just stare down at the churning water. The abyss. I want off this boat. I shed all my soaked clothes, even the underwear, drop the ladder, and dive in.

The water is warmer than the air. It's almost nice in here like a warm bath. I surface and start treading water, resting my head against the water and letting the rain pelt my face. When my cheeks start going numb from the wind, I allow my body to fall completely under the water again. Much better. Let's see if I can break my holding my breath record of forty-five seconds. Some good should come from this day.

At twenty-three, a heavy splash above me draws me from my isolation. Before I can process this, something grabs me around the waist and hauls me to the surface. I'm so shocked I inhale water. Suddenly, I'm airborne and coughing up the ocean. As I glide through the air toward the boat, I glance up at my assailant. Of course.

Nightingale sets me gently on the deck before landing himself. I'm still hacking my lungs out when he asks, "Are you okay?" He smacks my bare back until I can breathe enough to talk.

"Jesus fucking Christ, were you trying to fucking kill me?" I ask through the coughs.

"I..." At that moment I think he realizes I'm naked, as do I. His eyes rove from top to bottom.

"Turn the fuck around!" I screech as I reach down for my clothes.

He doesn't need to be told twice. "I'm-I'm-I'm so sorry. I—"

"Well, you should be! You could have fucking drowned me!"

"I-I thought you were trying to...you know," Nightingale says.

My clothes are so wet I can barely get them on. "Kill myself?"

"Y-Yes. You seemed distressed earlier. I-I-I was worried."

"So you decided to *stalk* me?"

"Fo-Follow you," Nightingale corrects.

"Stalking me!" I start walking to the stern to get out of the rain. He trails behind. "Since when? The hospital?"

We go below deck where it's dry. "Be-Before that."

I need to change before I catch pneumonia. Nightingale takes a step into the stateroom, but I hold up a finger to stop him. "No." I shut the door, pick up the discarded sweats, and undress. "So you've been stalking me since the memorial?"

"Following," he says. I grab a towel and dry off before opening the door enough to toss another at him. "Thank you."

I shut the door again. "I know you're still in grade school when it comes to social learning, but you do realize it is batshit crazy and downright creepy to fly around all over town even into the middle of a storm, to watch me without my knowledge? You're a genius, you should know this." Now fully clothed, I throw the door open again with a scowl. He's still wiping his purple suit off. "And to top it all off, you try to drown me."

"I didn't try to—"

"You are not responsible for me. I am an adult, it's not your job to save me. I don't need saving."

"Okay," he says.

"I came out here to be alone. I don't want you here. You-You complicate my life. I don't like it. I-I can't do this with you anymore. I can't. Not today, not ever. Just leave." I slam the door in his face again, staring at it. It takes me all of three seconds before I feel like total shit. He hasn't moved when I open the door again. For some reason I didn't think he would. "I'm sorry."

"It's fine."

"No, it's not. I'm sorry. I'm *so* sorry. I just, I'm fucked up." I sit on the bed and pull the comforter around my freezing body. "I am *so* fucked up. I'm not fit for human consumption, especially today."

Nightingale strolls over and sits beside me. "Today is a bad day. Tomorrow will be better."

"Promise?"

He shrugs. "Could it get worse?"

I actually chuckle at that. "Oh, let's see. I've turned an entire city against me, am probably suffering from hypothermia, you saw me naked, oh and I could have possibly ruined things with someone I really, really care about. So yeah, it's gonna be hard to top all that."

"See?"

I half smile. "How'd you get to be so smart?"

A pause then, "Made that way." I chuckle but he doesn't smile back. "No, really. I was *made* that way. In a lab." My face falls in confusion. "They spliced my genes," he adds, mouth twitching. "Engineered me before conception. I was made to be…perfect. In every way. I'm a science experiment. So you're not the only one not fit for human consumption. If that makes you feel better." I just stare at him for a few seconds. "Please don't look at me like that."

"Like what?"

"Like I'm a freak."

"You're alive because of science, I'm alive because Pop forgot a condom. I don't think you're a freak. I could never think that."

He studies me for subterfuge, but of course finds none. His shoulders relax, but he looks away. "I've never even told the others that."

"But you told me?"

"I-I just wanted you to know you're not alone in feeling...like an oddity. Alone."

I half smile again, and hesitantly take his gloved hand. He doesn't pull it away. "Thank you."

"You're welcome."

I just hold his freezing, gloved hand for a few seconds in silence as he gazes down at the floor and I at him. "Your hand is like ice," I say.

"Yeah. I was hovering for awhile."

"Here." Before he can protest, I yank his glove off. I rub his hand with my slightly warmer ones. "You must be freezing. Why didn't you say anything?"

"I'm fine."

I grab his other hand, de-glove him, and rub the two together. "You must be soaked through."

"Really, I'm fine."

I shake my head. "I think there might be another set of sweats here somewhere. You really should get out of that suit."

He pulls his hands away. "I-I don't think that's a good idea. No."

His vehemence not only shocks me but cuts me to the core. Anger festers into the wound. I can't take much more of this bullshit. "What? You don't trust me not to look? You can go in the other room. I'm not trying to see you naked or get you to reveal your stupid-ass secret identify. I know I'm not trusted enough to be part of your inner circle. I just want you to be comfortable."

"I told you, I—"

"I know, you *would* tell me if you could," I say with an eye roll. "Forgive me, it's just, given my experience with your type, if I find that damn hard to believe. I mean, hell, we barely know each other. I am aware of this. I shouldn't expect you to…" I rub my temples and groan. "Okay, we shouldn't have this conversation now. I'm too emotional. I'm bound to say things I don't mean to." I scoot away from him and lay down on the bed again. "You should go. I'll be fine. I promise no more skinny-dipping."

He turns around, face expressionless behind the mask. "I don't think I should go anywhere right now."

I glare. "I told you, I'm fine. I'm not a danger to myself, okay?"

"I don't…you shouldn't be alone." He pauses, his jaw setting. "Justin wouldn't want me to leave you alone in this state."

"And how the hell would you know what Justin would want?"

He's silent, then, "Because. He asked me to look after you, and I promised I would."

My eyes narrow. "When the hell did this happen?"

"During your…ordeal last year. He said should anything happen to him, I was to look in on you from time to time."

I scowl. "Is that why you've…" No. No way. The thought is too horrible. "Never mind. Look, I am not a charity case. I absolve you of your stupid promise, okay? You don't have to…just go, okay?"

"I'm not…" He moves up the bed closer to me. "I *want* to be here. With you. I do."

I don't have the energy to fight him, especially when I don't want to win. I don't want him to leave. "Thank you," I whisper. He smiles, which brings one to my face too. I look away again before I turn red. Time to change the subject. "What was he like? With you? Justin?"

"Professional. Intuitive. Stubborn. Take charge. He and Tempest butted heads, but we respected him."

"You obviously knew who he was. His real identity."

"And he knew ours. A situation arose, and we all needed to know."

"Did he ever talk about me?"

"Oh, yes," he says with a proud grin. "He compared you to a lioness. Strong, capable, intelligent, fierce. He told me you would walk through the fires of hell if it meant saving someone, even a total stranger. He loved you very much, Joanna. So much."

Fresh tears spill from my eyes, but when I try to blink them away they fall. "Do you think," I choke out, "he was proud of me?"

Nightingale scoots even closer to me, visibly disturbed by my tears. He cups my head in his hands, and I place mine over his. "Of course. How could he not be?"

"I…" I chuckle wryly and shrug. "Panic attacks, moodiness, alcoholism, cheating, take your pick. Not quite the lioness he pitched, huh? How disappointed you must have been."

"God no," he says almost breathless. "I think you are…the most infuriating, challenging, frightening…breathtaking, insightful, astonishing woman I have ever met." He moves in even closer. "You awe me. You're a marvel." His thumb wipes a tear away. "An absolute marvel. And I'm blessed every second we share together."

I can't do this anymore. I surrender.

Not taking my eyes from his, I press my cheek against his hand, enjoying the softness and gentility of it against my skin as a fire alights inside me. I kiss his wrist where the veins cross and his pulse thumps double time. He doesn't move but his breath grows ragged as I trail my lips up the palm to his little finger before nuzzling his hand again. With my other hand, I reach up to his face, lightly brushing his exposed chin before tracing his lips with my thumb. They quiver. "I've dreamed about these lips," I whisper as I smile, "almost every night since we've met."

Lust flips to confusion in his eyes. "You have?"

"Yeah."

"I…this is wrong," he says, pulling away from my touch. "This cannot happen. Not-not like this. Not now. I'm sorry. I should—" He leaps from the bed and backs out of the room as if I was about to suck out his soul.

I lay still with shock for a second, trying to figure out what happened. Instinctively I know what I have to do. What I should have done weeks ago but was too afraid to. I jump out of bed and run to the galley. He is at the top of the stairs being pelted by rain when I shout, "You're not crazy!"

He spins around. "I'm sorry?"

"I said you're not crazy," I say, taking a step toward him. "And you're not imagining this." Another step. "I feel it too."

We stand staring at one another for a second, his body trembling a little as those words and their meaning penetrate that genius brain of his. His eyes search me to see if this is real, that this is really happening. I take another step. A mistake. He rockets up the hatch into the storm. "Jem, wait!" I rush over to the hole but am greeted by nothing but a face full of freezing rain and darkness. Shit.

He's gone.

Chapter Ten

Bad Seed

He gets one day. I give him a day before chasing after him in earnest. Enough time for him to process, assimilate, and figure out what he wishes to do next. At least that's what I assume he was doing because he sure as hell wasn't returning my calls, e-mails, or texts. I even drove by his building, leaving a note with the doorman, and his secretary Miranda assured me she gave him my messages. I've never been one to be ignored, especially with something this important. It's the lioness in me. So he's got thirty-six hours before I throw on my best dress, get my hair blown out and stylized, and strut into the hospital ready for battle.

Since the direct route has failed, I have to get creative. Once more being on the hospital board proves useful. I order one of the nurses in the ER to page Jem. Three agonizing minutes later he hustles in, as always hair as unkempt as the rest of him. The nurse gestures in my direction. One glimpse at me, and his face falls. Not the reaction I was hoping for. As I walk over to him, he glances around the room for an escape route. He is no fool. I say the words every man dreads: "We need to talk."

"Not here."

"We can use the small conference room. It's isolated. No one will hear us."

"I—"

"Please."

He's silent, then, "Fine."

I breathe a literal sigh of relief. That was easier than I thought. Didn't even have to pull out the big guns: begging or eye fluttering. He follows me out of the ER, through the main entrance foyer, and down another hall off to the side. This conference room overlooks the Falls and river walk through big bay windows on this bright, blue day. Hopefully the majesty of Mother Nature will promote a calm productive conversation. He closes the door.

"You didn't return my calls," I say.

"I know. I had no idea what to say to you." He pauses. "Have you told anyone?"

"Of course not," I spew out, more than a little offended. "How can you even ask me that?"

"I-I'm sorry. You're right. I don't know why I…" He shakes his head and looks down at the carpet. After a few seconds, he gazes at me with an apologetic smile. "How long have you known?"

"I figured it out when we were working on the missing explosives. When I was giving you the massage, I saw your eyes. I'd know them anywhere." I smile. "Lexie and Brendan took longer."

Those same eyes bug out of his head. "Wait, you—" His mouth snaps shut.

"I'm not an idiot, Jem. The only reason I never figured about Justin was I spent all of ten minutes around Justice my whole life. I've spent *days* with all of you both in and out of uniform. Plus there was the whole Independence angle, and Lexie practically pushing the two of us together even though she barely knew Jem Ambrose. Danforth's party was a set-up, wasn't it? She gave us both makeovers, forced you to go, then ditched me so you'd have to drive me home. Right?"

"I-I didn't know about that last part. I just knew you'd be there. I-I was actually surprised she wanted me there. We have a strict rule about our real selves fraternizing. We avoid each other socially as much as possible. There are no ties between us for safety reasons. We've only broken the rule once so Lexie and Brendan could publically meet and begin dating. I couldn't even attend their wedding."

"Then I'm flattered, I guess. You guys risking your secret so we could…you know."

We stand in silence for a few seconds just staring at the other neither of us sure what to say next. His face falls a little. "Why didn't you say anything?"

"At first I kind of liked that the tables had turned. That I knew but you didn't. That I was smarter than you all, at least in that. Then as things, you know, progressed, I was waiting for you to tell me. My thinking was if you trusted me, then you would." He opens his mouth to protest, but I say, "And I know you said you would have told me if you could, but after everything with Justin, I just, not all of me believed you. Any way you look at it, you were still keeping a huge part of your life from me. Our…whatever the hell this is, couldn't have gotten far if we weren't letting each other in."

"Do you think I didn't consider that? Do you have any idea how much I've *agonized* over keeping my secret? I lost sleep over it. I fought for it. I approached them individually, together, a dozen times since the beginning. It killed me I couldn't tell you, but I had other people to consider."

"If you really wanted me to know, you would have told me," I say, voice hard.

"We have been acquainted for less than two months, Joanna. Only six people, yourself included, have ever been privy to that information. And I still wanted to tell you. I *told* you I wanted to. You said you understood the reasons. But it was all a test, wasn't it? You were testing me because *you* didn't trust *me*." He starts pacing back and forth on the other side of the table. "I swear to God I could kill Justin right now. I didn't do anything wrong, and I'm the one paying for his sins." He stops moving and looks me dead in the eyes. "I am not Justin, Joanna. Just because he lied to you does not mean I will as well. Just because he let you down and brought you abject misery does not mean I will. I am not responsible for his mistakes, and I resent you flogging me for them."

"That is not what I—"

"And for God's sake, admit the real reason you lied. Because this," he says, gesturing to us both, "frightens you almost to the point of madness. I know it does me. If you had told me, you knew there would be nothing left in our way, would there? Nothing but your fear that maybe, just *maybe*, this could be, that *we* could be the real thing. That you can let me in, and I won't run away, and I won't shun you for being less than perfect. That I can potentially hurt you. Believe me, I understand. Because I feel exactly the same way when it comes to you." He shrugs. "But I was willing to take the chance. Because I trusted you. Because I thought you were worth the risk. I don't think you're there yet. I don't know if you ever will be." He turns his back to me and begins toward the door.

"I want to be." He spins around, understandably skeptical. "And that is *epic* for me. Hope has always let me down. It damn near destroyed me three times over. Never, not once, has it come through for me, so forgive me if this doesn't come naturally. It's not you, I swear it. A person can only be knocked down so many times before it becomes impossible to get back up. And the last time almost killed me. Literally. But I'm…finding my legs." I take a step toward him. "And you did that. You picked me up. Just…please help me the rest of the way."

He studies me, the anger fading. "Oh, Joanna. I—"

BOOM!

A huge explosion slices through the rest of his sentence. I have no idea where it comes from, not this building I don't think, but close enough I jolt. Before I can ponder this further, Jem throws me to the ground and covers my body with his just as the bay windows beside us shatter into a trillion pieces, glass and scorching air filling the room. I'm too stunned to even breathe. Motherfucker.

Jem lingers a few seconds before removing himself from me. "Are you okay?" he asks, examining me.

"I-I'm fine. I think," I say, voice shaking. He isn't. Tiny pinpricks of blood begin blooming on his white lab coat from the shards of glass. "You-You're—"

"I'm fine. I'll heal in a minute."

As we rise, car alarms wail in the distance, but I can still make out the sound of metal twisting on itself. Both our mouths drop when we view the source.

Oh, dear God.

Less than a quarter mile away what remains of the Pendergast Bridge is a twisting, splintering inferno. Flames shoot up from not only the unlucky cars on the bridge, but as the structure itself collapses, parts falling into the river where the hundred foot gap is. I gasp as a car that angling over the edge loses its battle and plummets as well. Black smoke billows where support beams and tension wires used to be. Another wire snaps and falls onto the already shaky bridge. Panicked people flee from their cars away from the wreckage. Jesus Christ.

Jem's face has solidified into stone. Without a word, he dashes out of the room with me at his heels. Uninjured hospital visitors and staff help those in need away from the glass. It's pandemonium with people screaming, crying, and bleeding all over. Jem ignores them. We run toward the elevators. He pounds the button. "Come on. Come on."

"What—"

"I have to get to the roof. My costume's there. I have to—"

"Oh, my God! The bomber's on TV!" someone shouts.

Like everyone else we rush to the overhead television. One look at the cracked screen and the color drains from Jem's face. I recognize the villain from my Triumvirate research. Emperor Cain stands in a dark room surrounded by pipes illuminated only by the light on the camera. Steam rises in the background. A boiler room of some kind. The Emperor wears his black and red costume with black cowl hiding all but his mouth. From far away the outfit could be mistaken for regular clothes with black pants and red top with "EC" entwined on it complete with a black cape. Wish I had done more research on him, but I do remember he was presumed dead after their last battle nine months ago. That was what the heroes told everyone anyway.

"...your attention," he continues. "For those of you not familiar with my work, my name is Emperor Cain, formerly of the great city of Independence, and you may be asking yourselves why I have chosen to grace the presence of this podunk, rat infested cesspool. There are three of your new residents who know the answer to this question." I glance at Jem, who if possible has grown paler. "Hello, old friends. Didn't think you were rid of me, did you? The location may change, but the game remains the same. Feeling nostalgic, yet? I was. *First* time for everything." He pauses. "And I do apologize to the citizens of Galilee, that you must be brought into our fray, but that is the price you pay for giving quarter to mine enemies." His smile sends a shiver down my spine. "Principal rule of warfare for those less educated: leave your enemies nowhere to go to ground. I've often alleged these quote unquote heroes they care not for the collateral damage inflicted by their antics, but today I give them a chance to prove me wrong. The Royal Triumvirate has one hour to vacate this city. For every fifteen minutes they do not comply a bomb, such as this one," he steps aside to show a huge, complex bomb with a dozen wires woven into blocks of C-4 wedged between two boilers, "will detonate in the hearts of this city, which might be closer than you think, and thousands will die." He leans toward the camera. "Citizens of Galilee Falls, are your newest so-called heroes really worth all this? I think not." The screen goes black then returns to BNN, the anchor carrying on interviewing Senator Harden as if the interruption never happened.

Jem is so deep in thought I can practically see the gears spinning. "Jem?"

Without a word, he runs over to the wall, smashes the plastic container for the fire alarm, and engages it. His gaze jerks to me. "We have to evacuate the hospital in the next fifteen minutes."

I do a double take as he sprints to the stairwell. I reach him just as he enters it, and we run down. "We can't do that. This is the closest hospital to the bridge. County is four miles away. We don't even know if there's a bomb here. Besides, it'd take triple that to fully evacuate. It can't be done." People pass us in a panic, running up the stairs in the opposite direction. "Jem, are you listening to me?" I grab his lab coat. "Jem!"

From the shock on his face, I think he'd forgotten I was here. "You shouldn't be here. You need to leave. You need to run as far and fast as possible. He—"

"What? I'm not going anywhere."

"You don't understand. He said, 'closer than you think.' He mentioned nostalgia. The first battle we ever had was in the boiler room at my hospital. He could be down there now."

"Then there's no way in *hell* I'm letting you go down there alone."

"Joanna—"

I pull out my .22 from my purse. "You need back-up. No time for debate. Come on." This time I lead, but he quickly passes me. This is stupid, *so* stupid, but I follow anyway. I can't not.

The stairs to the boiler room are blocked by a chain-link door that hangs open. I grip the gun tighter as we descend. The stairs end at another open door. Machines rumble though the space, so it's hard to listen for voices, if there are any. It's also dark, the only light emanating from the incinerators. We'll have to go in blind and deaf. Jem stands at the door to listen anyway. "Stay close," he whispers. I nod. I follow a step behind with the pistol pointed. We make it five steps when his foot hits a toolbox. I damn near leap a mile up as the tools clatter out. So much for the element of surprise. We wait a second in case of attack, but none comes. Jem retrieves the flashlight that's rolled out and switches it on. Still nothing. "This way," he whispers.

We move through an avenue with two scalding machines on either side. When we clear them, the flashlight reveals something silver down the path. A video camera on a tripod. "Why would he leave that here?" I ask as we sprint toward it. Jem isn't listening. I glance where he stands, my stomach dropping. A bomb. A huge fucking bomb with at least ten pounds of explosives and a timer counting down the seconds. A little over twelve minutes. This thing could blow up the hospital twice over. "Fuck me."

"I need tools," Jem says, more to himself than me.

"We need to call the bomb squad."

"They may not make it in time. I need tools. Wire cutters, screwdriver, electrical clips, just bring everything in the toolbox."

"You know how to defuse bombs?" I roll my eyes at my stupidity. "Of course you do. I'll be right back."

I run the way we came to the toolbox. I have basic knowledge of bomb squad equipment so I know all that's useful here is the exacto knife, a screwdriver, and electrical tape. With those in hand, I rush out of the boiler room in search of a utility closet or mechanical room. The utility closet is locked, so I shoot the lock. "Just me!" I shout to give Jem peace of mind. I search furiously through detergents and cleaning supplies for another tool box. Shit. The mechanical room is beyond the now empty laundry room, the staff evacuated already, and I have to shoot this lock too. I have more success here.

When I return to the boiler room, Jem is pulling a disk out of the camera and stuffing it in his pocket. "Did you get everything?"

"I hope so." We move over to the bomb with now less than ten minutes left. I drop my collection. "Here." He hands me the flashlight, and we bend down next to the tools. "You defused this type before?"

"Once or twice," he says, picking up the wire cutters. "The only problem is Cain knows I have. He'll have it booby trapped. Tilt and trembler switches, anti-tamper devices, a hidden detonator or two. He will not make it easy on me." He takes a deep breath to steady himself. "I really wish you'd—"

"Not happening. Get to work."

He does. The bomb has almost two dozen wires and Jem examines, cuts, or ignores them all like a virtuoso whose instrument is a bomb. I try to keep my eyes off the counter but it's fucking impossible. Seconds ticking down to destruction. About a minute into this unbelievably tense process, my cell phone rings and I jerk in surprise. Jem glances at me, breath shaky. "Sorry." I pull it out to check the screen. It's Harry. "Harry?" I say into it.

"Where are you?"

"The hospital. The first bomb is here in the boiler room."

"Have they found the others yet?" Jem asks.

"Who is that?" Harry asks.

I put Harry on speaker. "Lord Nightingale. He's defusing the bomb."

"What? Joanna, no. Get the hell out of there. The squad's on the way. I—"

"Tell him the other three bombs are most likely in the boiler rooms of city hall, the library, and the Justice statue, and if not found there, try the airport, The Falls, and Pendergast Industries."

"Did you get that?" I ask Harry.

"We found one at city hall. It's set to go off in twenty-five minutes. They're working on it now."

"No!" Jem shouts. "There could be half a dozen anti-tamper devices or false switches. He'll have back-ups for his back-ups. I've already found two on this one. He knows your techniques and thought processes. Tell them to wait for me. I'll finish here and get to the hall as fast as I can."

"We're not waiting—"

"Captain O'Hara, I know how this man thinks! He wants you to try. They had to re-build the President Wayne Memorial and two bomb techs lost their lives because they underestimated him. Order them to wait!" He bobs his head to indicate that I should hang up. I do. His full attention returns to the problem at hand.

"Do you really think there's a bomb at Pendergast?"

He's quiet as he places clips to bypass wires, then says, "Yes. They need to evacuate."

"They're already doing it. It's company policy to evacuate after a terrorist attack. This qualifies." I watch him work for a whole thirty seconds before I can't hold in my question anymore. "This is all for you, isn't it? It's a test for you, to get your attention."

Silence, then, "Yes." He yanks a wire out and throws it aside.

I pause this time as I decide if I should ask the real question. Like I could ever stop myself. "He's your brother, isn't he? Jordan?" For the first time, Jem stops working and looks at me, mouth slack. "You both have the same, exact smile and voice."

"Oh." Jem returns to work, slowly starting up. "After Uma, I went looking for him. Scowered the globe, but he…" He shakes his head. "It was a fool's errand. If my brother doesn't want to be found, he won't be. After a year, I gave up. I took a post in Independence but something had changed. I couldn't sleep, I barely ate, the bitterness and frustration were eating me alive.

"Then one night, it had to be three in the morning, I was walking the streets as I often did when I came across a pimp beating a prostitute in an alley. For a second I thought about continuing on. Then she noticed me, met my eyes, and blind rage overtook me. I beat the man within an inch of his life. But…for the first time in over a year I felt as if I could breathe again. So I went out the next night, then the one after that. While I was out patrolling, I felt close to content. Then one night I was almost arrested, so I commissioned a suit. Became 'The Nightingale' after my favorite Keats poem. A few months after that, we formed the Triumvirate and the work really began."

"Then Jordan resurfaced."

"Yes. Because I was happy," he says, words dripping with venom, "or as close as I ever could be. I had moved on, found a measure of peace, and he couldn't bear that. I was respected, and he had to tear me down. Destroying a city and killing over a hundred people were just, as he said, collateral damage. He was actually upset I was helping people as I was. It was exactly what our father had wanted, why he tortured us for years. Made us train, pushed us over our limits. 'How could I?' my brother asked." Jem scoffs. "It was another betrayal. We'd sworn we'd never use our not so God given gifts if we could help it. Just because we were made to be freaks didn't mean that would be our fate. He acted as if I had spit in his face. I had to be taught a lesson."

"He sounds like a fucking psychopath," I say.

"That's what nine out of ten of out psychiatrists said," he says, snipping a wire. "I'm just so sorry for all this. I thought he—" He shakes his head and cuts another wire. "This shouldn't have happened."

"It's not your fault."

He quickly glimpses at me. "Yes…it is." He takes a deep breath, wipes his sweaty brow and continues working. "I think I've almost finished. You should leave now."

"I told you twelve times I'm not going anywhere."

"Joanna—"

"If you're here, I'm here. End of discussion."

"Don't be so damn—"

"I am not leaving you!" I shout. "*I'm not.* So save your damn breath."

His mouth sets straight. "The-The problem is there are two wires I can cut, and I don't know which is the correct one. Look."

I move over beside him. In the tangle of wires, I view a white and black wire inside a second timer. Both are positioned exactly the same. "Oh."

"You have less than five minutes to clear the building. *Please go.*"

And for a second I do consider the option. Running away and leaving him in this dark basement with a bomb to potentially die alone attempting to save thousands of lives. But I can't. The thought of losing him too…nope. I'd rather die. "Choose," I say.

"What?"

"Do it. I'm right here."

His eyes search mine for something. I just smile. "If I'm wrong, I'm killing hundreds still in the building," he whispers.

I cover his hand holding the clippers with mine. "Then we'll do it together. It's on both of us. Choose."

"But—"

"Just…trust."

He glances down at my hand on his, then back at my smiling face. The fear vanishes into the ether. With his free hand, Jem grabs the back of my neck and pulls my mouth hungrily against his. Our lips are so in line, it's as if they're made for one another. As we devour each other, I run my hand through his soft, thick curls like I've been wanting to since we first met a year ago. A kiss to die for.

He draws away first, completely breathless from the need. We just stare into each other's eyes for a few seconds before grinning in unison. "Sorry," he says, "I just didn't want to leave this earth without doing that at least once."

"I know exactly how you feel," I say before going back for seconds. It's a little softer this time but just as wonderful. I can die a happy girl right now. I'd rather not, but still.

We break apart a few seconds later and look at the bomb in unison. As me move our entwined hands toward it, the oddest sensation washes over me. I've never felt it before. Serenity. Faith. I know, I *know* that we're going to be okay. That this is not the end. Not by a long shot. We aren't dying today. Don't know how I know, but I do. I rest my head on Jem's shoulder as his free arm wraps around me, pulling me in close. We position the clippers on the black wire, and I take the other handle. "Ready?" he asks. I nod. "On three. One…two…" I bury my face into the crook of his neck, and he squeezes me even tighter. *Oh please, oh please…* "Three."

Snip.

Nothing happens. At least I think nothing happens because this close to the bomb I wouldn't feel a thing if it exploded. But I'm breathing and Jem's fingers are digging into my side hard enough I'll bruise, and I doubt heaven or even hell stinks like a boiler room, so I'm pretty sure we're alive. I open my eyes and stare at the bomb. The counter's stopped. The bomb's intact. We did it. Never had a doubt.

I gaze up at Jem, who peers from the counter to me, mouth agape with shock. I burst into laughter, nervous at first but joyous a second later. He catches the bug instantly. We just laugh and laugh as he kisses my hair and down my cheeks to my mouth. This kiss is swift but just as yummy. The man sure can smooch. The laughter subsides as the mirth drains from his face. There's something on mine that almost startles him now, even more so than even the bomb. He draws away as if I was the one about the explode.

"I shouldn't-I-I have to go." He leaps up and begins to walk away. He's quickly out of view, but a second later he rounds the corner again. "Wait outside for the bomb squad. Please show them down here, then go straight home. Lock all the doors, and don't leave until I or one of the others arrive. Don't let *anyone* else in."

"Jem—"

"Joanna, please! Just do this for me. Please," he begs, not hiding his desperation.

"Okay," I say with a nod.

"I'll be by when I can. Be careful."

And he leaves me alone in the dark beside a bomb, my lips tingling from his touch, without another word. I shake my head. Supermen.

CHAPTER ELEVEN

POST MORTEM

The bomb squad arrives minutes later. Two minutes longer than the bomb would have allowed them. Jem saved the hospital and no one will ever know. A crying shame. I escort the squad to the bomb then return upstairs to help the overwhelmed hospital staff in the parking lot and river walk where they've set-up a makeshift M.A.S.H. unit. Despite the evacuation, patients stream in from the smoldering bridge, which still crumbles into the river as fire crews try to control the blaze and continue rescue efforts. With the patients from inside, the ones from the bridge, and those injured from the flying glass, it's bedlam. I've had first-aid training so I make myself useful bandaging and ordering people around. As I channel Florence Nightingale, no pun intended, once or twice Liberty and Tempest fly in with someone from the bridge, but if they see me they don't let on. They dump their cargo and zoom off to save more. As time passes, and there are no more explosions, I assume Jem is successful with the other bombs. I'll chalk that down as a victory.

It's dark by the time I drag my exhausted, bloodstained body home. Pendergast Bridge had ceased smoldering but lost a hundred feet of road and probably won't be usable for a minimum of over a year. Long way home from here on in. I take a quick shower, toss on some sweats, and literally run down to the command center. Tempest and Liberty, both still splattered in dust and blood, are already typing away on Doris. Liberty sits in front of the computer where an image of Cain from the transmission fills the screen. "I told you, I don't know how to do that!" Liberty shouts to her hovering husband.

"Do what?" I ask as I walk down.

Both turn and seem relieved to see me. "Jesus Christ, there you are. We were getting worried," Liberty says.

"They needed help at the hospital. Jem's not back yet?"

"Not yet. He—" Tempest realizes his mistake. "What?"

"He *told* you?" Liberty asks, mouth agape.

"No, I figured it out weeks ago, Lexie."

She and her husband exchange an uncomfortable glance. "But—"

"I think we have more pressing concerns right now. Get up." She does, and I plop in the computer chair. "What are you trying to do?"

"Analyze the background noise in case we can hear his accomplice," Tempest says. I pull up the program and fine tune it. "How much do you know?"

"Most." I shake my head. "There's too much ambient noise from the boilers to isolate it. Sorry." I spin in the chair to face them. "Have you spoken to the police? Have they lifted any prints from the camera?"

"No, and they're still processing all the prints on and around the bomb," Liberty says.

"Jem's will be on the one from the hospital. He wasn't wearing gloves."

"Shit," Tempest says. "That fucking…" He groans. "That'd be all we need."

"I'll take care of it." I sigh. "I think we should tell the police who Cain really is. Get his picture out there, his name."

"GFPD have all his past aliases, of which I'm sure are useless as he's using a new one now," Tempest says. "He also disguises himself in public. We've been through this three times before. And there are other considerations. It'd put Jem Ambrose on their radar. He'd be placed under surveillance, or worse. He could be exposed."

"Trust us, we've had this debate a dozen times before," Liberty adds. "Jem's our best hope of finding the prick. He can't do that if he's being followed. We'll only pull that pin if we have no other option."

"Fine. So what do we do now?"

"All we have at present are the bombs and this broadcast," Tempest says. "He hacked into BNN's signal like before. The man he used last time is serving five years in prison, so he must have found someone else. I already pulled a list from the database. If you can track them down, we can cull the list. We know it was filmed in the boiler room but when? He left the camera for a reason, though."

"Jem took a tape out of it," I say. "I don't know what was on it."

The duo exchanges an angry look, and Tempest shakes his head. "Did he now?"

I don't like his tone, and the last thing we need is antipathy amongst ourselves. "Maybe we'll get a print off it. I don't know that much about Cain. Would he make his own bombs?"

"Yeah," Tempest answers. "And we're still no closer to finding who helped him steal the explosives from the military base, assuming the two are related."

"Like anyone doubts they are," Liberty says. "And that trail's cold."

"What else do we have?" I ask. "Does he have known accomplices in town?"

"Not that we're aware of," Tempest says.

"We have nothing. Nothing! Twenty people are dead and we have nothing!" Liberty all but shouts. "Not a fucking thing, as usual!" Her eyes grow wide. "You! You bastard!"

Tempest and I spin around as Liberty stalks toward the beach entrance. Nightingale stands in full regalia staring at his oncoming pissed friend. When I lock eyes on him, a giant weight lifts. Since he left, in my few spare moments, I've been playing out a hundred scenarios where heinous events had befallen him. I suppress the urge to race over to him and throw my arms around him. Liberty beats me to him anyway. "You son of a bitch! You lied to us! You said he was dead. You told us you *saw* him die!" she screams as she shoves him.

"I'm sorry. I couldn't do it," Nightingale says. "I couldn't watch. I left him unconscious on that plane seconds before it crashed into the ocean. He couldn't have survived."

"That's what you said the last time too," she spits out. "We could have been hunting him down all this time! How the hell are we supposed to trust you if you keep lying to us?"

"I'm sorry," is all he can muster.

"Fuck your sorry," Liberty says as she turns around to walk away. A moment later she spins toward him again. "Oh, and thanks for telling your fucking girlfriend who we all are, even though I *distinctly* remember multiple conversations where we asked you not to!"

"He didn't tell me," I say.

Her gaze whips to me. "Excuse me if I find that a tad hard to believe from Justin Pendergast's best friend," she says with a sneer.

"Okay, enough!" Tempest roars. "Enough! It's done, it's all done. Cain's alive, Joanna knows, nothing we can do will change either. The question is, where do we go from here? What's his game this time?"

"Yeah, does he want to throw a hissy fit like the first time? Kill us all like the second? Or is he just bored like the third?" Liberty asks in a snarky tone.

Nightingale removes the tape from his belt. "This should answer your question."

He moves over to us, putting the disk in Doris without even a glance my way. Ignoring me. Stellar. Once again Emperor Cain's smiling face fills the monitor. The brothers' smiles really are uncannily similar. "Hello, old friends. Miss me? I certainly missed all of you." I glance at Nightingale, whose mouth is set vice tight. "Liberty, you're looking as beautiful as ever. I hope that napalm from our last sojourn didn't leave a scar."

"Fucker," she mutters.

"And Tempest, still barking orders and cowing my poor big brother?" He tsks. "I don't hold it against you. He never did enjoy thinking for himself. I don't know how you can stand him as a partner, weak as he is. It always disgusted me." Cain shakes his cowled head. "I suppose I should be grateful for it, though, his weakness. I'm still convinced it was he who uncoupled my handcuffs on the plane last time." We glance at Nightingale for a reaction but don't find one. "Even after all our fights, all we've been through my dearest Jem, you still could not let me die. It touched me, brother. It really did." I actually believe him. I move my hand to touch Jem, but he won't let me. He yanks his hand away. Another sting to my ego. I don't allow it to show.

"I gave considerate thought as to why that is, brother dear." Cain continues. He leans toward the camera. "I believe everyone in the room knows the answer as well. They may pretend they understand you, even that they care about you, but it's underneath their eyes, isn't it? You're still a freak even among the freaks. But worry not, Scout's back, and it'll be just like old times big brother.

I promise. See you soon." He kisses at the camera then it cuts to black. Thank you, Jesus.

No one speaks for a few seconds as we process this new information. Liberty breaks the tension. "So...he's bored."

"No. He's lonely," I say as I glance at Nightingale, who hangs his head.

"Jesus Christ, cry me a fucking river," Liberty snaps. She takes a step toward Jem. "This is all your fault. We had a deal last time. You—"

I rise between them, acting as a human barrier. My eyes burn into Liberty's. "Stop it," I hiss. "Leave him alone. Right now."

"No! Joanna, you don't know the absolute hell that psychopath's put us through. The beatings, the shootings, the burns. I-I've held *children* in my arms as they died because of him."

"He's a fucking monster, you get no debate from me on that, okay? I'm just saying, right now, if you continue this, you are letting him win. This is what he wants, can't you see that? That's his endgame: The World versus Jem Ambrose."

"What do you mean?" Tempest asks.

"Think about it. He made those bombs damn easy to find. There were no stipulations about how or who could defuse them. The only one that went off was right outside Jem's work, the rest he all but left a damn map to. Cain went on national television saying he was only killing people because of you. People are already screaming for you to leave town. Now that tape for only you to see. It's Uma all over again. He's trying to take away the one thing he feels is keeping their reconciliation from happening, the one thing brings him happiness. Saving people. This. You." I turn to Nightingale. "Right?"

"Yes," he says quietly.

I spin back around to the others. "See? So stop dwelling on the past and concentrate on how we're going to stop him this time."

"She's right," Tempest says, placing his hands on his wife's shoulders. "We need to start working on strategy. Cain—"

"Not here," Jem cuts in as he steps around me. "This is the last time any of us sets foot in this house in uniform until he's found. She has nothing more to do with this, with us."

"What?" I ask. "No."

"We have to assume he'll have people following me, if he doesn't already," he says to the other two. "If Joanna's not already in his sights, I don't want to put her there now."

"You two have been playing kissy face all over town," Liberty says. "There's already gossip."

"We were never publically affectionate, and I've been telling people they've just been business meetings, in part for this very contingency." His gaze whips back to me. "Call board members and begin asking about investing in my drug company now you have enough information about it. Maybe start…publically dating someone to quell the rumors, someone who won't mind lying to the press about when you started the relationship." I'm about to open my mouth to protest, but he turns away. "If you have to come over here, come as yourselves. In case her phones and e-mails are being surveiled, no shop talk. Regardless, she's no longer part of this."

"Excuse me, I am right her—"

He spins around again, grabbing me hard by the arm and dragging me toward the couch. "This is not up for debate. One of those bombs was in your office building. If we didn't need it so badly, I'd smash that computer so you wouldn't be tempted to use it. You're done. Finished. This is not your fight. You are to have nothing more to do with this. With us. In any capacity. What happened today between us, all of it, was a mistake," he says, lowering his voice. "I shouldn't have…" He shakes his head. He can't even say it. "I'm sorry."

"No. No way you're benching me. I—"

He squeezes my arms even harder. "He'll kill you!" he says desperately through gritted teeth. "He. Will. Kill. You. *No.*" He releases me, literally casts me aside and looks at the others. "I have the old communicator, we'll keep in touch that way." He pauses. "I am sorry for this. All of it. I…bye."

Without a glance my way, he walks out the way he came, then flies down the dark tunnel to the beach. I think I've just been sucker punched in the gut, it sure feels like that. I've lost him before I ever had him.

"Someone should go after him," Tempest says to his wife.

She scowls. "Fine," she says before lifting off the ground to fly away.

"Are you okay?" Tempest asks me.

"Um, fine," I say, clearing my throat.

"He's right, you know," he says, stepping toward me. "If Cain even suspected—"

"I know!" I shout, voice echoing through the cavern. Tempest is taken aback as I am. "Sorry. I'm just going to…" I point to the exit, bow my head, and start up the ramp to the living room in a daze. I've shut down again. Everything's gone one degree fuzzier than before. It's damn stuffy in the living room, so I walk outside to the patio in case that helps. It doesn't. I sit in the chair and unclip my cell phone before I even realize it. I still have work to do. If Cain has tapped my phones, he knows I'm in this game already. I'll risk the call. He picks up on the fifth ring.

Over the commotion in the background, he says, "Captain O'Hara."

"It's Jo."

"Hold on a second." I can hear him walking to shut the door. "Are you okay?"

"Yeah, but I need a favor. Have you processed the prints from the hospital bomb yet?"

"Just about to. Why?"

"You're going to find the one from the hospital has prints all over it. I need you to…lose that report."

"What? Why?"

"The prints on it don't belong to any of the perps, they'll belong to the person who defused the bomb. And his life will be ruined if word gets out he's in anyway associated with this. You know I wouldn't ask if it wasn't absolutely necessary."

The other end is quiet for a few seconds. "If you're withholding evidence, Jo—" he warns.

"I'm not," I lie. "Look, I know it's a lot to ask, but I swear on Justin's grave the man whose fingerprints on that bomb had nothing to do with this. Not directly, anyway. I saw him handle the bomb, and we are damn lucky he did. I can't get more specific than that. I know I have no right to ask, but I am. I am asking you to trust me. Please."

More silence, more tense fucking long horrible silence, then, "You have been working with them, haven't you? I knew it! Jo, what the hell are you thinking? After everything—" I think he moves the phone away in an attempt to regain his composure. I do have that effect on him. On all men it seems. "Jo," he says, calmer now, "whatever you're doing, or thinking of doing, don't. Get out. Get away from those people before you become too involved."

I don't know what it is about that last word, but it makes tears well in my eyes. I bite my lip to stop the fuckers. "It's too late for that, Harry." *Get a hold of yourself, for Christ's sake.* "Um, I assume you're helping the Feds with this one, so I'll send you all I have on Cain. We think he was responsible for an explosives theft a few weeks ago. I'll send you that file too. Just please get rid of that report or you'll ruin a great man's life. *Please.*"

"I'll see what I can do," he says.

"Thank you, Harry. Bye."

I'm about to end the call, when he says, "Joanna? Look after yourself, alright?"

No one else is going to, right? "I will. Bye, Harry." I hang up, pulling my legs up so I'm hugging them to my chest, and stare up at the starry sky.

Here I am again. All alone.

Fuck hope.

*

I didn't want to see any of them after that so I retreated into my bedroom, passed out after five minutes, woke at 5am, and returned to work. I've never been good at doing what I was told. Never. Rebel with several causes, me. I review all the progress the others made—very little— save for IDing a partial print on the disk. Only problem is that the man it belongs to a man that has been dead for over five years. Danny Watkins, Alkaline henchman, was presumed dead after being shot during a police raid led by Justice. The body was never recovered because the place then exploded. Watkins specialty was bombs. The search on him through the databases came back empty. He hasn't used any past aliases or been flagged in any worldwide search since his "death." Our best lead and it is a literal dead end.

They also reviewed the CCTV footage in and around the bombing sites last night. The cameras on the bridge were too high to get a decent look at who planted the charges, but it does show a five man construction crew working around 4am yet no permit was authorized. They did get a shot of the license plate. The truck used was stolen that same night, and it was found torched in the Ward last night. Even less luck at the hospital. There are no cameras in the boiler room or stairwell that far down and with thousands walking in daily, and no idea the time it was planted, we can't identify who carried it in. Pendergast Industries footage wasn't much better, and city hall's cameras were bypassed as best we can tell. The park footage was a bit better. The bomb was in a shopping cart pushed by a homeless person. A few cameras caught the face of a man in ratty clothes leaving the cart by the fountain. After Doris works her magic, he'd ID'd as Gary Acevedo, thug for hire. Per his wrap sheet, he worked for Alkaline too. Small world. I send all the information to Harry as promised.

Now know thy enemy time. From my earlier search on Jem, I know Jordan Ambrose has been wiped from records almost as if he never existed. No birth or death certificates, no social security number, no drivers license ever issued in that name. The only time his name pops up is in a newspaper article about the death of their parents and in a witness statement regarding the death of Uma Gupta. He was never a suspect. Bought himself an alibi. His past aliases prove more fruitful. Jackson Adler, Lee Harper, Finch Adams, one or the others pop up in South America, various countries in Asia and Europe, and even in New Urbana all connected to high profile hits and criminal organizations. Jordan seems to spend his time between terrorist attacks as a hit man or consultant. He's wanted by Interpol, the Moussad, and is on a terrorist watch lists in many countries. Per reports, he mostly works alone, and the few who have ever evoked his name during interrogation shortly never uttered another word. The few surveillance photos of him are fuzzy and he has a different hairstyle, facial hair, even noses in them. This fucker is good.

"Emperor Cain" first appeared four and a half years ago by planting a bomb in Jem's hospital then taunting the heroes on TV.

The oldies never die. There were several more bombings and taunts until, as soon as he arrived, Cain vanished. The Triumvirate announced he was gone for good and left it at that. The real story is they cornered him in a warehouse, Cain knocked them out, and vanished into thin air. Why he didn't kill them hell if I know but a year and a half later he resurfaced. For his opening act, he set off Sarin gas at a charity gala, then set up a series of elaborate traps for the team. He attempted to drown Tempest by flooding a sewer, burning Liberty at the botanical gardens, gassing Jem at the gala, and between those crimes blowing them up a few more times just for shits and giggles. Guess he regretted leaving them alive the previous time.

I'm not sure how long I'm down here, but long enough to get eyestrain. Time to stop. I pull myself away from Doris and flop on the leather couch with my eyes shut. What I need is a plan. I know they want to freeze me out for my own protection, but many have tried and all have failed with that maneuver. No one dictates my life. This asshole's in my town, blowing up my bridge, and keeping Jem from…*he's going down*. I just don't have a clue as to how.

The good news was they caught him, the bad was before he could be processed, he escaped custody and went underground. It came as no real surprise when he returned for a command performance a year later. He made the heroes jump through hoops just to toy with them. These hoops included kidnapping the First Lady, who Justice helped find. The three weeks he was active that time came to a head when the superteam plus one caught him attempting to hijack a plane. They managed to save the passengers, but the plane took off with Nightingale and Cain still aboard. Only Nightingale returned. Everyone thought that was the end of him. Until yesterday.

I'm not sure how long I'm down here, but long enough to get eyestrain. Time to stop. I pull myself away from Doris and flop on the leather couch with my eyes shut. What I need is a plan. I know they want to freeze me out for my own protection, but many have tried and all have failed with that maneuver. No one dictates my life. This asshole's in my town, blowing up my bridge, and keeping Jem from…*he's going down*. I just don't have a clue as to how.

Think. He's using local talent so I can discreetly put out feelers to old CIs and childhood friends and ask them to keep their ears open. My fucked up childhood in Diablo's Ward has to be worth something. I'm sure the Triumvirate can hit the local henchmen hangouts I already clued them into. I may be a partner in this endeavor, but I want to remain as silent a one as possible. I'm stubborn but I ain't stupid or suicidal. Anymore.

Thinking of stupid. An idea comes to me that makes me grimace. There is one person who can really help, but I'm not quite sure the gains exceed the costs. Or that he'd assist us. Or that I'm strong enough to even start that ball rolling. He did work with both accomplices and all but controlled the underworld for years. It wouldn't surprise me if their paths crossed at least once. Might be worth a shot. Just need to visit the Wizard for some courage.

My eyes open when I hear footsteps descending the ramp. Lexie, in her designer pink jumpsuit, stops when she spots me. She frowns. "Bren owes me ten bucks."

"Why?"

"I bet him I'd find you down here," she says as she struts over to my couch. "Scoot." I remove my legs and she flops down next to me with a long sigh. "I am freaking exhausted. We finally gave up wailing on punks around four this morning. Got nothing to show for it but bruised knuckles. Ruined my manicure, see?" She holds out her chipped nails. "Don't know why I even bother." She lowers her hand, glances at me, and half smiles. "Guess we need to talk, huh?"

"If you say so."

"I do." She crosses her long legs. "This whole situation sucks, huh? All of it. Cain's like the one person on this earth who scares the shit out of me. You know Brendan actually died when he flooded that sewer? If I hadn't shown up and performed CPR, that would have been it. When he woke up, sputtering disgusting water all over me, *that* was the moment I realized I was in love with him, you know? Our first kiss was in that sewer." She shakes her head. "Anyway, I know it's pointless, but I wouldn't be a good friend if I didn't warn you away from this one. You're already too exposed, don't want to make it worse. He finds out about you, and that's it. We might as well fit you for a toe-tag, especially since Nightingale's...you know, *fond* of you."

"I don't have a death wish. I'm not going to advertise my involvement. And despite what you think, I am good at keeping secrets," I say, narrowing my eyes.

She looks away with a sigh. "We probably would have told you. Eventually."

"Gee, thanks for the vote of confidence."

"What? I can count on half a hand the people who know. My own sister doesn't even have a clue. It's need to know, and you didn't, okay? Don't take it personally." She pauses. "How long have you known?"

"Jem for about a month, you and Brendan the day you took down Boneshaker. The blonde wig's a nice touch, but you have the same posture and phrasing as both."

She frowns. "This is why we work alone." She folds her arms across her chest. "So he really didn't tell you?"

"Of course not. He'd never betray you like that." I shift on the couch so I'm facing her. "But, for the record, that was a pretty shitty thing. Not trusting me. He and I got into fights because of it."

"I know. He came to us like every other day begging for permission. I almost gave in a few times—he was so pathetic—but Bren held the line. It cut Jem up something fierce keeping it from you. I think he was ready to bare his soul to you the moment we touched down in town. You made *quite* the impression on him last year. And the moment I realized you were into him too, I decided to help things along. It was such a pain in the ass to get him to that party, let alone getting his hair cut. Never knew he could be such a babe. Should have kept him to myself, huh? Huh?" she asks, nudging me. Her smile drops when she notices my miserable expression. We sit in silence for about thirty seconds. "If it's any consolation, he *really* likes you. I've never seen him so happy as when he's talking about you."

I stand. "It's not." I move over to Doris and sit, pulling up the file. "I sent all our data but the partial print ID to Harry O'Hara. I have to warn you, he might suspect—"

"Let's just can the shop talk for now, okay? I know you're hurting, and let's face it, I'm the only person you can talk about it all to."

"I don't want to talk. I want to find this bastard before he sets off another bomb. My fucked up love life can wait." I spin in the chair to face her. "Besides, there's nothing to talk about. We hung out a few times, we weren't engaged or anything. Never even went on a date. The relationship never made it past the gate, and that's probably for the best. It never would have worked, even without his psychotic brother showing up. He's too…smart for me.

Too shy. Not to mention the whole superhero angle. It's weird. No offense."

"None trying to be taken."

"We had a few laughs, but it was bound to end sometime, why not now? Okay? End of conversation." I spin back to the screen. "So, we know of two accomplices, Danny Watkins and Gary Acevedo, and that he had at least three more. The question is how did he recruit them?"

"To the best of my knowledge Cain's never worked here before, at least not *as* Cain."

"Well, he's basically a mercenary. It's not a big leap to think someone here hired him once upon a time. According to the files the only known connection between Acevedo and Watkins is James Ryder. I've sent this information to GFPD as well. I'm sure they'll try to interview him, but I can't see him being cooperative. Our best bet is to let Doris do her thing. Now, there's too much footage for her to go back in time all over the city, but I've programmed her so if Acevedo or Watkins show up anywhere, she'll alert us right away."

"Sounds great."

"I know you said Cain changes his appearance a lot, but on the off chance he gets sloppy I'd like a picture. I know Jem has some of him as a child, so I can send it to a colleague who has software to age him up."

"He didn't tell you?" she asks, eyes narrowing.

"What?"

"They're twins. Identical twins."

My face falls. "Oh. I-I didn't know." Christ, what else didn't he tell me? "That'll make it harder then. Doris will just spot Jem and alert us." There goes that plan. I lean back in my chair. "What do you think Cain's next move's going to be?"

"Not a damn clue. If you're right, and he wants people to hate us, he might continue the bombings. He still has a shit load of explosives left. Or, if he's really serious, he'll attack Jem Ambrose, not Lord Nightingale."

"Has he ever done that since he became Cain?"

"Strangely, no. I mean he showed up at his apartment or the hospital before to taunt him, but he's never gone after him as a doctor or threatened to out him."

"Maybe he's proud of that aspect of Jem's life," I offer.

Lexie slips into the chair beside me. "Total possibility. Those two have the sickest relationship I have ever come across. I don't know how much he's told you about his childhood, but it was seriously fucked up. The fact Jem turned out half as well adjusted as he did is a miracle."

"I know."

"He won't be able to kill him," she says more to herself. "I don't think he'd do it for anyone or anything, and that's the only way Cain will stop. Not a doubt in my mind of that. Sometimes I think Jem can't kill him because he just wants to punish himself." She sighs. "He was so...*happy*. You make him so happy. Now it's all fucked up again. He's petrified something will happen to you, so don't let it, okay?" Her cell buzzes, and she pulls it out to check the text. "Bren. He might have a lead on who hacked into the BNN footage. Miles Raitt?"

I plug the name in. "Known computer hacker. One arrest eight years ago. Served a year for accessing the city's CCTV footage and traffic system during a museum heist. He never gave up the crew he was working for. Other alleged employers are Nocturne, our old friend Oleg Casanov, a semi-retired mobster Mario DiAssini, and...James Ryder. Alkaline. Shit."

"Feed his photo into Doris along with Watkins and Acevedo. That his last address?" she asks, pointing to the screen. She types it into the phone. "Send all this to GFPD. They can get to Casanov and Ryder. I'll take DiAssini." I pull up his file, and she notes the address. "Oh, before I forget. Here." She pulls out a small cell phone. "This is a prepaid cell completely untraceable to any of us. Any shop talk is done on this. The three other numbers are programmed in. Use it if you need it." She rubs my arm, stands, and runs out of the lair.

I stare at the computer screen but really stare past it into the dark recesses of my mind. Maybe they'll find Raitt. Maybe he'll lead them right to Cain. Maybe...I sigh. Yeah. Right. Shit. I don't see any other option.

I have to face my boogeyman.

Chapter twelve

True Evil

I knew this day would come. I've dreaded it, had nightmares about it, but I still prepared. He broke out of prison once, there was no way I'd let there be a second. Alkaline is housed in the protection wing underground at Xavier Maximum Security Prison. They keep him doped on Thorazine, he only leaves his cell twice a week for a shower and the other to walk around the gymnasium with full restraints. He watches television an hour a day, reads, works out in his cell, but will never see the light of day again. The guards aren't allowed to speak to him so the only human contact he gets are phone calls to his lawyer. A visit from GFPD and the Feds must have been a welcome change, not that he showed his appreciation by spilling his guts or anything. He said he didn't know who Cain was and hadn't had contact with Watkins, Raitt, or Acevedo for years. I know this because I got the full report from the guard in the room. Every guard on his block is on my payroll. A grand a month to send me progress reports but mostly for insurance. Ryder escaped last time by having a guard in his pocket. I just took a play from his book. It also makes it easy to arrange meetings such as this.

I'm not as nervous as I thought I'd be. No sweating or shaking hands. My foot isn't even twitching. I sit at Doris waiting for the video link-up to the laptop I had smuggled in. I decided on a video conference so I can see if he's lying, something not as easily detected through the phone, so I have to look at his handsome face and dead eyes. Goody.

I sigh. I don't want to do this. I wouldn't be doing this if there was any other option. In the past three days we've made no forward progress. None. Doris hasn't picked up a visual on the men, the criminal element hasn't heard any whispers, and no new evidence has surfaced. Every potential trail is cold. Brendan and Lexie are frustrated, probably Jem too but I haven't had contact with him. It still stings thinking about him, which I seem to do twenty times a day. He'd try to talk me out of this, the others as well. Probably why I didn't tell them. Or I might have listened to them.

The black computer screen is suddenly alight with the image of a white door and the sound of a turning key. The webcam on the laptop jostles as the person holding it opens the door and walks into the cell. My stomach twists when I see him. His dark hair is shorn short and he has a beard, but the rest is exactly as I remember. Handsome face, dark eyes, and amused expression as he takes the computer. "Thank you," he says to the guard. I watch as he lies on a cot and adjusts the screen so we can see each other. A huge grin fills his face, crinkling his shark eyes of his. "Joanna Fallon."

"James Ryder," I say curtly.

"You're looking very well. Immense wealth agrees with you." I don't utter a word, just glare. He studies me for a few seconds. "You do look well, Joanna. I'm serious. I was certain you'd end up a shell of a woman, drinking yourself to death or finishing what you started all those years ago."

"I wouldn't give you that satisfaction."

He pauses. "It wasn't personal, Joanna. You were a means to an end, just like the doctor and her daughter. He had to be taught a lesson."

I almost stop the call, my hand even lurching toward the button but stop myself. Gonna have to be on top of my impulse control today. "I'm not here to talk about that."

"I know. I didn't think you arranged this to rehash the past, but it's not very often I have anyone but my four walls to speak to. No matter how hard I try the guards won't say a word to me."

"Gee, poor you," I say, emotionless.

He grins again. "I hope you're paying them well. Though I am surprised I haven't received any late night visits from Mr. Truncheon or fist. That always seemed your style. At least it would break the monotony."

"Can't say the thought never crossed my mind. But I'm not you. Your need for revenge put you and your girlfriend in your current states. You're just not worth that."

His smile drops. "How is Grace?"

"Not great. She's tried to kill herself. Twice."

His mouth sets straight, and he looks away. I give him a few seconds for that fact to sink in. Oddly, I get no joy from his pain. I'm just numb. His gaze returns to the camera. "Is there anything that can be done?"

"No. And eventually she will succeed. That'd be another death on your conscience. If you had one."

"Don't be cruel, Joanna."

"Why not? I've been taught by masters."

He glares at me for a few moments, but I remain impassive. "Ask your questions. I assume this is about my replacement on Galilee Falls Most Wanted List. I'll tell you what I told the police: I know nothing."

"And that's total and utter bullshit, and we both know it. One of your old cronies is understandable. Three? Not so much."

"And why the hell should I tell you a damn thing?" he snaps.

"Besides the fact I can make your life an unimaginable hell, to say nothing of Grace's, I think you want to. Said it yourself, he's replaced you. Collected your old playmates, probably using your old hideouts," I scoff, "and let's face it, he's already proved himself a better villain. Got a body count higher than yours in one shot. At this rate Galilee will forever be synonymous with him, and you'll just be like…what's his name. Whoever was top dog before you." I lean back in my chair. "And *I'm* asking. Went to all this trouble too. Gotta be worth something, right?"

Once again he's silent as he stares at me. "Why are you doing this, Joanna? Why join in this fight?" he asks, sounding genuinely concerned. "Didn't you learn anything from last year? Nothing good can come from this, not for you. No mortal has fared well in a battle between gods. You'll be nothing but cannon fodder. Justin wouldn't want this for you."

My back goes ramrod straight. "Don't you *dare* utter his name. You have no right. And you don't have a fucking clue what he'd want for me."

"I was there, Joanna," he says with a scoff. "I saw his face when he let go. I think I understand him better than even you."

"We are not discussing this. Stop trying to distract me."

"I can't imagine the guilt you feel," he continues. "If only you hadn't stopped him from murdering me. If only you had been the strong one and let go. If—"

"Shut up!" I snap. "Shut the fuck up! Answer my damn question."

He pursues his lips, I think in disappointment. "Temper, temper," he chides before pausing. "I'll make you a deal. You do that with your other informants, I believe."

"What?"

"Judging from the décor I view behind you, and your zeal to gather information, I assume you've more or less taken over Justice duty. You're probably even in league with his replacements. I'm a useful asset with priceless information regarding the city's underworld. I'll provide you this information as needed if you arrange weekly video chats with Grace."

"Monthly. I don't pay off her guards, and she's under constant observation. That's the best I can do."

"Then I'll settle for weekly calls from you, plus the monthly with Grace. Any port in a storm, right?"

Fuck, fuck, shit. "Fine. Tell me about Cain."

"I recognized one of his aliases, Jackson Adler, code name 'The Mockingbird,' which it seems your police friends knew nothing about. I hired him six years ago for a hit that required a finesse I knew myself and my enforcers incapable of. I'm not going to tell you who the person was, but I will say that Adler's specialties are accidents and natural causes along with the bombing talent you've already seen. He was worth every penny."

"How did you hire him?"

"Danny Watkins knew him. Before he moved here, Danny did some work in Columbia for the cartel. Adler was building his reputation with them at the time. They stayed in touch. I also think they were lovers judging from Danny's leanings and the way he spoke about Adler."

"Cain's gay?" I ask with a raised eyebrow.

"Just a theory. Anyway, I met the man once only. Adler didn't want to, but I insisted. I wasn't about to pay half a million dollars without meeting the man I was hiring."

"What did he look like? What were your impressions of him?"

"Medium height, thin almost to the point of lanky, brown eyes, black hair and beard, square glasses, and I believe a fake nose. He seemed incredibly smart, more so even than me. The job was impeccable."

"Where did the meeting occur?"

"The library. We both insisted on a public location."

"Do you know where he was staying or—"

"No clue. We didn't exactly chat. I try not to ask personal questions of the help."

I frown. "To your knowledge has he ever taken any other jobs in town?"

"Not that I'm aware of. He only handles a few jobs a year, that I know of. Apparently he met his quota for the year, and if not for Danny, he wouldn't have taken mine."

"What about Danny? Did you help him fake his death?" I ask.

"After the explosion he was taken to one of our clinics. I helped him get a new ID and put him on a plane to Rio. Haven't heard from him since. There was a rumor he was in Russia."

"What was the new name?"

Ryder thinks for a second. "Ralph Comstock, I believe. It was years ago, I can't be certain though."

"What about Acevedo and Raitt? Did Cain have contact with them?"

"No, but Danny did. They were all on my payroll at the same time."

"So Cain contacts Watkins, who in turn reaches out to his old co-workers," I say, more to myself. "Who else was Watkins close to in your organization?"

"Afraid that's where I draw the line, Joanna. I won't give up anyone else. I will not penalize those wily enough not to get caught. They have families, I do have some loyalty left."

I want to lunge at his image and strangle him, but all I can do is glare. "How did you contact Raitt and Acevedo? Where'd you find them?"

"Acevedo was pure muscle. An idiot, but loyal. He came to me though Gearhead, but last I heard he was working for Oleg Casanov." Whose organization was just decimated thanks to me. "Miles is a contractor. He has a website, MRBakery.com. Send an e-mail asking for chocolate croissants and give your phone number."

"Do you have any idea as to where Cain might be holed up? He has a large quantity of explosives and needs privacy."

"I owned over a dozen properties, which as you know, were taken by the city under the RICO laws."

"You must have one or two we never found. The subway station you held me in for example," I say with a fake grin.

"Good memories," he says with a matching smile. "None that Danny would know of. Anything else?"

"Know any of Watkins' old lovers names?"

"Never had the pleasure of meeting them. As I said, I tried to keep business and personal separate, otherwise things get complicated."

"As your present circumstance proves," I say with a genuine smile.

He smiles back. "How true. I let my emotions get the better of me and am now paying the price." His grin widens. "But it was *so* worth it."

I have to stop myself from spitting on the webcam. "I'll get started on the Grace thing. Just hope it won't come too late."

That fucking smile grows even wider. "Wear something sexier next week, Joanna. I'm awful lonely in here. Until then, good hunting." He makes a kissy face, then the screen goes black.

The moment it does, my façade crumbles and the breath I've been holding sputters out. If I wasn't already sitting I'd need to. My legs shake even now. I close my eyes and will myself to calm down. It takes awhile. When I can, I open my eyes and stare at the black screen. Why do I feel like I've just made a deal with the devil? Because I have. Better be worth it.

*

To maintain the status quo, Lexie is in New Urbana for a photo shoot the next two days and Brendan has football practice during the days, and I'm not even allowed to think about Jem let alone contact him, it's up to me and the GFPD to run down the plethora of new leads Ryder provided. I sent Harry the new info on Cain's alter ego, "The Mockingbird," Watkins alias, the way to contact

Raitt, and instructions to ask all the male escorts to keep their eyes and ears open. Everyone needs companionship, even terrorists.

Doris and I tackle the rest. First I review the INTERPOL file on Jackson Adler A.K.A. Lee Harper A.K.A. the Mockingbird. Jordan must really like *To Kill a Mockingbird*. I have no doubt he's the one who gave Jem his nickname. I start playing with my hair as I imagine their nanny reading the boys the book as they fell asleep, dreaming about the perfect father who adores them and fights for justice. I shake my head to clear it.

Anyway. The Mockingbird. The authorities only attributed two hits to him: one in Prague and the other in Guatemala, both car bombs. Watkins must have taught him that skill. The alias Jackson Adler hasn't popped up since it was traced to an order for the knock-out gas he used on the First Lady's guards when he kidnapped her. That must have been when he retired Adler and became Lee Harper. There's only a grainy photo taken from the security camera in that INTERPOL file. His hair is down to his shoulders and blonde. A wig complete with sunglasses and moustache. Only if I squint do I see the family resemblance. Hard to hide those cheekbones. The fact there's so little information on him or any of his aliases does not bode well. If he's been an active mercenary for almost two decades, and they barely have a picture of him, it tells me he's either incredibly smart, ruthless, lucky or all which is where my money lays. But I do have one thing he doesn't: Doris.

Assuming he started plotting his re-emergence when he heard Jem was moving here approximately three to five months ago, I change the search parameters from then to the present. I plug in every alias and *To Kill a Mockingbird* reference I can think of and Doris culls through all property sales, rentals, and utilities for those key words. While she does that, I rest my eyes on the couch, waking when Dobbs brings me breakfast six hours later. Yesterday was a hell of a day.

As I eat my cereal, I review her results. Out of a hundred fifty possibles, two look promising. The Scout Group, owned by Lee Jordan, is renting a building by the airport. When I look the company up, I see they're advertising plane parts. The company was incorporated a few months in New Urbana. So far so fishy.

The other is Mockingbird Inc, owned by J.A. Dill, who purchased a warehouse in the Ward two months ago. The company was founded eight months ago, also in New Urbana, and specializes in book distribution. The CCTV near the airport shows the outside of the Scout building but none of the cameras around the warehouse are functional. Good old Ward. People will steal even things that *are* nailed down. Guess it's up to me.

I grab a few cameras from storage and the instruction manual on how to set them up before going upstairs to shower and change into baggy jeans, a black hoodie, Angel's baseball cap with my hair tucked in, sneakers, and bulletproof trench coat Justice gave me. I don't expect trouble but in case I also bring an untraceable gun from Justin's collection, my Taser, Triumvirate phone, and brass knuckles. Better safe than sorry.

It's a damn good thing I kept my old Acura because an Aston Martin wouldn't last two seconds in the Ward. Since the bridge blew up it takes me thirty minutes longer to get into the city, not that I'm in a rush. Condemned buildings, junkies and pushers on the corners, bars on every window, my old stomping grounds. I certainly have moved up in the world.

The warehouse is surrounded by equally dilapidated, empty buildings with nary an intact window to be found. There are no signs of life inside as I drive past. It's small, only about a thousand square feet with no trucks or workers outside like a normal working warehouse. Either they haven't begun filling the warehouse with books or there's something rotten in the state of Denmark. Since it'd be suspicious for me to climb a telephone pole like a monkey to place a camera there, I park behind the abandoned three-story office building across from the warehouse. I pass fleeing rats as I climb to the second floor. After half an hour of cussing and even throwing the instruction manual against the wall, I think I finally get the damn camera working. It has the perfect vantage of the main warehouse door. I check the feed on the laptop. Camera's operational. Hurray for me.

Just as I'm packing up to move onto the next building, through the window, I notice the warehouse door open and two men step out. I vaguely recognize one of them but can't place him. They light cigarettes and begin chatting. I sit down to move out of their sight. I pull the laptop from it's hiding spot to watch on it as they continue social hour. Come on, brain. How do I know—Matt Lucas. I busted him six years ago for assault. He beat up some college kid who couldn't pay his gambling debts. If memory serves, we later linked him to Ryder's organization.

As they shoot the shit, an SUV turns down the street then pulls up to the warehouse. Lucas runs to open the sliding door for the car to enter. From the glimpse I get, the inside of the warehouse is mostly empty with a table and at least two other cars inside. Lucas closes the door and returns to his buddy. Book warehouse my ass. The door opens again a minute later. Gary Acevedo pokes his head out and gestures the men in. My mouth falls. Holy shit. Not expecting that.

What the hell am I supposed to do now? Call the cops? What if Cain was in that SUV? What if the place is wired to explode? I get my prepaid and dial Brendan. It rings about ten times before I leave a message, giving my location and the situation. He's probably still at practice, and Lexie's across the country. No choice.

"Hello?" Jem asks after the fourth ring.

"I found Acevedo. Possibly all of them. Meet me at 18765 Eisner St, brown brick warehouse, second floor. Get here fast." I hang up. I'd be nervous to see him again after he sort of broke up with me, but I'm too damn excited by this lead. *God* I've missed this feeling. The thrill of the chase. Almost as good as sex.

Of course on a roller coaster what goes up must come down. Ten minutes pass and all is quiet. No one exits or enters. Just as I start getting bored, I hear a thump inside this building and unholster my gun just to be safe. Fast footsteps moving toward me make me clutch it tighter, unlocking the safety. I relax when I see a flash of purple, then him. Damned if even now the butterflies don't begin. He, on the other hand, seems less than happy to be in my presence.

"What the hell are you—"

I stand. "There are three I know of inside, probably more. I definitely saw Acevedo."

"You shouldn't be here," he hisses as he approaches.

"Well, I am." I give him the rundown on everything I've learned from Ryder to Matt Lucas. With each sentence, the sides of his mouth move lower until he's downright frowning.

"Have you lost your senses? What were you thinking conversing with that psychopath? What if everything Ryder told you was to lead you into a trap?"

"Oh, come on. Give me a little damn credit."

"You came here. Alone. You're exposed."

"I took every precaution. Look, can we please stop fighting and figure out what we're going to do?"

"*We* aren't doing anything. *You* are going home."

"I'm not leaving you here alone. You need back-up," I insist.

"Tempest will be here when he can."

I shrug. "Then I'll wait until he gets here."

Nightingale takes an angry stride toward me, and instinctively I move back a little. "I don't need you." Something about those words unnerves him. His lips twitch. "*Here.* I don't need you here. Please. Just go. *Please*," he pleads.

Part of me wants to go. To get away from the anger and disapproval I sense from his every pore. But no. This was my lead, my investigation. I refuse to be dismissed like some flunkie. And I sure as hell am not leaving him alone here across from a warehouse full of goons no matter what he says. I fold my arms across my chest. "Do you think I'm weak?"

"What?"

"Do you view me as some weak damsel in distress who faints at the first sign of danger?"

"What? Of course not."

"Then stop fucking treating me like one," I say through gritted teeth. "I have been taking care of myself practically since the cradle, and I will till the grave. And I know you…care about me. You don't want anything happen to me, and I do appreciate that more than you can imagine. But I do not need or want a knight in shining armor shielding me from the big bad world. I'm a smart woman. I know my limitations, and I sure as hell know when to cut and run when I'm in over my head. So I'm telling you, this stops *now*. I almost lost my life because someone close to me was trying to protect me and didn't give me the chance to do it myself. I know the risks. My eyes are wide open to the dangers, but I'm in this. I am in this fight. All the way." I move toward him. "So you can avoid me, even order me to leave until you're blue in the face, but catching your psycho brother takes precedence over your chivalry streak or anything going on between us. The job comes first. I think we can both agree on that." I plop down in my original position on the floor near the laptop. "I'm staying until Tempest gets here. You don't have to talk to me, but I am not leaving. Get over it."

He stares down at me, I can't see his eyes behind the mask but I know they're not filled with kindness or approval judging from the balled up fists. I don't think anyone's challenged him like this in a long time. He could pick me up and fly me out of here, but we both know he won't dare lay a hand on me. All he can do is suck it up and let me be. After a sigh, he slowly walks over to me and sits down against the wall near me, leaving a few feet between us. I gaze at the monitor at the quiet warehouse for a full minute. Out of the corner of my eye, I watch my partner shift uncomfortably beside me.

"Ants in your pants already?" I ask. "I hate surveillance work too. Hours of nothing with no guarantee anything will come of it. I've gone through entire Sudoku and crossword puzzle books on one shift. I brought microphones. If you want, you can place them on the warehouse for something to do."

"No. I don't want to...I'll wait for Tempest. Just in case."

"Not confident with your stealth skills?"

"No, just better safe than sorry." We return to silence. Even though he's probably pissed at me, the quiet isn't uncomfortable. I'm quite happy to see that hasn't changed between us. "So, is this footage transmitted back to Doris?"

"Yeah."

"What about the other location? By the docks? Did you check that one out as well?" he asks.

"Not yet. There were also a couple others that had potential too, but this was a goldmine." I smile. "Your brother sure does love *To Kill a Mockingbird,* that's for sure."

"Our um, governess gave it to him for Christmas when we were six. He devoured it. We lost count of how many times we read it. The movie as well. I can quote the entire thing."

"Let me guess. He's the one who christened you 'Jem'?"

"Yeah. I'm older by ten minutes, so he thought it fitting."

"I can see it."

"What?"

"You. Jem Finch. You're a lot alike. Smart, brave, protective, does the right thing no matter the personal cost." I notice him staring at me, and I turn to face him. "What? I had high school English too. I've read it."

"That's not…I…" He glances away, the visible flesh on his face turning red. "Never mind."

"You really can't take a compliment, can you?"

"Not one that's so undeserved, no." His thin mouth sets straight. "I am nothing like Jem Finch. He…protected his sibling. *He* was the strong one. When we were growing up it was Jordan who fought for me, for us both.

"When we were nine," Nightingale continues, "Dr. Ramone, Father's lead researcher, was testing our healing capabilities. Normally Jordan volunteered to go first, but he was angry at me for not wanting to go swimming with him earlier. Anyway, Dr. Ramone…strapped me down on the examination table and began his incisions. Shallow at first, down my arm, and then…into the muscle. I managed not to scream until he hit bone."

"Jesus Christ."

"When Jordan heard my cries for him, my brother rushed in, barreling at the doctor. Broke his arm and knocked the man out. We escaped to our secret spot, the tree house we built near the lake. They found us later that night. Father was livid, even threatened to 'end the experiment.' He grabbed my still tender arm, and that's when Jordan attacked him with the scalpel he'd stolen. Father received stitches, and Jordan received a week locked in the lab being forced sedatives and reprogramming techniques. Basically, they tortured him for seven days and nights. When he returned to me, he was different. Angrier. And still after all he endured, he volunteered to be first every time after that. *He* was the brave one. And it destroyed his soul."

I don't say anything for a few seconds because I can't think of a damn thing *to* say. I've never been much of a hugger, but an overwhelming desire to embrace him must be fought. I'm afraid if I touch him he'll freak and run away. Instead, I don't even look at him. I stare straight ahead. "You know…for such a smart guy, you can be dumber than a sack of hammers. It's a damn good thing you're cute."

"Excuse me?"

"I was twelve when my Pop died, and I was *convinced* for years I had some part in it. If I hadn't insisted on us leaving my mother, if I hadn't needed new shoes, blah blah blah then he wouldn't have been driving that cab and wouldn't have gotten shot. It made me angry, furious at the world but especially at myself, and I wasn't born little miss Zen to begin with," I chuckle. "But with time, and a lot of help from Justin, I came to realize I'd spent years being a fucking idiot. Blaming myself was just a way for me to control a situation that I had no control over. All I could control was my reaction. I worked hard to stop hating myself, at least for that. Of course then I did other things to hate myself for but…" I chuckle again. I glance over at him but can't tell much with the mask. I look away. "My point is you didn't create this monster. In fact I think you're the only thing keeping him from going nuclear. Literally. You and I both know your brother was born a sociopath. It was just a freak thing. A genetic mutation. He doesn't kill people because you didn't stand up to Dr. Mengele when you were a child, he does it because he has a mental disorder. A crossed wire. You couldn't have done a whole hell of a lot from stopping him down his path anymore than I could have stopped the man who shot my Pop at twelve years old. You have to let go of this misplaced guilt because you're drowning in it. And until you do, you will never have control of your own life. You'll never be able to stop him right here, right now. You'll just be alone with your pain. And then he wins."

I shake my head. "I don't know about you, but I'm not okay with that. *He* doesn't get to win. He doesn't get to travel the world, doing whatever he damn well pleases while you're back here flogging yourself for his sins. Unless that's what you want. Hell, maybe you're happy in misery. Some are. My mother was. If that's the case, then you must be like a pig in shit right now. Alone, pushing people who care about you away, suffocating in guilt and leaving no room in your life for anything or anyone else. Good times." I turn to him, catching those gorgeous blue eyes. "So, are you? Happy?"

We stare at one another for a second, my impassive eyes challenging his hooded ones. I know I'm victorious when he says, "I know what you're doing."

"Is it working?" I ask with a smirk.

"Yes."

"Good." And I lean across, my lips finding his before the spell breaks. His stiffen at first as I'm sure warning bells chime in his mind, but I don't pull away. I'll win this war no matter how many dirty tricks I have to pull. But this battle lasts all of three seconds before he accepts defeat, moving his lips against mine tentatively at first then with the ferocity of a man lost in a desert who tastes water for the first time in days. I thought he'd be shy, tentative, but as usual with him I'm in for a delicious surprise. His tongue pushes past my barrier, finding mine to dance their dance. The only time he withdraws is to nibble on my lower lip. His fingers dig into my back, drawing me in even closer.

Not close enough.

I crawl onto his lap, straddling him, holding him, igniting parts of us both that we'd forgotten about in our self-imposed miseries. I don't know how long we make out like teenagers in this rat infested hovel, but I love every millisecond, every sensation of it. I just wish we didn't have all these clothes on. I want to run my fingers through his soft, wild hair. Burrow my fingers into the flesh of his back as he does the same to me. Why the hell have we waited so long? This is fucking amazing. I'm about to supernova. No more wasting time. I've never felt this much…intensity. Longing. Passion. Even with Harry. Or that night with Justin by The Falls. Didn't hold a goddamn candle to this.

Eventually we have to break apart to breathe, both of us panting as if we'd rounded home base. This close I can actually see those blue eyes as he gazes up at me with that same amazed, frightened, and loving expression he had on the hospital rooftop. This time it doesn't scare me. I won't let it. I run my finger across his swollen lower lip. Mine pulses in time to another area south of the border. Our smiles move in unison before he leans forward to kiss me again.

"Ahem."

Oh, shit. I practically leap a foot in the air off him. When I land beside him, I find Tempest smirking in the doorway smirking. Thank God it's only him but still. I'm mortified. "Um…"

"Hey, don't stop on my account," Tempest says.

"We were just—" Nightingale says.

"Killing time on a stakeout? Yeah, Lex and I sometimes kill time the same way."

"You do?" Nightingale asks, shocked by this unprofessional revelation.

Tempest scoffs at the hypocrisy. His gaze moves from us to the camera and laptop on the ground. "So, I got your messages. Sorry it took so long to get here. Looks like you've got things well in hand here though. If you want I can leave or—"

"No," Nightingale says forcefully as he jumps up. "We-We still have a lot to do. We need to place the bugs, there's another warehouse to surveil, there are other leads to follow up." He glances at me. "Alone."

"What?" I ask.

"We can manage from here. Go home. *Now.* Please. It'll be fine now."

Fuck a duck. His barriers shut like a steel trap again. I recognize the posture and expression. I did the same thing to Harry and just about every other person who tried to get close to me. Most gave up, save Justin. I'm still amazed he ever put up with me. I'm fuming at my dismissal, and I really want to dig my heels in, but know it won't do any good. Not with Tempest here. The interloper knows this too as he shoots me a sympathetic smile. Shit. I swallow my emotions and plaster on a poker face.

"Um, fine. I'll let the big, strong men handle it from here. I need to go to my office anyway. Nightingale can get you up to speed."

"I'll swing by later tonight if I have any questions or anything else develops," Tempest says, really meaning he'll come by to check on me and make excuses for his friend.

"Whatever. Have fun with the rats. Call if you want me."

As I move, Nightingale takes a tiny step away in case I accidently brush against him. This should sting, but instead I feel a sense of triumph. He's afraid to touch me. Afraid of what he might do. As I walk out of the room, the corners of my mouth move up into a smirk.

Most people never understood me and Justin. Why two people from such different backgrounds and temperaments could be such good friends. What they never understood was we were basically the same person. Kindred spirits. Soul mates. And like him, I am as stubborn as a mule when something really matters to me. He didn't give up on me until the day he died. Hell, it's why he died. So as long as there's a glimmer of hope, even a half chance in hell, I'm not quitting on Jem. He needs me, especially now. No matter how many times that man pushes me away, I'll keep going back. Because he's worth it. Even in death my best friend is looking out for me. Giving me strength.

And if Jem's half as much trouble as I was, I am gonna need it.

Chapter Thirteen

Cuckoo's Nest

Mansion, sweet mansion. Cleaning things up at the office took longer than I anticipated, so all the happy feelings from earlier were sucked from me by international phone calls and paperwork. Tracking terrorists might be more dangerous but it sure beats mergers and acquisitions. I'm usually praying for someone to shoot at me after the second dull as hell hour.

I'm fucking starving. Right on cue, as I pull off my jacket, Dobbs hobbles out from the kitchen sans food though. "I was getting worried," Dobbs says as he takes my coat.

"Sorry, impromptu conference call. Is dinner ready?"

His eyes narrow from confusion. "I thought you and Dr. Ambrose were dining out tonight."

"What? No. Who told you that?"

"Dr. Ambrose. He's been waiting in the living room for almost an hour."

"What? He's here? Why didn't you call me?"

"He told me he had."

What the hell? "Um, thank you, Dobbs. That'll be all."

As I walk toward the living room, I check both my phones. No calls. What—

Oh, fuck.

The moment I see the man on the couch, I know I'm as good as dead. It's Jem from tips to toes. Same exact haircut, glasses, face, posture, even crumpled clothes and aftershave. But it's not Jem. My eyes say yes, but something deep inside knows there is no way in hell that's him. Which can only mean I have a mass murderer in my living room watching the news as if it was the most natural thing in the world? I manage to keep my face neutral as his eyes move to me a second after I step in. Even the nervous smile he shoots me is pure Jem. It sends a chill down my spine.

"Hi," the doppelganger says with his voice.

A million different scenarios flash through my mind. Excuse myself and call the guys? Suspicious. Scream for Dobbs? He'll kill us both. Attack him? Um, no. He can snap my neck with two fingers. Play along wins by a landside. "Hey," I say with a grin. "This is a surprise."

"I, uh, know," he says nervously. Jordan shuts off the TV and rises. "A pleasant one, I hope."

"Always." Oh, shit I think I just entered a mental chess game with Bobby Fucking Fisher. What does he know? What does he suspect? Why the fuck is he here? Attacking him now seems like the smarter option. Damn, my purse with all my weapons is by the front door. To buy time, I move to the bar with my eyes averted. "Though, if you're here to discuss an investment in Ambrose Pharmaceuticals, I am in no mood."

"That's not why I'm here, and we both know it."

Shit. My heart starts pounding in my ears. "I figured." I pour myself water, using sheer willpower to stop my hands from trembling. *Keep it together*. I spin around with annoyance on my face. "So say your peace."

"You have to stop investigating Cain. I know you haven't, even though I begged you to."

"And how exactly do you know that?"

He scoffs. "Please. I know *you*." He leaves it at that. Clever. "This isn't your fight."

I scoff this time. "Please. The second that cowardly, psycho fuck set foot in my town, it became my fight."

If I've offended him, it doesn't show. "You don't have to do this. You can sit this one out. Leave town for awhile."

Okay, now I'm really confused. What the hell is he playing at? He moves toward me. Lord even his walk is all Jem. Jordan stops two feet in front of me, too damn close for comfort. Now I notice the subtle differences. The faint smile lines around the eyes and mouth. He smiles more than Jem. Not surprising. Villains always seem to be having more fun than heroes. Really, it's the eyes. Same color, same shape, but there's nothing in there. No sparkle. No light. No soul. He's doing a better than average job of hiding this fact, seeming sympathetic and concerned as he stares. Fuck, this is creepy.

"Please. You cannot fathom what you are up against in that man. *Please*. If you care about me, you'll just leave. I can't keep going with you here. I worry all the time. Where you are, what you're doing. I can't concentrate. You're in my every thought every minute. He can get to you anytime. Anywhere. I...the mere thought paralyzes me. Please, just go."

Oh. I get it now. My eyes narrow in confusion. Two can play this game. "Look...um, your concern is sweet and all, but uh, you're kind of making me uncomfortable here. Like, a lot. This is sort of coming out of left field here," I say with a nervous chuckle.

"It is?" he asks, sounding hurt. Nice touch.

"Uh, yeah. I never knew you felt this way. I mean, you're a nice guy and all, but I don't...consider you in that way. *At all.* I mean, I like working with you and teaching you to sail and whatnot, but that's it. I just think of you as a friend." I gaze down at the floor. "And I'm, uh, actually, um, seeing someone. He's stopping by soon." And he can't get here fucking fast enough.

"I-I had no idea. Why didn't you tell me?"

I narrow my eyes. "We're not exactly close, Jem. I don't know who you're seeing, if anyone. Come on," I say, placing my hands on my hips. "Where the hell is this coming from? Really? You've barely said twenty non-work related words to me since we've met. The only time I ever came close to flirting with you, you were horrified. You're obviously not thinking straight. All this bullshit with your brother is doing your head in. Get out of town for a few days, get some perspective. Jesus." I sip my water. "Now, I'm exhausted and I gotta get ready for Brendan."

"Brendan Darby? The football player? Isn't he married?"

"Spare me the lecture, okay? It's none of your damn business. Just go, okay? God!" Rolling my eyes, I take a step away. Checkma—shit! I make it only the one step before his hand clamps on my arm to stop me. I let out a gasp and almost jump out of my skin. The look on his face, complete with wide grin, stops my heart. "What—"

"You're good. Real good. Had me fooled there for a moment."

"Jem, what—"

He squeezes my arm hard enough I wince. "Please don't insult my intelligence."

"I don't…" His glare stops my denial dead. The jig is up. Surprised I lasted this long. I wipe the confusion off my face to match his expression. "Damn it."

Plan B time. Old Faithful.

I knee him in the balls with all my strength while at the same time smash my glass against his head, shattering it. Pain ripples through my hand and hopefully his head. He releases my arm, and I make a mad dash toward the door. I get all of five steps when a hand clamps my hair, snapping my head back hard enough for whiplash. Before I can process the pain, I'm flung over the back of the couch, landing on the cushions before bouncing onto the hard floor. My bleeding hand stings when I land. *That* was a stupid idea.

"Get up," Jordan orders. I manage to rise, and when I turn I spot the gun pointed at me. Of course. At least his head is bleeding. One point for effort. I lift my hands in surrender. "Nice try. Now, sit down. Time for a real chat." Glaring at him, I do as he says. Jordan rests on the other end of the couch. "Know that if you scream for help, I kill you then the butler."

"I won't scream. I wouldn't give you the satisfaction."

Sighing, he rolls his eyes. "Save the tough girl act. We've done enough lying for one evening, don't you think?" He wipes his blood with his sleeve. "Just out of professional curiosity, what was it that gave me away? A lot of time and research went into this meeting. Surveillance, breaking into his apartment, rehearsal. What was it?"

"You're here for one. They don't come to the house, not since you literally blew into town. No contact anymore, at least not with me. But I knew for sure when you said *you* were the one who begged me to stop investigating. It wasn't Nightingale, it was Liberty," I lie. "Your brother and Tempest just backed her decision. I haven't heard from a one of them since. And third, your brother would never, not in a million years, hit on me. I've given him a dozen chances to, and he stared at me as if I was crazy. I don't think he has a lustful bone in his body, at least not for me. I would have found it." I scowl at him. "Not surprising, though. After what you did to him, you might as well have cut that part out yourself."

"You really expect me to believe there's nothing between you two? I've been following him almost since he arrived in this hellhole of a city. I've seen the two of you together on multiple occasions looking rather cozy. He apparently even informed you of his double life."

"That wasn't by choice. I figured it out early on. Came to town at the same time. Same height, weight, eyes, desire to shrink away whenever I touched him. I confronted him, he fessed up. Which is why we had so many meetings. Not only is my company thinking of investing in his wonder drug, but we were trying to take down a syndicate, which we did. We're both busy people, we found time whenever we could. But that's it. He's a colleague, and yes, a friend. And when you kill me, which I'm guessing is what you're here to do, he'll feel bad. You might even make him cry, but you won't destroy him. Just like you didn't before with Uma or all those times you attacked Independence in an attempt to gain his undivided attention. You know why? Because he's better than you. Smarter. Stronger." I meet his blank eyes, giving him the full force of my glare. "You will not win. He will beat you. Every. Time."

"You know, for just a friend, and knowing him such a short time, you certainly do hold him in high regard."

"Just calling it like I see it. I know his type. Like I know yours. You're nothing but a selfish man-boy throwing a tantrum because your brother is ignoring you."

"A bit simplistic, don't you think?"

"Is it? When your brother might, just *might* be starting to find a glimmer happiness, of normality, you have to show up, to what? Save him from this horrible fate? Or maybe you just can't accept the fact he can live without you. Because from where I'm sitting, it doesn't seem like you can live without him. You're acting like a psychotic, jealous ex-girlfriend whose boyfriend has moved on. Is that it? You want to fuck your brother, and if you can't have him no one else can, Jordy?"

He pauses, and then raises an eyebrow. "Who says I haven't? Fucked him, that is. It was just the two of us for many years. Many cold, lonely nights in that compound with only each other for comfort."

His grin grows as the revulsion on my face intensifies. "You're lying," I say.

"Don't you wish I was," he says. "No, you don't have a sibling, let alone a twin, so you wouldn't understand. Since birth you have a built in friend and built in competitor all through life. A comfort and a nightmare. And there are times you feel like one person. You're both in your own microcosm, a hostage to one another, and yes, there's no room for anyone else. And try as you might, you cannot be happy without them. And you hate them for it. But how can you hate someone you love so much?"

"I don't know," I say.

"Because you *can't* know, so please refrain from judging and commenting on concepts you know nothing of," he says with an undercurrent of anger. Cain's quiet for a few tense seconds as he studies me. When his shoulders relax, I know I've passed his test. "No, my brother could never love you. You're far too low-brow. Uma had class. She was bright. Beautiful. You're just…common. You couldn't turn his head if it was on a top."

"Fuck you asshole," I hiss.

"Have I hit a nerve? I suppose I must have. It must be hard having a penchant for falling in love with men above your weight class."

"You don't know what the fu—" I stop myself. I'm getting too emotional for this conversation. "Look, if you're going to kill me, then just fucking kill me already. I'm bored with you."

His grin grows. "Really? I'm having fun." Those sapphire eyes catch mine, and the smile slowly falters. He points the gun to the side, away from me. "I'm actually not here to kill you. I mean, I will if I must, but that is not the purpose of my visit today."

Those words should bring relief, but I'm still at Defcon 1. "Then what the hell do you want?"

"I wanted to meet the newest addition, gage your threat level." His nose twitches. "Minimal. Which is a disappointment. Your work with Alkaline was impressive, but it must have been the exception, not the rule. All bark, no bite. Shame." The gun returns to my chest. "But really I want access to your computer. I have research to do. I searched the majority of the house but couldn't locate it. *You* will show me where it is and how to use it. Were you lying when you said you had a gentleman coming over?"

"No."

"Well, then we best get to it. Don't want you to miss your adulterous fun. Get up."

Fuck. Going to a second location never ends well. With the gun still on my person, we rise. Cain picks up the satchel from the floor he must have brought. I don't like it, but I lead the way toward the fireplace. For a second I'm convinced he's lying, that he's going to shoot me in the back of the head. I press the button under the fireplace, and it slides open. Still no shot.

The psycho keeps the gun against my shoulder the entire way down the ramp. "Huh. It's smaller than I imagined." I slowly march toward Doris. I'm about to enter the password that sends a warning to the others, but Jordan moves the gun to my temple. "No tricks, Miss Fallon. And familiar faces show up while I'm here you're the first to go, then your old friend upstairs. As I said, I don't want to kill you, but I will. Correct password please." Fuck again. I do as he says. The main screen pops up. "Looks simple enough. Suppose it'd have to be for you to use it."

"Gee, I can't tell you how wounded I am by your low opinion of me," I say, deadpan.

I get a quick smile from the villain. "I am sure you'll recover from the disappointment." He sets the satchel down and reaches into his pocket. My breath catches when he pulls out a syringe, using his teeth to get the cap off.

"What—"

Before I can form a defensive tactic, the needle pierces my neck. Whatever's inside burns through my veins. As the darkness envelops me, and I lose function of all my limbs, I hear the words, "Say hello to my brother for me."

Fade to fucking black.

*

A stinging chemical smell. Brendan and Dobbs above, shouting my name. Black.

Sirens. Jostling around as a car moves. Black.

Bright lights. Doctors and nurses circling me. Black.

When I open my eyes for the fourth time, I manage to keep them ajar for more than a second. Four walls, machines attached to my arms, antiseptic smell, and a gurney. Hospital. The right side of my head throbs, and when I touch it there's a bandage over my matted hair. My neck where that fucker injected me is sore too. At least I'm alive.

Brendan is asleep in a chair in the corner snoring lightly. My attempt to sit up fails the first time, but the second successful one alerts my guard. He lets out a snorting snore, and his eyes fly open. "Oh, hey," he says, sitting up as well.

"Evening," I say as I settle into the gurney.

He checks his watch. "Actually, it's just past two AM." The gentle giant stands and walks over. "How you feeling?"

"My head hurts."

"Yeah, you whacked it when you hit the floor. They already gave you a CT scan. There's no swelling so probably no concussion. Just a couple staples for the gash and some blood loss. Jem said they'd do more tests when you woke up."

"Is he here?"

"He's around somewhere, but…"

"But?"

"We both thought it best he keep his distance. Because of, you know. So I pulled guard duty."

"You know it was Cain?"

"Yeah. I came over around nine to check on you, but your butler told me you were out with Jem, which I knew was a lie. I'd just left him at the docks an hour before. When you weren't in the living room, I opened the fireplace and found you bleeding and unconscious on the floor. We tried to revive you, but when we couldn't, your butler phoned an ambulance and I moved you upstairs. Seems Cain injected you with an anesthetic. It's not dangerous or anything, no long term effects, just knocks you out for a couple hours." Brendan sits on the edge of the gurney. "I called Jem while we waited for the ambulance to make sure he'd be the one to examine you. We checked you in under a fake name, but there have been a few calls. We've just kept silent."

"That's why I pay a PR firm buckets of money to handle things like this. How long do I have to stay here?"

"That's a Jem question but minimum overnight for observation. I'm gonna go tell him you're awake. He was…" He ceases speaking to find the right words. "Well, let's just say he'll be very, *very* relieved you're up. As will the nurses he's been haranguing at non-stop. Be right back."

My friend squeezes my hand before walking out. When the door shuts, I let out a long sigh. The last time I was in a hospital bed I'd been Tasered, kidnapped, shot at, burned with acid and had a subway station fall in over my head. A measly gash and tranquilizer are an improvement. I guess.

Jem must have been nearby because five seconds after Brendan steps out, the men return. My doctor looks as horrible as I probably do. His dark hair is wild as if it hasn't seen a brush in years, and his clothes are mismatched and rumpled except for the white doctor's coat. The moment he lays eyes on me, that striking face falls with relief but only for a second before he shuts off again.

"I'll leave you two alone," Brendan says. "I'm gonna call Lexie, tell her you're up if she's not already on the plane."

"She didn't have to fly back," I say.

"Too late. We need to get ahead of this thing, if possible. Come get me when you're done with your...examination." He smiles at us both before departing.

Alone again.

Jem refuses to move from across the room, not sure how to proceed from here. I'll make it easier for him. "Aren't you gonna examine me?"

"Oh, um, yes," he says, shaking his head to clear it. He takes a tentative step, then another. "Do you have—"

He's too surprised by what I do next to finish his thought. The moment he's within reach, my arms spring around his chest, drawing him into an embrace. Jem stiffens as if I was Medusa and he just looked into my eyes. He even stops breathing.

"Just so you know, I'm not letting go until you hug me back like I know you want to. You know how stubborn I am. I'll hold on for hours if I have to, so you might as well just do it now." I pause. "Please."

He begins breathing again right away but it takes ten seconds before his arms encircle my body, and another three to give into the sensation of comfort this should afford us both. He relaxes and clings to me as hard as I to him. "I'm okay," I whisper. "I swear I'm okay."

I shouldn't have spoken. It brings too much reality to the situation. He moves away, once again refusing to look at me. "Do you have, um, any double vision or nausea?"

"Little nausea. I've had concussions before, and this isn't like that. *I'm fine.* Really. Besides drugging me, he barely laid a finger on me. He said he just wanted to size me up and use Doris."

"How did he even get in?"

"He was there when I got home. Dobbs let him in. He looked *exactly* like you, right down to your mannerisms and aftershave. It was uncanny."

"What did you say to him?" he asks, fear level rising a few notches.

"Jem, I knew it wasn't you right away," I say, sounding more offended than I intended. I take him through the whole ordeal only leaving out the incest revelation because I can only face so much right now. That's a whole other conversation.

"Do you think he believed you?"

"He left me alive. Supports the theory."

"Maybe. Or he has something bigger planned," he offers.

"You don't buy he just popped over for a chat and to use the computer?"

"Do you?" I just stare at him. "Didn't think so."

I put my hand on his. "So, what are we going to do?"

He pulls his hand away and stands. "*You* are spending the night here, then tomorrow you're being released into Brendan and Lexie's care. Then you can either stay with them until we've defeated him or do the smart thing and leave town."

"We've been through this. I didn't run from Ryder, I'm not running from your brother."

"Yes, because your decision to remain in town had such a good outcome last year. You really want to go through an ordeal like that again?"

"Your brother is an international criminal. If he wants me dead, which he could have accomplished today, he could do it just as easily in France as here."

This realization doesn't assuage his fear, or mine for that matter. If possible his long face collapses even further. "I'm sorry. I'm so sorry for putting you in this situation."

"Stop saying that. It's not your fault. I don't blame you."

"I blame me. I know my brother. I should have known this would happen. I just—I don't know what to do, Joanna. I—"

"Hey." Jem's still close enough for me to take his hand again. He doesn't pull away. He doesn't even put up even a tiny fight when I hug him again. He even sits on the bed and embraces me back, squeezing me even tighter than I am him. "We'll figure this out. It'll all be okay. I know it." I kiss his cheek. "Just don't give into him. He wants you distracted. He wants you torturing yourself. Don't. Just don't. You don't deserve it."

Jem moves back enough to see my face, I think maybe to see if I'm sincere. I smile and cup his chin in my hands, rubbing my thumbs across his cheekbones before leaning in for a kiss. I anticipate hesitation but he allows this, though he barely kisses me back. He breaks away first, resting his forehead on mine. "I have to go. Any longer could raise suspicions."

"Okay," I whisper.

"I won't let him hurt you again."

I peck his lips. "Ditto."

He kisses my forehead before standing and walking to the door without looking back. I lay down against my pillow and sigh. Fuck. Oh, fuck. I'm scared. Not because a demented psycho has me on his radar, although that is a big, damn concern. No, because I recognize look I just viewed in Jem's eyes. Once in mine when I was twelve then in Justin's twenty years later after he lost everything. There's nothing worse in the whole universe than hopelessness. Nothing. Justin saved me from its clutches, then I saved him, at least temporarily. If there is a God in heaven please give me the strength to save Jem. Please.

*

Two things I hate more than anything are being beholden and being an invalid. Thanks to Jordan Ambrose I'm now both. Asshole. I did have a minor concussion and the anesthetic still in my system made me lightheaded so I can barely stand, which meant I had to be observed outside the hospital for at least a day. But even if I was the picture of health, it was three against one in the "Joanna can be alone" vote, so for the foreseeable future I will inhabit the guestroom at Casa Darby. As I'm not a total moron I saw the logic and didn't put up a fight. At least not today. I was released mid-morning and Lexie swung by in her Mercedes to pick us up. I rest in the backseat slumped like a sullen teenager while my parents in front discuss my curfew and rules of the house such as no going out alone or leaving without telling them. Oh, and no food in my room. This should be fun.

We drive to the mansion to pack my bags, pick up Brendan's car, and check the damage to Doris. There are a few paparazzi outside my gate as we pull in. People seem to think I was drunk and fell down. Let them. My PR team will sort it out, and I'll play along. Dobbs must have been listening for the gate because even before we park behind Brendan's Hummer, he steps out. The old man's face falls when he sees me, as Lexie's did before. I haven't looked in the mirror but I know it ain't good. I meet Dobbs halfway to the door.

"Oh, Miss Joanna. I am so sor—"

I hug him. His body stiffens. He must not know what to make of my uncharacteristic PDA. "You didn't do anything wrong. There is nothing to forgive. I'm fine." I release his frail body. "But I am starving, and we have guests. Come on."

Everyone follows me inside. Dobbs retires to the kitchen to fix me a sandwich while the heroes and I go assess the damage. The living room bears no signs of the night before. Dobbs must have cleaned up the broken glass. I was worried I'd be apprehensive, possibly even have a panic attack, but feel nothing. Yippee, I can live in my home without losing my marbles.

I open the fireplace and down we go into what easily could have been my crypt. Still no strangeness. I suppose after having a subway collapse around you and almost plunging to your death, someone inviting themselves over for a chat and putting me to sleep isn't high on the horror scale. The only sign of my assault is the faint bloodstain on the concrete. Dobbs must have spent an hour on his hands and knees scrubbing. It'll never fully come out. Maybe I'll put down a carpet or rug. Something gray and depressing to match the rest of the room.

"Looks intact," I say after I boot up Doris to run a diagnostic. "I'm still going to call Lizard to check for viruses. We shouldn't use her until then." I twirl around to face my friends.

"And what about the warehouses? I don't want to pull up the uplink now."

"I'll do a fly-by on my way back from practice," Brendan says. "I've actually gotta go. You got this?" he asks Lexie.

"We can manage."

"Okay." He kisses his wife's cheek before turning to me. "You gonna be okay?"

"Yeah. Thank you. For everything. For finding me, staying with me, you know."

"Of course." He puts his arm around my shoulders and rubs my arm up and down. "You're family now." He releases me and kisses his wife. "See you later, babe. Be safe."

"Love you," Lexie says.

With a grin, Brendan strolls off to live his normal life. I miss having one of those. My own house isn't even safe anymore. "Fucker took us out of commission," I say. "We gotta get back up quick. I'll call—"

"Uh, you will do nothing. At least not today."

"He chose to surface yesterday for a reason. He probably has something huge planned and needed Doris out of pocket."

"Maybe, but that isn't our main concern right now. You are. You're in his crosshairs."

"I have been for over a month. We just happen to know it now."

"Regardless," she says, "we are going home, and you are resting. Doctor's orders. Come on. I'll physically carry you out of this house if I have to."

"But—"

"That was also doctor's orders. I mean it. Let's get your clothes and get the hell out of here. This place always gives me the creeps. Don't know how the hell you live here."

I'm too tired to put up much of a struggle. I need a shower too. Still have blood in my hair. I follow Lexie up and out, the fireplace shutting itself five seconds later. "How long do you think I'll be staying with you guys?"

"Until we catch the asshole."

"Then what?" I ask.

"Up to him. Personally…I hope to kill the son of a bit—"

The all too familiar sound of an explosion toward the front of the mansion shocks us both almost out of our shoes. What the…? Oh God. We stand slack jawed for a second before glancing at one another and sprinting out of the room. Dobbs is already at the front door, about to open it, when Lexie reaches him. The moment the door opens, a gust of scorching air assaults us. This doesn't stop Lexie for a moment. I'm the last out just as Lexie lets out a bloodcurdling scream.

Oh, God. No.

Brendan's Hummer is engulfed in flames with the driver's side completely destroyed. Black smoke curls up to the sky like a pitch black snake. The smell of burning human flesh causes me to gag. Lexie starts shrieking, "Brendan, Brendan," and starts toward the inferno, but Dobbs has the wherewithal to grab her by the shoulders to stop her. "No, Mrs. Darby. No. He's gone. He's gone."

He's right. Inside the flames, I can see a smoking arm still holding onto the steering wheel with nothing attached, and even that burns into nothing but dust. Obliterated. Gone. Not even he could have survived this. Lexie crumples to the ground, folding in on herself as she gasps for air. Tears fill my stinging eyes as I join her down there. He's done it. He's destroyed the Triumvirate. The King is dead. And God save us all.

Chapter Fourteen

The End

I seem to be hosting a Priority Homicide reunion in my living room. Past and present colliding. The gang's all here: Kowalski, Mirabelle, Cam, and this homicide is such a priority even Harry's left his office to pitch in. And by pitch in I mean shoot me worried glances as he bosses the others around. They've been here half an hour and besides saying hello and hugging me the guys have left Lexie, Dobbs, and me alone as they process the scene in my driveway. Good thing too because Lexie is almost catatonic, and I have no idea what to say let alone do next. I just want to crawl into my bed and yank the covers over my head until this is all over.

"Mr. Dobbs," Mirabelle says as he steps away from Harry whose taken position by the fireplace. "Will you please come into the other room so I may take your statement?"

Dobbs glances at me, and I nod. "Yes, sir."

As they leave, Cam and Harry move toward the couch where I sit with Lexie. "Joanna?" Harry asks. "You look like you could use some fresh air. Come outside with me?"

I glance at a red-eyed Lexie for approval, but she just stares down at the shreds of the tissue in her hand. She's beyond caring about anything now. I'm almost there too. Almost. Don't have that luxury now. My turn to be the strong one. I stand and step toward Cam, whispering, "She had nothing to do with this. Go easy on her." My old partner nods. I squeeze his large bicep and walk over to Harry. "Fresh air would be great."

Harry half smiles and gestures toward the sliding glass doors. The air is less than fresh when I step outside with the stench of smoke and Brendan still lingering. Harry shuts the door as I sit at the patio table. My ex doesn't move from the door, he just stares at me with a mixture of anger and concern. As if anyone ever gazes at me any differently.

"Is your life in danger?" he asks, voice hard.

"Yes," I say without hesitation.

"You were in the hospital last night. Did someone attack you?"

"Yes."

"Was it the same person who killed Brendan Darby?"

"I assume so. Yes."

"Is that person Emperor Cain?"

"Yes."

Harry blinks furiously as he processes this. "And I assume Darby was—"

"King Tempest. Yes."

"And his wife is—"

"Lady Liberty."

Harry nods as he deeply inhales and exhales. He does this when he's angry. *Very* angry. It happened a lot when we were an item. "Jesus Christ, Joanna. What the hell am I supposed to do with this?"

"Not a clue."

Harry takes another deep breath probably in an attempt not to throttle me before sitting across from me. "What the hell were you thinking? After last year—"

"I don't need a lecture, Harry. I know it all. The fact is, I'm in this situation now. The question is how do we proceed from here?"

"You leave town."

"He's an international criminal. He can find me anywhere."

Harry's face falls as he comes to a realization. "You know who he is, don't you?" I keep my mouth shut. His anger overtakes concern. "Jesus Christ, Joanna! The man killed twenty-seven people not even a week ago. He's a fucking terrorist, and you know his real identity?"

"I can't tell, okay? It will ruin a good man's life if I did. Besides, I have the most sophisticated computer system around searching for him along with the best crime fighters on the planet doing the same. He changes his appearance, his name, everything. You wouldn't find him."

He falls back in his chair. "And how dare you not give us the chance? What happened to you? You haven't even been off the force for a year. You used to be true police."

"But I'm not anymore. I'm doing the best with what I got."

"Well, your best apparently isn't good enough, Jo. You gotta trust me here. You used to."

"I still do. Of course I do." I stare at my old boyfriend, my old mentor, my friend and sigh. We need all the help we can get. "I will tell you everything I can." I take him through almost all that I know leaving out only his real name and connection to Jem. It's not my secret to tell.

"I want everything you have. All the files, all the footage, *everything*," he demands.

"Okay."

"I have to give it to the Feds. I'll say it came from a CI."

"Do whatever you have to. But what about Brendan? Paparazzi were outside when it happened."

"We tell the truth. We suspect Cain put a car bomb in Brendan Darby's car. If your new friends want to elaborate, we will. But don't be naive. People *will* figure it out."

"I know, but it's up to them to go public. I probably shouldn't have told you as much as I have."

"It's good you did. You're only three people, I have access to hundreds. We'll check out the properties on the list. Discretely." I nod. "I'd feel better if we put you in protective custody."

"And place good police in the line of fire to shield me? Hell no. I'll be fine. If he wanted me six feet under, I'd be there." I rise from the table. "I'll e-mail you the files as soon as I know the computer's clean."

Cam is still interviewing Lexie when I step in. "...if I knew, I'd tell you," she snaps.

"You might as well tell him. I already did," I say.

My old partner and new one stare at me with equally puzzled expressions. Lexie realizes what I mean, face contorting with anger. "You did *what*?"

"I trust these men with my life. Literally. They're in this now. You said it was need to know, they need to know. They'll keep it close. They're on our side. They can help us, and we sure as fuck need it."

"What exactly did you tell him?"

"Everything they *needed* to know. The warehouses, Lee Harper, Ryder, all the way back to the explosives theft. He already figured out who you and Brendan were because he knew I was working with you."

"What the hell is going on?" Cam asks Harry.

"Let's step into the hall," Harry says to Cam. "I'll fill you in."

Cam glances at Lexie before departing to pow-wow, leaving me with a woman on the verge of a nervous breakdown. "I'm sorry," I say. "I didn't know what else to do. Harry already pieced it together. He probably won't be the only one. It's only a matter—"

"Shut up," she hisses. "Shut the fuck up you stupid bitch." All of a sudden my friend leaps up, bridging the gap between us, the menace on her face intensifying with each step. "How did he know? *How did he know*, Joanna? Years. The three of us have been together for years. We were careful. He never figured it out until today. Until *you*. I know it wasn't in the computer. Couple minutes with you then a few hours later my husband's dead? *Brendan Darby* is dead, not King Tempest. So how long did it take for you to give us up? One minute? Two?"

"You think I told him? He didn't even ask me about the two of you. And even if he did, I wouldn't say shit. I don't know how he knew, but it didn't come from me."

"Yeah. Right." She sneers at me before turning her back and stalking out of the room. Just as she reaches the door, she spins back around. "Oh, and when you see Jem, tell him I told him so. Tell him next time he's face to face with his brother, he damn well better make sure that fucker stays dead, or I'll kill them. Both." She walks out without looking back.

As I stare at the spot she inhabited, I slowly lower myself onto the couch, clutching my clenched, churning stomach. I think Cain just succeeded in tearing apart the Royal Triumvirate right when we need them most. I'll bet wherever that son of a bitch is he's popping the champagne, toasting to his victory. I hope the bastard chokes on it. And he will when I get my hands on him.

He may have drawn first blood, but I won't settle for anything but a bucketful.

*

Lizard can't come over for a few days to fix Doris but walks me through the virus scanners and firewalls over the phone. There was one Trojan horse and a worm, whatever those are, but I killed them with Lizard's help. Still, I'm hesitant to use her. Besides those treats, I find that Cain deleted all the files on himself, the explosives case, and cut the feed to the warehouses. Back to square one in that regard, but in the grand scheme of things he did minimal damage. *That* worries me.

The police and CSI techs still work out front three hours later with the press clamoring at the gate, recording every second. My PR machine is grinding overtime with my hospitalization and the blown up footballer in my driveway. For my part I don't intend to leave the house or speak to anyone until the funeral. If I'm even invited. I texted Lexie half a dozen times but no reply. If anyone knows what she's going through, it's me. I can actually help in this situation. If she'll let me.

I used up my remaining brain cells working on Doris so complex thought is hard. Every time I try to figure out why he came here, how he knew about Brendan, it's like I'm banging into a glass door. I can see the answer but can't quite reach it. I should just crawl into bed and watch shit TV until I fall asleep, but I can't bring myself to leave this room. It'd be as if I'd given up. Two crimes in less than twenty-four hours against a specific group, obviously related, but did the first spurn the second? Had to. Too big a coincidence otherwise. Was there a clue to his real identity in Doris I never saw? Did he already suspect and Brendan showing up just pushed those suspicions over the edge? Hell, does it fucking matter anymore?

Yes. I'm still in danger. Lexie too. I just have the distinct feeling that if I crack this, I'll finally be on the right path to—

Footsteps. Beach entrance. Just as I turn, the exact person I want to see steps into the room. Dear God, he looks terrible, even worse than last night with hair a rat's nest, cheeks ruddy from the cold, and plaid shirt untucked. I didn't think he'd ever set foot in here again. I was worried he'd receive the news and just fly, away never to be heard from again. Or dive off the hospital roof. I tried texting and leaving messages with no reply. I didn't realize how petrified I really was something happened to him until just now when I know he's okay. The knot in my stomach dissolves. "Jem," I say, almost breathless.

"I-I was in my lab. I-I-I just heard. What—"

"Oh, Jem," I say, voice cracking. I stand and rush over, throwing my arms around him. "I'm sorry. I'm so sorry."

He doesn't hug me back, doesn't move at all until he pulls me off him and takes a step away. "What happened?"

"Car bomb. Brendan's Hummer. I don't know how he knew, Jem. I don't know how he figured it out. I didn't say a word, I swear on Justin's grave I didn't."

"I know."

"It doesn't make sense. I said Brendan was coming over because we were having an affair. He wasn't in costume, he didn't fly me out, he was just…Brendan Darby. I'm missing something. What did I do wrong? How did I slip up? I-I—"

"This is in no way, shape, or form your fault. It—"

"It's not yours either," I cut in. "I swear it's not."

"I think Lexie would disagree with you." He gazes down. "How is she?"

"Devastated. Scared. Pissed. At you, at me, at life. I'd give her a few days before you reach out."

"I'll take whatever she needs to give me. I deserve it. Everything I touch, *everything*, I damage. Destroy. My best friend is dead. No matter your viewpoint, if I hadn't come into your lives, you wouldn't have been attacked. Lexie would still have her husband, and Brendan wouldn't be in a body bag right now. You'd all be better off."

Dear God. I am having a massive dose of déjà vu. It's as if I'm back at Rebecca's funeral in a church office standing across from Harry, except in this case I'm Harry. Almost those exact same words spewed from my mouth then. The guilt was so heavy inside, I was a millisecond from being flattened by it. If Jem feels half of what I did then, my heart breaks for him.

"Okay. I'm not gonna lie. I won't sugarcoat it. Would I have been in the hospital last night if we weren't in each other's lives? No. He attacked me because of you." Jem's face contorts into agony before turning away. I touch his cheek and move his eyes back to mine. "Hey. Let me finish." I remove my hand from his tense face. "You come with baggage. More than most even. But I'm still here. Brendan would be too. He and Lexie were for years. They put their lives on the line for you time and time again. So ask yourself: why? We know the risks. Been though them firsthand with the scars to prove it. So why don't we go running for the hills?"

"Why?"

I reach for his hand and stare into his beautiful blue eyes. "Simple checks and balances, genius. Because you're worth it." I entwine my fingers with his. "And I can't speak for the Darby's, not really, but...you brought *me* back to life. You," I roll my moist eyes, "I don't know, restored my faith that good things are possible in this God awful world. You gave me hope. That's...worth a psychopath or two in your life. And I don't know about you, but I'd rather have a year of brilliant than ten of just okay. And you, sir, are *brilliant*. *Never* doubt that for a moment."

We stare into each other's eyes, his searching to see if I'm full of shit, determined to prove I am. I'm fighting through a lifetime of hell, of self-doubt, of dysfunction, anger, and self-hatred. But I just need one crack in the wall, one tiny pinpoint through the mortar. When I see a small smile crossing his face, sad though it may be, I know I've succeeded. I've won. I step into him, folding his arms around my body before doing the same to him. I've never been a hugger or physically affectionate in any way, but I can't stop touching this man. He just brings the tenderness out of me. Never thought it possible. *Never*.

"You're brilliant too," he whispers.

"Only around you."

Shit. The mood is destroyed as Doris starts beeping to let me know someone's calling for a video chat. I've only used that feature once or twice before, so I don't know who could possibly have the number. We break apart and look at Doris, then one another. I have a feeling I should take this call. Jem sidesteps out of view of the webcam as I move to the computer. I pull up the tracking system in case it really is who I think it is before I accept the call.

"Motherfucker."

"Hello to you too, Miss Fallon," Jordan says onscreen. "Looking well."

The villain sits in what looks like an office with bookcases, file cabinets, and I believe a map slightly out of shot. Nothing distinguishable to allow me to glean where he is. And least he resembles his brother less than yesterday with his hair slicked back and fleece sweatshirt sans glasses. It's still eerie, same face and all.

"Go fuck yourself, psycho."

"Charming. You attempt to kiss my brother with that mouth?" He moves his head to my left. "Has she, Jem? Tried to kiss you?"

"He's not here," I say.

Jordan raises an eyebrow. "You were a far better liar yesterday. I know he's there."

"How?"

"That's for me to know and you to find out." He gazes past me again. "You hiding under your girlfriend's skirts now, big brother?"

"She's not my girlfriend," Jem says harshly behind me.

"Oh, thank God for that. From all I've uncovered in my research, she's something of a whore. Cheating on her boyfriend, an abortion at fifteen, sleeping with a married man. Oh, forgive me, that last one was total malarkey wasn't it? Or not. She does have a thing for superheroes. You do battle a little above your weight class a lot, don't you Jojo? I did warn you about that."

"Leave her alone," Jem says, walking beside me.

"*I* didn't bring her into this, big brother. You knew this would happen eventually. You're just selfish. Selfish, selfish, selfish. And weak. Always have been. Sad, pathetic, weak, in—"

"Wow, pot meet fucking kettle there, Jordan," I say with a sneer.

"Pardon me?"

"Joanna…" Jem warns.

"You heard me. *He's* the sad, selfish, pathetic one? You follow him around the country throwing hissy fits when you don't have his undivided attention. Sad. You killed his fiancée because he liked her better than you. Selfish. You have no real life outside him. Pathetic. But let's not forget to add coward to your list of more admirable traits. I mean, really. A car bomb? What, were you too afraid to be within ten miles of Tempest, is that it? Because you knew he'd kick your ass without breaking a sweat?"

"Jem, leash your bitch please," Jordan says, rolling his eyes. "Her yapping is grating."

"Not hearing a denial asshole."

"Joanna, stop," Jem orders.

"Yes, he can fight his own battles. He doesn't need *your* help."

"What do you want, Jordan?" Jem says before I can speak. "Really. *What do you want?*"

"Peace on earth and goodwill toward men?" he retorts with a smirk. "No, I suppose I don't really desire a thing. I'm quite content actually. I just found myself with some time on my hands. You know I've never handled boredom well."

"Then take up fucking fishing," I snap.

"Shut up, whore. You know, car bombs are cheap. One down, two more—"

"Enough!" Jem shouts. Both our mouths snap shut. The peacemaker takes a deep breath before looking back at his brother. "Scout, *please*, whatever you want me to do to stop this, I will. Whatever it is, I will do it, just don't hurt anyone else."

Jordan cocks an eyebrow at the prospect. "Really? If I told you to rob a bank, you would?"

"Yes."

"Give all your money away?"

"Yes."

"Jump off the highest building to your death to save them?" he asks, glimpsing at me.

"Absolutely," he says without hesitation.

It's only for a split second, and I don't know if Jem sees it as well, but like lightning a ripple of intense fury crosses his face, eyes blazing and nose twitching. Shit. Not what he wanted to hear. Jordan recovers with a smile. "I have no idea where this nobility comes from. Certainly not our sperm and ovum donors or those not-so-well-meaning morons who raised us."

"Guess he's just a better, stronger person than you," I say. "He didn't use his crappy childhood as an excuse to become a terrorist."

Jordan rolls his eyes again. "Yes, we get it, Joanna; you're madly in love with him. Won't have a harsh word spoken against him. So on and so forth. Hurrah for loyalty. But do shut up now."

For the first time in a long time I'm stunned speechless. "I'm not...I..."

"Finally," Jordan says. "If you ever do enter into a relationship with that thing I suggest investing in ear plugs or a muzzle. At least your last love interest had some class and knew when to keep her mouth shut. Even when I blew her head off, she managed to die silently."

"Don't talk about her," Jem warns.

"Why not? It was years ago, you must be over it by now. If you're not over a past lover then how can you ever move on?" He looks at me. "Really, Joanna, he is a loyal sort. He waited years after our sexual relationship ended before he entered into another with that Indian cow."

"Shut up," Jem says through gritted teeth.

"I never did ask. Was she better than me? Did she make you come as hard as I did? Do you still imagine it's my hand jerking you off on all those lonely nights—"

"SHUT UP!" Jem roars with insane ferocity. Even I shrink away, especially when he grabs the chair beside me and smashes it against the monitor. I leap out of my seat away from the onslaught. "Shut up!" He hits it again. "Shut up!" And again. "Shut up!" And again, until there's nothing left to demolish but shards of glass and plastic. He tosses the chair across the room and takes off running toward the ocean exit.

At first I'm too shocked to move. I just stare at the sparks shooting from the exposed wires. He actually did something I didn't think possible. He scared me. But I push it away and sprint after him. "Jem!" The passageway is dark with the only light from a bulb on the stone every ten feet. Jem has just reached the exit when I round the corner. He presses the button to open the cavern door onto to beach. "Jem, wait! Goddamn it, you wait for me Jonathan Ambrose!"

He reluctantly ceases moving and pulls his hand away from outside as if the waning sun would scald him. He doesn't turn around, just hangs his head like a man who has given up. When I reach him, I try to touch his arm, but he jerks it away and spins around, face scrunched up as if I were attacking him. "Don't touch—don't touch me. Please, just..." he whimpers. Despite his protests, I grab him by the collar and wrench him into my arms. I squeeze him as tight as possible in case he attempts to escape. He breathes heavily, the spurts hot against my hair, but when he realizes I'm not letting go, the pace lessens. I feel tears sprinkling into my hair. He raises his arms, lowers them again as he reconsiders, but does hug me back. "I can't take this anymore. I just can't," he whispers. His chest heaves against mine as if he's sprinted around the planet. "What-What he sai—" His voice cracks, choking off the rest of the words.

"You were young. You were scared. All you had was him. Whatever happened, happened. I don't need to know any more. And I don't think any less of you. I'm just *so* sorry that happened to you." I pull away enough to wipe the tears streaming from his eyes. "I'm so sorry," I whisper.

He presses my hand against his cheek with his own and closes his eyes to savor the tangibility of it, breathing heavily as my compassion, my lust, my hunger nourish him. When those eyes fly open his breath stops, and he stares at me with laser sharp focus. Before I can say another word, his lips are on mine with enough force our teeth collide. His tongue enters my mouth as insatiable as the rest of him. As the rest of me. His zeal infects me. We grow enflamed as only fear, death, and desperation can stoke. I return his ardor stroke for stroke. I crash against the stone wall as he backs me against it. Using that to brace me, I lift my legs up to wrap around his waist. Though there are two pairs of pants separating us the heat of him pressing into me almost makes me lose my mind. I think I very nearly do as his hands move under my shirt and bra. He's not gentle either, instead squeezing and pinching in all the right places. I let out a pained moan, and the hands vanish along with his lips.

When I open my eyes he's staring up at me, unblinking with sad wonderment. I want to ask what's wrong but those eyes terminate further thought. Awe transforms into terror, then anguish. We gape at one another for a tense moment before he breathlessly croaks, "I lov..." but nothing else comes. Like a man who has just cheated on his wife for the first time, he's disgusted by what he's done, mouth twisting into a sneer and nose wrinkling up. "I can't do this. I shouldn't have done that. I'm sorry."

My feet drop to the ground as he springs away. "Jem..."

He retreats backwards. "Ju-Just stay away from me. I can't..." he whimpers again and presses his temples with the palms of his hands as if the voices were yelling at him. He lowers them and once again on the verge of tears says, "I'm sorry. I'm so sorry."

And he takes off like a rocket out and into the bright blue sky. Shit. This one step up two steps back is making me exhausted. I just hope the dance hasn't ended for good. I still have a few twirls left in me.

Chapter Fifteen

Cockroach Psychology

Abandoned and alone. Why do superheroes always leave me abandoned and alone? Dozens of messages to Lexie and Jem left unanswered. Everyone else on the planet has phoned, reporters mostly. I can't even leave the house anymore without them following. They've been parked on the street and inundating me with calls for days. The theories are running as rampant as the gossip, quite a few even coming close to the truth. I've "no commented" until my tongue is sore, barely left the mansion except to go into the office where I locked myself in all day. I hate to admit it but I think I'm afraid to go outside or climb in a car. The first time I had to drive, I popped the hood and checked under the seats and undercarriage for bombs. Even still took five minutes of willing myself in a cold sweat to turn the key. Hasn't gotten much better in the passing days. Hell even inside the office and home I'm on high alert. The house creaks, and I damn near yelp. It's hard waiting for a hammer to drop on my head. Calling a genius psychopath a pussy might not have been the smartest move I've ever made.

The self-imposed tension has gotten so thick I can't even focus on my real work for the past five days. All the monitors were destroyed and Lizard, when he finally agreed to come over, wiped the hard drive and had to re-install all the programs and backed up information. Took days. We did upgrade the monitors to state-of-the-art touch screens. While he was pimping my ride, I spent the time attempting to wrap my head around how Cain discovered the truth about Brendan. And in my hours of contemplation I've come up with nothing. Zip. I thought my affair explanation was pretty damn believable considering that rumor was already swirling around town. From what I've gleaned after interrogating Dobbs, there was nothing super heroic in his finding me and getting me to the hospital. No superpowers displayed at all.

Something else nags at me during my sleepless nights. That video call. It was too…on point, time wise. Jordan could have a tracker on Jem or someone watching the ocean exit from a boat and knew when he arrived here. Possible but not probable. Jem would have considered those possibilities and taken the necessary precautions. Five days and nights of working all the angles with nothing to show. I'm missing something important, something Jordan said or did when he was here that will blow the confusion away. It hasn't happened yet. But I do have a Hail Mary pass up my sleeve. After all I did promise to call him, and my word is my bond no matter how much that promise turns my stomach.

I've only allotted twenty minutes for this torture. Memorial to get to and all. I've been to far too many in the past year. One expects to attend five funerals in a year when in your eighties, not at thirty-three. I wasn't officially invited but decided to fly to Independence anyway. Even if Lexie turns me away at the church door at least she'll know I put forth the effort.

I sit at the new and improved Doris to wait for the call. I'm not as nervous as last time. Guess there's a new monster under my bed to fill my nightmares. He won't like that. I must make sure to tell him.

The video chat music begins tinkling, and I accept. Ryder sits on the other end looking exactly the same as last week: cheerful and handsome despite his pasty skin and need of a shave. His smile drops a little when he sees me.

"Oh, my. You look dreadful."

"You're one to talk, vampire Grizzly Adams."

"I was expressing genuine concern, Joanna," he says snidely. If he were capable of feelings, I'd think I just bruised his. "You're obviously under considerable stress. Not sleeping? You haven't become a wino again, have you?"

"No." Came close a few times, but my sponsor talked me down. "Things have gotten a lot more heated with Cain, that's all."

"Was my information useful?"

"Yeah, but then he attacked me and…got the upper hand."

Ryder's face falls. "I'm sorry, Joanna." He pauses. "He didn't violate you, did he?"

"No, he's not a rapist, unlike some," I say with venom I can't contain.

"Excuse me, I've only committed the act once, and it had to do with principals, not sexual deviance."

"And that makes it okay?"

His mouth remains shut for a few seconds. "I don't like where this conversation is headed. You're growing angry. Let's try and keep this as pleasant as possible, alright? Despite what you may think, I don't want to add to your apparently mountainous troubles."

"Forgive me if I find that a little difficult to believe."

"Understandable. But you're a smart girl. Consider my motives for speaking to you. Boredom. Access to Grace. If I piss you off, they won't be serviced. Besides, I never had anything against *you*. As with Dr. Thornton and her progeny, you were a means to an end. In fact I hold you in quite high regard. I truly do. I know you hate me, and not without cause, and I blackmailed you into these calls, but I don't want this to be torturous for you. I'll remain on my best behavior if you will. Agreed?"

I roll my eyes. "Fine."

He settles into his yellow plastic chair. "So. If the Emperor didn't molest you, and you seem intact otherwise, what exactly occurred during your time together?"

"We talked. He made me show him the command center. He knocked me out and installed a few computer viruses."

"That's all?" Ryder asks, surprised.

"As far as we can tell. Why?"

He shrugs. "Just seems a little…light, is all."

"Like I got off easy."

"Exactly. I mean, did he even interrogate you? Attempt to gain the true identities of his sworn enemies? Not to mention the fact he made you privy to the fact he was using your computer. Doesn't that strike you as odd?"

"Of course it does. I mean, I'm not that big a threat, but I am…friendly with them. They would care if I died. In that respect, I'm worth more to him dead than alive. So why the fuck am I alive?"

He considers this for a moment. Who knows what a cockroach is thinking better than his brethren? "From what I know of him, nothing this man does or says is on the fly. It's been planned, rehearsed, then planned and rehearsed again for every contingency. I'm the same, all of the legends are," he says with a smile. I roll my eyes again. "Everything done has an endgame. For example, why do you think I killed Dr. Thornton first?"

"Shock value? Easier prey? She and Daisy were the most important to Justin?"

"Are you a poker player, Joanna?"

"No."

"I am. A good poker player works the odds. He knows the cards and often uses simple addition and subtraction to determine what the most likely outcome is. A *great* poker player more or less ignores the cards. He plays the players."

"I see prison has turned you into a Zen master."

"I do have nothing to do but meditate, but no, you're missing my point. He can work the odds, sure, but in the end it all comes down to the people around the table. Our player has done his homework. He's determined the other player's psychology, quirks, etc. as the game wears on."

"What does this tutorial have to do with Rebecca and Daisy?"

"You were right. Part of the reason I disposed of them first was for the shock. To all of you. The act sent all my players into a panic, exactly as I anticipated. That was the face value, but ask yourself, what did the Thorntons really signify to Justice?"

"Love. Family. Hope for the future."

"Justin Pendergast was a rich, dashing man who due to his orphaned state craved a family. Their deaths were a tragedy, no doubt, but in the end they were replaceable. Pretty faces are a dime a dozen. And supplemental. *Justice* was his real self, Justin Pendergast was the front. And to Justice, *you* were the lynchpin to his destruction. The living, breathing, cussing embodiment of all his sacrifices and the importance of his life."

I want to protest but can't open my mouth.

"I knew all about your mutual history through Grace, who continued the research during my first unfortunate incarceration. I knew you were the first person he rescued so soon after his father's death. I knew that you were in love with him, and he was oblivious. I also knew you had no idea of his alter ego. Logically, with my maelstrom swirling, that tidbit would have to be revealed. And when it was, and you loathed him to your very core, I pounced before you could forgive him. Well, tried anyway."

"How did you know when I found out?"

"Multiple avenues. One, I knew you brought Logan in. Then my surveillance team followed you to the mansion, then the apartment where I heard you venting to your then boyfriend."

I blink. "Wait. You bugged my apartment?"

"Of course. Yours and Rebecca's houses had surveillance cameras. We attempted to hide some in the mansion but the butler was always there, so we settled for Justin's office and phones. So, with all this intel, I could plan, rehearse, adapt, and plan again. *This* is what you're up against, Joanna dear. And Cain's IQ reportedly topples even mine. I do not envy you."

"So, what should I do?"

"Only one thing to do." He pauses. "Pray."

I sit in silence for a few seconds staring at the monster who demolished my life and feel...nothing. "I have to go. Plane to catch."

"My meeting with Grace?"

"Working on it."

"Thank you. I do hope I was helpful. Really."

"You were." The words stick in my throat, but I say, "Thank you."

"Just keep in mind what his endgame is and do your best to circumvent it. Might give you a chance."

"I will. See you next week." And the pieces finally fit. I was right. One cockroach just helped me figure out the other.

After jotting down a quick note, and slipping it in my pocket, I rise from the chair. I find Dobbs in the kitchen wiping the counters. "Hello, Miss Joanna. Ready for the airport?"

I move beside him. "Almost," I say, covertly palming him the note. He reads the paper with confusion, and then shakes his head to answer no. Still. "I wanted to borrow that book for the flight. Is it in your room?" I ask, eyes jutting toward the door.

"Yes. Come with me," he says. I follow him through the other kitchen door into his apartment. Like the rest of the house, it's filled with antiques and faded red carpet. I shut the door behind myself. "What is going on, Miss Joanna?"

"I know you said Cain didn't enter the kitchen, but we should be careful. He didn't come in here, did he?"

"No. I was in here the majority of his stay. I know he was upstairs for a time as we spoke when he was descending the stairs. He said he was using the bathroom, which I found odd as he had a satchel with him at the time, but you know all this."

"Do you know anywhere else specifically he went?"

"Just the living room, but I didn't watch him. He had free reign of the house."

Wonderful. "Okay, I need you to walk me through what happened after he left again."

"I heard the front door shut about thirty minutes after you arrived home. I thought you two had gone to dinner as he claimed. Perhaps two hours later, Mr. Darby was at the gate. I let him in and told him you were at dinner with Dr. Ambrose. He appeared shocked by this, but wanted to use the computer regardless. Five minutes after that, he began screaming for me. He had you on the couch in the living room attempting to revive you. The ambulance arrived ten minutes after that, and I escorted them in. Mr. Darby told them he found you out on the patio, then went with you to the hospital."

"So Brendan was the one who found me in the secret room? You didn't open the fireplace for him?"

"No."

And pop goes the weasel. I scoff and shake my head. Of course. "He bugged the house."

"I'm sorry?"

"Cain put cameras and listening devices all over the house. He saw Brendan walk right up to the secret switch, which he shouldn't have known about if he were only my secret lover. Cain put two and two together."

That's also how he knew the exact moment to call when I was comforting Jem. I was ruining the impact of the execution. He couldn't have that. Crap, I have to wade through five days of actions and speech to figure out how much I gave away. Oh God, did he or his cronies watch me undress?

"What do we do? Find and disconnect them?" Dobbs asks.

The gears in my mind turn and turn for a few seconds. "No, not yet. For right now, act normal, but do cancel the cleaners until I say so. I don't want one of them to stumble on a camera and say something. Just keep your eyes open, and assume there's surveillance in every room. Patio too. He probably also tapped all the phones so be careful there as well." I check my watch. "Shit, we have to go. Just…act normal. I'll figure out what to do."

I walk out of his room and even though he said Jordan never came into the kitchen, it's as if I can feel his eyes on me. As I make my way up the stairs to my bedroom, the wheels keep spinning. For the first time since this ordeal began, I think we have the upper hand. The question is how to effectively use it.

Time to play the player.

*

I'm not turned away at the cathedral door, probably not because my name is on the list but because the press behind the barriers instantly recognize me and go into frenzy.

"Were you and Brendan Darby having an affair?"

"Are you working with the Triumvirate?"

And my favorite. "Did you kill Brendan Darby like Justin Pendergast because he was about to end your love affair?"

I keep my eyes down and mouth shut before being waved into the church by security..

I estimate about three hundred mourners milling around the pews, aisles, and the picture of Brendan in his Independence Eagles uniform surrounded by flowers, some arranged to resemble footballs or helmets near the pulpit. Members of both the Eagles and Galilee Angels are chatting with each other, old rivalries forgotten for the day. You can always tell the players by how wide they are. There's a cluster up front forming a semi-circle around a person in the front pew. Though her back is to me, judging from the dark hair, it's Lexie. Another group is on the opposite pew talking to a large man with red hair and tiny woman in a black hat. The parents. I wonder if they knew about King Tempest. If they're proud of him. They should be.

As I scan the crowd I don't see any other familiar faces, but they all seem to know me. Everywhere I look people keep glancing at me then whispering to their companions. Almost a thousand miles from home and I'm still the talk of the town. I ignore them. All I care about is finding that one familiar face. He might not attend out of respect to Lexie and the near cracked secret between them. But if it was my best friend, I'd want to be surrounded by the others who loved him too. For closure too or the beginnings of it. Why else do we hold funerals? They aren't for the dead person, that's for sure.

I sweep the cathedral twice and don't find him. Damn it. Okay, might as well get this over with. Making sure the letter I wrote on the plane asking her to meet later is folded and concealed in the palm of my hand, I maneuver down the aisle toward the widow. I sense at least over a hundred pairs of eyes moving with me. Probably waiting for a catfight. Lexie's parents notice me first, both sets of brown eyes narrowing. She takes after her father with the same dark hair and mouth. Lexie sees me a second later, her expression matching that of her parents' the moment she does. I don't know whether to hug her or run.

"Lexie," I say.

"Joanna," she says with little affect. "Thank you for coming."

"I…" I don't know what to say. Nothing. I just extend the hand with the note to her. "I'm sorry. For your loss."

She glances at my hand with derision, but shakes it anyway, retrieving the note. Her nose twitches when paper hits skin, but there's no other reaction. "Thank you."

I nod and amble away. That went better than anticipated. Now hopefully she'll read the letter, realize she's angry at the wrong people, and rejoin us. I choose a pew at the very back to watch those who enter, but the one I want to arrive doesn't. Stupid respectful bastard. Ten minutes after I arrive, the priest takes his position behind the pulpit and people sit. As the priest begins his sermon, my nervous tension raises a notch. I thought for sure he'd be here. I *need* him to be here.

The sermon is short and sweet. Time for the eulogies. Brendan's brother Martin is first. He speaks of their growing up in the suburbs of Jericho and happy afternoons playing football. Poor Martin breaks down in the middle of the speech and takes a few seconds to collect himself. God, I hate funerals so fucking much. I start wiggling around in my seat like a Mexican Jumping Bean. I can't stop it. The people around me keep glaring. I would too. Rudeness should be frowned upon. Yeah, this was a bad idea. I did what I came to do. I can leave now before I have a freak out as I did at the last two funerals I've attended.

I wait until Martin finishes so as not to been seen as completely rude, and while the priest announces the next eulogizer, I get up and make my way down the pew. More glares follow. When I reach the large reception area, also filled with flowers and pictures of Brendan, I take a deep breath. I lasted longer that I thought I would.

Quick movement to my left of the lobby draws my attention. I knew it. I'd recognize that thin frame and dark hair anywhere. He's rushing down the hall toward the side exit. He must have been watching the funeral from the door and took off when he saw me get up. I'm right. He turns, sets eyes on me, and quickens his pace. I can't shout in church but I can run. I kick off my heels, pick them up, and take off after him. He's out the door when I'm halfway up. By the time I'm through it too, he's climbing into a cab. A few vultures snap my picture and shout questions, but I plow through them to reach the cab. Just as the car starts moving, I throw open the back door and it comes to a skidding stop.

"Lady, what are you—" the driver says.

"Sorry," I say, out of breath. "Keep driving."

The cabbie glances at Jem. "It's fine." The driver turns back around and pulls away from the curb again. "What are you doing?" Jem whispers. "We shouldn't be seen together."

"I had to talk to you, I'm sorry," I whisper back. "I figured it out."

"What?"

"Your brother. How he learned about our friend. The real reason for his visit. He put cameras and microphones all over my house. He saw our friend enter a room he couldn't have known about."

Jem's silent, then says, "It's logical. Have you removed them yet?"

"I considered it, but…you know what this means, right?" He shakes his head no. "We have the upper hand. He doesn't know we know. We're a step ahead."

He stares at me, eyes slowly narrowing. "You have a plan."

"Hell, yes. Someone very smart and very ruthless reminded me of something. Pride is the deadliest sin of all because those afflicted rarely realize they are. Hubris has taken down many a great man. It's gonna take down your brother too. We've just got to give him exactly what he wants."

"And what is that?" Jem asks with trepidation.

"You, hero." I grin. "*You*. I'm going to destroy your life."

And it's gonna be a hell of a show.

CHAPTER SIXTEEN

CENTER RING

The stage is set, the costumes ready, the cameras are in place, now I simply have to wait for the players. Who are late. If they show up at all. Jem seemed cautiously optimistic this will work, but since he's the one who'll suffer the most, I understand his reluctance to fully commit. Lexie's the wild card. God, please let her show up. Operation Three-Ring Circus needs her.

I'm exhausted. Five hours of flying, a funeral, the realization I'm living in a fishbowl, fear this won't work as planned, it's all caught up with me. I don't even have the energy to change from my funeral clothes. Dobbs drove me home, and I came right downstairs to the lair to "work," pretending to review footage around the church. I've never been much of an actress so even *this* farce is taking a lot out of me. They need to get here before I fall asleep on Doris or run out of fake things to do. I don't know, maybe this whole thing is insane. Cain'll see right through it in five seconds flat. Of course that—

I sense someone staring at me and pivot around in my chair. Jem's still dressed in his clothes from earlier as well. I don't stop my smile. And it's show time. "Jem. You came." I rise. "Thank you."

"Three heads are better than one."

"Oh. Right," I say, sounding a little disappointed. I sit again. "I was just, uh, going over the memorial footage. I don't think he was there today."

"Should you be using the computer?"

"Lizard and I wiped everything. It's safe now."

Jem ambles over, standing close next to me and resting his hand on the back of the chair. I visibly tense and glance at him. "I can review it. If he did come, he would have been in disguise. I'd recognize him before you would."

"Good idea." I click the mouse and rewind the footage. "So, how are you? I didn't get to ask earlier before you kicked me out of your cab."

"Yes, I apologize for being so abrupt. I just didn't want—"

"I know. Keeping your distance in public. I shouldn't have done it." I pause to steal another glimpse of him. "So. How are you?"

"Some days are better than others. I alternate between melancholy and infuriated on an hourly basis. You of all people know how it is when you…lose a best friend. I just, I sincerely hope I didn't lose them both. She is coming, correct?"

"I-I really don't know. I just gave her the note, I didn't see her read it. If she doesn't, then we'll just…come up with something together."

"Yes," he says with little enthusiasm. "Suppose there'd be no other choice."

Once again, I don't hide my displeasure, nose crinkling as if he just shoved literal shit under it instead of emotional shit. "The footage is cued up." I rise and allow him to sit in my place. I take his former position, getting as close as I can without touching him. Jem glances up at me giving me an uncomfortable smile. "Do you think he was there?"

"Possibly. Him or a minion."

"Ryder sent Grace to Rebecca's with a camera in her pin. Jordan might have done the same. He gets to revel in the misery without any of the risk."

"I should have stayed longer. Done my job better. I let my emotions get the better of me."

"It was your best friend's funeral. Of course work wasn't on the forefront of your mind."

He gives me a genuine smile. "Thank you."

"For what?"

"Always knowing the correct thing to say. For not blaming me. For being on my side, even though you shouldn't be."

I force a blush. "Well, Justin always said I was loyal to a fault. I'm only that way when the person's earned it though."

"I'm, uh, honored you count me in the same regard as Justin."

"You're welcome," I say, beaming at him with admiration.

Jem smiles nervously and looks back at the computer. "Um, would you mind getting me some coffee? I, um, want to finish this tonight."

"Of course." Like a dutiful love slave, I totter to the machine and start preparing his coffee. God, please let Lexie show up. I don't know how much longer I can keep up this charade tonight. I return with our coffees. "Here. Just how you like it."

"Thank you," he says with a sip.

After pulling up a chair, I sit next to him to watch the footage. Occasionally, I point to someone who could be Jordan just to make myself relevant while sneaking a coy glance at Jem. After ten minutes of this bullshit I'm getting nervous. She isn't coming. She *needs* to come. The wheels spin in my mind, attempting to think up ways to salvage this. Postpone so I can work on her? We've already begun. Jem meets my glimpse with a concerned one. He's thinking the same thing. She's abandoned us. She has to—

Jem's head whips toward the beach tunnel. I turn just as Lexie, dressed in jeans and a red sweater, steps into view. She stares at us, mouth vice tight. "Well. Aren't you two cozy?" she asks with a sneer.

"Lexie," Jem says breathlessly as he rises.

"You didn't mention he'd be here," she says, ignoring him. She removes the note from her pocket. "Though you didn't say a lot in the note. But I guess its good you're both here. I only have to say this once. *I'm done*."

"Lexie…"

"Shut up, Jem. *You* do not get to talk to me ever again," she says, nostrils flaring. "You are as dead to me as my husband is. He…*we* trusted you. With our lives. And you lied to us! You had him! You knew what he was capable of, and you let him go! This, all of this, is on *you*."

I take a step. "Lexie, stop."

"Oh, shut up Joanna. If you had half a brain, and weren't thinking with your pussy, you'd do what I am and run the fucking other way from him as far and fast as possible. Not concocting harebrained," she crumples the note and tosses it at us, "stupid, fucking schemes to trap a psychopath. Because no matter how much you want him to be Justin, he never will be. Given the choice between you and his brother, you will lose every time. My husband is proof of that."

"Lexie, shut up," I say through gritted teeth while signaling to the computer with my eyes.

"What? Can't handle some down home truth?" Face hard as stone she stalks toward me. Her cold eyes bore into mine. "Well, tough shit. Here it is. You will not win against him," she says, drawing out every word. "You will die. So whatever you're thinking of doing? Don't. It will not work. Run. Just run. Run for your fucking life away from this man. While you still can. Just run and do not look back. I'm not." She wipes a falling tear from her cheek with a trembling hand. My entire body has knotted itself up. "I'm sorry. Good luck." She turns on her heels and starts back the way she came.

With a near panicked expression, Jem glances at me but finds a similar expression. He strides toward Lexie. "Lex, please. We need you. Don't—" He touches her shoulder. Out of nowhere, she pivots around and decks him in the jaw. I gasp as he crashes to the ground.

"Don't touch me! You have no right to touch me!" she shouts.

I dash over to the man. "I'm sorry," he says as I help him up. "I didn't…I'm sorry."

Lexie scoffs, voice cracking. "Not good enough. Nowhere near good enough. But you never were, were you Jem? Not strong enough, not brave enough, and sure as hell not honorable enough. I just wish I'd seen it years ago as clear as I do now."

She takes a step toward the door before I rush in front of her to stop her. "What about Cain?" I whisper. "Don't you want to see him brought to justice? We can't do it without you. Just listen—"

"Don't you get it?" she says, voice breaking with emotion. "You can't do it period, Jo. And even if you could…I'm done. I've given enough. I'm not going out like Justin and Brendan. *I'm not.* Not for you, not for anyone. Keep me out of this." She kisses my cheek. "I'm sorry." And with that she lifts off the ground and flies down the tunnel.

My mouth hangs open from shock. That was…horrible. God awful. I take a moment to compose myself before turning to an equally wide-eyed Jem. "What do we—" he begins.

"Let's get some ice on your jaw," I cut in. "Sit on the couch."

Still a little dazed, he obeys as I get the ice pack out of the first-aid kit. "Just keep going, Jo," I whisper to myself.

Jem cups his jaw and looking at me expectantly when I sit beside him. "What do we—" he whispers.

"Keep going," I whisper back. "Here."

He takes the pack and holds it to the side of his face. "Thank you," he says loudly.

"Are you okay?" I ask.

"It just aches. She didn't—"

"Not what I meant. *Are you okay?*"

"I...understand."

"She didn't mean it. Not really."

"She did. And she's right. If I had just been honest, with them, with myself, we might not be in this untenable situation. Whenever it comes time for me to...vacate him from my life, I can't do it. Maybe I don't *want* to," he admits, voice quaking. "Maybe...deep down...I need him. He's been the one constant in my life. And no matter how many heinous acts he's committed, I can't...believe that little boy who stood up for me, who comforted me, who protected me, is dead. That love came from somewhere. He *has* to still be in there somewhere."

I scoot closer to him and take his free hand. "Jem, I know you want to believe that. I would too. But...Jordan killed that little boy a long time ago. If he ever really existed. Sociopaths are born that way. They cannot change."

"You didn't know him then."

"I know him now. He blew up a bridge with innocent people on it. He put me in the hospital. He murdered your best friend. Uma." I shrug. "And you in a sense. You're the biggest victim of us all. That man tortured you, tormented you, molested you. He's killed you in all but body. He keeps you from happiness. From friendship." I meet his eyes. "From love. Who but a monster would do that?" I caress his good cheek, and he tenses. "But I'll help you stop him. I'm all yours. If you want me."

"Joanna, I—"

My kiss stops his words. I give it my all, but he doesn't kiss me back. His lips remain rigid under mine. After a few seconds I break away, eyes narrowed in confusion. Jem just hangs his head. "What? What is it?" I ask.

"I…don't-don't do that."

"What? Why-why not? No one's here. No one will see us."

"It's not…" He stands. "I should go."

He makes it one step toward the exit before I leap up to block his path. "No. Don't. Please. Don't leave me."

"Joanna, I-I don't want to hurt your feelings."

"What do you mean? Why would you hurt my feelings?"

"Because I don't…share them," he says hesitantly. "I'm sorry."

My face falls. "What? No, you…I've seen the way you look at me. How you are around me. I've *felt* it," I say, agitated.

"No, I-I don't…" He looks horrified, mouth opening and closing like a dying fish. "I'm sorry. You're my friend, without question. I care about you. Very much. I probably wouldn't have gotten through this without you. Really. I value you, *so much*. I just…don't think of you in that way. I'm sorry."

For once having a surplus of rage comes in handy. I unleash the flames. All through me steam practically shoots from my ears as real tears fill my eyes. "What?" I ask, voice cracking again. "No, you…no. You…" I glare at him hard enough to cut diamonds. "What? I'm not *good enough* for you or something?"

"No! No, I…" He tries to touch me, but I recoil.

Vibrating with anger and torment, I take a step away. "*You* don't think *I'm* good enough for you? *I* am the one who has stood by your side through all of this! I-I-I have defended you, lied to people I care about for you, been your support, your rock, and you…" I chuckle and run my hands through my hair as I force a horrible realization into my mind. "I'm never enough, am I? Not pretty enough, not couth enough, not…" I swallow the rest of my words. "Get out."

"Joanna, please. I'm—"

"*Get the fuck out of my house!*" I shriek at the top of my lungs. "Please. Fuck. Go. Just go."

"I'm sorry," he whispers desperately before backing away. Like Lexie before him, he flies out.

Even when he's gone I just stand staring at the spot he was in with such hatred he may as well have been there still. *Bring it home, Jo*. I start shaking my head like there's a rock rattling in there I want out. I thought it would be difficult to cry on cue, but the sorrow's been building for days. I let 'er rip. A blubbering sob escapes, and I cover my mouth to stop them, but they continue on. I crumple on the couch and sob my heart out. For Brendan, for Lexie, for Jem, even for me. Because if this fails, I really will lose him forever. And that really would break my heart beyond repair.

The curtain falls.

*

She's gone. The next day, after the funeral, I take a walk along the beach to see if I can talk to Lexie, but instead of her, I find men boxing up the house and moving furniture into a truck. One of them men tells me she's already left for Independence. I slowly meander the way I came to my house. I hate the place now more than ever. Even in the damn bathroom I swear I can sense his eyes on me. And it's hard being "on" all the time. I've been moping around the house like a less cheery Hamlet, or on occasion snapping at Dobbs or Shannon. I even called my sponsor on my tapped phone. That was actually helpful. If I get through this farce without a real drink, it'll be a miracle. I already had Dobbs fill a whisky bottle with ice tea in case I need a prop. Luckily, I had twenty years experience of heartbreak to draw on for this performance. Method acting at its finest. Hope Cain enjoys the show.

I trudge up the stairs to the mansion, but stop just before I reach the top. Game face. My body becomes slack, my shoulders hunched, and the scowl I've been sporting since Jem fled is plastered to my face. Rejected, depressed, unloved, pissed. Got it. I make my way up to the patio. Pretty sure I've spotted a camera attached to the light fixture. That makes five already. Big bastard brother is watching. I open the sliding glass door, stepping into the living room (camera on the map above the fireplace) where my ex sits watching the news and sipping a cup of coffee. Thank God. Another one I didn't think would show. After all he's swamped trying to catch a terrorist. Little does he know that by coming over today that's exactly what he's doing.

"Shit. Harry. I'm sorry, have you been waiting long?"

"Only five minutes or so."

"Oh. Good." I shrug off my coat and move around to him. "Thanks for coming over. I would have come to the precinct, but I just…" I shrug and scoff as I sit. "Lexie Darby's left town apparently."

"Really? Does that mean—"

"Yeah. Galilee Falls has managed to kill or scare away two more heroes. We're pretty much on our own. Again."

"Oh. Sorry. I know you were all close."

I scoff. "Yeah. Right." I unleash the image of Justin and Rebecca when they announced their engagement into my brain. Still feels like a punch to the gut. "I think I was wrong, Harry."

"I'm sorry?"

"I mean, I *was* right. Before. I've just been wrong the past few months."

"What are you talking about?" Harry asks.

"Superheroes. All those years I despised them. Everyone said I was wrong. That they were good for us. Powerful. Righteous. They were on the side of the angels. Gods that walk the earth to protect us. I realized…those people are morons. Because they forgot, *we* forgot, with God comes the Devil. I forgot this. I drank the Kool-Aid, and I kept drinking it even though the first time I did with Justin, it brought me to death's door. I guess I'm just a glutton for punishment, huh?" I chuckle, which turns into full blown cackling. Harry just stares at me as if I've cracked. Good. "Oh, life is just so fucking ridiculous, isn't it? Good Lord."

He lets me continue cackling like a loon for about thirty seconds before I taper them off. I really need to make sure I don't overact. Harry believes me, though. He shifts uncomfortably on the couch. "Are you…okay?"

I cackle again. "Yes, I'm fine. Completely fine. Can't you tell?" I shake my head and chuckle some more. "Oh, Harry." I fall back into the couch in defeat and roll my eyes at my own fake stupidity. My wonderful ex gazes at me, so sad for me. Perfect. The man is so damn close to perfect. "Why did you like me?"

"I'm sorry?"

"You were the only man worth a lick who ever gave me the time of day. Why on earth did you do that?"

"Joanna…"

"No. Really. I *really* need to hear it."

He stares at me, hopefully seeing a lonely, desperate woman ruined by a broken heart. Once again, years of experience pay off. Glad my pain was finally good for something. "Your tenacity. Your loyalty. Your ability to think on your feet. How you never put up with people's crap, even when it costs you. How you fight with all you've got when you think the cause is worth it. Your smile. Your wild hair. That noise you make right before you..." He blushes. "You know. You're a good person, Jo. If I, of all people can say it, then know it's true. But for the life of me, I just don't know why you can't believe it."

"Because you seem to be the only man to ever see it, Harry. And I threw you away." I sit up and smile sadly. "I'm happy you found someone, my hand to God I am. You deserve every happiness in this world," I say sincerely. "I just...I don't know." I flop back against the couch again. "I miss you. I miss Justin. I miss the guys in the squad. I am...completely alone. All I have is the work now." I gaze down at my wringing hands. "Maybe that's all I'll ever have. Maybe it's all I deserve. But by God if that is the case, I'm gonna do it right. If this city and its citizens are all I got, then no matter what, I have to do right by them. To protect them. And I will do whatever is necessary to achieve that." I pause for effect, pretending to struggle to get the next few words out. "Dr. Jonathan Ambrose."

"What about him?"

"You might want to question him about his twin brother, Jordan, and their...destructive rivalry," I say with venom. Harry's eyes narrow behind his glasses. "What you choose to do with this information is up to you. I trust you. If you feel the need to distribute what you discover from him, I will back you fully in your determinations. With documented evidence and eyewitness testimony if needed."

At first he's confused, but that only lasts a second. "Lord Nightingale."

"Yes. I shouldn't have kept it from you, but at the time my loyalty was misplaced. I've had some sense knocked into me since. I shouldn't have let emotion cloud my judgment. Consider me cloud free and completely on your side from here on. Just go talk to him. As I said, if you feel the need to release information to the press, such as a picture of Jordan Ambrose, by all means."

"Okay. Thank you."

I rise from the couch and smooth my pants. "If you have any follow-up questions, I'm here. Just don't say anything over the phone. I'm fairly sure Jordan's bugged them."

"Good to know." He stands too. "Are you sure you're going to be okay?"

"I'm fine, Harry," I say with a proper smile. "Really. I'll see you to the door." We walk out and through the long hallway, past the disapproving Pendergasts, to the front door without a word. I keep my eyes straight ahead, but Harry keeps glancing at me with trepidation. I open the front door with a gracious grin. "Thank you for coming. Really. If I learn anything else, I'll contact you. I promise. And good luck with Dr. Ambrose. Just keep at him. He's not as tough as you might think," I say with an undercurrent of scorn. "Bye."

As I shut the door, Harry says, "Joanna?"

I open it again. "Yes?"

"Look, I don't know what happened, but whatever it is…you deserve to be happy. You really do."

For whatever reason this sentiment makes me burst into a real giggle. "Oh, Harry," I say, shaking my head. "When has anyone ever gotten what they really deserved in this life?" Still laughing, I shut the door on the man I never, ever deserved.

*

With that piece of theater complete, I return to the plethora of work calls and e-mails I've neglected these past two days. It actually feels good to focus on something non-Cain related. Depressed Joanna always did throw herself into work when the going got tough. Of course I can't stop glancing at the clock as I satiate my workaholic side. I don't know if Harry will go directly to Jem or wait a day or two after he's gathered more information. He will visit, though. For all our sakes I hope it's sooner rather than later. Harry's probably really concerned about me, even kicking himself for leaving me in such an agitated state. Jem will set him right. All part of the plan.

When I'm finally done with work, a million hours later, I burn myself a frozen pizza and curl up on the sofa to watch TV. I have to be ready if he arrives tonight. Around nine-thirty, I'm about to abandon my vigil when the moving fireplace startles me. Jem, in full Lord Nightingale uniform, steps into my living room, lips twitching in anger. Ready for round two. *Fight*!

"Jesus Christ! You scared the hell out of me!" I say with a hard tone. "You know, I think from now on if you have to come here, you should send a text first or something."

"Our phones are bugged, remember?" Nightingale says, matching my tone.

"Even better. Don't come over at all." I switch off the TV. "When you do, you might as well just paint another target on my back." I stand with a sneer. "I have no desire to be scraped out of a bombed out car too, thank you very much." I walk past him as I say, "Do what you came to do and leave. I'm going to bed."

"I was called into your old precinct today," Nightingale says as I reach the door. I spin around. "Captain O'Hara had several questions for me about my brother. Jordan."

"Did he? Imagine that."

Nightingale's mouth drops open. "Why? Why did you do that? He was talking about releasing a photo of Jordan to the press. What…" He's stunned into speechlessness. "W-Why?"

"He's in charge of the case. He *needed* to know. I trust *him* to do the right thing for this city."

"And what transpired between us last night had nothing to do with your sudden decision?"

"Of course it did. Because after you left, I had an epiphany. I realized exactly how selfish I was being."

"Selfish?"

"Yeah. I was letting my idiotic feelings for you blind me from seeing what any asshole could. That you need to leave. You need to run, or fly, or whatever out of this city and don't look back. I don't care where you go, but I suggest a deserted island where you and your brother can kill each other or fuck each other or whatever you want to do without hurting innocent people. It just won't be here. Not if I have anything to say or do about it."

"You cannot be serious."

"Deathly. I will do everything in my considerable power to save my city from you and your psycho brother."

"You're going to run me out of town on a rail?"

"If needs be."

His shoulders fall. "Joanna, you're not thinking clearly."

"Don't you dare fucking patronize me," I snap. "I see things very clearly. You leave, your brother leaves. Simple math. Can you honestly say you've improved things around here? Or should we ask Brendan and the dozens who died on that bridge due to you?"

"You're just being cruel now."

I take a step toward him, ice cold eyes boring into him. "Well, I've been taught by masters, babe. And unless you leave and leave now, I will school you too. Your job at the hospital? Gone. The few friends you have remaining? The things I can tell them. And, if I have to, the entire damn world will hear just how warped the Ambrose Brothers are. I will spill to any reporter who will listen the tale of a certain respected doctor who moonlights as a superhero and his twin brother whose twisted love resulted in a triple digit death count. The only reason I haven't yet is out of respect for Lexie and Brendan. But that respect extends only so far. So before I blow up your life, I suggest you go home and type up a letter of registration, pack your bags, and pick an island. You can show yourself out."

I turn on my heel again and walk to the door until his voice stops me. "Don't do this, Joanna. It's…beneath you. We need to work together. Now more than ever. I'm sorry I hurt you. I'm sorry. I—"

I twirl back around. "You didn't hurt me, Jem. It takes a hell of a lot more than some socially stunted, incestuous, second rate superhero to hurt *me*. What you did was knock some sense into me. Now I'm just returning the favor. Leave. Or I will *crucify* you."

With one final glare, I stalk out of the living room like the evil queen in a fairy tale with a satisfied grin on my face without a glimpse back. Yet it slowly drops with each step as the weight of the situation starts stacking. I have to do this now. Him being on board doesn't make it easier. That man's just going to stand by and watch as his livelihood, his reputation, hell his life burns to ashes all for the greater good. And I'm the bitch who lights the match. And I always thought being a villain would be a hell of a lot more fun.

CHAPTER SEVENTEEN

TO SHREDS

A week and a half and nothing. A week and a half of me ripping his brother to shreds in almost every conceivable way, and Jordan remains silent. He doesn't crawl out of his hole in any capacity. No notes, no telephone calls, not even flowers. At least there are no more attacks. He's probably too busy watching the soap opera taking place in my house and out in the world. I've been a right good diva, chewing up the scenery and spitting acid about Dr. Jem Ambrose to anyone who listens. Hospital board members have received several calls each where I lay out all my reservations about Jem's drug trial. That I've heard he's not following guidelines and protocol, that he's mismanaging his staff. I even faxed them information about one of his trials several years before where the drug caused brain aneurysms that left subjects blind. I even called the FDA to demand an investigation into his latest one. All that made its way to the press too.

The diva really bared her fangs in the social scene. I attended two charity events, one to restore Pendergast Bridge and the other to support art in schools. Of course everyone wanted to know the story about the bombing and my hospital stay. I neither confirmed nor denied their theories, but I know they suspect the truth. King Tempest hasn't been seen since Brendan's death, and Lady Liberty was spotted in Independence fighting Harridan. She still won't return my calls. But in-between dodging and weaving the gossips, I threw in tirades about how worse our city's grown since the Triumvirate arrived. Most were in agreement with little persuasion necessary. And depending on the person, i.e. - those affiliated with the hospital, how unprofessional Jem's being, including the tidbit he's been inappropriate with male staff. The gossip swirled within hours as it always does.

The biggest blow, the one that I was positive would bring Jordan out from hiding, was when I employed my PR firm to get the conversation about the causality of heroes and villains spinning nationwide. Almost every talking head and newspaper began condemning the property damage, the violence, the deaths associated with their battles, every head drumming home that if there were no heroes there would be fewer possibly no villains. I made sure they mentioned the Triumvirate, especially Lord Nightingale. The smear campaign cost a pretty penny but was damn effective. Today's polls show that 59% of Galilee citizens want the Triumvirate to decamp. And still nothing. Not a peep. I'm running out of ideas short of literally throwing acid in Jem's face or kicking him in the balls. Not that we've seen or spoken since that night. He calls, but like a good scorned woman, I don't return them. I just talk badly about him behind his back like a normal gal.

So the charade continues. I'm short with my staff, I sneak glasses of "whiskey," I stare into space with a scowl. Anger used to fuel me, now it exhausts me. I almost want Cain to kidnap or kill me already, anything but this damn waiting and bile spewing. I don't know how Jem's coping with it all. I miss him so much. Talking to him, working with him, his smell, those penetrating eyes of his, the feel of his lips on mine. I've had more than a few X-Rated dreams the past few nights. When I do sleep. I get maybe four hours on a good night. I can quote all the infomercials.

Oddly, I'm looking forward to my Ryder chat today more than the opening of the Thornton wing. The video chat music chimes just as I send Harry all the info Doris acquired on a rape last night. That's another thing getting me through this, focusing on plain old ordinary crimes. Cain isn't the only asshole in town who needs an ass whooping. I close my e-mail, and accept the call. Like all horrible things in life, seeing him gets easier each time I do it. I don't feel a damn thing when he pops on screen.

"Hello, Joanna," Ryder says. "I was beginning to think you weren't going to call this week."

"I've been busy. I'm here now. Besides, you already had a call this week."

"Yes," he says with little enthusiasm. "Thank you for that."

"I always keep my word, Ryder. Always. So, how is Grace? I haven't spoken to her since she tried to shoot me."

"She is…" He grimaces and shakes his head.

"That good, huh?" I fold my arms across my chest. "Well, what the hell did you expect? A super-max ain't exactly Rio, especially to someone like her. She didn't grow up hard like us.

And she did help you murder a prison guard. Hell, I'm surprised she's lasted this long."

"Are you attempting to get a rise out of me?"

"No, just telling the truth. I mean, did the thought you two would get caught ever cross your minds? Do you feel any guilt for dragging her into your ridiculous vendetta?"

"It was not ridiculous," he spews out.

"Ryder, I had a front row seat. It was fucking ridiculous. 'You bested me, you think you're better than me, you think you can't be corrupted, I must destroy you, gurr, argh!' Anyway you dress it up with long winded speeches about superheroes as gods and balancing scales, when it came down to it, you were pissed he arrested you, and you had to punish him. End of story. If you had just broken out, and met Grace in Rio, neither of you would be behind bars now. You demolished the life of the one person you claim to love for next to nothing. For hubris." I lean back in my seat. "So, do you? Feel guilt? Are you even capable of it? Do you even love her?"

"I love Grace with my entire heart and soul," he says in a hard tone.

"Just keep telling yourself that, Jimmy, maybe it'll become true. You're a sociopath. You're incapable of empathy, and it's kind of a big requirement for love. Real love, true blue love, requires sacrifice. You would do anything, give anything for the other person, including your life if needs be. *That* is love, James."

The villain glares at me for a few seconds. I don't know why I've wasted my breath. Talking about love to a sociopath is like trying to describe the color twelve. "I have no desire to continue this avenue of conversation."

"So, what do you want to talk about? The weather you never get to experience?"

"Any luck finding our friend the Emperor?" Ryder asks.

"Not yet." I lower my arms. "Let me ask you something. Say Justice had moved somewhere like New Urbana or India, would you have followed him? Set up your reign of terror there?"

"Most likely. Is that your plan? Make Cain someone else's nightmare? How mercenary of you."

"Desperate times."

He cocks an eyebrow, I think in approval. "Have the Triumvirate agreed with your logic? I suppose it is all just geography to them as well."

"Two down, one to go, but he seems dug in. I've turned the majority of the city against him, come close to ruining his personal life, but he just won't leave. He's starting to really piss me off." My eyes narrow. "What would you do?"

"I assume killing him is off the table?" My eyes narrow to pinpoints. "Right. We all have our limits, I suppose." He considers the dilemma for a few seconds. "What it boils down to is blackmail, correct? Well, he does have one hell of a secret to exploit. Use it."

"Expose him?"

Ryder shrugs. "Remember what happened to Johnny Law when his secret identity was revealed? The press hounded him. He lost his job, his family, and then Helter Skelter resurfaced for payback and paralyzed him. Probably would have killed his family too if they hadn't been smart and run for the hills early on. But you know all of this. You just want what? My take on this drastic move?"

"Other people could get hurt if I do it."

"Of course they will. No man is an island. Of course I am preaching to the enlightened on that front. And you will be essentially destroying a life, possibly even signing his death warrant. Justin being a perfect example. But since we're being mercenary, what are one or two lives against all the innocent Gallileans you can save if they flee? You just have to ask yourself if you can carry the hero's damnation on your conscience forever. Would you like my approval or condemnation?"

I sit stony still staring at him for a few seconds. "I have to do it, don't I?"

"Doesn't mean you have to enjoy it, Joanna." He grins. "But it does make it far easier. It can actually be quite thrilling ripping someone to shreds, especially when they've wronged you. That power. Knowing you're hurting them more than they've hurt you. It can be quite cathartic."

"This isn't personal. I'm not getting any satisfaction from it."

"Keep telling yourself that, Joanna," he says with a grin.

"I'm not," I insist.

"Last time we spoke you were desperately trying to arrive at ways to aid your new friends, now you're talking about obliterating them. No one has that colossal an about face without personal feelings entering the equation. I mean, even when you discovered Justin's deception the thought of outing him never crossed your mind. So either a hero *really* wronged you, or you've come over to the dark side. Knowing what I do about you, I very *very* much doubt the latter. We recognize our own kind."

I scowl. "I just want him gone. For the greater good."

"Then you know what you have to do." He pauses. "Poor Joanna. Superheroes just keep breaking your heart, don't they? Will you never learn?"

"Fuck off, Ryder." I end the call. "Asshole." Now it's said aloud it's really a tangible possibility, one I've barely given a second thought. Now…

I stare at the black screen with a grimace. Shit. I can't do it. I can't out him. It'll destroy him. No question. His medical career, his entire fucking life will vanish. The press will hound him. Any villain he every fought will come after him. People will loathe him, spit on him for his brother's sins. Hell, the Feds can even arrest and sue him for billions in property damage. A few store owners did with Justin, going after Pendergast Industries. Our lawyers are still sorting it out. I can't do it. Even evil Joanna isn't that cruel.

Well, I'm not doing it today, that's for damn sure. I rise from the chair and go upstairs to change. I'm late to honor the saint who brought Jem into my life after I just chatted with her murderer. Life is so fucking ridiculous sometimes. It makes you want to cry.

*

At least I did this right. I can leave this planet with absolute certainty I did one pure, good thing for this miserable world. The Dr. Rebecca Thornton Pediatric Recovery Wing is as perfect as its namesake. All the bedrooms, the kitchen, the living room, even the nurse's station turned out better than I envisioned. There's even a stocked fridge. It's homier than my own home.

As with the opening of all new wings, there must be a ribbon cutting ceremony attended by various contributors, the hospital board and chronicled by the press where we congratulate ourselves on being so selfless and charitable. Danforth Mills stands beside me in the kitchen with the rest of the board and selected families already milling around the living room. In the next room, on the other side of the red ribbon, are a handful of reporters and doctors and nurses who have come to see the show. Shannon, who really deserves the credit for this project, stands off in the corner working her Blackberry as always. Thank God Jem isn't here. Just get through the speech, and get the fuck out of here, Jo.

"Good turnout," Danforth says.

"I suppose." No rest for the wicked. I raise my voice so the whole room can hear, saying "Did you look over the reports I sent you?"

"Which one? The one about the aneurysms where Dr. Ambrose was one of ten doctors on the project? Or the one from the society pages about his inappropriate behavior with staff, which as far as I know has no substantiation? I checked, there hasn't been a single complaint against him in his entire work history."

"People are probably too afraid to make an official complaint against your newest golden boy. Wouldn't be the first time."

Danforth rolls his brown eyes. "Where is this coming from, Joanna? A few weeks ago you were gung ho about adding him to staff, now you can't wait to pillory the man."

"Everyone makes mistakes. But when we do, they must be corrected. Dr. Ambrose is definitely one of those mistakes. He needs to go before the entire hospital is dragged through the mud behind him. You just need to trust me on this, alright?"

"Absolutely not. Short of the man embezzling from the hospital or murdering someone, he stays. His drug will earn billions." He leans in and hisses in a low voice, "You do realize all this muckraking you've been doing is only making yourself look bad and tarnishing the reputation of the hospital."

"I'm not a moron, Dan," I say through gritted teeth. "I know that. You think I wouldn't be doing this if it wasn't necessary? Him being here puts us all in danger." I glance around the room at the staring others, meeting a few eyes. "He needs to go."

"Then give us something better than gossip and an old report," Danforth says.

"I—" The words won't come out, and my mouth snaps shut. I gaze around the room again at the concerned yet titillated board members. Not a one is on my side. They all think I'm crazy. Let them as long as this story makes the rounds around town tonight. "I will. But not today. Today's about this wing. But when I do, you're all going to wish you'd fired his ass sooner." I snatch up the big scissors from the counter. "Let's get this over with." I step toward the door, stop to plaster a smile on my face and lead the procession out.

The audience perks up when we walk out, but my smile falters when I spot my glowering speckled new enemy by the entrance. He seems none too pleased to see me. I meet his eyes and match his glare for a moment before flipping my frown upside down for the crowd. I stop in front of the ribbon and keep my gaze focused on the reporters. When everyone's in position behind me, I start. "Thank you all for coming today to the opening of the Dr. Rebecca Thornton Pediatric Recovery Wing. I'll keep this short as I'm sure the children and their families are itching to settle into to their state-of-the-art home away from home.

"Dr. Rebecca Thornton, for whom this wing is dedicated to, graced this hospital for far too short a time before her life was cut unnecessarily short by violence. Most of you didn't know her, didn't…know her heart." I glance at Jem whose eyes are glued to the floor. "It was the fullest of anyone's I have ever met. Full of her friends, her family, her patients. She and Justin Pendergast had that in common. And this wing is the physical manifestation of that fact. They wanted to heal the world one person at a time, and though they are not here in body, I am positive they are in spirit. And with every child whose both body and soul are renewed within these walls, may they and what they stood for live on. Strength. Compassion." I stop speaking and Jem stares up. My hard eyes bore into his. "And above all, doing the right thing even when it hurts." I look back at the cameras and hold up the scissors. "To Dr. Rebecca Thornton, Justin Pendergast, Daisy Thornton, Marnie Beesley, and anyone else whose life has been touched by darkness. May this wing tip the scales in favor of the light." I snip the ribbon. Everyone claps. I'm getting better at this speech thing.

I pose for photos with board members and patients, but my mind is elsewhere. I watch as Jem examines the painting he knocked down the second time we met. He was so bumbling and nervous, I almost OD'd on cuteness. The memory brings a small smile to my face. Feels like we've had a lifetime since then. He must feel me staring because he peers my way. I wipe the smile off my face and return my attention to the reporter.

Just as Danforth and I finish with this sound bite, Jem makes his move. "Excuse me, Mr. Mills," he says to Danforth, "may I please borrow Miss Fallon?"

"*Ms.* Fallon," I correct.

"*Ms.* Fallon," he says, matching my nasty tone. "Excuse us." He gestures toward the back. I follow him toward the nurse's station where there are fewer people but still some. This upcoming performance piece would be pointless without an audience. "You have to stop this," he begins.

"Stop what? I have no idea what you're talking about."

"This war you've decided to wage against me. Spreading rumors about my love life? Petitioning the board to fire me? Bringing the FDA in? They could force me to abandon my drug trial. My work could potentially help millions of people."

"Mine too," I parry.

He's silent for a moment to swallow his anger. "Going after my work is low."

"I'll go as low as necessary, buddy. I've waded through shit before, and I'm not afraid to get dirty again. But this can all stop, Dr. Ambrose. You know my condition. You can easily do your work, in peace, back in Independence or Pacific City or even a deserted island. You can save your millions there, just not here. Not in my town. *We* don't want you here."

"No, *you* don't want me here," he says, lowering his voice.

"Well, I think the current polls and general animosity around town supports my view more than yours," I counter with a smug grin.

"Yes, I suppose you should be congratulated for spreading your hate so far and wide in such a short time. How much did it cost? A million? Two? Your soul?"

"If it gets you gone, it's worth every fucking penny," I sneer. "You claim to have the city's best interest at heart. If that were true, you would have packed your bags the second he showed up. You didn't. People died."

"You're not seeing the bigger picture, Joanna. You—"

"No, *you're* not. Just. Leave."

"*No*," he says, hard as titanium.

I fold my arms across my chest. "No?"

"I am not going anywhere. I'm close to finding him," he says, lowering his voice even further. "If I leave, I'll have to start all over. Can't you see that?"

"All I see is half the hospital without windows," I say quieter. "I see people missing limbs with burns covering half their bodies when they were brought to the hospital after the bombing. I see, and smell, Brendan's corpse as it smoldered in my driveway. I see your brother holding a gun on me then injecting me with God knows what. It's on you. That's all on you. So just leave. Or I am not responsible for what I do next."

"Meaning?" He actually seems shocked and horrified as he studies my hard face. "You wouldn't."

"As I said, I'm not responsible for what I'll have to do next." Great exit line. After raising an eyebrow, I step away. His hand clamps around my wrist, stopping me. I spin around and jerk my hand away. "Do not touch me or I'll have you arrested for battery," I say loudly.

"Stop it. Just stop this. You're acting like a lunatic."

"And now we can add slander to your list of crimes!"

"Will you listen to yourself? Do you know what will happen if you do what you're threatening to?" he asks in a low whisper. "Forget about what it will do to my life, what about Lexie? It will spill over to her."

"It already has. That one's on you too."

"You cannot do this," he whispers desperately. "It will destroy everything. All I've accomplished. Do you really hate me that much?"

"I don't hate you. I feel *nothing* for you," I say through gritted teeth.

He's silent for a second, then says, "That's because you have no soul," he states as a fact. "Dress it up anyway you like

Joanna, but what this comes down to is the fact that I don't want you. And from what I've experienced, I'm not surprised that no one ever has. And they never will. There is something twisted, something *wrong* inside you. At least Jordan admits his exists. You hide yours, dress it up as doing the right thing. If Justin could see you now, he'd be as disgusted with you as I am. Or maybe he did see it, and that's why he could never return your love. He saw how pathetic you really are."

I'm brimming with such hate and hurt it has to come out. Really I just want him to shut the fuck up. With all my might, I slap his face. The room goes quiet except for my heavy breathing. Jem looks as shocked as everyone else in the room, myself included. "Fuck you, cocksucker." And for good measure, I slap him again. "*Fuck you.*"

Still breathing heavily and shaking with unharnessed emotion, I stalk out of the room, past my staring and whispering audience, then out of the wing with what little dignity I can muster. Shannon rushes over to me, but I hold up my hand to stop her. I need to be alone for a few minutes. Away from prying eyes and ears. I all but punch the two elevator buttons. The one going up opens first. Perfect.

When the doors open onto the roof, a gust of wind knocks me back a little. I still walk out. The cold air is bracing, stinging against my exposed skin. I'm past caring. I take large buckets full as I pace around the roof. Tears stream from my eyes, and I swipe them away. I can't keep this up. We're going to end up saying or doing something that will truly be unforgivable. I'm losing it. We—

Out of the corner of my eye, I spy the stairwell door open. Jem steps out with his shirt open, revealing his costume and a pained expression matching my own. He was running away too. Flying away all alone until he could face the world. After a moment his gaze whips in my direction, the misery weighing down his long face all the way to the river thirty stories below.

"I'm sorry," he whispers, near tears. "I'm so sorry I said those things. I—"

I sprint toward him, stopping those words with a kiss. No hesitation this time. He kisses me with the same fervor. I always thought those women who claimed they almost swooned when they kissed a man were full of shit. Being overly dramatic. They're not. If he wasn't holding me and I him, I'm pretty sure I'd be on the ground. I could kiss this man until Armageddon. He breaks away, resting his forehead on mine and tracing circles on my cheeks with his thumbs. "This is hell," he whispers. "I'm so sorry."

"It was my plan. We knew what we were getting into. I just didn't think it would be so fucking hard." I put my hands over his. "I miss you so much. I hate this. I hate it. You don't deserve this. Hell, I don't even know if it's working. What if I'm ruining your life for nothing? It's a stupid plan. What—"

"Hey," he whispers before kissing me again. God, he tastes delicious. "Stop. Just stop. It will work. It will. And then he'll be gone. He'll never bother us again. He'll be gone."

"I can't go back to that house. I can't keep this up much longer, I can't. I *feel* him watching me, like he's right in the room. Waiting for me to slip up. Give it all away."

"Then don't. Go for a drive, get a hotel room. Go out on the boat. Take a break. After what just happened, it would make sense if you did."

"Makes sense you would too," I point out.

"I don't think that—"

I meet his eyes. "One night. Just one fucking night before the shit really hits the fan. God knows we've earned it. Hell, God knows I need it. *We* need it. We've never had a proper date."

He smiles. "You want to go on a date? Now?"

"We'd just have to be careful. I take the boat out, I text you the coordinates. I had Dobbs check *The Athena*. It's clean of bugs. And he really can't track you if you're flying around. So fly to me. One night. Who knows when we'll get another chance? Really." I pause. "One night, just one night where I'm just Joanna and you're just Jem, and there's nothing and no one in this world but us." I kiss him again. "Please."

It's a gamble in a lot of ways, but I don't care. Jordan could kill me tomorrow. We have such a small window, I sure as hell want to take advantage of it. He can give us just one night, damn it.

Jem kisses me this time. "I should go. You too."

He moves away and once again won't look at me. He turns around and starts shedding his clothes. "Jem?" I call to him. He turns back around. "We deserve happiness. We deserve each other.

We've earned each other." I smile. "I'll be here. Waiting for you to realize that. Just try not to keep me waiting too long." My smile grows before I walk to the stairwell door. When the door closes, I let out a sigh. "Dear God, please let me win this one. Please?"

Guess I'll get my answer tonight.

CHAPTER EIGHTEEN

ONE NIGHT

Jesus Christ, I'm more nervous about having sex now than I was when I lost my virginity a million years ago. *The Athena* only has a small bathroom so performing a full body beauty ritual proves difficult. Shaving, showering, dealing with my crazy hair, it takes forever. The one good thing about celibacy is you don't have to waste hours on this bullshit. I do look damn good though, and it gets me in the right mindset, which used to be the alcohol's job.

I can count on one hand how many men I've slept with sober. Even with Harry once or twice I was blotto. Hell, I barely remember the last time I had sex, except I hated every second of it. Two drunks in a seedy hotel fumbling around. I can't even call up his face from memory. I never did get his name. Sex was always just something that ended up happening, and in the end mattered very little to me. Just some fun. I'm too fucking nervous for this to be "just fun." A tiny part of me hopes he doesn't show. As time draws on, I fear I may get that wish. I texted him two hours ago with the coordinates but no text back and no Jem.

After an hour and a half, I give up pacing the deck, staring up at the stars, hoping to catch sight of him as he approached. I go below deck to the stateroom and lie down. It does feel good to know no one's watching me. Even if he doesn't arrive, I will do my damndest to enjoy this. The eye of the storm. On the drive to the dock, I phoned Dobbs and told him I was taking the boat out. I also called V at the paper saying I wanted to give her an important story. Hope I don't have to keep that appointment. I do try to fight it, but with the rocking of the boat, I give into the Sandman.

It's cold, so cold the snow swirls around me in a vortex as the wind howls in agony. In a millisecond, I'm chilled to the bone and not only from the Arctic weather. I sense his eyes on me. When I spin around, all I see is darkness. "Joanna!" I hear Jem call me from inside the frost crystallized labyrinth. Oh. So that's where I am. I recognize it now. I pull my bullet resistant coat Justice gave me around tighter and step inside the midnight black maze without hesitation. I'd step into a volcano if he needed me too.

Twist, turn, Twist, turn. It has more avenues than I remember. The moment I move down one, another maneuvers me even deeper. Twist, turn. Twist, turn. Minutes that feel like hours pass as I make what feels like a hundred course changes. And the walls. With every step, they grow tighter and taller until I can barely see the top. After what must be half a chilling hour, I must stop my pilgrimage or my knees will buckle. This is pointless. I'm getting nowhere.

But *he's* getting closer.

The bastard's mimicked my footsteps so I can't hear him, but I know he's there. Stalking me. Waiting for me to fall. To crumble. I hear him breathing around the corner. In, out, in, out like a pervert on the other end of a phone. Me, his prey, remains still, holding the air in my lungs. He knows I know. A second later, I hear the crackling of snow as he takes a step. Shit. I take off again as fast as I'm capable of into the labyrinth with him only a few feet behind. I want to look back, but I don't dare. Every millisecond counts.

"Joanna!" Jem yells again.

Just make it to the center. He'll save me. Don't give up, never give up, just get to the center. The tears on my face freeze as icicles, and I don't even wipe them away.

It just won't end. It never ends.

Hours. I've been running for hours. It's the same. It all looks the same. My ankles feel like they're made of glass and about to shatter. Keep going, just keep going. *He* won't stop. *I* won't stop. I just need to reach Jem. He'll be there. Just please let it end. I've run long enough. I'm so tired. It needs to end. He'll get me. I've worked too hard for the bastard to get me now. It isn't fair. All I want is to get to the center. To him. I've earned it.

"Joanna!" I'm close. He's so close now. And I see it! The light amid the darkness. The center. If I had breath to whimper, I would. "Joanna!"

It ends.

I've found it. The center. It's glorious. So vast compared to what came before. The lights on the ground make the snow almost twinkle like fine diamonds. A winter wonderland. "Jem?" I ask with a grin. But he's not here. No one's here. No. *No*. He has to be here. I sprint all around the circle, checking every shadow, but he's gone. It was all a trick. He was never here. *NO*!

"Joanna," Jem whispers behind me as light as the wind.

I twirl around, but my smile becomes a silent scream. Justin, my phantom, stands a foot away as he was in my last memory. Caked in blood, skin blistering with pus from acid, missing a hand, face bruised and pulpy from the beating Alkaline gave him. But his eyes are what fill me with unspeakable terror. As cold as this night. No one has stared at me with this much ire, this much scorn in my life. That I'm substandard. Inhuman. Despicable. Then I blink, and it's Jem in the same horrific state, a shell of a man drowning in spite. I blink again. He's gone. They're both gone. And I'm all alone in the cold wasteland.

Tears still stream down from my eyes when I wake, the sobs wracking my body as I curl into a ball. But it takes a moment for me to realize someone's holding me, shushing me while he pets my hair. I cling to him tighter. I open my eyes and through the tears see Jem in full costume except for the cowl. He's perched on the edge of the bed, cradling me in his lap as if I were a child. "Don't cry," he whispers. "Why are you crying?"

"You weren't there. Then you hated me," I whimper.

"I'm right here." He hugs me tighter. "I'm right here. It was just a nightmare."

I force myself to calm down, each stroke of my hair wiping the misery to a manageable level. It was a dream. Just a dream. "I didn't think you were coming."

"Neither did I," he says. He stops stroking my hair. "Here."

I pull away to find him holding out a handkerchief. "Thank you." My great seduction scene is ruined. I'm about as sexy as a hundred-year-old man in a Speedo right now. Oh, God I'm all snotty, and I'm sure splotchy. I blow my nose. "I swear I was a stone cold fox a few hours ago." He watches with a smile, and when I'm empty, I smile back. "We never get anything right, do we?"

"I don't know." He meets my eyes, and his smile grows. "I think we manage the important things."

My smile matches his. "Such as?"

"Respect. Friendship. Acceptance."

"Is that enough?" I ask.

"Absolutely not."

He grabs the back of my neck and brings my lips to his. Even in my less than pristine physical condition and emotional vomiting, he still wants me. And God knows I want him. In this moment, I want him more than I've ever wanted a man before. Even Justin. Yet that fear from before whacks into me with the force of a car crash. For a split second, I have the urge to push him away, but fight it back with equal force. I'm not letting anyone sabotage this, especially not me.

When I imagined this, and I've lost track of how many times I've played this potential scene over in my head, *I* was the aggressor. He was the virginal, blushing flower who only ever slept with one woman years and years ago. This astounding man continues to surprise me. He literally rips off my shirt, buttons flying everywhere. My pants and underwear receive similar consideration. He has me at a disadvantage. I haven't a clue how to remove his uniform. All my groping and nary a zipper is found. He takes care of that too. There's a secret zipper around the waist, a fact I'll file away for next time. He's not shy, that's for sure. He stands naked for a moment, allowing me to snap a mental picture. He may appear skinny and weak while dressed, but without clothes he's chiseled and powerful looking, like a wild cat. He pounces like one too.

The world falls away as it always seems to do whenever we're together. There's nothing but him. The feel of him. The taste of him. His smell. And those eyes. I've never gazed into a man's eyes as he moved inside me. Every time I close my eyes, he caresses the eyelids, and I open them again. It's beyond intimate but makes this already blissful experience so much better. He seems instinctively to know where to touch, where to nibble, when to change rhythm. We just fit. And when we bring each other to nirvana, I have never felt so close to another being before. Like we're one. And this one, I'm never letting go. I'll die first.

We lie together on the small bed with my head resting on his chest and a dopey smile on my face. "Now, aren't you glad you came?" His grin changes and I realize what I actually just said. He chuckles, and a second later I join in. "Shut up. You know what I mean. Lord, you get laid once and all of a sudden your mind needs a good scrubbing."

"I've always had a filthy mind. I just hide the fact better than most."

"Oh huh, yeah. Just keep telling yourself that."

"What does that mean?"

"Let's just say on more than one occasion I've caught you undressing me with your eyes. I was just too much of a lady to say anything."

"You are one to talk, Miss Fallon. The night we met, you were all but licking your chops while we talked. I feared for my virtue."

"Yeah, it took a lot of willpower for me not to drag you upstairs to a hotel room and have my way with you."

"I wish I had known that. When you vanished, I thought I'd done something wrong. I flagellated myself over it for months."

"I'm sorry." I bite my lower lip and smile mischievously as I move up closer to his mouth. "I'm sure there are multiple ways you can think of for me to make up for it. In multiple positions." I give him a smooch before resuming my position right over his heart. "Just give me a few minutes to recover. Not all of us have super-stamina."

"Oh. Shame. Guess I'll have to end things then. No other choice that I can see." I playfully nibble his chest in retaliation. "Ow!"

We both chuckle for a few seconds before growing quiet. "I am sorry, you know. About that night. About how I've handled a lot of stuff."

"As am I. But…my view is that whatever has gotten us to this point, this moment, is fine. It was necessary. It's forgiven. Because without it, we wouldn't have *this*."

"When you put it that way…" We grin again. Mine drops first. "But seriously, why did you decide to come tonight? The few times we almost reached this moment, you put the brakes on. I know you thought it was for my own good, but still."

"You can be incredibly persuasive when you want to be." He smiles, but I don't. I want a real answer. "'All that is necessary for the triumph of evil is that good men to do nothing.'" My eyes narrow in confusion. "He does not get to win, Joanna. He does not get to dictate my life anymore. I refuse him that power over me. And as I was flying around the city tonight, blindly searching for him, I realized how idiotic I was being. How there was this brilliant, sexy, astounding woman waiting. For *me*. A woman who I wanted to be with more than anything in this universe. And if it only allows us tonight or a million tonights, I don't want to waste a second of the gift it finally bestowed upon me."

"Good answer." It earns him another kiss. I will never get sick of his lips caressing mine, I know that now. I do break our seal first. "But since I'm a greedy bitch, I'm gonna hold you to the million tonights. One just ain't gonna cut it." There but for the grace of God.

"We are in full agreement there."

I wasn't wrong about superhero stamina. It is a wondrous thing. The galley, the deck, the shower are all put to very, *very* good use. It'll be a miracle if I can walk tomorrow. And when we finally wear each other out, I drift to sleep with his naked body pressed against mine and his arms around me.

I dream of a million more nights. For once, may my dreams come true.

*

His absence in our bed stirs me from pleasant dreams. The warmth has vanished, and once again I'm left in the cold. My eyes flutter open. He isn't beside me. He's gone. I immediately jerk upright with a gasp, but my panic subsides when I see him across the room putting on his pants. He pivots around. "Are you alright?"

"What? Yeah," I lie. I smile to reassure him and lay back down. "Fine. What time is it?"

"Almost dawn. I need to get going. I disappeared down a sewer, I have to be seen coming out."

"So, you literally crawled through shit to get to me."

"More like flew over, but yes."

"That is both disgusting and romantic at the same time. Quite difficult to pull off, Dr. Ambrose. Kudos." He smirks before continuing to dress. My smile drops. "I don't want you to go."

"Believe me. I don't want to go," he says, sounding exhausted.

I sit up again, holding the sheet to my chest. "Then don't," I blurt out, shocking even myself. "Let's just…sail. We'll dock upstate in Cumberland, withdraw a shitload of money, buy a new boat with cash, and just go. Disappear. We'll figure out a way to get new identities and start over in New Zealand or somewhere."

"See you put some thought into it."

"Had to do something while I was waiting last night. People without our massive resources do it every day. They just opt out. Vanish and start fresh. Why not us?"

Jem's face falls as he realizes I'm serious. "Joanna…" He lowers himself beside me on the bed. "That is the last resort. We both have people who rely on us. A lot of people. We'd never be able to return. Never. We'd spend our lives constantly glimpsing over our shoulders. And Jordan could very well level the whole city to get us back, if he doesn't find us, which would most likely happen. He has contacts in every city in every country in the world."

"Put some thought into it, huh?"

"I'd be a fool not to. I guarantee you almost every person in my situation has protocols in place should they need to disappear. Even going as far as…faking their death," he says with a quick smile. "In our case, that line has not yet been crossed."

"And if it is?" I ask with a rock in my stomach. "I've thrown everything but the kitchen sink at you, and he still hasn't crawled out. We're down to the last move Jem, and I can't…" I cover my mouth as I swallow the fear and sadness down, "I cannot be the one to destroy you. I can't. And if I out you, it will. Without question. Your career? Gone. Your anonymity? Vanished. Us? How…?" I cover my face with my hands, I guess in an attempt to hide from the situation I've created.

"Hey, hey," Jem says as he peels my hands away. "Look at me." I meet his tender eyes. "I knew what I was agreeing to with this plan. The cost. You laid it out clearly. This is still our last, best hope at apprehending Jordan. I still believe that. We simply have to keep pushing, to the edge if needed. And if that means you revealing everything, then you do it." He squeezes my hands. Hard. "*You do it*. You do it without hesitation. I will not blame you for what happens. I will not hate you. I could never hate you." He cups my cheek in his bare hand. "I love you."

Those last three words wallop me as if another bomb just went off. My eyes grow double their normal size. "Did-Did you just say what I think you just said?" I ask desperately. "Bec-Because if you just told me you love me, and you don't mean it, you have exactly five seconds to take it back or I will kick your ass, I swear to fucking God I will."

"I'm not taking it back," he says, just as desperately. "I mean it. Every syllable. I love you. I think I've loved you since the first time you smiled at me the night we met. That smile and every one since has brightened my world more than a million suns combined. I think…no, I *know* I agreed to move here for you. I couldn't get you out of my thoughts, I couldn't. And all the time we've spent together, every single solitary moment it has been the happiest time of my life. Really. You are the first thing I think of in the morning, the last at night, and when I'm not near you, I literally ache for you. I love your strength, your loyalty, your tenacity, the way you kiss, the way you move, even the way your eyes narrow right before you're about to rip someone to shreds. I love *you*." I'm too stunned to move or even blink. Too much. This is too much to deal with today. "Please. Say something."

It takes me a few seconds to find my voice, but I shrilly croak out, "*Now*? You tell me this now? Today? When-When I have to ruin your life? Jesus fucking Christ, Jem!" I wrap the sheet around my naked body and leap out of bed on the opposite side of the bed from him.

He rises. "I-I-I'm sorry?"

"*What*? Why the fuck are you apologizing? I-I'm the one acting like a crazy person right now!" I start pacing like one too.

"Okay, I'm *not* sorry? I-I-I don't know what you want me to say right now. This-This is not how I envisioned you'd react."

"Me neither!" I say, still pacing. "I have no idea why I'm acting like this! None! The man I love just told me he loves me back, and I have a nervous breakdown in front of him! Yeah, not exactly how you picture the moment when fantasizing about it."

"Wait. You-You love me too?" he asks with a dopey smile.

I stop pacing. Holy shit, I did say that, didn't I? I take a second to verify with my brain, heart, and soul that I meant it. Fuck me. I did. I love him. My wide to the point of pain eyes meet his.

"I do. I love you. Shit. Fuck. Shit. Oh, my God. Oh, fuck. I'm sorry."

"You're sorry you love me?"

"What? No! Of course not! I'm just…this is a lot. Right now. I'm not used to good things happening to me, and this is a…fucking doozey. I never thought someone as wonderful as you could ever love me, so I'm kind of freaking out right now."

"Sh-Should I leave?"

"No. Yes. Maybe. I-I-I don't want you to, but I-I think I need you to. I kind of don't want you to see me like this. I-I'm kind of worried you'll see sense and fall out of love with me."

"That is never going to happen. Never."

"Let-Let's not, I'd rather not test the theory right now. You need to go away. Sewers, remember? Alibi? Crazy brother? Go. I promise I'll be fine. I will."

"O-Okay." He nods and collects the rest of his clothes from the floor as I slump onto the edge of the bed. He doesn't even put them on, just hustles shirt and shoeless to the door. But at the threshold, he spins back around. "Just-Just for my own edification, if you do out me and I do need to vanish, would you come with me? Leave this city, your life behind? For me?"

Without hesitation, I say, "Hell yes. No question."

That brings a smile to his face and fresh tears to his beautiful eyes. "Then do it. I can take it." His smile grows. "I love you."

My lip begins trembling because I'm about to burst. I wipe away a tear. "I love you too."

"Bye." He walks out of sight.

For a few seconds, I just stare into space, my mind whirling like a cyclone. He loves me. I love him. We're in love. How the fuck did that happen?

Still in a daze, I lie on the bed that still smells of him and curl into the fetal position, closing my eyes. He loves me. *He loves me.* No bullshit, no lies, no conditions, he loves me. And I love him. This is it. He's it. Why the hell didn't I realize it sooner? Why now? Why today? Because he's right. I have to steer the boat back to Galilee, meet with Veronica, and blow his life to smithereens. *Our* life.

God, give me strength.

CHAPTER NINETEEN

ALL IN

I hate Jordan Ambrose.

I thought I hated people before. The unknown gunman who killed my father. My drunk, abusive mother. James Ryder. If I pooled together all the hate I had for those three, it still wouldn't come close to how much I despise, abhor, and detest Jordan Ambrose.

He's really going to make me do this. He's really going to let me obliterate the brother he claims to value above everything else. What, he wants more of a show? He wants me to murder his brother with my bare hands? Or maybe I was wrong. Maybe he hasn't been watching us or he saw through everything and is laughing his ass off. This was a stupid plan. *Stupid*. This all hinged on me getting into the mind of a psychopath, knowing how he'd react to my every move. But I don't know. I thought I did, but I don't. And my damn hubris is going to be the man I love's downfall. The man I love. Jesus Christ, thinking of him like that is gonna take some getting used to.

Fuck, I hate this. I hate him. Fuck, fuck, fuck.

"Miss Joanna, Miss Lilley is here for your appointment," Dobbs says.

A second later, V steps out onto the patio, all smiles. My unwitting accomplice in the character assassination of a Lord. She's right on time. I called her this morning on the drive from the dock before I lost my nerve, told her I had exclusive information about a certain well respected self-professed Lord and his connection to Emperor Cain, but wouldn't say anymore on the phone. I thought for sure that would do it. He'd hear that and immediately make contact. That buried deep, deep, deep down he actually loved his brother and wouldn't let me do this. Nope. I'm playing chicken with a mass murderer, and neither of us is veering. Pedal to the metal, Jo.

I rise from my deckchair and kiss my cousin's cheek. "Hey. Thanks for coming."

"You look terrible," V says with her usual delicacy.

"Didn't sleep much. Had a hard decision to make."

"Make it?"

"I called you, didn't I? Come inside. Dobbs made some ice tea and scones."

"Good," she says, following me inside. "I haven't had any caffeine in two hours. I'm dragging."

We sit on the couch right in front of the hidden camera, and I slip my cell phone into my pocket. Come on, you bastard. Swerve. Dobbs pours us drinks and hands out scones before leaving. As V chugs her ice tea, I take a moment to center myself. I must remain calm with an undercurrent of righteous rage. I cannot cry. I cannot scream. This is the correct thing to do. A necessary evil. I just wish it wasn't my evil to commit. But I can—

A hand waving in my face breaches my center. "Whoa, ground control to Major Tom. Jesus, did you sleep at all last night?"

"An hour or two. I was out on the boat. Alone."

"Yeah, I tried to call you back last night. Your cell was off. Are you okay?"

"Why wouldn't I be?"

"Oh, I don't know. You were hospitalized? A guy blew up in your driveway? And I've heard you've been running all over town taking chunks out of your new best friend Jonathan Ambrose. You're not drinking again, are you?"

"Not...as much." Her face, like mine, falls. "I take a drink here or there. I have it under control this time."

"Fuck, Jo. You were doing so well."

"I can stop whenever I want. Really. I just have to eradicate a problem, and I'll stop completely. Don't tell your parents, okay?"

"'Eradicate a problem?' Is that why you summoned?"

"You're my greatest weapon, V. I just wish that asshole had seen reason so it didn't have to come to using you."

"What asshole? What problem? Will you please stop with the riddles?" She sighs. "You're drunk now, aren't you? It's barely noon, Jo!"

"I am not drunk," I assure her. I wish I was. "I'm sorry, I'm just...this is harder than I thought it'd be," I chuckle. "I mean, I did warn him. It has to be done. It's good for us all if he goes, both of them, I know that. You'll see it too."

V suddenly grabs both my hands, squeezing. "What the hell are you talking about?" she asks, drawing out every word.

I need a few precious seconds to encase my heart in a steel box and weld it shut. I can do this. I can. *I'm sorry, Jem.* "Get out your tape recorder." As she obeys, I fall back in the couch with a sigh. She clicks it on. "I've been working with the Triumvirate since they arrived in town. Not out in the field or anything, just using the Justice computer to help with investigations. Including the one into Emperor Cain. I know why he's so fixated on them. Why he blew up our bridge. Why he came to this house and attacked me."

"He attacked you? That's why you were rushed to the hospital?"

"Yes. He discovered my involvement, so he came to my house, injected me with a sedative, and demolished my computer."

"Jesus. Was the Darby bombing related?"

"I have no direct knowledge, but I assume so. It might have been done to punish me, by killing one of my friends, I don't know."

"So Brendan Darby wasn't King Tempest?"

"No comment."

"Come on, Jo. Everyone knows he was. Tempest hasn't been seen since the bombing. Liberty became active in Independence right after Alexia moved back there. It's damn suspicious."

"No comment. All I will say is I have nothing but the utmost respect for King Tempest and Lady Liberty. We owe them a debt of gratitude for all they've done, all they've sacrificed. And I know for a fact, despite what some of their dejectors say, *they* are in no way responsible for unleashing Emperor Cain on Galilee. It falls solely on one man's shoulders. Cain's brother." I pause. "Lord Nightingale."

V's eyes narrow. "Wait, what? Cain and Nightingale are brothers?"

"Twin brothers, actually. Cain has a sick, incestuous relationship with his brother, and I believe vice versa."

"*Incest?*"

"That's what Cain told me, and it was later confirmed by Nightingale. He also informed me the last time the brothers fought, Nightingale allowed Cain to escape then lied to everyone about his demise, including his team mates. Those two are playing out some twisted love saga and the citizens of Galilee are caught in the middle. So I couldn't, in good conscious, keep silent a moment longer. He has betrayed the trust we all placed in him. He does not have our best interests at heart as I once assumed. I have begged him to leave the city, but he won't. And as long as he is here, as long as he continues to play this game with his brother, we are not safe. Cain followed him from Independence, he'll follow him out of Galilee Falls."

"You know how he is," V says with an astonished smile.

"Both of them. Cain is also known by INTERPOL and our government as The Mockingbird. General mercenary work and assassinations. According to a source, five years ago he carried out one such assassination for James Ryder's syndicate, victim unknown. Since returning to the city, he has used several former employees of Ryder's, including Danny Watkins and Gary Acevedo."

"Do the police have this information?"

"Yes. You should contact Harry O'Hara for verification, though he might not be able to comment on an ongoing investigation."

"Why have you waited to share this?"

"I was…protecting Lord Nightingale. When all the evidence came to light, and I realized just how culpable he was for this entire fiasco, and how he wouldn't do the one thing to keep us safe—leave—I couldn't remain silent a day longer. He doesn't get to sit in his lab and walk our streets with impunity while his brother murders our citizens. Not anymore."

"His lab?" V's face almost lights up as it dawns on her. "It's Jonathan Ambrose, isn't it?"

Here we are. Moment of truth. Just rip off the Band-Aid, Jo. "Y—"

RING RING!

Oh, thank the dear Lord. My cell phone rings in my pocket. Its melody is sweeter than a million symphonies combined. Thank you, thank you, thank you God. I'm donating hefty sums to a church of every denomination, I swear it. With a shaking hand, I pull it out. "Sorry, V. Give me a sec." Unknown caller. "Joanna Fallon."

"Is your cousin still there?" a familiar voice asks.

"I'm sorry, who is this?"

"You know damn well who this is. Get out of earshot of your cousin. We have to talk."

I smile at V. "I'm sorry, I have to take this. Just watch TV or something until I get back." I rise from the couch and return to the patio on shaky legs. Adrenaline surge. Getting damn sick of those. "How do you know my cousin's here?"

"I have my ways. Just as I have my ways of knowing the reason for said meeting. I'm resourceful." He pauses. "Quite a vindictive bitch, aren't you? A man turns you down for sex, and you're ready to serve him up to every reporter, two-bit villain, and citizen with a pitchfork. In other circumstances, I believe we could have been friends."

"I have no idea what you're talking about. I'm doing this to rid my town of *you*. Your brother is just collateral damage. He leaves, you leave. I gave him several opportunities to do it the easy way. He declined."

"And what makes you believe I'd just up and abandon my new home just because *he* does?"

"Well, you're not blowing up Independence anymore, are you? You saying I'm wrong?"

The other end is silent for a few seconds. "What exactly do you want, Miss Fallon?"

"Simple. You gone. Galilee safe. That's it. And right now the only way I can see to accomplish that is for the pitchfork and torch brigade to run your brother out of town. They will, you know. I have the money and resources to make sure of it. Your brother will be given no quarter anywhere in this world. I am about to make him the most famous, reviled man on this planet, with you right alongside him. Both of your faces, all of your aliases, your entire sordid history is about to become front page news. Maybe you don't care, although many of your business associates probably don't want to hire an unhinged, incestuous homosexual I'm guessing. Even if you don't care, the brother you profess to love sure as hell will. So leave. And never return."

More silence. "You'd really do it, wouldn't you?"

"Hell, yes. So, come on. Be your big brother's hero. Save his life. Agree to leave."

"And you'd take my word for it?"

"Oh, hell no. My private plane, with me onboard, will take you to the destination of your choice far, far away. And should you hit town again, I release the information. Should I not return from our trip, I've taken steps to make sure the information is released."

"Not good enough. There's no guarantee for *me* that you won't disseminate it just because you've had a bad day or are on your period or something. Or perhaps this is all just a set-up? Police will be waiting on the plane."

"I'm open to suggestions," I say.

"Mutually assured destruction. I want ten million in untraceable diamonds. And I'm going to require photographs and audio of you paying me off and giving me the royal treatment on my way out of town. Aiding and abetting a known terrorist, a big no no."

"I can live with that. I am going to need a day or so to get the diamonds."

"You have twenty-four hours."

"Fine."

"Also, a few ground rules. This stays between us. No police, no supers, no weapons, no tracers or bugs. If I get even a whiff of subterfuge, not only will I kill you, your cousin, your butler, even your assistant, but I'll blow up Pendergast Industries with everyone inside."

"Got it."

"I shall call in twenty-four hours. It's a pleasure doing business with you." He hangs up.

The breath I was holding raggedly escapes, and I have to take a few more to calm myself. With him watching I can't appear happy. I go with shit scared instead. Not difficult. I clutch my churning stomach and stare into space. Tomorrow I have to meet face-to-face with a psychopath who loathes the very air I breathe. Alone. Defenseless. Me and my brilliant fucking ideas.

V is texting when I stumble back in. She finishes and glances up at me. "Everything okay?"

"Sort of. That was just, um, a source of mine. I can't get into much right now, but…I need you to hold off on the story for a day or two."

"What? Hell no!"

"Listen, it's for my safety, okay? Besides, I came to you with this. It's an exclusive, only you have it and will have it, I swear on Pop's grave. I just have to do one thing, and I'll give you the whole shebang. The full story. From start to finish. You just have to wait a few days. Please? You know I wouldn't ask if it wasn't necessary."

She mulls this over, but I can tell from her eyes she's not happy about this. I don't know what Jem finds so cute about my narrowed eyes. On V they're fucking terrifying. "Everything?"

"Even the proof. I promise. Exclusive, all yours."

"Two days. That's it," V says.

"Thank you."

She begrudgingly nods. After wrapping up three scones, she collects her tape recorder, placing them all in her purse and standing. "Just answer one last question. Was I right? Is Lord Nightingale Jem Ambrose?"

I pause, then, "No. He's not."

"Oh," she says with a frown. "Then why do you have it out for him? Off the record."

"To save his life. I have a target on my back. Didn't want him in the crossfire like Brendan. That's why I've been staying away from everyone. You, Harry, Lexie. For your own good."

"And here I thought you were just a bitch," she says with a smirk.

"Well, there's that too." I smile back. "Two days, and I'll hand you the Pulitzer."

"Okay. Just…whatever you're doing, be careful. Really."

I hug my cousin. We're not really touchy-feely people, so she stiffens. "I promise."

I release her, and she looks almost disgusted. "Jesus, now I am worried."

"Don't be. I know what I'm doing."

My friend nods and after a second, concerned glance walks out.

With a deep sigh, I lower my exhausted body onto the couch. It worked. I can't believe it. I called his bluff. He took the bait. Too bad I'm bait. But it's done now. Onto Phase Two. He's mine now, Jordan. You can't have him anymore. I just hope I'm alive to reap my reward come tomorrow evening.

*

Getting ten million in diamonds proves harder than I imagined. I know from Justin's will I have five million in a safety deposit box, but for the rest I have to send various Pendergast minions to known diamond dealers, both licensed and not, to acquire the rest. Even I'm up all night hitting up every black market vendor in the database with suitcases full of cash. I'm more than sure Jordan has people following me, so I keep everything above board. No calls, nothing suspicious. A text to my fellow co-conspirators with the details while in Dobbs' room on the secret cell and nothing more. They know what to do.

By ten the next morning, when I stroll into First National Bank to access my box, I have five million in diamonds in my office safe and my three favorite men waiting in a high security, private room at the bank. Technically I just saw him yesterday, but when I set eyes on Jem it seems like a million years have passed. He looks ridiculous in disguise with a fake beard and black knit cap on. Doesn't stop the lust. Don't think anything could. Harry and Cam are dressed in their usual suits and serious expressions. My own supersquad.

"Gentlemen," I say with a grin. I shut and lock the door. "We don't have much time." I set the safety deposit box on the table and retrieve the bag of diamonds. "Jem, you bring the computer?"

"He already showed us how to use it," Harry says, putting the laptop on the table. "We'll be able to track you using CCTV. We also uploaded the GFPD duty roster for today. We'll know where the closest unit is to your position at all times. If you stay in the city limits, someone should be able to get to you within two minutes."

"We should check the tracker," Jem says, moving to the laptop.

"If she already has one, why'd we bring this?" Cam asks, holding up a plastic kit.

"Despite what Cain said, he'll expect me to be low-jacked. I'd have to be insane not to at least try. There'll be one in my watch, one in my shoe, and the one you brought."

"He'll most likely sweep her and find the sub-dermal we're injecting today. When the others are gone, and the sweep is done, she'll activate the fourth."

I hold up my left middle finger. "Just above the knuckle. Press it, activated. Press it again, deactivated in case they do a second sweep. Had it sent from R&D. Dobbs injected it the night after Brendan's funeral in case Cain kidnapped me at some point." I press the spot. "Got it?"

Jem taps a few keys, then checks the watch Shannon snuck into his desk the day of the dedication. "Affirmative."

I press it again to shut it off. Only has a ten hour battery. "If I switch it on and off five times in quick succession, then nothing, that's the S.O.S. Everything and everyone advances in. Three, just Nightingale. This guy's a bomber. Wherever we go, I expect booby traps. The fewer people in, the better for everyone involved."

"I can't believe I agreed to this," Harry says. "This is insanity. You are going to get yourself killed. He could just shoot you walking out of this bank."

"If he wanted me dead, it would have happened by now. Remember, he thinks he's smarter than us. He'll want to prove it. And I'm not the real objective, Jem is. This *will* work. It has so far. It's simple. I lead Nightingale to Cain, he arrests him, the city's safe. We're heroes. And if I die, you can say, 'I told you so' in the eulogy."

"That's not funny," Harry says.

"Look, I'm well aware of the risks, but they're mine to take." I glance over at Jem. "And I'm all in. So no more discussion. We're doing this."

"Okay," Cam says.

"Fine," Harry says.

"Thank you."

Jem clears his throat. "Um, gentlemen, I need a minute alone to inject her with the dummy tracer. Could we please have the room?"

"Um, sure," Cam says. "We'll meet you in the men's room."

"Thank you."

Harry and Cam take one last weary look at me before walking out. And then there were two. Jem and I gaze at one another for a second. "They really care about you."

I move around the table to his side. "And I really care about them. I just pray this doesn't backfire on them. On all of us." I plop down in the chair beside him, roll up my sleeve, and hold out my forearm. "Tag me, your lordship. I have an appointment to keep."

He picks up the box and opens it. "I won't put it in too deep in case they—"

"Cut it out of me," I finish. "Yeah, I'm really looking forward to that." He doesn't give the smile I wanted. Instead he extracts the thickest needle I've ever seen, easily a millimeter across. Another toy from R&D department I had sent to the station months ago. Thought they could use it. Never considered it'd be on me though. "Can you promise me one thing?"

"What?" Jem asks as he adds the bug to the saline solution.

"Never grow a beard. You look ridiculous."

"That's a promise I can keep. I only put it on to imitate Dr. Barnes."

"That how you sneaked out of the hospital?"

"I hacked the hospital signal days ago then filmed myself working in the office for two hours. Good thing I'm incredibly boring and only wear a few different outfits, huh? This will be cold." He wipes my arm with an alcohol swab.

"Jem, you are many things, but boring is not one of them. Sexy, brave, bonkers in bed, ow!" He injects me with the tracker, and it hurts like a mother. "Fuck!"

"Sorry. Here." We wipes the blood away and seals the hole with superglue so it's not completely obvious. "It needs a minute to dry. Don't move." He tosses everything back into the box. "Are you alright?"

"Well, my arm hurts."

"You know what I mean. It's not too late to back out."

"He threatened my family. He even threatened to blow up Pendergast. All in, remember? You didn't flinch with the possibility of your life ending, neither will I. This ends today. One way or another."

Jem nods. "I just…I can't believe he actually stopped you."

"Well, he loves you." I slide my hand into his. "Miracles happen. I mean hell, you even unfrosted *my* cold, dead heart."

"Did I now? I wasn't sure."

"Yeah, sorry about that," I say with a grimace. "Mind if we erase it from our memories and try again? I promise no nervous breakdown this time."

"Suppose we can give it a shot," he says with a smile. He pauses and that brilliant grin grows. "I love you, Joanna Fallon."

"I love you too, Jem Ambrose. With all my heart. I love you."

He grins, then leans across to kiss me again. The moment we touch, the tears rise. This could be the last time we do this. He knows it too because his desperation and ardor matches my own. Oh, I do love this man. I love him so much I'm afraid I might burst from it. Thank you God for this man. He breaks away first, resting his forehead on mine. "I don't want you to do this, I don't want you to do this, I don't want you to do this," he whispers as desperately as his kiss.

"I have to. You know I have to," I whisper back. I kiss him again. "Just like you know what you have to do. You have the much harder job here. Can you do it? Look at me." I move his chin to meet my gaze. "We will give him every opportunity to come in alive, I promise you that, but if he doesn't…can you live with what might have to happen? Because it may come to that. He will keep coming after us. You just need to be prepared for that eventuality." I pause. "And the chance something may happen to me too."

"No," he says, shaking his head.

"There are a million ways today can go wrong. The odds are not in our favor. And if it does, I just need you to know…I don't regret a second I've spent with you. Not a one. You healed me. You brought me back to life, and I would rather have one night with you than a million without. So don't you dare blame yourself if I don't make it out of this. It was all my choice, and I'd do it all again in a heartbeat. Because you're worth it. Because to me you're perfect. You have blessed my life in ways you cannot fathom, and from the bottom of my heart thank you. Thank you for loving me and making me a better person. I love you. Just keep my family, friends, and city safe, okay?"

He cups my head and wipes my tears as they fall. "Okay," he says breathlessly.

"Good." I give him a quick peck and pull away before I completely lose it. "I have to go now." I kiss him again. "I love you."

I can't look at him as I retrieve my diamonds and rush out of the room. It isn't until I get to my car that I really break down and cry. Because I'm scared. I've never been so scared in my life. Because I finally have something real to live for. And I am going to fight with my dying breath to keep hold of it. And I know I'm going to have to prove that today.

All in.

Chapter Twenty

My Hero

Diamonds? Check. Tracking devices in my sneaker, another in my collar? Check. All black today. Fitting for a funeral. Plane on stand-by, though I doubt I'll make it there? Check. I assume my co-conspirators are in place. No way to find out though. Faith, Jo. Faith. I pace around my office like a caged panther clutching my cell hard enough to break it. I haven't sat still for fifteen minutes. I am sure Jordan is watching my meltdown with amusement from the camera in the credenza. It's five past one and no call. Fucker. He's late just to drive me crazy. Keep me on edge. It's working like a fucking charm, asshole.

There's a knock on my office door, and I gasp in fright. "Joanna?" Lane asks on the other side.

Oh, good. A distraction. "Come in."

Lane steps in with a file folder. "I've been reviewing your data on the acquisition of Ambrose Pharmaceuticals. I just, I can't see it, especially considering the offer we just received from Goliath to sell our existing pharma."

"Huh?" Oh, right, I have to keep the hating Jem farce alive. "What about purchasing the hospital from the city? Privatizing it?"

"That's more viable, especially with Dr. Ambrose's drug trial showing promise. We buy the hospital, we own the patent."

"He'd never go for that. Too much of a do-gooder. Push the offer forward regardless. Even if Ambrose resigns in protest, it's still a moneymaker."

"I doubt the board—"

Another knock stops this pointless conversation. Shannon scurries in without invitation, holding an envelope. "I'm sorry. This package just arrived. It's marked urgent."

And away we go. About fucking time.

"Would you please excuse me? Lane, we'll continue this later." Hopefully.

Shannon escorts Lane out as I stare at the package in my free hand. Medium sized, brown, small. And ringing. It begins ringing. For a split second I anticipate an explosion, tensing and even holding my breath. All that comes is a second ring. I rip open the package, finding a cell phone, a strange looking Bluetooth, Metro card, and black velvet bag. I quickly place the Bluetooth in my ear and receive the call. "Joanna Fallon."

"The phone has a webcam function. The camera is in the Bluetooth," Jordan says through my earpiece. "There's a switch on the side. Flip it on." I do. "It's transmitting. Think of me as the angel on your shoulder, I see, know and judge all you do. Now, remove everything in your pockets and show me as you do. You are to leave here with nothing but what I've provided." I have nothing in my pockets, and I show him such. "Where are the diamonds? Show me as you place them in the bag provided." I move over to the office safe behind the Dali painting, following instructions to the letter. Diamonds in the bag "Now with only the bag, walk out the door to the elevator."

"Can I take my jacket? It's cold out."

"You'll just have to suffer. Go now. And remember, I have eyes and ears in the sky. No funny business."

"I'm not feeling humorous today, don't worry." *Just put one foot in front of the other, Jo.* Go. With a sigh, I amble out of my office. "I'm leaving for the day," I tell Shannon. "Something came up. I'll be back in a few days. Hold down the fort."

I don't wait for her response, I just keep moving. In exactly thirty seconds, she'll send a text to Cam that I've left for the meet. "Ground floor," Jordan says as I enter the elevator. "Then walk to the Gaines Street Metro station, South platform."

"I could just take a taxi to the airstrip," I offer.

"You go where I say the moment I say it or the bomb set to prime in the Thornton wing blows."

Oh shit. "That's not necessary."

"Simply insurance. You asked for this, Joanna." He pauses. "Metro. You have five minutes."

The elevator ride takes an eternity as workers keep getting on. A few attempt conversation but my glare stops their words. Boss of the year, me. Like most, I get off on the first floor and trek through the lobby with its water features and golden "PI" logo a story tall. No one stops me as I rush out to the street. Somewhere Kowalski sits parked, waiting to pull out in a fake cab in case Jordan went for my suggested mode of transportation. He'll still trail me as he's linked to the tracker in my shoe.

I wasn't lying. It's damn cold, low forties, with the wind pounding against me. I hurry the three blocks to the Metro, occasionally glancing back to see if I have any shadows. Only one person I recognize. "Yes, you are being tailed," Jordan says. "Eyes forward, Joanna."

The station is bustling with commuters. Thank goodness not a one pays me any attention. I swipe my Metro card and walk to the south platform. "Find the bench in front of the poster of Our Lady Hospital, then get in the train car directly in front of it. Hurry. The train's arriving."

Shit. Advertisements line the entire red and white tiled wall. Just as the train pulls in, I find the spot. I dash into the car as told. This ordeal just began and already I'm exhausted. "Remain standing and don't get off until I say so."

"Roger."

The train jerks to a start. Bye, Kowalski. Hope you made the train, Mirabelle. Three, four, five stations pass, all the opposite direction of the airport. Not that I expected to arrive there. That would be far too easy. I wall up my terror somehow and brick by hard won brick until I'm numb. Alert, but numb. I'm aware of everyone around me. No one is above suspicion. The college student with the purple hair. The tourist checking me out without his wife noticing. The businessman beside me chatting to his mistress on his cell. Mirabelle keeping an eye on me through the glass partition between the cars. I learned hand to hand combat skills at the police academy, even how to disarm someone, I'm ready to strike if necessary. The doors begin closing at the sixth station when Jordan yells, "Get off the train! Now!"

Shit. I leap through the doors just before they shut. Bye, Mirabelle. "Go to the opposite platform and embark the next train." I'm like a trained seal jumping through hoops. I keep leaping though. This time I only ride two stops before he orders me off. "Find the hospital poster to your left." I walk down the wall and spot it. "See the maintenance door beside? Enter."

The door opens without issue. I take one step inside when a hand clamps on my free wrist, yanking me all the way inside. I gasp and try to pull it away. "Stop struggling," Jordan says. "He won't harm you unless you make him."

I recognize Gary Acevedo as my assailant. "Hi, Gary. James Ryder says hello," I say as he shuts the door.

"Strip," Jordan says over the Bluetooth.

"Excuse me?"

"Take off all your clothes, underwear included. He won't touch you."

Wonderful. I've gone from seal to stripper. Without hesitation, I remove my sweater, pants, jewelry, undergarments, the whole lot. To his credit, Acevedo doesn't leer. He's all business. "Yes, sir?" Acevedo listens over his Bluetooth. He picks up the bag beside him, removing a white bra and panties.

"Put those on," Jordan says, "then spread your arms and legs. He's going to check you for trackers." Ugh. I assume the position as Acevedo sweeps a black rod over my body. It buzzes when it reaches my arm. Jordan tsks over the earpiece. "I told you no bugs."

"Can't blame a girl for trying."

"And you can't blame me for this. Present your arm. This will hurt."

Acevedo receives his instructions before pulling out a scalpel and tweezers. I can't look. I stare at the broom and pan in the corner as the scalpel slices me apart. "Think happy thoughts, Joanna," Jordan says in my ear. I whimper as the tweezers plunge into the hole and root around in there. Fuck that hurts! I bite my lower lip to stop from crying out. "Who is on the other end of that bug?"

"Dobbs," I wince. "He's tracking me from the manor." Of which I am sure you are verifying on the surveillance camera right now. As planned, Dobbs will be sitting by Doris until the signal goes dead.

"So, what's the plan?" Jordan asks.

"If the signal dies, or he doesn't hear from me in the next hour and every two hours after that, the information on Jem is released and he contacts the Feds."

Acevedo finally locates the bug. The torture is over. "Just leave it on the floor?" He listens again and nods before handing me the first-aid kit.

"Fix your arm then put on the rest of the clothes," Acevedo says.

As I do—just jeans, gray sweatshirt, and white sneakers—Acevedo places the bug on the floor before swiping the diamonds with the baton. No tracers. He replaces the diamonds in the bag. I slip on my new shoes and tuck my hair under the Galilee Angels cap provided. "Now, follow Mr. Acevedo. And remember: bombs, children, no fleeing." Acevedo yanks on my arm and maneuvers me out of the closet. I activate the fourth tracker in my finger.

We file to the opposite platform to embark the southbound train. After two stops, we switch again, riding three north then switching to westbound for five stops, then south to the end of the line. I suppose it's not really paranoia if they are out to get you. Like a good hostage, I don't struggle or say a word when I'm led from the subway up to a parked car near the docks. Ah the fresh ocean air. May your enjoyment not be ruined by the day's events. "Don't you even want to know where you're going, Joanna?" Jordan asks as I climb into the car.

"Does it matter? Wherever it is, I'm going there anyway."

We don't drive far, only six blocks to a private dock. Once again, I'm manhandled down a wooden landing with half a dozen johnboats, to the small blue speedboat where I'm promptly shoved onto the bench while Acededo fires up the engine. Charon guiding me down the river Styx. No one made it out of that boat ride alive either.

"Guess we're not flying to our final destination," I say to Jordan.

"No shit, Sherlock. Just sussed that one out?" Jordan replies.

Acevedo maneuvers the boat through the busy shipping lines filled with steel cargo boats as long as a city block. My fear, which I was doing a fine job of keeping at bay, spikes and spikes through my defenses the further we zoom out to sea. Thirty seconds in I'm trembling and not just from the cutting wind and splash of the freezing water. There are GFPD Marine boats patrolling the harbor, but it'll take longer than two minutes to get to me. Wonderful.

Just as the city's landmass is about to fade completely from view over the dark blue horizon, Acevedo lowers the throttle to slow us. I'm guessing our destination is the stopped carrier about a hundred yards away and closing. Even from this far I can tell she's no ordinary shipping boat. There are no containers on the deck with only a few tiny people milling around on deck. It's smaller than a typical freighter too but still enormous, easily the length of three football fields and as tall as a three-story house. As we pull up to its rusting side, a rope ladder falls from the deck. Acevedo hands me the diamonds. "Up."

Hades, I have arrived.

I knot the bag's tie around my wrist and climb up the side of the ship. I make it about five rungs before Acevedo guns the engine again and zooms away, back towards land. So much for stealing the boat to escape. Swimming to shore is out too as my arms ache by the time I reach the deck. A minion has to help me up the last step. When I stand fully erect, I spot a familiar face strolling toward us with a huge grin plastered on his stolen face. He's dressed casually for our showdown in beige chinos, loafers, and black fleece sweatshirt with his dark hair slicked back. "Welcome aboard."

I remove the Bluetooth, and start pressing the transmitter to signal Jem. "What the hell is this? Not that I don't love a good sea voyage, but a plane is a hell of a lot quicker. I can't see you wanting to spend more time with me than you have to. So what the fuck is going on? I thought we had a deal."

"All shall be revealed shortly. This way."

The two goons with machine guns flank me as Jordan leads us toward the metal staircase down into the massive, cavernous and almost empty cargo area. Well empty except for the bomb the size of an SUV sitting center ring with a million wires attached to bricks and bricks of explosives. Sitting on top is a wooden platform and tall metal rod with a circular top that was probably attached to a crane to lower it, complete with small ladders on either side.

My mouth dries up at the sight of this weapon of mass destruction. And of course we stop the tour right beside it. Damn it's two times taller than me. If he's attempting to scare me, it is damn sure working. "Nice bomb."

"Don't worry, it's not primed. Yet. There are also smaller devices planted across the freighter in strategic points. Engine room, hull, etc."

"All for little old me? I'm flattered." I pause. False bravado is the only thing keeping me from crumbling. Just keep it together until Nightingale arrives. "Before we begin what I assume is a re-negotiation of terms, can you please call the police so they can remove the bomb in the hospital?"

"Do you honestly think I'd plant a bomb in a children's ward?" I just glare at him. "Yes, of course, you're right. I did. But fret not. My dear brother is, as we speak, disarming it. I wanted to keep him occupied while we conducted our business. I made it relatively easy. I try not to kill children. Unless I'm paid extra for it."

"Noble. So, can we please just get on with this?" I raise the bag. "I brought your diamonds. Want them now or…what? Are we sailing to another port and a plane will meet us near there?"

"Possibly," he says with amusement.

This garners another glare. "Then *possibly* you should keep in mind the guillotine hanging over your brother's head. This isn't a complicated equation: kill me, kill him. So, why don't we just stick to our agreement, Mr. Ambrose? I've kept my end. We can all walk away winners. You go, I leave your brother alone. You get away scot free to continue tormenting whoever your black heart desires, just not in my town. So stop posturing and let's get on with this."

Jordan stares at me impassively for a few seconds before a large, sickening grin crosses his face. "Oh, Miss Fallon, you are *good*. You are really, truly good," he says as if surprised. "Even now, under all this stress and duress, you remain in character. Kudos. Really. I like you far more than his last paramour. You're miles more entertaining. Still going to kill you, though." He glances at the minion on the right. "Bert, handcuff her to the bomb, please."

"What?" I shriek. Bert slaps a cuff on before I can fight back while the other henchman points the Uzi at me.

"Keep the diamonds. I have loads already."

"We had a deal!" I shout as Uzi man shoves me toward the bomb.

"And she keeps on going! Way to commit!"

"I don't know what you're talking about, Ambrose!" Bert has already climbed onto the bomb's platform. Uzi presses the gun in my back to get me to climb too. "This is a mistake! A huge mistake! Your brother is dead. He is so fucking dead!"

"You know, you almost had me going there once or twice," Jordan continues.

"Sit and raise your hands," Uzi orders. Having little choice, I obey. *Just buy time. Just buy time, Jo.*

"Especially yesterday. Whoa!" Jordan chuckles. "Tense. You were really going to do it, weren't you?"

With the Uzi still pointed at my vital organs, Bert passes the open cuff through the metal loop and attaches it to my free wrist. Both cuffs are so tight even breaking my thumbs couldn't get me out of them. I am now handcuffed to a bomb. Brilliant plan, Jo. "Look, I don't know what you think is going on, but you have it dead fucking wrong. I am not playing you here!"

"Oh, now you're just growing tedious," Jordan chides. He whips out his cell phone and holds it up to take a picture. "Say cheese!" He snaps a picture of me on the bomb.

"What the hell are you doing?"

"Texting our lover," he says, fingers tapping. "'Come and get her.' Short and simple, just like you."

"Goddamn it, Ambrose! You have this all wrong. I—"

"Shut up!" he roars, face becoming almost feral as his voice echoes through the metal space. "Just shut your fucking mouth. You lost. Maintain some damn dignity, woman. *I know.* I know it all! I know you discovered you were under surveillance. I know you and my brother concocted some ridiculous scheme to make it appear you loathe one another so I'd leave you in peace. I even know you must have some hidden tracker so he can locate you now. It was a decent plan, and you played it masterfully. I will concede that. As I said, you almost had me believing your ire on more than one occasion. You really went for it, but you simply…underestimated me.

"I've been following my brother since he touched down in this city. I have photos of you and him pitching woo all over town.

I knew about you long before you knew about me. And I sure as hell know my big brother. You're exactly his type. Damaged. Trashy. Dumber than you realize. And more important, you showed him the time of day. I know you had to do all the heavy lifting, I have the recorded conversations to prove it. And do you know why that is, Joanna? Because he doesn't love you!" the maniac bellows, fury echoing through the ship. "He could never love you! You are nothing! Just some whorish, drunken, ugly, fucking gash! You are so beneath him you are not even fit to be the shit he scrapes from his boots! I just have to make him realize that!"

"Then why not just kill me? Blow up my car or shoot me in the head like the coward you are?"

"Haven't you been listening? Because you were no threat, bitch! As is illustrated by your current predicament. The only reason he went along with your absurd farce is out of some misplaced sense of loyalty for drawing attention to you. And I will admit, I was entertained by your little soap opera. Absolutely riveting. Four stars. And spending millions to have the press braying for Lord Nightingale's blood was masterful." He holds out his arms, gesturing to the entire ship. "But I still win. You overplayed your hand. So a bullet? A bomb? Dead is fucking dead."

"So you just spared me until now because I'm a good actress and you wanted to gloat? Show me you have the bigger dick?" I shake my head. "If that's what you need to believe, then knock yourself out. *Please.*"

Jordan wryly chuckles, and I'm sure would say something pithy back but Danny Watkins, his lover/bomb expert hustling out from the corridor with something in his hands. "Jordan, it's all set up. The detonators are rigged to this controller."

"Wonderful. Thank you, love." He pecks Danny's lips.

"Oh, so you're allowed to have a significant other, but not your brother? That's fair." I catch Danny's eyes. "Just so you know, my boyfriend is gonna kick your boyfriend's ass. Run while you can."

"Ignore her," Jordan says as he examines the detonator.

"Actually, attention everyone on the boat," I shout. "The megalomaniacal maniac was just handed a detonator to blow up the entire boat! If you have any sense of self-preservation, you will abandon ship! Now!"

Jordan raises an eyebrow. "Done? Good. Trent, punch her in the face, please."

Uzi's fist makes contact with my right cheek hard enough I see spots. It hurts like a mother, instantly bringing tears to my eyes. Fucking hell.

"Looks good," Jordan says to Danny. "Oh, did you send the video about the bombs in the subway trains?"

"Went out just when she reached the dock," Danny says. "Every available officer is en route now."

Jordan's attention returns to me. "Don't worry, *that* one was a lie. It was just in case your police friends were enlisted as back-up. Best we keep this in the family, so to speak."

If I wasn't so focused on the throbbing pain in my head, I'd probably be concerned.

"And don't worry your vacant little head, Joanna. My brother should see through that ruse. I've used it once before." He stares up at the sky through the open ceiling. "Yes, I think we've covered everything. Now we just have to wait. Place a bag over her head, please."

Trent places tape over my mouth then a bag over my head. Wonderful.

"Positions, gentlemen!" Jordan shouts. "We don't want to make it too easy for him. Injure, but not fatally. He's mine. And close the deck."

Footsteps against metal recede as the men run off. The deck partition above my head must close as I hear machinery whirring and gears spinning, then what little light I can see through the burlap vanishes. Then I'm alone. Alone with a bomb. All I can do is wait. My jaw throbs in time to my racing heart. Well, I'm still alive. That's oddly surprising. I haven't been raped or tortured. Putting that in the win column. Handcuffed to a bomb? Not so much. I'm putting my odds at surviving 1,000 to 1. *No, no bad thoughts*. Faith. Trust.

How much time passes is hard to gage, but awhile as my arms go from pins and needles to numb. All that keeps me company are my hopes and plans. I'm going to take some time off from crime fighting, maybe a month or so. Jem too. We'll take the boat out. Sail for a week or two. Just us and the open water. Making love on deck, exploring exotic locales, talking for hours. And maybe I'll get an apartment in town. I don't want to live in that mausoleum anymore. It's just not me. If I get out of this, I'll make a lot of changes. I swear it. Please just let me survive this, and I will. Don't take us from each other. But if I'm meant to die here today so be it. Just give him the strength to find someone else to love and who loves him as much as I do. Let him find peace. And love. Above all, love. He deserves—

Automatic gunfire above my head jerks me out of prayer. It last two seconds, followed by a hollow thump as I assume a body hits metal. One bad guy down. Poor minions. I did warn them. It happens again, this time there are two bursts of gunfire and the clinking of bullet against steel aft. This time I faintly hear a man groan in pain. He's inside the ship. Running footsteps, four pistol shots, a thump, silence. Closer. Again. Shots, groans of pain, silence. I struggle against the handcuffs, but like the previous dozen times it fails to work. Fuck! Two loud thuds against the walls, then a man howls in pain. Silence.

"Joanna!" Jem shouts, voice echoing through the ship.

A metal door shuts just as more continuous automatic weapon fire begins, bullets hitting metal, ricocheting as a man roars in anger. It lasts five seconds of hell. "Come out, you fucker!" a man shouts. Another thud as he must kick open the door as it hits the wall a millisecond later. More gunfire. Two men screaming, then another thud as someone slams against the wall. Silence. And more silence. It's fucking deafening. Nothing. I don't hear a damn thing beyond my own heavy breathing. He's hurt. If he was hit multiple times, he could bleed out before his body repairs itself. Jordan—

Wind whips behind me then someone lands on the platform beside me. He rips the bag off. Jem. He's a little worse for the wear with an oozing gunshot to the arm and a trickle of blood smeared on his exposed chin. He's still the most glorious sight I've ever viewed in my life. I spot the worst hovering in a dark corner of the ceiling in full red and black villain uniform pointing a rifle at us. Oh fuck! I signal with my eyes, but Jem's too busy ripping the tape from my mouth. "Are you—?"

"Four o'clock!"

Just as Jem pivots, Jordan fires. There's an almost deafening pop. Before I even blink, Jem is knocked off the platform by what looks like a harpoon to his shoulder. I shriek as he's impaled to the floor. The large metal rod has to be four feet long with a ball on top. That is it. This is over. I press the transmitter to summon back-up.

"Sorry about that, brother," Jordan says as he glides toward us. "I know it hurts."

"You fucking bastard!" I shout.

He ignores me and lands beside the still stunned Jem. "I really don't want to fight you. It's not necessary. We're above that, don't you th—"

Jem sweeps his brother's feet from underneath him. The moment the villain flattens, Jem brings the heel of his foot down on Jordan's stomach, knocking the wind out of him. As Jordan's dazed, with a guttural roar, Jem yanks the harpoon from his shoulder. I feel his pain down to my soul. Jem manages to rise and with his good arm, raises the rod over his brother's chest like a vengeful Poseidon. Just as it's about to make contact, Jordan rolls aside. The rod sticks in the floor. As Jem realizes what happened, Jordan removes another gun from his belt, firing almost point blank into Jem's chest. Jem's knocked onto his stomach, holding onto his chest with his arm underneath. He doesn't move. He doesn't draw breath. Oh. God.

"No!" I cry

Jordan moves toward his brother to check him. "Jem?" Jordan asks. He nudges his brother's body. "Jem?"

Like lightning, Jem flings his arm from under his chest and jabs a knife into his brother's foot. Jordan shrieks in pain as the blood pours under his heels, and Jem uses his momentary shock to rise. Not quick enough. The moment he's up, Jordan backhands his brother with all his super might, sending the stunned hero flying backwards into a nearby wall, head first. Jem crumples to the floor like a string-less puppet. Jordan yanks the knife from his foot, stares at it with fury, and tosses it to the floor. Jem slowly sits up. "I don't want to fucking hurt you!" Jordan bellows at the top of his lungs. "And you don't want to hurt me!"

Though still dazed and hobbling, Jem rises to his feet for the next bloody round. He charges his brother with a roar, but the head wound must be grave because he's slow. Too slow. As they make contact, Jordan knees him in the stomach. With a groan, Jem folds at the waist, giving Jordan the opening to elbow the hero in the back of the neck. He lands jaw first on the metal floor, a sickening crack echoing through the arena. I cringe. "Why are you doing this? Stop it!" Though in the fetal position and panting in pain, we both see him reaching into his belt for another weapon. "Stop it!" Jordan says as he kicks him in the forehead. Jem collapses onto his back.

"N-No," Jem whimpers. "Y-You have to die."

"What?"

"You have to die. I see that now."

Jordan stares at his brother, dumbfounded. "You-You came here to kill me?"

"You're a monster," he gasps through the agony. "You're insane. I can't save you. I never could."

"No!" Jordan explodes. "You-You love me!"

"No. No," Jem says sadly. "Any love I ever felt for you, you destroyed years ago. I detest you. I hate you to my very core."

Jordan vibrates with anger as those words sink in. "No. Take it back."

"Never."

"Take it back!" he shrieks. In a blink, Jordan has picked up the rod and hovers over his brother. "You're lying!"

"I'm not."

He plunges the rod into Jem's chest. "Stop lying!" Out it rises from my love's damaged body, spatters of blood raining all over, until the monster plunges it in again. "Why are you lying to me?" In again, this time right near the heart. He's going to kill him. "Why are you making me hurt you like this? I love you! Why are you making me do this?"

"Because of me!" I blurt out. "It's me! It's all my fault."

Jordan turns, and his mouth drops open almost surprised I'm still here. "Shut up, bitch! This has nothing to do with you."

"No matter how much you don't want that to be true, deep down you know it is. Because no matter how much you think you love your brother, it doesn't hold a fucking candle to how much he and I love each other. Think about it. We planned this whole thing together, including me unmasking him. That wasn't my idea,

Jordan. Unlike you I'd rather die than hurt your brother, but he convinced me to. He was willing to sacrifice his entire life, his career, just to keep me safe from you."

"Stop it, Joanna," Jem says.

"Shut up!" Jordan yells with a punch to Jem's already tender face. "You're lying."

"I'm not. And you know I'm not. Because you stopped me yesterday. And you may have told yourself it was because you loved him, that you wanted to save him. But really? You knew what it meant. That he would do anything to save *me*. Just like I knew what coming here would mean. That even if I die here today it's worth it because I die knowing I gave him a chance to be free of *you*. Because that's what love is. Love is crawling down into the pits of hell, fighting tooth and bone and nail to drag his ass out no matter the cost. *This*," I say, gesturing to the bomb and Jem on the floor. "Us…" I meet the love of my life's tear filled eyes so full of love, and the world fades. "Is true, pure, once in a lifetime love. It's *everything*. And you can't fucking touch it."

It's so quiet for a few seconds we can hear the blood dripping. I'm vaguely aware that Jordan glances from Jem, to me, then back at Jem, but I don't take my eyes from my hero nor him me. And for a moment all is right in the world because it's just us. As it should be. Until Jordan punches him in the face again. "*Her*?!?" He bashes again. "Her?"

Jem's head lolls to the side as Jordan stalks toward me, picking up the knife Jem lost on the way. "She's nothing!" The knife wielding maniac leaps onto the platform. "This bitch?!" he bellows as he slices my cheek with the blade. White hot pain brings tears. Jordan spins around so we're both facing the terrified Jem. He attempts to pull out the rod but after all the damage, his strength has left him. There's so much pooled blood that still pours from his chest a normal man would be dead already.

"Leave her alone," Jem says.

"Leave her alone?" He grabs my right ring finger, snapping it back with a crack. I can't stop the howl of pain. "*Leave her alone*?" He snaps the pinky, and I almost vomit in agony. "She can never love you as much as I do!" He punches me in my slashed cheek. For a moment everything goes from black to fuzzy. "Me!" he says, sounding far away. "I'm the one who protected you! Who loved you when no one else would?" He socks me in the chest, the sound of cracking ribs hurting almost as much as the physical sensation. "I am the only one who understands you!" He hits my face again, cracking my nose. Blood spews down. "We have the same soul! We're the same person. We are all we have in the world. I love you. Tell me you love me." Jem doesn't say a word. I'm still seeing spots, but I know Jordan leans beside me, wraps his arm around me, and presses a knife to my throat. "*TELL ME YOU LOVE ME!*"

Jem glances at me for confirmation. We both know no matter what he says, I'm dead. I slowly blink. No more games. If I die, I die from the truth. He owes me that. Jem glances behind me, his mouth twitching before meeting his brother's eyes. "I don't love you. How could I? You took advantage of me. You destroyed everything and everyone I ever loved. Including the brother I looked up to. Who kept me sane. Who was my best friend. You obliterated him, even from my memory. He ceased to exist in the one place he ever really lived: my imagination. You are dead to me. I will never love you. I *loathe* you. And it has nothing to do with her, or Uma, or Tempest, or anyone else. It's *you*. You're *wrong*. A mistake. An abomination. I wish you'd never been born. And death is preferable to spending another moment on this earth with you."

The knife trembles against my throat. I glance up at Jordan. Tears stream down his mask as his lip twitches. If he had a heart, I'd swear it was breaking. "Well. Then. I live to serve you, brother." He reaches into his belt and pulls out the detonator. "Nothing left to do then, is there? We came into this world together, we'll leave the same way." The monster's gaze moves down to me. "You first, though cunt."

"Now!" Jem shouts.

We both glance up at the ceiling as the machinery whirrs to open the panels. What...? The whoosh of air behind us draws our attention again. I turn and see a yellow flash zooming mid-air toward us. There isn't time to react. Liberty, force field glowing around her, grabs the arm holding the detonator, twisting it to almost a hundred eighty degrees as tendons and bone crack like kindling. The detonator drops. Before it completes its descent, she kicks Jordan in the crotch, grabs his shoulders to bend him down, and knees him in the jaw. He collapses on his back right beside me. Fuck.

Before he even opens his eyes, she seizes the villain by the wrists and takes off like a rocket into the air. Twirling as fast as she can, she spins and spins Jordan by the wrists to gain momentum before releasing him. He hits a nearby wall head first, even leaving a dent in the metal. Momentarily unconscious, he plummets down to earth. Good—

She's behind me, breaking the cuffs at the middle, when he lands. I don't even have time to process that before she yanks me to my feet. Holding me around the waist we lift off, my neck snapping backwards and my stomach following a few seconds behind. The spots return. I'm vaguely aware of passing through open space and everything being blue. The sky. Then down we drop toward the dark churning water. About a second later, her arms vanish. Wind whips around me as I plummet to earth. The last thing I see before the water overtakes me is Liberty gliding toward the ship. Crash.

The water's freezing, shockingly so. In my dazed state, it takes me a moment to realize why I'm so cold and why my lungs don't like what I'm breathing in. I'm in water. Fuck. Oh shit. Which way is up? When I try to expel the water already in my lungs, more enters. I open my eyes and notice the light. Up. That way. A few kicks and I surface, coughing all the water out along with the crackers I ate earlier. What the…? I stare at the open water. There's movement. Something white. Oh, a boat. It's coming. Not my boat. Where's my boat? I need… The spots become full darkness for a few seconds. What's—

BOOM!

I spin around just as an orange and black fireball shoots up and sideways from the carrier a hundred feet away. The noise reaches me first. Then the massive, oppressive heat and rocketing fire coming right for me. Even in my wretched state, instinct knows the score. I plunge underwater as the flames turn the light above red. The water ripples like an earthquake, churning me every which way, but I keep my eyes on the light to find my way back. When the red's vanished, I surface again. The sound of cracking, twisting metal is almost deafening. Jesus, Mary, and Joseph. The ship folds in the middle as smoke and flames rise to the sky. Wow.

Planks of metal and other debris rain down all around me. I just watch it burn and sink until a minute later the darkness can't be kept at bay a moment longer. I let it transport me from this hell. I've earned that.

*

What the…?

I force my eye open, but the florescent lights sting as if I were inches from the sun. The other won't open. I close it again.

Shouting brings me back this time. I unglue my eye and turn toward the commotion. There's a flashing light through a window, and Cam shoving someone out the door. I close my eye again.

Pain. Ungodly, intense agony. My chest. My hand. My face. Once again only one eye opens. The pain won't allow me to pass out this time. I glance around. A hospital. Tubes in my arm and other unnatural places. My fingers are splinted. The cut in my arm from the tracker is bandaged. There's something wrapped tight around my chest, an ACE bandage I think. I touch my face with my good hand. I think the cut is bandaged too, but my cheek, nose, and eye are swollen to fuck. Even lightly touching them sends pain through my head. I reach for the call button. All considerations about sobriety are swallowed by the agony. About ten seconds later, a nurse walks in.

"Oh, good, you're awake. We were starting to worry."

"Pain," I croak.

She prepares a syringe. "Right on time too." She injects my IV. "Quite the ordeal you went through."

"How long have I been here?"

"Only a day. You've been in and out of consciousness. You're very lucky to be alive, Miss Fallon. Your guardian angel sure earned her wings yesterday." The nurse picks up my chart from the end of the bed and starts scribbling. I close my eye as the drugs kick in. Oh, that's wonderful. "The press have been camped outside all day. You're national news. The sole survivor of Emperor Cain's reign of terror."

I survived. I can't believe it. It's really over. I won. I…My eye flies open. "What?"

"That's what they're calling it anyway. I have to ask. Were you really working with—"

"Wait...so-sole survivor?" I attempt to sit up but don't have the strength. It's taking all my willpower just to stay awake. "N-No. Lex-Liberty and Nightingale were there. They-They made it off."

Her chubby face plummets. "I-I," she stammers, "I just know what they're saying and what I saw on the news. The police boat that pulled you out of the water, the officers watched Lady Liberty fly out, drop you in the water, then fly back in. No-No one came out again before the explosion. I'm sorry."

I stare at this pitying woman for a few seconds as the rage billows up, choking the air from my lungs. No. *No*. Not... "Get out."

"I'm sor—"

"Get the fuck out!" I shriek.

"I-I'll just go find your doctor," the frightened woman says before running away.

No. *No*. He can't...not again. No, no, no, no, no. You can't be that cruel. No, oh, fuck. I can't breathe. I can't fucking breathe. Every choked attempt and no air enters. This can't be happening. No. If it was anyone this time, it was supposed to be me. *Me*. I can't. I can't...

The door opens again, and it is official. I've gone insane. Lexie stands in the doorway holding a cup of coffee, staring at me with concern as I choke on my grief and pain. "Jesus Christ." She sets down the cup to rush to my side. "Joanna? Shit, breathe. Just breathe." She touches my arm, and I actually feel it. Oh, fuck. I've really gone mad. "Shit." She hustles back to the door, throwing it open. "Dr. Ambrose!"

She's almost back at my bedside when Jem dashes in. At the sight of him what little chance I had at breathing vanishes. I'm starting to see spots. "Joanna?" Jem asks.

"What's the matter with her?" Lexie asks.

"I think she's having a panic attack." Jem sits on the bed and takes my good hand, placing it over his heart. It's beating. It's actually beating. His sapphire eyes lock with mine. "Joanna Fallon, listen to my voice. Listen to my words. You are safe. You're with us. You're safe. But you need to breathe. Please breathe, my love.

Like me." He takes a deep breath, chest rising and falling. With a wince, he exhales. Then again. "I am right here with you. I am not going anywhere. I promise, just please breathe. Joanna, *breathe!*" I gasp and expel the stale air in my lungs. Thank God. Thank you, God. I breathe in and out in time with him. He chuckles as tears fall from his eyes. He wipes them away and kisses my forehead as I pant. "Excellent, my love. Excellent."

"She-She-She told me you were dead," I say when I can finally speak.

"We are," Lexie says. I look to her. "Well, Liberty and Nightingale anyway."

I glance at Jem. "It's for the best. For Lexie. If they think Liberty's dead, and Lexie isn't, suspicion should dissipate. I'm sorry. I'm so sorry, my love." He kisses my forehead again. "One of us was supposed to be here at all times until you woke."

Lexie pulls up a chair to my bedside. "My fault." She touches my leg. "You gave us quite the scare there."

"*I* gave *you* a scare?" I hold up my demolished hand. "What the hell took you so long? When the fifth signal popped up, you were supposed to swoop in and attack. *That* was the plan."

"I'm sorry, okay? It took longer to fly in from Independence than I thought. I couldn't exactly come commercial, and I had to instruct the decoy and fight Ache in the morning so Cain would believe I was still there. It was your plan. And it worked. He's dead, and we're alive. We win."

I stare at Jem, who doesn't remove his gaze from the floor. "He's dead? You're sure?" I ask. "What happened?"

"Well, I rescued you," Lexie begins, "went back in, yanked the rod from Jem, picked him up, and flew us out just as the boat blew. My force field shielded us from the worst of it. Guess the marine unit missed little old us as we were a hairsbreadth from that huge fireball. Knocked us into the drink."

"You're sure Jordan was on the boat when it exploded?"

"Oh, yes," Lexie says with a miniscule smile. "I saw him right before we took off."

"He must have regained consciousness when Lexie reached me," Jem says solemnly. "Pressed the detonator. Tried to take us out with him."

"But he didn't have—"

I stop myself. Though Lexie's face has frozen and her slightly scared, downcast eyes tell all. Understanding fills me. I can even picture the scene. The avenging angel swoops in to save her friend, yet on her way to Jem picks up the detonator from the platform. Jordan remains unconscious on the floor as she saves Jem, then triggers the bombs as she glides out. She murdered him. She could have gone back to arrest him, instead she blew him up. And his goons. Holy fuck.

"But he didn't have what?" Jem asks.

Lexie finally meets my gaze. All I see inside their dark pools is pain. I'd recognize that look anywhere. The same look I saw in mine whenever I thought of Justin. Cain tormented her for years. He beat her, burned her, tortured her. Then he slaughtered the love of her life. He'd escaped custody once, escaped death another. He'd keep coming for all of us. Without question. She did it for love. For us. How can I condemn that? And what good could it serve for him to know? I'll carry this one for him. For them both.

I break our wordless exchange to turn to Jem. "What? I'm sorry?"

"You said something. 'But he didn't have' what?"

"What? Sorry, the drugs are making me loopy."

"I'll, uh," Lexie says as she stands, "go tell your police friends you're awake. Give you two lovebirds some time alone."

As she's about to step out, I call, "Lexie?" She stops to look at me. I give her a reverent nod. "Thank you."

"Thank *you*." My friend nods back and steps out.

Just the two of us now.

"Can-Can I get you anything?" he asks.

"Can you just hold me?" With a content, sweet smile, the man I love nods. I turn over on my good side as he climbs onto the small bed, spooning me. I hug the arm he drapes over me. The entire process hurts, but is so worth it. I relax for the first time in weeks. It's over. It is really, truly over. And here's my prize. "Are you alright?"

"Far better now," he whispers.

"Are you really retiring from the superhero racket?"

"I think for awhile at least. Why? Would you love me any less if I did?"

"Oh, absolutely. No question. I love the cape, not the man."

"Well, I do still have the cape. Perhaps we can get you one too."

"No, thank you Dr. Ambrose. I've faced two supervillains. I've met my quota for life. I'll do my life saving from behind Doris or through charity work from here on in." I squeeze his hand. "Besides, I promised you a million nights. And I always keep my word."

The love of my life remains silent for a moment, then kisses the back of my neck. "You saved my life, Joanna Fallon. In every conceivable way." He pauses. "You're my hero."

"I'm no hero, Jem. I'm just the woman who loves you."

"As I said…" His lips curl into a smile against my neck. "My hero."

CHAPTER TWENTY-ONE

BREAKING DAWN

"My goodness, you look like hell."

"Sensitive and considerate as always, Ryder. Thank you."

I sit curled up in our new comfy black leather lounge chair. Our first purchase together. I told him if I was staying at his apartment for the foreseeable future, I'd need one piece of furniture not rock hard or worth a fortune. The matching sofa arrives in two days. The laptop linked to Doris rests on his coffee table with Ryder's face filling the screen. Jem's out picking up our dinner, so I thought I'd take this opportunity to make my obligatory call. A promise is a promise.

"Seriously, Joanna. You look dreadful."

"Well, you should see the other guy. He's in pieces at the bottom of the ocean."

"My my."

"Yep. I finally met a man more twisted and depraved than you, Jimmy. Jealous?"

"I assume we're discussing Emperor Cain. I saw the news. Quite the ordeal you endured."

The official story is Cain found out my affiliation with his sworn enemies, threatened my life, then killed my friend in retaliation. That was when I discovered the connection between Nightingale and Cain and decided not only to finally involve the police but to force the hero from town. It was also when I started fighting with Jem so Cain wouldn't make him a target as he had Brendan. The day of the boat, I received word Jem was injured and contacted the police, but Cain still grabbed me to lure the Triumvirate in. Nightingale and Tempest arrived first and while they were battling Cain, Liberty rescued me, then went to help her friends. Cain blew the boat with all inside. A tragedy. V even interviewed Lexie for confirmation. She claimed we had a falling out after I informed her why her husband was murdered. Still, she rushed to my side after the event. There were people who swore they saw her in Independence when the boat blew then boarding a plane with records to back up her story. I love it when a plan comes together.

"You don't know the half of it, Ryder."

"Called to gloat?"

"No. To say thank you."

"Thank you? Why?"

Oh, just tell him, Jo. You know you want to. And who is he going to tell? "You're really going to like this. Actually, you're the only one who can really appreciate it. It all goes back to something you said during our second conversation. 'Don't play the cards, play the player.' But first you need to know your opponent. Cain realized this first. When he broke into my house it wasn't for the computer, it was to plant cameras and microphones. He hid them all over my house. You said it yourself, you wanted eyes and ears in the mansion yet couldn't get in. He found a way. Now, my first instinct was to use this fact to feed him false information. Act as if I didn't know about them and misdirect him."

"Simple but smart."

"Nope. Stupid. Because he was listening to *our* conversation. He knew you planted the idea in my head about surveillance. He thought I was stupid, not a total moron. He also knew his brother and I were in love. I was on borrowed time regardless. He was going to kill me as soon as I lost my usefulness to him, if not sooner. So I knew I had to do something, not only to keep myself and Liberty alive but draw him out.

"So I thought about you, and asked myself the same thing I asked you: why didn't you just leave? Sail off into the sunset? And it came to me: hubris. You came after Justin because he deigned to challenge you, and he won. He believed he was better than you, and you had to prove he wasn't. So I considered this, what really drove Cain, and my two goals: stay alive and lure him from his hole. Thus began the farce.

"I knew he'd see through my crap plan, but he didn't know *I* knew he would. I stuck that farce until it hurt, giving Cain exactly what he wanted: his brother. Alone. Afraid. Weak so Cain could pick up the pieces. And while I was being entertaining, while I was acting as if I were smarter than he was, he'd keep me alive. It also ensured he'd want a face-to-face to lord it over me that he saw through my pathetic display, that I wasn't a worthy opponent or competitor for his brother's heart. That I was beneath him. Not up to the game. But that still wasn't enough. Deep down he's a coward, so he'd only surface if he thought he was losing control of his players. When the game wasn't fun anymore. We had to *prove* our love. Our devotion. So I had to out Nightingale. And as I anticipated, when Cain realized his brother would risk everything for me, the person who truly had his heart, *that's* when Cain surfaced. And in that moment, it was all over. We got him."

"But he could have killed you."

"I was dead already. Borrowed time, remember? Besides, once again, he underestimated me. He was so dazzled by our two person play, he forgot about the third player. Liberty. Liberty, who stormed into the Justice lair, practically shouted I tried to enlist her in my plan, then stormed out. Who was hundreds of miles away, making herself visible there every day, including D-Day. Nightingale did technically get her husband killed. She had a *real* reason to hate him, and me by association. What Cain didn't know was this entire plan was detailed in the note I slipped her at the memorial, and any changes that I thought necessary, I passed to Dobbs or Shannon, who then texted her on a secret cell."

"So the one bad con was to hide the two good cons. Clever."

"Don't play a player. Would you have fallen for it?"

He smiles. "No, but only because I learned my lesson the last time."

"Which was?"

"Never underestimate you. Never. It would be a gross injustice."

I grin. "If only you could have known that sooner, right?" The front door opens, and Jem steps in with our Chinese food. I glance back at the screen. "Sorry, Ryder. Dinner's here. Oh, and you might not hear from me for awhile. I'm taking a long vacation with a very gorgeous man. I'll call when I get back. I need to pick your brain about the Albanians. Till then." I shut off the webcam.

"Albanians?" Jem asks as he unloads the cartons.

"They're a major drug supplier." I stroll over to him. "New target for the resurrected Captain Moonlight and his lovely silent partner and her supercomputer."

"Captain Moonlight?"

"Just a thought."

"One for *after* our vacation."

"Of course." I root around in the bag. "Crap. They forgot the sauce again."

"You mean…" He reaches into his pocket, revealing three packets of orange duck sauce, "this sauce? I grabbed some on the way out."

A huge smile creeps across my face as I move toward him. I throw my arm around his neck, slowly drawing him into a deep kiss. Oh, how I love this man. I break apart and stare into those eyes of his that melt me every time. "*My* hero."

Guess sometimes there is some justice in this world.

The Galilee Falls Trilogy will conclude with Book Three:
FALL OF HEROES
out 2014

ACKNOWLEDGMENTS

First, thanks to Damonza for another beautiful cover. You're the best for a reason.

Thanks to my Betas: Susan, Jill, and especially Ginny.

Thanks to all who spread the word about this and my other series. I mean it, you are all my champions. Really.

To my family who put up with me. And thanks to Mom and Liam for helping me come up with the ending.

ABOUT THE AUTHOR

Jennifer Harlow spent her restless childhood fighting with her three brothers and scaring the heck out of herself with horror movies and books. She grew up to earn a degree at the University of Virginia which she put to use as a radio DJ, crisis hotline volunteer, bookseller, lab assistant, wedding coordinator, and government investigator. Currently she calls Northern Virginia home but that restless itch is ever present. In her free time, she continues to scare the beejepers out of herself watching scary movies and opening her credit card bills. She is the author of the Amazon best-selling F.R.E.A.K.S. Squad, Midnight Magic Mystery series and *Justice*, the first in the superhero thriller trilogy. For the soundtrack to her books and other goodies visit her at www.jenniferharlowbooks.com

www.ingramcontent.com/pod-product-compliance
Lightning Source LLC
Chambersburg PA
CBHW070845250626
47159CB00003B/938